BLOOD THAT BINDS

MELISSA WINTERS

WINTERSGATE PRESS

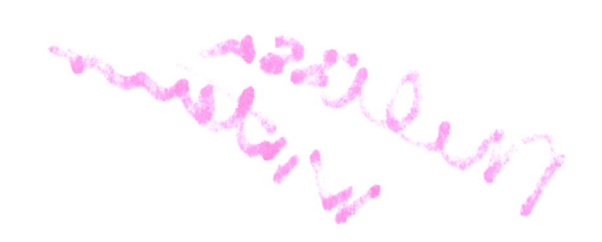

Copyright © 2022 by Melissa Winters

All rights reserved.

No part of this book may be reproduced in any form or by any electronic or mechanical means, including information storage and retrieval systems, without written permission from the author, except for the use of brief quotations in a book review.

This is a work of fiction. All of the characters and events portrayed in this novel are products of the author's imagination.

Edited by Per Se Editing

Cover Design by: Regina Wamba of ReginaWamba.com

To #14 for supporting my ideas even when they seemed a bit fantastical. I'll love you forever.

CHAPTER 1

My nerves are shot.

I don't want to be here, but it isn't my choice; it never has been. I've been forced to see a professional my entire life. This time it's to deal with my grief. At least that's the bullshit my parents fed me. It was a decision they came to together, which is a miracle these days. Communicating is not their forte, and being sober is an even greater challenge for them. Yet somehow, they managed to speak to each other long enough to sentence me to this purgatory. My parents mean well, but at this point the only one that can help is my sister. I need her.

She's gone.

Eyes fixed forward, I watch as the woman's red lips move, but I don't hear the sounds or words she speaks. The incessant tapping of the pen she holds has my complete focus, and it promises to sever the thin string holding my sanity together.

I'm not ready to talk about what happened, but she is hellbent on forcing me to relive every brutal minute of it. It's a memory I'm trying hard to repress. It's too painful.

My gaze finds the silver wall clock positioned just above Dr. Tilney's head. Ten more minutes.

"Marina, did you hear me?" Dr. Tilney manages to make her question sound like a scold.

I groan in response, sitting further back in my seat. For as sterile as this office is, the chairs are oversized and comfortable. So much so, I just want to close my eyes and sleep through the rest of this hellish session.

"Marina, I can't help you if you don't talk to me."

Lowering my eyes to meet hers, I muster the strength to speak.

"I don't want your help. I *want* to sleep."

Dr. Tilney's eyes narrow slightly, and that damn pen finally stops, suspended in air as the good doctor ferrets out the meaning in my words. She probably thinks my words mean something more. It's likely she believes me to be suicidal like Maggie, my sister. I'm not; I'm just tired.

"Are you sleeping well?" She switches her tactic.

I know this game. I've been playing it all my life. From as early as I can remember, I've been seeing someone from Dr. Tilney's practice. I rarely make it a year before I'm back through these doors, subjected to the same old mind games. As much as my parents would like to forget, I suffer from the same plight as Maggie. The only difference was that I learned to deny I saw the same monsters, while she refused, desperate for help.

"Marina," she repeats.

I shrug. "Define sleep." Her face remains stoic, so I relent. "No, I'm not sleeping. I've been having nightmares," I cringe at my slip.

The worst thing I could've done is admit that. Telling a shrink you're having nightmares is the worst idea when you're me. I've had to get really good at formulating my stories on the fly. Dr. Tilney has radar for bullshit, so perfecting lies has become my sport of choice throughout life. But this time, I don't have to lie. I haven't been having the same endless dream from my childhood. It's different this time.

It's so much worse.

"Again?" She doesn't miss a damn beat.

They never really stopped.

I'd never tell her that for so many reasons. The most important of them all is that it would prove I inadvertently killed my sister. Lies of omission are still lies, and mine caused Maggie to jump.

"Tell me about them," she demands, and I relent.

"They aren't the same as before." I take a deep breath and chew on my lower lip. I need to feel pain. Pain is better than sadness.

"Go on," she prods.

"They aren't . . . monsters," I blow out a puff of air. "This time they're about Maggie." I close my eyes and like clockwork, the dream resurfaces. Every last detail spilling out behind my lids. I can't escape it, so I decide to play nice and relay exactly what I see to Dr. Tilney. "She's lying on a gurney. They begin to zip the bag up, but her eyes open," I take a deep breath. "She looks right at me and whispers, 'I love you.'"

Dr. Tilney purses her lips, which could quite possibly be more annoying than the tapping.

"The same words she spoke before she jumped from the cliff."

I flinch at the verbal smack in the face. All memories of that day are burned into my mind, playing on a constant loop. It's another reason I'm not sleeping. If it's not the monsters or my sister laid out in a morgue replaying on a loop, it's that horrible day. Every night, I see her. Yellow sundress. Long blond hair blowing in the breeze. Her head turning to look at me. The words whispered on the wind ... *I love you.* The sad smile right before she turns away from me and jumps.

"I don't want to talk about that." My voice is edgy, and Dr. Tilney knows she's hit a sore spot.

"You witnessed a traumatic event, Marina. It's normal to have nightmares."

I turn my head away from her, willing away the tears that threaten to fall. She's leading me to places and memories I don't want to talk about. Isn't it enough that I can't forget them? That I'm forced to replay them nightly?

"All right, we can talk about something else." She clicks her tongue, unhappy to relent. "Start with the conversation you and Maggie had four days before her death."

I stiffen at her words; every sentence she speaks only drives the knife in deeper. Heat spreads through my body as my blood boils. The fact that everyone just assumes that Maggie is dead makes me livid. Without a body, I'll never believe she's dead. To me she's just ... gone.

"Marina, are you all right?"

"Her body was never found. She could still be alive," I snap. "She's *not* dead."

She taps that damn pen to her mouth.

"What makes you think that?" Her eyes narrow. "The experts all agree she couldn't have survived."

"She's my twin. I would know. I'd feel it." I run my hands through my hair, tired of this conversation. I've had it a million times with a million different people over the past four months. Every one of them says the same damn thing. She didn't survive that fall.

"In your dream, you see Maggie on a gurney. Perhaps,

subconsciously, your mind is trying to help you come to terms with the events of that day."

"No. It's just a dream. I can't control what I dream."

She doesn't respond to my comments, but forges ahead, annoying as ever.

"Tell me about the conversation you two had four days before," she presses.

"Ugh," I groan, annoyed at her probing. "She was scared and the medicine *you* provided wasn't working." My voice rises as I dig my fingernails into the skin of my legs, desperate for more pain. I need to stifle the sadness creeping toward the surface.

"Why do you say that the medicine wasn't working?" Her brow tilts upward.

"It made her tired and intensified the things she was seeing."

"Tell me about the things she was seeing."

I sigh, frustrated.

"This is my session. Not Maggie's." My words are biting, but she doesn't react. She doesn't say a word.

Dr. Tilney is a dog with a bone. She won't stop until our time is up or I walk out, which I'm currently tempted to do, but in the end, I won't. I'll give in and tell her what she wants to hear. It's the only way I'll ever be free of her. I need to play nice and appear rehabilitated. Like before.

"She was seeing monsters."

She knows full well what Maggie was seeing. It hasn't changed since we were three. She just wants to hear me say it. She believes that facing your problems head on is the first step in rehabilitation. I think she's a sadist.

"Just in her dreams?"

I shake my head back and forth.

"Everywhere."

Dr. Tilney places her pen back on her desk.

"The same monsters you used to see?"

Inhale. Exhale. Lie.

"My monsters weren't real. They were a figment of a childhood imagination created by the shadows in the dark." I grit my teeth at the lies I'm forced to tell. The rehearsed words I've repeated constantly since I was ten years old.

I know my monsters were very real. They hid in plain sight, disguised as people, but I saw their darkness. The way their eyes glowed a blazing red, burned holes into my being every time I saw one. They bared their elongated canines as if to prove they were to be feared. It wasn't necessary; my body shook when it sensed their presence. I didn't have to see them to be scared.

"Your sister was diagnosed with schizophrenia with paranoia. The medication was to help her."

"Should you be sharing your patient's diagnosis with other patients, doctor?"

"I'm not telling you anything you don't know. I'm simply reminding you. Based on your years of joint therapy, I'm not outside of my rights to discuss Maggie's diagnosis."

I bite my lip, trying desperately not to say the things on my tongue. I want to tell Dr. Tilney that I never really stopped seeing the creatures. I only said I did so I wouldn't end up in a straitjacket. I want to tell her how much I hate her smug face and condescending attitude, but I can't. Ever.

"She wasn't crazy, and the meds didn't help," I say, defeated.

"I don't use the word crazy. If she felt the medication she was prescribed was making things worse, she should've called me. There are always situations in which medication can cause worsening symptoms."

She didn't call because she would've been institutionalized. Both Maggie and I were threatened with that on numerous occasions by our parents. While I heeded the warnings and hid my paranoia, Maggie didn't. She couldn't, and she knew it was only a matter of time before they made good on those threats.

"Marina, your sister was sick."

My shoulders sag at her words. If she was sick, so am I.

"You're angry and you have plenty of reason to be. You were close to Maggie, and her decision hurt you."

"You don't know anything about her." My teeth grind in anger.

All her questions and prying over the years have piled up, making it very difficult not to break her in half. I'll never believe that Maggie chose to end her life and leave me. Something else had to have happened. Someone caused her to jump and I've made it my life's mission to discover who it was.

She leans back in her chair, crossing her arms, clucking her tongue a few times before speaking. "I'm sorry, Marina." For the first time today, there is a break in Dr. Tilney's armor. "I cared about Maggie too. She'd been my patient for years, and her death weighs heavily on me as well."

There is sadness in her eyes, and it forces me to admit that maybe I'm being unjustly hard on her. Her job is to help, and medicine is all she knows. For years I've been combative, and perhaps she's as tired of these sessions as I am. Then again, every time I've given her the benefit of the doubt, she's proven me wrong. She's good at playing games, and I've always struggled with getting caught up in them. I have to do better. Maggie didn't, and it cost her greatly in the end.

The world isn't privy to the things that Maggie and I know. There is a whole other world out there. One where the shadows in the night are not just tricks of the mind, but actual monsters. They give it fancy terms like schizophrenia, but we're not crazy. Everyone else is. It's hard to face reality when it includes the stuff of nightmares.

I sigh, lowering my eyes in ignominy.

"Tell me what you're thinking."

Inhale. Exhale. "It was my fault."

Because I lied about seeing the monsters too.

"I could've stopped her." The words escape without permission.

"Did you know she was considering suicide?"

My body jerks back at the question. It's ludicrous. I loved my sister and I would've done anything to stop her, had I thought she was contemplating that.

"No. Of course not." I shake my head vehemently.

"Then how could it be your fault?"

I didn't know, but I should've. She was my best friend, my sister. The signs were all there, yet I did nothing.

"It just is."

"It isn't. She didn't ask for your help. You couldn't help her, Marina," Dr. Tilney states.

She did, though. She begged me to admit to our parents that the monsters were real. I didn't. I kept quiet.

"She told me she was scared. I should've done something."

Her eyes soften, and she changes tactics once again.

"What happened earlier that day?" she asks softly.

I reflect back on that day, even though I don't need to. It's all there, clear as day.

"Maggie said they were coming for her, but she had a plan."

"Who was coming for her?"

"I don't know. She was hysterical. All she said was that she had to leave before she led them to us."

"Led them to your family?"

"Yeah, I assumed."

The only people that Maggie cared about was our family. She wouldn't have left unless she thought we were in danger, and based on her paranoia that day, she did. Something *had* happened, but she was too distressed to tell me. I had tried to uncover what had her upset, but she was insistent that she was running out of time. I should've forced her to talk to me; instead, I let her go.

"You followed her, but you didn't tell your parents?"

I narrow my eyes. She knows I didn't tell them. We've been over this. They would've driven her to the nearest hospital and dumped her there. Our mother was over the delusions—as she called them—and that would've been the final straw.

"My parents have their own issues."

So many issues. Yet nobody drags them to see a professional. Nobody's come to help me help them.

I'm alone.

"Tell me about that."

I sigh in agitation. My parents are the last people I want to talk about. They abandoned me when I needed them the most, and I'll forever harbor resentment for that.

"Marina?"

"My dad abuses pain medications, and my mother pretends it's not happening," I say flatly. "As long as her wine glass is never empty, she's fine."

She compresses her lips and I wonder what she's thinking in this moment. Has she realized that my family is gone and I'm alone?

"Have you spoken to them about how this makes you feel?"

I huff, exasperated at her lack of understanding about how pointless that would be.

"No. It wouldn't do any good."

"Why do you feel that way?"

Has she forgotten everything we've told her over the years?

My mom has never been okay. Since the day we were born, she's been absent. Grief will do that to a person. Maggie and I survived, while our triplet, Molly, was stillborn. We've never had our mother. A piece of her died the day she lost Molly, despite the fact that she had two other daughters that needed her.

After years of trying to pull my mom out of her misery, my dad gave up. Nothing worked, and their marriage was never the same. Instead of family outings, it was just our dad, Maggie, and me. He'd take us everywhere. For a moment, I allow my mind to drift to better days. Our favorite pastime with him was fishing. We loved those times with him, and some of my greatest memories are of the three of us down by the river. I smile absently at the memories. They seem like a lifetime ago, because those days didn't last long.

One day at work he threw out his back and was introduced to Vicodin. Since then, it's all been downhill. The father we knew and loved vanished, and we were left alone. If he isn't high, he's mean. I don't know which version of him I hate more.

I never told Dr. Tilney everything about my dad, because it would've led to CPS digging around. Who knows where Maggie and I would've ended up? No, she only knew about my mom, and that's not something I'm going to rehash. We've had this conversation numerous times over the past several years. I'm starting to feel like a broken record, and besides, it'll only lead to more "how does that make you feel" questions. So, I stick to less complex answers.

"I can't even hold a conversation with them." My voice cracks. "Because every time I try, they stare at me as if I'm Maggie."

She inhales, leaning her elbows on her desk. Exhaling, she brings her hands together and steeples her fingers. Her eyes find her clock and just like that, I know. As much as I want to mean something to someone, I don't. Her time will always be more important. Just like my dad's pill haze and my mom's numbing alcohol.

"This week I want you to work on communication."

I frown.

"Sit down and make a list of the things that are bothering you in regard to your parents. Ask them to have a family meeting and lay out your list of grievances."

I internally cringe. *Never happening.*

"I'll try." I collect my things and stand to go.

"Marina."

I turn back to look at Dr. Tilney.

"If you need to talk anytime, day or night, please call. I'm always here, not just during our sessions." Her eyes are kind and sincere, but I know better.

It's dollar bills that she's seeing when she looks at me. It's always about the money. I school my features, refusing to show any sign of weakness or hurt.

"Thanks, Dr. Tilney," I say, shutting the door and therapy behind me for the day.

On my way to the car, my phone lights up in my hands. I consider just stuffing it in my pocket and ignoring its existence, but I've been doing that for too long. I've slowly pushed away everyone from *before*, yet they don't give up. Groaning, I lift the screen to my face, shielding it from the sun.

SHANNON: **I miss you. Dinner tonight?**

I AUDIBLY SIGH, because deep down I knew this was what it would be. I'm not really up for it after the session with Dr.

Tilney, not that I really need an excuse to opt out. I've avoided my friends for weeks. The fact Shannon still tries is a testament to how good of a friend she is. I don't deserve her loyalty. It would be so much easier if she'd just give up on me.

Me: Let me get back with you. Just leaving the gym.

I lie. I always lie. Telling my friends about seeing a shrink is never going to happen. They probably suspect as much, but I don't see a point in confirming it. My friends don't need to worry that I'm losing my mind again. They know about before.

Shannon: Please! You ditched us last week...

And the week before that. I truly feel bad pushing off Shannon, but it's never just her. I'd be forced to hang out with our old group, and that's not something I choose to do to myself. It's easier to avoid them rather than being dragged into conversations that I don't want to have. At twenty-one years old, they've experienced things I've never even dreamed of. College, dating, typical milestones. Things I've never experienced because my life isn't normal.

No matter how much I care about my friends, it's hard to not be bitter. They've moved on while I've stayed rooted in this state of perpetual hell without Maggie. I know it's not their fault, and at the end of the day, I have to remind myself of that. They loved Maggie and they miss her too. It's just that they have the luxury of moving on. I don't. I've been unfair and the first step in making things better is stepping out of my comfort zone.

Me: Okay, fine. I'll see you tonight.

Shannon: Yes! Head to my house.

I blow out a breath, trying not to let the events of the day hover over me like a black cloud. If I'm going to have to put a smile on my face tonight for my friends' benefit, I need to start working on it now.

As I unlock my car, a familiar feeling of unease washes over me. I stop in my tracks as every hair on the back of my neck stands at attention.

No. No. No. Not again. Someone is watching me.

I glance around at the parking lot. Empty. My eyes dart toward the alley to my left. Empty. Across the street, the park is also vacant. In fact, it's eerily quiet for this time of day. *Where is everyone?* A hoarse cawing noise has my head snapping to a pole across the road in the park.

A large black crow sits stoically, staring directly at me.

"Creepy freaking bird."

At that, the thing takes flight, coming right at me. I practically jump into my Volkswagen, locking the door behind me. Putting the key into the ignition, I turn the car on and yelp at the blaring music coming from the radio.

"Jesus Christ." My hands come to my chest, my breathing heavy.

Pull yourself together, Marina.

My head falls to the steering wheel as I try to calm my racing heart. My paranoia isn't good. It's just like before. It's how everything started with Maggie too. First the delusions, then the hallucinations. Or so we thought. *You beat it.*

I run both hands through my hair, pulling at the roots. All the anger, frustration, and sadness are coming to a head. A primal scream bursts from my vocal cords as my fists pound the steering wheel, over and over again, until all the fight leaves me and I'm nothing more than a weeping girl in a deserted parking lot. *Alone.*

CHAPTER 2

Coming through the front door to my parents' home is anything but comforting. Where most of my friends would be greeted by an overeager mother desperate to spend time with them since they've been away at college, I'm met with silence.

The television is on in the great room, and my father is in his typical position, feet up and conked out. I call his name several times, but he doesn't stir. He won't. He's passed out, per usual.

It's getting worse.

Looking around, I cringe at the state of my home. Dishes are piled up in the sink, a layer of dust coats every inch of wood, and not a single photo is to be seen. Unlike other homes, mine has never had walls lined with family photos or pictures of Maggie and me from childhood. We didn't even have graduation pictures taken.

No wonder Maggie and I are so screwed up. It's the product of our upbringing. If I'd just told Dr. Tilney, maybe we could've gotten out of here. Maybe we could've had a different life. *It's too late for that now.*

Creeping by my mother's half-open bedroom door, I peek my head into a dark room devoid of sound. My mom is likely three bottles into her nightly wine consumption and passed out. So I close the door a little more and head for the steps. My foot lands on the bottom stair when I hear her raspy voice call out, "Maggie?"

I stiffen at her words, wanting to pretend I didn't hear her and run up the stairs to the safety of my room. But I don't. No matter how little I mean to her, she still means something to me. Absent or not, she's my mom and I want—no, need—her in my life. Even if this is the only way to have her, drunk and confused, calling me by my missing sister's name.

"It's Marina, Mom. Can I get you anything?" I call in from the threshold, not wanting to go any farther. The room smells like stale cigarettes and vomit. My stomach can't handle the combination on a normal day, but on an empty stomach, I'm afraid it'll revolt.

"Ah," she sighs. "I thought you were Maggie, finally come home."

"Nope. Just me," I say grimly. "Need some water?" I prompt, knowing full well she'll never accept it.

"No," she says before silence falls around us once more.

I'm about to turn and head back to my room, but she speaks again.

"You know she's with Molly," she grates out in that voice that sounds as if she's smoked an entire pack—or two—of Marlboro Reds today alone.

I breathe deeply, not in the mood for her nonsense. I've heard it all before. When she's really hit the bottle hard, she starts in on her conspiracy theories about Molly not really being stillborn. After an afternoon with Dr. Tilney, this is the last conversation I want to have.

My parents' delusions and addictions are what the doctors should be focusing on.

"The hospital and that doctor of yours are working together. My girls are important," she goes on, and I try my best to tune her out. Over the past couple of weeks, she's brought Dr. Tilney into her crazed ideas. I want to remind her that she's the one who pushed me back into therapy with the "doctor of mine."

The longer I stand here, the longer she'll go on. Sometimes I let her, if only to have some sort of conversation with her, even if it's dysfunctional and encouraging her delusions. I take what I can get. It's the only relationship she's capable of having with me.

"I'm going to sleep now. Make sure you lock your door."

"All right, Mom. Get some rest," I say, exhaustion closing in.

I turn to walk away, but not before she gets in one last chilling thought, "They'll come for you too."

As I close the door, my whole body shudders. Not because I actually buy into her nonsensical ideas about Molly and Maggie being together, but because of her last words.

They'll come for you too.

I shut myself in my room, close the blackout curtains, and sit cross-legged on my bed. Running my hands roughly down the length of my face, I attempt to push away the incessant chills. I'm on edge and damn near ready to jump off my own metaphorical cliff.

Grabbing the picture of Maggie and me that sits next to my bed, I study the photo. Anyone who looked at it would think we were normal, happy teenagers, but I know better. Maggie's smile doesn't quite reach her eyes like I know it does when she's truly happy. She stares off to the side, looking distracted.

That night she had me up for hours because she swore

someone had been standing at the foot of my bed. Watching me sleep. I still get goosebumps thinking about it. It wasn't the first time and it wasn't the last, but she had been different. She had been frantic. I shake thoughts of that night away and replace the picture where it belongs.

I try to catch an hour of sleep, but it never comes. Instead, I stare into the dark and think about what my family could've been like. How different Maggie's and my childhood should've been. I wish for things I'll never have.

I'M NOT ready for a night out.

These girls have been my friends since grade school, and maybe I need them, but the last thing I want to do is mingle. I'm liable to break out into hysterics at the mention of old times. Memories from the past that are actually good. Fun times with my sister, which I'd give anything to have back. Those conversations might break me tonight.

I ring the doorbell and run my fingers through my hair, smoothing out the knots. Shannon opens the blue door with a wide smile plastered across her face.

"Rina," she exclaims, pulling me into a tight hug. "Why the hell did you ring the doorbell?"

Shannon has been my friend since kindergarten. She was the only one who never felt like a third wheel with Maggie and me. Her parents, Bob and Susan Cline, took us in and treated us like their own. My sister and I came through these doors more times than I can count. I've never rung the doorbell before, but tonight it just seemed weird to walk right in. I can't explain it; maybe it's because everything in my world has changed. But I don't say that.

"I didn't want to catch Bob in his underwear again," I tease instead, hoping to lighten the mood.

"Ew. Don't remind me." She mock gags. "The 'rents are not here, and the girls are having a drink before we head out."

I force a smile. They're drinking, which is another reason I tend to avoid them. With my parents' issues with booze and pills, the last thing I want to do is follow in their footsteps.

"What can I get you? I have beer, wine, shots, Pepsi." She grins, knowing my pick of poison far too well.

"Coke?"

"Obviously." Her body shakes as she laughs. I appreciate the fact that Shannon never pushes me to partake. She knows my feelings on the subject and she's never questioned it.

We walk through the arched doorway leading into the kitchen. My two other best friends, Jill and Andrea, dance around to old-school eighties' music like they don't have a care in the world. *That used to be me.*

When Maggie and I got out of our house and could just be kids, we enjoyed ourselves. Those days seem like an eternity ago.

"Woohoo, she's here," Andrea shouts over the music.

"I'm here," I exclaim in the most contrived cheerleader voice I can muster, complete with spirit fingers.

"Rina!" Jill shouts, standing and walking my way. She pulls me into a delicate hug. It's as if she's afraid if she squeezes too tight, I'll break right here in front of her. I have to force myself not to roll my eyes. She's the mother hen of the group. Always has been.

"We're heading straight to The Shack, so drink up." She nods to the Coke in my hand, smiling. I purse my lips before tipping it back and drinking it like I'm chugging a beer.

"Attagirl. You get that caffeine," Jill snickers, receiving a choice finger salute in return.

"The Shack? For real?"

Shannon raises a brow.

"Is there somewhere else that magically sprang up overnight?" she teases.

Liberty is a small town, population twelve hundred. There is exactly one bank, one library, one part-time café, two gas stations, and one pizza joint—The Shack. The next option is a ten-minute drive away. Shannon's parents' house is in town and a two-minute walk to The Shack, so it just makes sense. She's home for fall break, making it a convenient meeting place for a night out.

I take another drink, hoping to get a spike of energy. If I'm going to do this, I might as well try to stay awake.

"Let's go." Shannon bounces on her toes.

I've never quite understood the excitement at going to the same place that we've been hundreds of times. In a town this small, you're guaranteed to run into at least a dozen people you graduated with.

"Do you think Jason will be there?" Andrea asks the group, only proving my point.

Jason has been Andrea's crush since high school. They were the perfect match—captain of the football team and head cheerleader—but they could never get their crap together. The awkward exchanges were painful to watch. He adored her just as much as she did him, and their fierce love made them both incapable of holding a conversation that wasn't full of stuttering. They both went off to college, ending any chance of something actually happening between them.

"I heard he's in town on break. He might be there," Jill says reassuringly.

Andrea squeals and we all laugh at her giddiness.

Despite my reluctance, I have to admit it's nice to just be normal for a night. No talk of absent parents and dead sisters.

I'm in my happy place when something large and black swoops low over our heads. Shrill screeches sound as we all duck to avoid the massive creature.

"What the hell?" Shannon cries.

My eyes dart around wildly, trying to find the perpetrator of our near heart attacks. Perched upon a lamppost is a black crow, gawking keenly in our direction.

"It's just a crow," I say as my voice pitches slightly.

"Stupid freaking bird," Andrea calls.

What the hell is it today with me and birds? I shake off the lingering chills and start off toward The Shack. When my hands reach the knob of the door, a harsh, guttural caw sounds behind us. I turn in time to see the large black bird fly off into the moonlit sky. A cold shiver runs down my back, but I stuff it down, eager to have a normal night. *No monsters allowed.*

Walking into The Shack, I am both saddened and overjoyed to see it's exactly the same as the last time I was here. Nothing has changed within these four walls, yet *everything* has changed. The simple pleasures that most people my age take for granted are lost on me, because I'm lost. *Maggie should be here with us.*

Dim lights hide the peeling paint and grime of the unkempt bar that lines the back wall. This establishment serves as both the local pizza place and bar. At one time, the state of the place wouldn't have bothered me, but today I seriously consider opting for the ten-minute drive to avoid food poisoning. Through the door from the kitchen comes the same weathered woman who's tended the bar for as long as I can remember.

"Hey, Maggie," her throaty smoker's voice calls to me.

I wince at her misstep.

"Marina," I correct, but she doesn't seem to care.

"What'll it be for ya ladies?"

"Can we have one minute, please?" Andrea says. "What does everyone want?"

The girls discuss their choice of toppings. My lips purse, nothing sounding good.

"I could really go for a shot of tekillya," Jill chimes in.

I internally cringe. Maggie had always called tequila *tekillya*. Senior year of high school, Jill had tried tequila, and after several hours of holding her hair back while she got sick, Maggie dubbed it tekillya. It stuck with all of us, but it was always Maggie who would yell it loud as we all raised our glasses—typically containing cherry soda—in celebration. It's a dumb high school memory, but it still causes a pang of longing for my sister.

Andrea rambles off the typical order. One large plain cheese and four side salads. The only difference is the addition of four shots of tequila with chasers.

"I don't want a shot," I call to the aged woman. "Just a Coke, please."

Nobody says a word, but everyone averts their eyes and looks genuinely disappointed. Yet another reason why I've avoided these kinds of nights.

The woman rushes off to put in our order, while the bell above the door chimes, indicating more people have entered. By the way Andrea's eyes light up, I can only assume it's Jason and his crew.

"Andrea," Jason says with a smirk, as he passes our table with four other guys. I only recognize two of them. He's changed since high school. He's bigger. Cockier. Less boy, more man. Yet one more thing that's changed.

Our drinks are placed in front of us, drawing the girls' attention back to our table. Everyone lifts their glasses just like the old days. Three sets of eyes watch me as I sit stone-faced and unmoving. We haven't so much as mentioned Maggie, and now this? I don't want to do this. I don't want to carry on traditions without her.

Looking at my friends, I can see how much *they* need this, and I promised myself I'd be there for them too. Slowly, I lift my glass of Coke and with a slight stutter call out, "Cheers." They all repeat after me with somber faces. They want to memorialize her, but tonight I want to forget. For a brief moment, I understand my parents' need for numbness.

We don't talk about Maggie past the salute, and I'm appreciative of that. Our pizza comes a bit later and we eat in silence, all in our own thoughts. When we're done and our table is cleaned off, Jill turns excitedly toward the table of guys.

"Wanna play a game?" she calls, a wicked smirk plastered on her face.

"What kind of game?" the blond muscle-head with Jason calls back in a flirtatious tone.

She taps her finger to her mouth in mock thought. "Never Have I Ever. Loser takes a drink."

"You're on," Jason calls, standing up and pushing another table against theirs.

"You coming?" Shannon asks, holding out her hand to me. "You don't have to play."

Her smile is genuine, with no trace of disappointment or frustration. She just gets me. I nod, smiling up at my friend, before taking her hand and allowing her to help me out of the booth. I squeeze to let her know just how much I appreciate her. We're not seated long before the game begins.

"Never have I ever played strip poker," Jill starts, laughing at Andrea as she lifts her drink to her lips.

"You bitch," Andrea chuckles, wiping the remaining beer from her mouth. "You did that on purpose."

"Obviously," Jill snorts.

My eyes volley back and forth, watching the exchange like

an interloper. Jill, Andrea, and Shannon all went off to college together, while I stayed back with Maggie, attending community college. These girls have had years together to form memories that I wasn't part of. It only furthers the divide I feel, but I try my best to not show it. I smile widely and laugh when appropriate.

The game continues and beer after beer is drunk. The group skips over me like I'm not even here. Clearly, I'm throwing out the *not happening* vibe. As much as I should appreciate it, it just drives home the differences. And it hurts. So much of my life has changed and I had secretly hoped that maybe tonight would seamlessly slip back to the good ol' days. It's heartbreaking that it didn't. I feel like more of an outcast than I did before.

An hour later we're still sitting here and they're still playing games. The girls talk about college, boys, and parties, shamelessly flirting with Jason and his friends. I continue nodding my head as though I have any experience with any of those things. It's exhausting and I'm ready for bed.

"I'm going to head home, ladies," I tell the group, standing to my feet.

"What? No way," Jill cries. "You can't leave yet."

"I'm lame tonight. My bed is calling." I smile, trying to convey that it's not them. It's me.

"We hardly see you anymore," Andrea whines, but it lacks conviction. If I had to guess, she isn't all that sad I'm leaving. She's only trying to act like a good friend.

"We'll do this again soon," I promise, but I don't mean it. There is not a part of me that believes I'll subject myself to this again anytime soon. I'll always have love for my friends, but we are different people, living in different worlds. I'm not the fun Marina they once knew. No, that girl is gone.

"I'm not ready to leave," Jill says to the group, and they all agree.

"You girls stay. I can walk home by myself. It's nice outside and I could use some fresh air."

"Are you sure that's a good idea?" Shannon's eyes narrow in my direction.

She's always been the overly careful one of all my friends. I love that about her, but tonight, I just want her to let me be.

"My house is only a few blocks away. What could possibly happen in Liberty?"

"Your house is like a mile away." Shannon quips, scrunching her nose. "It's towns like these that breed serial killers."

I bark a laugh at her paranoia.

"I'll be fine. I'll text you as soon as I'm home."

And I will. Shannon has been my friend longest, and I don't want to hurt her. She's the one I'll miss most when I stop hanging out.

"I'm walking you out." Shannon stands, ushering me toward the door.

Jill and Andrea give me hugs, making me swear to text the moment I'm home. I squeeze them a little longer than normal. A thank you for all the good years and fond memories. A goodbye as well. I lift my hand and say goodnight to the guys and head toward the exit.

As soon as we're out of earshot of the other two, Shannon swoops in with her questions.

"Are you okay?" Her voice is low and full of concern.

I blow out a breath, trying to figure out where her questions are going to go.

"I'm all right. It was just a long day."

"Do you wanna talk about it?"

I turn to her.

"Not really."

Lines form in Shannon's forehead. "We all miss her too, you know? You can talk to us."

I sigh.

"I know."

"Do you? Because I feel like you're pulling away every day."

She's too perceptive, always has been. How do I tell her she's right? Would she understand and let me go? Instead, I continue with the lies.

"I'm not trying to, Shan. I just need some time to myself."

"I miss you." A tear slips down her cheek and I lean in to wipe it away. "You two were like my sisters. I feel like I've lost you both."

I grab her hands in mine and squeeze. "Give me some time, please," I beg my oldest friend.

She nods.

"Love you, Rina," she says, pulling me into a hug.

"Love you too."

Shannon steps back, biting her lip.

"Call me as soon as you're home. Promise."

"I promise." Smiling, I turn and push through the exit door of The Shack, letting it slam shut behind me.

When I'm finally alone, I take a deep breath of fresh air, staving off the tears I've been holding back. Tonight was a reminder of what my life used to be. That life is gone. Maggie took it with her the day she decided to jump from that cliff and leave me.

I straighten my back, resolved to get home and attempt to get some sleep. Tomorrow, I start the process of trying to get my parents help. Anything to get some semblance of normalcy. I try to imagine what that would look like. Clean house. Home-cooked meals. Parents who are sober enough to ask about my day. The ability to go off to college and not worry about them.

The houses begin to spread out more the farther I walk, and it isn't long before I'm at the edge of town. The sidewalk ends, and I'm forced to walk in the dewy grass or on the street. Since there isn't a car in sight, I opt for the dry pavement. There's a slight chill, triggering me to pull my jean jacket tighter around my body. I walk past the last of the streetlamps, preparing to enter the darkness of what we consider to be the beginning of the country. It isn't long from here.

My parents' home is less than three football fields away when a sense of unease rolls over me yet again. I speed up my steps, annoyed at how jittery I've been today. When the disquiet intensifies, I stop, looking at my surroundings. Nothing.

Pull it together, Marina.

I begin walking at a clipped pace as the wind picks up, tossing my hair haphazardly over my eyes. Brushing the hair aside, I keep my head forward. A cry from behind has me whipping around to see the black crow sitting atop the last lamppost. Once again, it's staring in my direction. *Creepy ass bird.*

It's then that I notice a white van twenty yards away. *That wasn't there before.* A feeling of anxiety crawls into my bloodstream. Something isn't right. The engine is running, but the lights are off. Not wanting to waste another minute, I spin around, moving forward at the same steady clip. My feet carry me another thirty yards before my palms begin to sweat and moisture builds on my brow. I glance over my shoulder to see the van creeping toward me as if trying to go unnoticed. My inner voice is screaming at me to run. So I do.

My feet hitting the pavement doesn't drown out the sound of the van quickly approaching. I don't look, desperate to make it home. Only one hundred more yards until I will reach the safety of my parents' front porch. My arms pump faster, trying frantically to outrun the van. *I can do it.*

Another peek confirms my deep inner fear. They've caught up.

Looking to my left, I decide to make a run for the cornfield. Once inside the maze of corn, I hide about five rows back behind a large stalk. Stomping through the field will only make my location obvious. It's too loud.

Crouched down, willing my thumping heart to quiet, I don't breathe for fear someone might hear me. I listen for any signs that someone has entered the rows of corn but hear nothing. I swallow, continuing to work on my breathing. My hand feels around, trying to find something—anything—I can use to defend myself. My palm wraps around a small rock. I know it won't do much damage, but it's better than nothing.

The sound of the van moving away has me letting out the breath I had been holding. A sigh of relief escapes as my heavy breaths come out in pants. I sit shaking for what feels like forever before I muster the courage to stand slowly. The sound of the van in the distance encourages me to attempt an escape.

I make my way through the corn, thinking my best bet would be to remain hidden for as long as the field keeps me out of view from the road.

They'll come for you too.

My mother's unsettling words run over me, and I shiver at the ominous thought.

Stop, Marina. You have to keep your head on straight and get home.

I continue my trek, knowing the field is about to end, giving way to our property line. If I can just get a little farther...

The fleeting sense of hopefulness crumbles as stalks crack, indicating something is approaching. I take off in a sprint, weaving through the stems instead of running straight down one row, using my hands to push away the coarse leaves, but

I'm not quick enough. Beefy arms circle me from behind, picking me clean off my feet. High-pitched cries force their way from my throat, intermixed with pleas for help.

"Help me!" I scream, but what's the use?

Nobody's going to hear me out here. My parents are well past the state of consciousness.

Regardless, I continue to bellow at the top of my lungs, fists pounding into the thighs of the man. A large hand covers my mouth, muffling my screams. As I'm pulled through the field, husks of corn tear at my skin. My heart pounds and bile rises in to my throat. Kicking, I fight with everything I have to escape the clutches of this stranger. *He's too strong.*

I look up into black eyes devoid of humanity. His face is stone, unmoved by my pleas. It's then that I know this man is evil. He might not have the red glowing eyes, but that doesn't make him any less of a monster. His soulless eyes make him appear barely human.

He drags me around to the back of the waiting van, dropping me to my feet and releasing his hold with one arm to open the door. I use the moment to swing my half-closed fist, clutching the rock, into the back of his head. It hits with a sickening thud, but he doesn't react.

Doesn't flinch.

He pulls me in tighter, crushing me into his side as he opens the door with one hand. I'm pinned under his arm, but I continue to crash the rock into his skull, all the while screaming for my life, hoping that somehow, someone hears and comes to my aid.

No matter what I do, how hard I hit, it's not enough.

Once the door is open, he grabs me with both hands and throws me inside, nearly on top of another girl who's either dead or passed out. The smell of urine is strong, signaling she likely wet herself.

What happened to her?

I whimper, my whole body beginning to shake uncontrollably. The adrenaline is starting to wear off.

Pull yourself together.

Two is better than one, and maybe if I can get this girl to come to, we can formulate a plan while they're preoccupied up front.

"Wake up," I whisper, pushing on her back. "Get up. Fight." She doesn't stir.

It's dark, but the dim overhead light from the door being ajar allows me to see her chest move slightly. *She's alive.*

I sigh in relief, but before I have time to process anything more, a stabbing pain sears my neck, and everything goes black.

CHAPTER 3

My head is pounding.

Tap. Tap. Tap.

My hands come up to rub my temples to ease some of the throbbing so that I can open my eyes. The pain is too intense. Even a slight flutter of my lashes has the pounding intensifying.

Tap. Tap. Tap.

"What is that godforsaken tapping?" My patience is running thin. Surely my father hasn't chosen this one day to decide to fix up our crumbling house.

Tap. Tap. Tap.

I sit up feeling light-headed. Steadying myself, I try blinking a few times to help my eyes adjust to the dark. As the room comes into focus and the foggy haze that I've been in dissipates, confusion sets in.

Where am I?

I'm staring at a concrete wall. As I squint to see more, I question my own sight. Rubbing the sleep from my eyes, I look again. *Same concrete wall.*

My eyes dart wildly around, registering one concrete wall and bars to my left and right. Spinning on my knees, I moan when I see yet another set of bars. I scramble to my feet and pull my body up to a standing position. My legs are weak and wobbly, making me unsteady. Pushing with all the strength I have left, I try to open the large door. It doesn't budge.

"Help," I cry out. "Somebody help me."

My fists bang on the metal bars, and I pray that somebody will hear me, or they'll give way. The pain in my head intensifies with every move I make. The tapping continues overhead, and I cry out in hopes that I'll be heard over the ruckus of whatever is causing the noise. I scream at the top of my lungs. "Help! Please!" Nobody answers. I squint, trying to see as far down through the bars as I can, only to find each and every other cell empty.

Sliding down, I curl into myself on the dirty floor. Urine and filth coat my clothes, stinging my nostrils and causing me to gag. My stomach twists and vomit rises to the surface. I turn away from the bars and spill the contents of my gut onto the concrete floor. When there is nothing left to expel, dry heaves rack my body until every ounce of energy is gone, leaving me weak and hollow.

My thoughts run a mile a minute. *How did I get here? What happened?*

The events of the night crash into me. The van. The strong hands. The other girl.

Curling into a ball, I rock back and forth as a million horrific possibilities assault me. Every terror-filled movie I've ever watched, from *Taken* to *The Silence of the Lambs*, runs through my imagination.

I'm going to have my skin peeled off. Or worse . . . be eaten alive.

I cry out, but there isn't anyone around to hear me. I'm alone. Utterly and truly alone. At this stage I regret all the times I thought to myself that life couldn't get any crueler. Right now, in this cell, I know it can get *far* worse.

Shannon would notice, right? Maybe they have people out looking for me.

I never texted her.

"Fuck," I yell, grabbing both sides of my head and squeezing to try to stave off the thrashing headache.

No one is looking for me. I did this. It wouldn't be the first time I didn't hold up my end of a bargain with Shannon, but karma has finally caught up with me. They probably think it's like every other time. Shannon will check in within a week, but a week is too long. Will my parents even notice I'm gone? *Depends on what state they're in.*

I feel for my phone, finding it missing. My pockets are empty, purse nowhere in sight.

Of course. It's probably still lying in that cornfield, out of sight where nobody will find it for another month, if ever. Dread fills me. How long have I been in this place? There is no sense of time, no windows to separate day from night. It could be hours; it could be days. I don't know how long I slept.

The reality of my situation, coupled with everything from the past year, moves over me like a tidal wave of heartache. It's too much. This has all been too much. I'm a walking tragedy. Who else has this much bad in their life? Sorrow takes hold of me, pouring out as if the dam holding my emotions in check has given way. Tears run unbidden down my cheeks and I don't hold back. I let them out. Something I've refused to do for a long time.

Here in this prison, there's no one to witness me break. There's a sense of freedom in that. The ability to be vulnerable when nobody's looking.

I give into it. Allow it. Embrace it.

And when the last tear has fallen, I roll my shoulders and put my armor back in place.

Whoever has me locked down here will regret it. I will fight with my last damn breath.

What they don't realize is they've taken the wrong girl. Someone with nothing left to lose. I won't go out easy.

I'll need my strength. I start working through rounds of deep breathing. Eventually, my body gives in to exhaustion and I fall asleep.

I peer out over the heavy quilt into the darkness of my room. The small night-light by my bed illuminates just enough to see the area directly in front and to the sides of me. A noise near my closet has me fisting the sheets so tight my knuckles begin to ache. I dare not speak, for fear it'll hear me. It's been in my room every night for the past week. It leers at me from the corner. I know it's there. I can hear it breathe. Some nights I see the glow of its red eyes. Slamming my own shut tightly, I silently pray to God to keep me safe.

"Rina?" My mother's voice calls from the doorway.

"Y-yes?" I say quietly, afraid the creature will hurt my mom if she sees it.

"What was that noise?"

The light flicks on overhead and I hold my breath in anticipation of seeing the creature in the light, but nothing is there. My room is empty.

I exhale in relief, eyes scanning the area for signs of what I know was there moments ago. My mother walks to the side of my bed, pulling the covers away from my face and holding my hand in hers.

"Someone was here. I know it."

My eyes widen at her declaration. Finally, she's ready to hear my truths.

"Was it Molly? Did she come back to us?"

I deflate as she punctures the hope I had. It always comes back to Molly. No matter how many people try to explain to her, she doesn't get it. Molly never lived. She didn't even take one breath. I want to scream that Maggie and I survived. We're here and we need her, but that doesn't matter. It never has.

"No, Mom. It wasn't Molly."

It's easier to appease her. Just like my dad always has. We feed into her delusions that Molly might actually be out there somewhere.

"All right. Good night," she says, bending over to kiss my forehead, the potent smell of alcohol clinging to her.

I turn to my side, pulling the covers with me, and shiver at the sight of my open window. There is no doubt in my mind that it was closed. Once my mom is soundly asleep, I sneak out of my room and crawl into bed with Maggie. We have each other. We only have each other.

I AWAKEN WITH A JERK. It wasn't just any dream, but a memory from years past. It's been ages since I've thought of those days. Maggie and I were so young and vulnerable, but we were alone. My father thought that Maggie and I had inherited some gene from our mother that caused hallucinations. Therapists tried to explain to him that what my mother was dealing with was entirely different from what Maggie and I were describing, but he never believed that. He thought she transferred her grief and aberrations to us. Eventually, he convinced her of the same, and that was the start of our foray into years of psychoanalysis.

I try hard to repress those years, but with Maggie's disappearance and now this current situation, it's like a doorway has opened to my past. It's not enough that I'm living out my own version of hell, but my mind insists on reliving every horrible childhood memory right along with it.

Because they're connected.

I shiver in the cold air circling around me. There must be a vent somewhere. I stand, searching for the source of the draft.

A man's voice has me slinking back into the shadows, desperate to not be seen.

"Get in," he commands.

A scampering sound comes from the cell next to me, and hope rises.

I'm not alone after all.

"Please don't hurt me," a girl's voice cries out.

I slowly move backwards until my back hits the wall behind me. Huddled in the corner, I do my best to stay as quiet as possible, assessing the situation.

Whimpering in the cell next to me gives way to something akin to slurping. I strain to hear, trying to place the strange sound. It gets louder, and the cries from the girl intensify. I lean forward, chancing a glance, but my view of the girl is obstructed by a looming figure.

"Please," she begs.

Chills run down my spine and my hands come to my ears to block out the horrific sound.

A bloodcurdling scream has my eyes slamming shut and another bout of terror racing through me. My hands press on my ears so tightly that they begin to ache. *Please, God, please help her,* I silently beg, rocking on unsteady legs. Between my hands blocking out the noise and my heart beating so irregularly fast, I miss the man leaving the cell next door. I rush to the bars separating me from her.

"Are you okay? Talk to me," I command, but she says nothing. "What did they do to you?"

She's curled into a ball on the floor, unresponsive. I fear what that means for her.

I search the cell for anything that could lead to escape. There's nothing. No vent to be seen. No windows. The bars are sturdy, and the lock appears to be unpickable, not that it matters. There's nothing in this prison that I could use to pick it anyway.

I'll have to bide my time and strike when the opportunity presents itself.

Days have gone by and nobody has come or gone from this place. The girl net to me hasn't stirred, making it clear she's dead.

Dehydration is setting in. If I don't get fluids soon, I will die. My muscles ache, and I keep slipping in and out of consciousness.

My back is against the wall, knees pulled in to my chest, head resting on the cold concrete.

"Why aren't they coming back?" I say aloud, as if there is anyone to hear me.

"They will," a small broken voice says from the cell next to me.

I bolt upright, finding strength I didn't think I had.

"Y-you're alive?" I stutter around my dry mouth. "H-how is that possible?"

I'm falling all over myself, blinking hard as my eyes scan the girl, trying to determine if this is a mirage or reality. At this point, I wouldn't be surprised if I was dreaming this.

"They have to keep us alive."

I scamper to the wall of bars between us. "Who are you?"

The girl doesn't answer my questions. She just continues talking, her voice hollow.

"They're gonna sell us."

"What?" My scratchy throat barely allows me to say the word. My eyes are narrowed to mere slits.

"Haven't you figured it out yet? We're being trafficked."

My breath hitches. I'm not sure what I thought, but that never occurred to me. The thought is worse than anything I had imagined. I'd rather die than be some gross man or woman's plaything.

"We're going to be blood banks."

My blood runs cold and my entire body begins to quiver. Is that what the slurping sound was the other day? Were they taking blood from her?

"Oh, God," I cry out, voice hoarse. "We need to find a way out of here."

"Shh. They'll hear you."

"Who?" my voice asks shakily, eyes darting around, expecting to find someone lurking in the shadows.

"Them. The men with the glowing eyes."

I freeze at her words, decade's worth of memories flooding my mind. Red eyes. Glowing.

Monsters.

"What have you seen?" I grip the bars so tightly my forearms ache. "What are you talking about?" I yell, desperate for her to start talking. She's seen them. She's seen the monsters.

She turns her head toward me.

"They're not human," she whispers.

I jerk away from the cell. Her dead eyes look right through me.

Her head turns away from me, and that's when I notice the bite marks on her shoulder.

"What happened to you?"

Her hands fly to her collarbone, shielding her wound.

"Don't ask questions you don't want answers to, pet," a frighteningly low voice speaks from the entrance of her cell.

She scampers backwards, but I sit frozen in place, taking in the tall, ghostly man in front of me. My eyes widen, and a chill runs down my spine at the evil standing in front of me.

"Let me see your neck," the man roars angrily at the fragile-looking girl.

She cowers at his ire, whimpering pathetically and shielding herself from the man.

"Who the hell are you?" I say, willing myself to stand and meet his hard stare head on.

He bares his teeth but turns away from me, never answering my question.

"Ramsey!" the man yells. "Get in here."

Another man approaches, his footsteps heavy and echoing off the walls.

"Stop the screaming, Sarcos. These walls aren't that thick," he chuckles.

"What the hell happened to her neck?"

"How should I know?" He raises his hands like he doesn't have a care in the world.

"You and I are the only ones cleared to be down here." He glares in Ramsey's direction. "If I didn't touch her, that only leaves you. Now . . . what did you do?" His voice is lethal.

Ramsey seems to notice the seriousness of the situation and he stands up taller, so he looks down at the man he calls Sarcos.

"I did whatever I wanted to do, S. Do you have a problem with that?"

"If the Crown gets wind of this, we'll be dead. You know we aren't to touch the donors."

Crown? Donors?

"Bah, the new Crown is soft. He doesn't know the first thing about keeping us all sated. I take what I want."

The sound of the girl's door opening shakes away my questions about the man's strange words. Seconds later, an overhead light illuminates the area in bright white. I rub my eyes to clear the stars caused by the intense light. My hands lower and finally, for the first time since I've been down in this dungeon, I can see everything clearly. The man who must be Sarcos saunters toward the small girl and begins to examine her, lifting her hand and watching it drop limply to her side. When he seems to be satisfied with his inspection, he goes to leave.

"She'll live," he says to Ramsey.

At that very moment, the girl springs forward, knocking Sarcos over the head with a metal water bowl. He's momentarily dazed, giving her the benefit of a head start. It doesn't last long, and in a matter of seconds he's behind her, grabbing her neck and lifting her off the ground.

She shrieks in fear of what's to come. My head is screaming for me to turn away. Not to watch. But I can't. I watch the morbid scene play out, biting my lip so hard that the tang of copper coats my tongue. The events that occur in the moments after leave me paralyzed. She screams as the man bites into her neck, taking a chunk out of her skin. His mouth forms to the original wound and he gulps her blood greedily, lowering her body to the ground and feasting on her flesh until she's no longer moving. Screams of terror burst through my shock. I'm shaking violently, my hands over my mouth smothering my screams.

Make it go away. Make it go away.

I repeat the words over and over in my mind.

All the nightmares of my childhood come together in one horrifying moment.

This isn't real.

I try desperately to convince myself, like all the times before, that it's all in my imagination, but this time, the visions aren't vanishing. No matter how many times I blink, the monster in front of me won't disappear.

"Enough, Sarcos. I don't want a mess to clean up," Ramsey chuckles.

The man stands, wiping his mouth to rid it of the girl's blood.

"You won't find a drop of blood," he says snidely. "Now . . . go get food and water for the other. This was your fault, after all." Ramsey mutters something under his breath, but he doesn't argue.

With that, they both turn and walk out, leaving her body to taunt me.

"H-hello," I whisper, hoping like hell she'll answer me. She doesn't. Nobody could survive what I just witnessed. She's dead, and I'm alone again.

I lie down on the cold, hard ground and wait for whatever's to come. I'll fight with everything I have, but something tells me it won't be enough. Not this time. Tears no longer come, and even the shaking has stopped. Numbness envelops me like a security blanket.

I walk slowly down the deserted hallway, leading the gurney carrying Maggie's body to the morgue. The gray walls close in on me as the black-and-white-checkered floors seem to vibrate under my feet. My pace remains slow and steady. I'm in no hurry to deliver my sister to the coroner. The thin white sheet that covers her body begins to slip away and I don't even try to stop it. It's as though I'm frozen and the only function I'm capable of is walking. My eyes lower and widen when they see Maggie's pallid skin.

I want to reach out and stroke her cheek, like I used to when we were kids and she was scared. But I don't. I can't. I have to continue moving forward.

When we get to a large metal door, my feet stop. I walk around the side of the gurney to open the door, but before I get there, a cold hand grips my elbow. I stiffen, looking over my shoulder, but no one is there. My body pivots toward the gurney and when my eyes lower, they meet Maggie's. They're open and penetrating.

"*They're coming for you, Marina. Run.*"

WHEN I WAKE HOURS LATER, I'm still lying in the fetal position, shaking and cold. The disturbing dream I had left me even more frightened. My thirst is beginning to wear on me, and so are the millions of unanswered questions filtering through my head. Will I ever see the light of day again? Do I even care at this point? My mind wages a war against itself. One part wants to give up, while the other is screaming for me to survive.

You have to fight.

The sound of heavy footsteps coming down the hall has me pulling myself to a seated position. I watch as Ramsey drags the girl's lifeless body down the long corridor. Not a drop of blood is anywhere to be seen. *He drained her.* Sarcos approaches my cell. I refuse to whimper in fear as he nears. I slam my eyes shut, pulling in every last bit of strength I can muster, preparing to fight for my survival if I must. The door opens and closes very quickly. I dare a peek, and my eyes blink, confusion mounting. The man brought food and water and is now gone.

I scramble toward the water and gulp greedily as it trickles down my chin. Within seconds I've drained the container, moaning at the need for more. It was barely enough to wet my dry mouth. My eyes catch the plate of mush, and without thinking I shovel it in. It's not long before I'm retching in the corner, having eaten too fast and too much. The smell of my own vomit causes dry heaves to wreak havoc on my body. I swipe at my mouth and cringe at the vomit coating my hands.

The creaking of my door has me looking over my shoulders. I gape at the pale man hovering over me. His eyes seem to glow red, and I freeze.

Move, Marina. Do something.

"You should eat slowly. The next time I won't clean up your mess." He growls, throwing a bucket of water over top of the vomit.

Another pail of water is placed in my cell, and he leaves.

I'm kicking myself for not taking the opportunity to attack, but what good could've come from it? Even if I managed to get farther than the dead girl did, I wouldn't know how to get out of this place.

No. I need to bide my time and make plans. Be smart.

This time I sip slowly, hoping that my stomach can handle the contents. Hours tick by in the quiet of the dungeon. One could lose their mind in this silence. I'm forced to sit in this cell alone, replaying the horrific events of the girl's death over and over again in my head. *He bit her.*

She was drained of blood, just like all of the people from my nightmares growing up. My body shivers as I recall the girl's words from earlier.

They're not human.

I've been without food and water for so long, I'm hallucinating. Maybe none of that really happened? Perhaps it's my suppressed memories from a traumatic childhood resurfacing and playing tricks.

It happened. Keep your head down and remain quiet. You'll be okay.

The voice in my head sounds like Maggie's.

"Maggie?" I say quietly.

It'll be okay, Marina.

I go to sleep that night tired and utterly heartbroken. It's not normal to hear your missing sister in your head. Maggie and I had a bond that transcended this world. We both saw things that others said didn't exist. We both felt the presence of things not of this world, yet telepathy was not something we shared. If Maggie is dead, I have no doubt she'd try to contact me from the netherworld. I'm hearing Maggie's voice in my head, which leads me to conclude they were all right.

She's dead.

CHAPTER 4

I don't know how much time has passed since I've seen another person. It could be days, weeks, or only hours, but a commotion at the end of the hall has me springing to my feet and pressing my head to the bars. Girls of all ages, ethnicities, and sizes are brought down in chains. Some are crying, others shouting, and a few hanging their heads in defeat. I watch as they're herded one by one into individual cells. The doors clank shut heavily behind them. The soft cries of my new companions are abnormally comforting.

A *psst* from the cell next to mine has my back straightening.

"Where are we?" a girl who looks to be around my age demands.

Angry, swollen welts pepper the girl's dark skin.

"What happened to you?"

"I fought those bastards when they first grabbed me." Her voice is hard. "When I broke free, they threw some type of whip that coiled around my arm. It hurt so bad. I couldn't get away." Tears pool in her eyes, but she wipes them away harshly. "What do they want with us?"

I shake my head. "I don't know. The last girl in your cell believed it was a trafficking situation."

She nods. "What happened to her?"

"They killed her."

The girl sucks in a breath, and I realize I should've kept that information to myself. There's no need for her to know the horror I witnessed.

We sit in silence for several minutes. The days of solitude have left me even more awkward than normal. I want to ask questions. I want to talk, but I can't find the right words. I'm just about to blurt out the first thing that comes to mind when she finally breaks the silence.

"Where are you from?" she asks.

"Liberty," I reply, hoping to hell I don't have to elaborate on that.

"Liberty?" she questions, and my hope begins to sink. It is a small town; perhaps she's just not familiar with that part of the state.

"Yeah, you know," I begin, voice shaky. "Small town Ohio."

She sucks in another deep breath. "I'm from Santa Fe."

My stomach drops at her words. Despite my worry, I've been hoping I was wrong.

"New Mexico?"

She bobs her head.

We could be anywhere.

"Do you know any of the other girls?" I ask, hoping we can piece something together.

"No. After I was taken, I woke up in the back of a van. There were two other girls with me. One of them was asking a lot of questions and causing a stir. They killed her." She hangs her head sadly. "The other girl isn't here, from what I can tell."

"Did you happen to see any easy exits on your way down here? Anything that could help us run?"

She shakes her head. "It was a dark maze. I couldn't see anything."

I blow out a breath.

"We're going to die, aren't we?"

I want to lie to her. Tell her that we're going to be all right. That we'll get out of here alive. I can't.

"I don't know," I admit reluctantly. "But I'm not going to give up, and neither are you. We'll find some way."

Despite the earlier edge to the girl next door, she eventually breaks. Her weeping helps me to sleep.

One. Two. Three. Four. Five.

Craning my head, I count the number of girls I'm currently chained to. *Five girls.* At some point the two ghastly men dragged us each out of our cells one by one, chaining us together single file. My cell was the last one, so I'm at the back, able to take in the other girls in various stages of distress.

At the front of the line is a petite Asian girl with a short black stacked bob. Her head is held high, looking straight ahead. Behind her, a frail, mousy brown-haired girl is looking from side to side frantically. If I didn't know better, I'd think she were searching for an escape. *She wouldn't get far.*

Chained to the mousy girl's back is a willowy redhead who stands about six feet tall. Her head turns, and my eyes meet hers. I see fear in them but also determination. A look that must match my own.

I can't say that I'm not scared. Creatures that shouldn't exist—who are stronger, faster, dangerous—are leading us into the unknown. But I won't cower, and I won't allow myself to go down a dark path in my mind.

If there's a will, there's a way. And I plan to find it and get the hell out of here.

Following the redhead is a stout girl with a blond bob who shuffles along, periodically tripping over the chains that bind her feet. Directly in front of me is the Black girl from the cell next to mine. She doesn't say a word, head hung in defeat. We're being herded like cattle through a dark maze, the air thick with tension. The morose energy that each of us is emitting makes the feeling of doom intensify. I can imagine that all the girls have the same fear—we are being led to our death . . . *or worse.*

"Keep your eyes peeled for an exit," I whisper to the girl ahead of me. She glances over her shoulder at me, but there's no emotion. She stares at me blankly before turning back and lowering her head to the ground.

She isn't even going to try.

The concrete walls that surround us twist and turn in a never-ending labyrinth of connected hallways. No doors. No windows. Just empty gray walls that feel like they're getting narrower by the minute.

"W-where are we going?" The mousy girl asks our captors.

"Quiet, girl," Sarcos growls through his teeth.

"W-w-why us?" she continues.

"Stop talking," the redheaded girl hisses.

"I would do as your friend here says." His snake-like voice curls around my spine, sending shivers up and down.

"I don't w-want . . . ," she continues to stutter.

Everything inside me coils, knowing what's about to happen. All because she can't just shut up. Ramsey stops in his tracks, whipping around, stalking toward us. We all go still. Sarcos shoots his hand out, stopping him.

"We are two donors short already. You need to control

yourself." His eyes glow a brilliant red. I blink several times, but his eyes remain the same. He turns on his accomplice.

"If she can't learn to listen to us, she'll never get out of the auction alive." My back stiffens at his words. *Auction.*

We're going to be sold. Ramsey grabs the chains and pulls, jerking all of us forward. "This is your last warning. You will die in this hall if you say another word."

Her head falls forward and she manages to stay quiet the rest of our trek. We veer to the left down another hall, and the right side of the wall gives way to what looks like a communal shower.

"You will clean yourselves up. There shall be no dirt, vomit, or any other stink left to be found," Sarcos warns, unlocking the chains shackling our feet and eventually removing the cuffs from our hands. All of us look to each other hesitantly. "Move," he barks.

We all obey, filing in and going to stand under the spouts coming from the wall. Soaps and shampoos line a ledge that spans the shower area. I pick one up, fumbling to open the top. Steeling my hands to stop them from shaking, I bring the bottle to my head, catching a whiff of lavender. I breathe it in, relishing the first fresh smell I've encountered in days. No longer caring, I remove every piece of clothing.

Eagerly, I begin lathering my entire body with the shampoo. Scrubbing at my hair violently, I try desperately to rid myself of the grime and memories from the cell. The fact that I'm naked and surrounded by others doesn't deter me. I've never been more desperate to be clean. Standing under the warm water, I let go of everything. For this one moment, I enjoy a luxury I may not have for some time.

I'll survive. I know it in my bones. But only if I'm patient and prepared.

"Can I use that?" a familiar voice calls to my right. I look over to see the redhead, finger pointing to the shampoo I'd just used. "The shit at my station was practically gone . . . and it smelled vile. Not like that," she tilts her chin toward the bottle.

"Yeah, sure," I say, holding the shampoo out to her.

"Thanks. Not that I should be trying to smell nice. Whatever asshole pays for me doesn't deserve it," she says, venom lacing every word.

I simply nod, because what the hell else can I say to that?

She scoots closer to me, facing the spout. "What's the plan?" I sneak a peek at her out of the corner of my eye. "You don't appear to be weak like some of the others." Her voice lowers even further. "So what are we going to do, to get the fuck out of here?"

"Get in your own stall," Sarcos growls, and I don't have to look back to know he's speaking to us.

"Thanks," she says, giving me a small conspiratorial smile before making her way back to her stall.

Grabbing the bar of soap, I lather myself up once more. I think about the redhead and what she said. Although it didn't sound like she has a plan, I'm relieved to hear that someone else has no intention of forfeiting to these monsters.

My thoughts move to other things. Where did she come from? Who was she *before*? It helps me to relax slightly. For a few minutes I'm not thinking about the auction or the horrible red-eyed monsters. I'm thinking about escape.

"Time's up," Sarcos yells from the entrance. I don't bother covering myself. He doesn't seem interested in our naked forms, for as soon as he's made his command, he's gone. Lying on the floor in a pile are hospital gowns. I stiffen. Are we to be examined? I don't have time to waste on that thought. We all throw the plain blue coverings over ourselves. Anything to cover us from these creatures. Ramsey appears holding handcuffs, ready to bind us again.

We're all being pushed back into our line, chained and paraded down the maze of hallways. We walk for a short distance before coming upon two massive iron doors.

"You will remain quiet and only speak when you're asked a question. Do you understand?" Ramsey demands.

We each dip our heads, not knowing if we should speak. With that, he throws open the doors, showcasing a cavernous room. The walls are made up of some type of gray stone. There are no windows, save for the small circle at the top of the domed ceiling. Bright light filters down, meaning it's daytime. On one side of the large room, red velvet barber chairs are lined up in front of a row of mirrored stations. Statuesque men and women stand behind the chairs, unmoving. They are cloaked in black robes that reach the floor. Thick black collars cling to their necks. *Are they prisoners too?*

On the other side of the room is a line of elegant wooden wardrobes with circular platforms directly in front of each. *What the hell is this place?*

The enormous doors are shut behind us with a loud crash. We all jump at the noise, on edge and unsure what to make of the scene before us. Ramsey begins to unchain us while Sarcos slams a long iron bar across the doors, effectively bolting us in.

"You." He points to the mousy girl. "There." She scurries to the nearest chair. Every girl is placed at a station until it's finally my turn. A woman with purple-streaked raven hair motions for me to take a seat. She says nothing, but begins tugging at my hair with a comb. I balk at her lack of tenderness. Not that I expect anything else in this hellish prison.

"We should keep it natural and long." Her smooth Australian accent is beautiful in a place born of ugliness. "Your hair's natural highlights will draw attention from bidders. You're stunning." A small smile graces her lips. It's the first sign of kindness I've been shown. Fruitless hope wells to the surface, but I smash it down.

There will be no help from her. She's a prisoner too, if her mannerisms are any indicator. Her hand trembles and her eyes are downcast.

She begins to trim, blow-dry, and finally curl my strawberry blond hair. I want to smack her hands away and refuse anything from these people, but that wouldn't work in my favor. The goal is escape, and that won't be accomplished by causing a scene. I'd do well to remember that. My best chance at this point is to play by the rules and plan my getaway once I leave this fortress.

My face is powdered, eyeshadow applied, mascara added, and a gloss placed on my lips. After what feels like hours, I'm turned toward the mirror. I gasp at my reflection. The person staring back at me *is* stunning. But it's not my face that stares back at me. It's Maggie's. We were twins, but you could tell us apart. She was the one that liked frilly things. Her makeup was always exquisitely done, and her hair curled to perfection. I didn't have time for those things. They seemed ridiculous given our life and all the crazy that accompanied it.

The woman gives me a handheld mirror and spins me around so I can see the back of my hair, as if I had a choice about the style. "You will bring in so much money at the auction," she says, then leans into my ear and whispers, "Get out of here and find a way to help us all."

My eyes widen at her words. In the mirror, I see the choker on her neck turning red. The mirror slips from my grasp, shattering into a million pieces on the concrete floor. I spin around in time to see her hands come to her neck, desperately trying to remove the collar. "Help me." Her strangled cries have two men approaching, grabbing her by her wrist and dragging her away. I jump from my seat.

"Leave her alone." I pound on one man's back. "Let her go."

The second guy drops her arm and picks me up by my throat. I flail my arms and kick out, but my foot moves uselessly through air.

I'm struggling to breathe, clawing at his hand, when Sarcos bellows, "Drop her."

The man does as commanded and I fall to the floor in a heap, gasping in breath.

So much for not making a scene.

A lady with pink and purple hair and a clipboard comes over to me, completely ignoring what just unfolded.

"Number seven-seventy-six." I sit dazed and lightheaded. "Number seven-seventy-six," she bites. I raise my eyes to her. "You are number seven-seventy-six." She points to me. "I'm Ratilda, not that it matters to you." She tsks. "I need to pin this to your chest," she says, not waiting for me to respond. She bends down and attaches a piece of paper with the number 776 to my hospital gown. "You will go to the next station when they call your number. Do you understand?" She raises a brow.

"Yes. Seven-seventy-six."

She nods and walks away briskly. I don't know what to do from here, but a few other girls wearing their numbers are sitting on chairs. So, I go and take a seat beside the redhead from earlier. Her knees bounce, and she wrings her fingers. We sit in silence for a few minutes before she leans into me and whispers unsteadily.

"Do you think they killed her?"

"I don't know," I sigh. "Probably."

"We are being trafficked, right?"

I really don't know, after everything I've seen. If she had asked me that before I saw that girl killed in the cell next to me, I would've said yes, but now . . . my wildest guess would probably be inaccurate. The two men's eyes glowed red, like the monsters from my childhood. Maybe I've just lost my damn mind, and this is all a horrific nightmare.

"That scary guy said auction. We're being numbered. What the fuck else could it be?" she asks, but she isn't directing the question to me. Really, she's just talking aloud.

"It's my best guess. But I don't know," I admit.

She huffs before asking, "What's your name?"

"Marina."

"Stacey Ryan," she chokes. "I'm Stacey Ellen Ryan."

I smile, not knowing any other way to comfort her. She's clearly wanting to hang on to her identity, and I can't blame her. If she gives up on herself, it's all over for Stacey Ryan. She needs to be strong, and if repeating her name helps, maybe I should do the same. I'll let her hang on to whatever she needs. Something to give her hope. Hope fuels courage, and courage is what she'll need if she wants any chance of escaping with her life.

"You're number seven-ninety-five. Stacey Ryan no longer exists," a cold voice says from behind us. I see Stacey shudder—whether at the voice or the thought of losing her identity, it's hard to tell. "Now, seven-seventy-six, follow me." I stand, following Ratilda reluctantly.

"Hmm. You're a size four. Full C cup, approximately five foot seven." She taps her finger to her mouth, contemplating. My eyes narrow slightly. "I have the perfect dress. You'll be radiant." She beams, clearly pleased with herself. *How does she know all of that just by looking at me?*

She walks to the large armoire and shuffles through the gowns. "Here it is," she says, pulling a beautiful gold-colored dress from the back. "Drop your frock." The garment falls to my feet as I'm ushered onto the raised platform. She holds the golden dress near the floor and I step into it, waiting as she tugs and pulls it into place. When she's done fussing, she spins me around to the floor-length mirror, and my eyes widen at the beautiful rose-gold dress.

Exquisite beads are embroidered onto lace and tulle, which overlay satin. It molds to the curve of my body, flaring just slightly from my waist. Swarovski crystals showcase my slender neck and shoulders. The neckline scoops just enough to show the swell of my full breasts that have been enhanced by the corset hidden by a row of crystal buttons.

I hate it.

"Ah. The aristocracy will not be disappointed with you. I dare say we shall have a bidding war." She giggles while my insides rumble in protest.

I don't want anything to do with this. Nobody that engages in this sort of perverse and insidious act is anyone I want to draw attention from. I'd rather die now than be sold off to some sicko. And aristocracy? What royal needs to pay for girls?

No Prince Charming, that's for sure.

"One more thing," Ratilda says. "We need to draw your blood." I furrow my brow. *Draw my blood?*

More women with collars approach with a cart full of needles and other objects I vehemently object to. "No," I say, shaking my head. "No, I won't do this," I repeat, balling my hands into fists.

"Don't get blood on that dress," she warns the other women, ignoring my protest.

"If you hold still, I should only have to do this once," a woman with short purple hair says to me. "Let me see your vein." I yank away from her. "Don't be stupid, girl. Do as I instruct or they'll . . . hurt you." She whispers this last part, offering me a sad smile that has me wondering how she's caught up in this. She's not wearing a collar, which leads me to believe she isn't forced to be here.

It doesn't make sense, but I choose to heed her words.

With trepidation, I hold out my arm. She pokes at it with her finger. "Fabulous. This will be painless," she promises as she stabs a needle into my vein, drawing the blood through the syringe and into a tube with a bag attached. I wince, feeling even more light-headed. A few minutes later, a woman is removing the tubes, cleaning the area, and placing a Band-Aid over the tiny wound.

"There you go," she says, handing me a small glass of what appears to be orange juice. I gulp the liquid down and pick up the two cookies sitting on a plate in front of me. "See? It wasn't so bad," she chides. I nibble greedily on the chocolate confections, hardly hearing her words. This is fuel and I need it. "Now, now . . . you mustn't overindulge. We can't have you busting out of that lovely dress. Your future owner will want you at your best. Remember to remove that bandage before you enter the auction room," she chuckles, eliciting a hard scowl from me.

"No one owns me," I snark under my breath, but it doesn't go unheard.

"That attitude will get you killed around here. Best to keep your head down and mouth shut."

She doesn't say it to be cold or frighten me, but to warn. The corner of her mouth lifts into a semblance of a smile, conveying that she doesn't like this situation any more than I do, but she's been through it enough to know the ropes.

Minutes later, the final touches are being forced upon me by various strangers' hands. I don't pay them any mind. Instead, I plan my murderous revenge on them all. When I escape, I promise myself I'll hunt them all down. Even the unwilling participants. The lot of them will pay.

I take a moment to look at the other girls' transformations. Mousy girl is no longer mousy. Her hair has been colored a brilliant shade of caramel, and curls cascade down her back. The sweetheart top of her fuchsia dress showcases cleavage and makes her look confident. I can't help but admire the work that has been done to each girl in such a short amount of time. Every one of them looks magnificent.

Like dolls on display.

"It's time," Sarcos calls.

We are once again placed in a single file line, as if we are back in grade school. This time the chains are absent, not that it matters. Large men flank us on all sides. We aren't going anywhere other than where they want us to. My legs shake on the horrific heels they've shoved my feet into, while my mind races, imagining all the possible scenarios that could transpire wherever we're being led. Before long, Ratilda calls out for us to stop moving.

"All eyes over here," she commands.

We all turn to look at her like Stepford robots.

"Once we step up to the platform, you'll find the part of the stage marked with your number. Stand tall and still in your designated space. You do not talk. You do not move. Understand?" she demands. We all nod. "Well then. Let the bidding begin," she says, standing aside and waving her hand in the direction of a set of stairs.

I rip off the bandage for no other reason but to feel pain. Something to keep my mind off of what's to happen next. Who will bid on me? Where will I go? How much farther will they take me from home? Which of these girls will survive the night? Who knows what awful humans are waiting to buy other humans?

Monsters.

One by one we ascend the stairs, coming out onto a slightly raised stage. The colossal room around us is empty, giving us a clear view of the ominous space before us. "Move," Ramsey barks behind us.

I stagger my way to my spot, knees wobbling and hands trembling. Feeling helpless, I concentrate on the gold rhinestone-covered monstrosities I'm forced to wear on my feet. They are already causing sores, but that doesn't matter. Nothing does when you're being marched on to a stage for vile people to gawk at. I may not know what's to come, but one thing's for sure—it's not going to be easy to get away.

When I'm in place, I take in the muted space. All the seating has been removed, making one large open space in front of the stage. White and gray marble floors spread out as far as I can see. There is not an ounce of color to be seen. Everything is gray and white, making the elaborate and bold gowns we wear the central focus. We're the only color to be seen. The thought sends chills down my spine.

Men and women wearing black tuxedos roll in carts containing champagne flutes about a fourth of the way full of a dark red liquid. A cart is situated directly under each of us girls. *Wine tasting and auction . . . Disgusting.*

"Are we ready?" Ratilda addresses the tuxedo-clad waiters.

They all reply with a stiff yes.

"Wonderful. Let them in, let them in." She claps her hands. I vow to myself right here, right now, that I'm hunting her down and wiping that freaking smile right off her face. Permanently. My hands clench into fists. I don't have long to plan that out, as the room begins to fill. The closer the people get, the more peculiar this entire situation seems.

They are all dressed in lavish ball gowns and tuxedos, acting as though they're attending the event of the season. Cackles and shrieks fill the once empty space as the elegantly dressed meander about the room. Waiters move around the area, offering appetizers and flutes of champagne. Music begins, and couples begin to dance to a string quartet that is set up somewhere out of my line of sight. Nobody has paid us any attention and I pray it stays that way, even if it is a pointless prayer.

I'm horrified to see women partaking in such a vile activity, but quickly I'm reminded that evil doesn't know gender, color, age, or ethnicity. Their idea of fun is watching a group of young girls paraded around to be sold off to the highest bidder. They are in fact the definition of evil. There will be no help from any of them.

They're all monsters, with or without the glowing eyes.

CHAPTER 5

An hour or more must go by as the creatures mill about, chatting, eating, and thoroughly ignoring the six girls on the stage before them. Aren't we the entire reason they're here? They haven't so much as looked our way. The whole thing is strange. Not that human trafficking should be anything other than strange, but this is entirely different than anything I would've expected.

It's frightening as hell as I watch the group couple off and dance. Every one of them is passing their partners around like it's a swingers convention and the more time that goes on, the more it feels like just that. The champagne is flowing freely, and with every second, these people get looser. They grind against their partners a little more as their inhibitions disappear. Hands roam liberally, groping and fondling private parts, and nobody even blinks.

My knees are starting to quake, whether from standing in these heels or from the increasing awkwardness of being a voyeur to an expanding orgy. The weight of the dress I wear is pulling on my shoulders and I do my best to yank it up to hide my cleavage. I don't want anything to do with what I'm witnessing, and I won't give them any reason to think otherwise. Who knew ball gowns could be so daunting and so damn provocative? I hate it.

My eyes roam away from the dance floor, landing on Stacey. She stands stoically, her face masking any fear she may be experiencing. Her lavender gown flows to the floor in waves of tulle. She looks sophisticated and beautiful. Her head never moves, and I wonder what she's thinking.

Suddenly, the music stops and the feedback from a microphone sounds, pulling my attention away from Stacey.

"Ladies and gentlemen," Ratilda says into a microphone. "The auction will begin soon. Please take your places." The partygoers immediately stop what they're doing and head toward the stage, attention now on us. Everything in me tenses as the reality of what's about to happen sets in. We were mere decorations a moment ago, but based on the intense gazes of the bidders below, we're their central focus now. My palms begin to sweat and anxiety builds in my chest. I will myself to take deep breaths.

"The rules are the same as always. You may walk the line, examining the donors from the floor. A sample of each is provided below. Help yourselves to *one* glass," she stresses.

A sample of what?

My mind is fixated on what could be in the flutes and what it has to do with each of us girls. The answer is just out of reach and before I can grasp it, Ratilda's shrill voice bats it away.

"You'll have thirty minutes to peruse the fine selection. At exactly midnight, the auction will commence." The people begin moving even closer to the stage. I slink back just slightly.

If I was scared before, I'm petrified now. My entire body is shaking as the people descend upon us. The first person to stand in front of me is a portly woman wearing a white wig and a black dress. Her gothic guise is intimidating. She looks me over from head to toe, smiling widely. I don't like how she relishes my body as if I'm dessert. Taking a glass from the cart, she brings it to her nose and inhales deeply. A look of ecstasy transforms her face, and my stomach sours at the thought of her finding anything tied to me appealing. She swirls the liquid in the glass and brings it to her lips, tipping it back and swallowing. For a moment, I don't breathe as I await her reaction. She scrunches her nose and purses her lips. A promising sign that she didn't enjoy the wine on my cart. As she swiftly moves on from me, my shoulders relax, relieved that I've clearly been given a bad batch. Perhaps this will keep others away from me as well.

Men and women come and go, none giving me an impression—good or bad—until a tall, dark-haired man approaches. Something about him has me feeling as though a million spiders are crawling over my body. His cold eyes penetrate me, chilling me from the inside out. He oozes evil, and at this moment he's paying too close attention to me. His eyes rake over me, pausing at my breasts. He licks his lips, causing me to shudder in response.

This isn't good. He looks like the sort that enjoys torturing his possessions before finally discarding them. I know without a doubt if I leave here with him, I'll die. He walks closer, grabbing a glass of the red liquid. He doesn't waste time with formalities or etiquette, raising the glass right to his mouth and gulping the contents greedily. He moans in pleasure at the taste, and I wince at the sight of it. A droplet of wine spills out from his lips, slowly moving down his chin. It's then I can see how thick the liquid is. *Is that . . . it can't be. Blood.*

My head spins at the realization. Why would anyone want to drink blood? The answer is so obvious that it practically smacks me in the face.

Vampire.

Vampires aren't real. At least that's what's been drilled into me for years. Between my parents and Dr. Tilney, they tried to convince me that I was insane. *You knew better.*

My God. This whole time Maggie and I never had a name for what we saw, but they had to have been vampires. But why didn't they ever attack or drink our blood? It doesn't make any damn sense. Yet, as I look into the pale, scary man's eyes, they begin to change, to morph from soulless black to glowing red orbs. The very same as the monsters that have haunted me my entire life. The same monsters that caused my sister to leave me.

They took our blood earlier so that these *things* could sample us. Why an auction when they can simply take what they want? Vampires are powerful, aren't they? I rack my brain for anything I know about them, but the truth is, I only know what I've read in fictional books and watched on television. For all I know, I know nothing. My anxiety builds and I sway on my feet. Being in the dark makes it unlikely for me to have any chance of survival.

Inhale.

Exhale.

You've got to pull it together, Marina.

A woman joins the man, pulling him into her. She spots the red liquid and licks it from his chin in an intimate gesture.

"What do you think of her?" the man asks in a heavy accent.

"She's rather plain, don't you think?" Her brow rises as she surveys me.

"She's a virgin," he says roughly.

My spine straightens. *How the hell would he know that?*

"I know," she purrs. "I could taste it."

I jerk back, mystified. *Taste it? Our blood can tell them that much about us?*

"She'd be a fun plaything for a while," he croons. "Can you smell her fear?" he says, head turning in my direction. His eyes. They're more red than before.

Monsters.

"I only smell false hope. She actually thinks she stands a chance of evading her fate." She throws her head back and laughs maniacally.

"You're vile. Hideous."

The woman lurches forward at my words, but the man's hand juts out, stopping her.

"Leave her, pet. It will be far more fun taking your aggression out while she's chained to our wall."

I envision a wall of torture, with me secured to the center, naked and exposed for this disgusting creature to do to me as she pleases.

These animals are definitely the things of my nightmares. They feed off fear and lurk in the shadows. Their blatant sexual appetite pollutes the air and chills me to the bone. I'll never survive. None of us will.

Stop. Don't allow her to win.

It's a battle of wills and I'm stronger than this.

"Yes . . . well, I could be on board to torture her."

I gulp, hating that she voiced what I'd been picturing.

"What about the Black girl?" She licks her lips. "She's delectable."

"No. This is the one." He nods his head in my direction.

The woman pouts for a moment before cheering up. "Fine. But I choose next time."

"My darling, if you wish to have something in particular, you can have it anytime. This girl's blood calls to me," he all but purrs. "She'll be the perfect—on demand—donor. We won't have to hunt. We can enjoy Barbados without drawing attention to ourselves. Isn't that why we're here?" he runs a long, thin hand down the woman's cheek adoringly.

She purses her lips looking at me but finally agrees, "It is. It's the only reason I allow you to spend so much money on filth," she sneers in my direction.

Everything inside of me is screaming to take my chances and run. I can't leave here with them. My eyes scan the room for an escape. One door to my left is unoccupied. If I made a run for it, I might be able to make it. But what then? How would I get out? *You wouldn't.*

What's worse? Trying and failing or lying down and taking what's coming? I'd rather die a thousand deaths right here in this auditorium than be subjected to whatever "play" this psychotic creep and his deranged hussy have in mind. I take a deep breath, steeling myself for the inevitable.

Don't.

Maggie's voice in my head has me staying put. *It'll be all right,* she says.

I don't feel like everything is going to be all right. Between blood-drinking maniacs and my probably dead sister's voice ringing in my head, I'm far from all right.

"Please make your way to the center of the room. The auction will begin in one minute," Ratilda speaks through the microphone.

The odd couple saunter away, going to stand in the middle of the crowd. A tapping on the microphone draws everyone's attention to Ratilda.

"It appears as though the decisions have already been made," she chuckles. "No doubt it was a hard choice, with the exceptional donors we have this time."

That word again . . . donors. It just cements how delusional they all are. We're not choosing to donate a damn thing.

Most of these girls have no chance. I can already see their will to live has leaked from them. They'll be used as blood banks for these overly powerful vampires. Used and eventually discarded for another.

"This is your last call to sample the blood and make your final decisions."

The room starts to move in and out like a kaleidoscope. My body sways and my head feels light. There is a real possibility that I'm going to collapse right here on this stage, likely from a lack of food and water.

The faces of the men and women are going in and out of focus. Their eyes shine brilliant shades of blue, amber, but mostly red. A tsunami of frightening images appears. The faces of the people below me contort into hideous sneers, sharp canine teeth protruding from their mouths. *No.*

Perhaps I have already died, and this is some sort of purgatory. The room begins to spin as recollections of the girl from the cell, being bitten and drained of blood, flood my memory. I breathe in and out, willing myself to calm down. You can survive this, I repeat over and over again, trying to calm myself to no avail.

How can there be any possible way out of this alive?

A strong breeze blows above us. My head lifts to find a giant industrial fan moving the air around the room. I close my eyes, breathe, and allow the air to cool my clammy skin. Soon the spinning recedes, and I open my eyes to take in the actual monsters in front of me. *Vampires.*

"All right, ladies and gentlemen, it's time. Let the bidding begin," Ratilda announces over the speaker. "The auction is a tradition that's gone on for centuries. It was started by our beloved late Crown, Darius Bellamy. To him we are forever grateful for bringing our kind a way of survival, without the threat of wiping out our food source."

Chuckles, grunts, and hurrahs are heard around the room.

"Well . . . and it's a lot more convenient than hunting," she crows. "What else do we need all that power and money for? It's why men pay extravagant prices for sex . . . it's better when we have it on call at a moment's notice," Ratilda's voice grows low and frightening. "Blood from a fighter is better than blood from the willing."

Again, the room erupts into laughter and cheers.

Disgusting. The whole lot of them. They're not doing this to survive. They're doing it for convenience and because they can. We're nothing but human slaves to be fed off of.

"We'll start with number seven-ninety-one." She motions toward the short blond girl. "Seven-ninety-one hails from the Southern region of the United States. She's the perfect heavy lifter for those projects you have." The room erupts in laughter at the blonde's expense and I want to throw up. So not just to be fed off of, but for whatever warped purpose they choose to use us for. "Seven-ninety-one, please step forward." She does as directed, stepping forward into a bright spotlight. "The bidding will begin at two million US dollars."

"Two million." The plump woman in the white wig waves a paddle in the air.

"Wonderful. Do I hear three million?" Ratilda asks, looking around the room with wide eyes and a Cheshire cat grin. "Now surely you won't let this wonderful creature go?" She looks at the blond girl and tsks. "Or perhaps she should pay you." She throws her head back in laughter and the others join her.

I take a step forward, ready to start the fight, but my eyes catch on Stacey, who shakes her head slightly. I'm not sure why, but I trust her judgment.

Now isn't the time to act.

The blonde begins to weep, body shaking from what I can imagine is embarrassment and fear. I want to go to her. To wrap her in my arms and tell her to be strong, but nothing I could ever say would make things better.

"Fine then. Seven-ninety-one to Countess Devoir for two million dollars."

The woman nods her head in satisfaction.

The auction goes on for what feels like forever. The mousy girl is sold to a purple-haired woman for four million, the girl from the cell next to mine is auctioned off to a lesbian couple for 12.2 million, and the Asian beauty was just sold to a French man for fourteen million. The obscene amount of money these creatures possess nauseates me. Every girl seems to bring more dirty money to this detestable cause. Stacey and I are all that's left, causing my insides to toss.

"Who shall be next, friends?" Ratilda calls out.

My gaze meets Stacey's. She nods her head, a silent promise of solidarity.

We're in this together, no matter how little we know each other.

Neither of us is ready to be sold off, but we know there is nothing we can do to stop it.

The noise level starts to grow as those in the crowd shout their preferences. My eyes land on the strange couple from earlier, and fear coils around me like a snake does its prey. The man's lips turn up into a wicked grin. He must know how repulsed I am. It has to be written all over my face.

He can smell your emotions.

I steel my resolve, not wanting him or anyone else to see me cower. The more I try, the more I feel like I'm going to faint. Just as the room starts to sway again and my vision blurs, a loud bang sounds from the back of the room.

Everyone spins to look at the cause of the ruckus. The place is eerily quiet; not a monster speaks. The stage we are on is not tall, and with the spectators blocking the view, I can't see.

Standing on my tiptoes, I try to catch a glimpse of what has everyone still as statues. Seeing nothing, I lower myself, wringing my hands together nervously. These frightening people all appear to be confused. Whatever is going on can't be good.

My eyes land on Ratilda, and what I see there does nothing to ease my growing panic. She looks terrified. What could possibly have her frightened? She's the monster running this awful auction. I'm still watching her closely when her entire body relaxes and a wide, sinister grin transforms her face.

"Well, well, if it isn't the Crown playboy," she croons, all sugary and sanguine. "Welcome, Lawrence." Ratilda makes a low bow, smirking as she stands. I can't see the person she addresses, but whoever he is, she finds him to be attractive. The way her cheeks pink and her lashes flutter, it isn't hard to surmise. Her voice is flirtatious yet reverent, only providing further evidence that whoever this Crown playboy is, he's got her full attention.

"Ratilda, it's always a pleasure to see you." The boyish voice sweeps across the room. "I've brought a friend today. I'm sure you all know him, so why is nobody showing their respect?" the man says stonily, and every single one of these creatures bows low. The other man, whom I've yet to see, doesn't say a word.

"Please, excuse my brother and his stiff formalities. I'm only a spectator today. Rise." His voice washes over me. Smooth and masculine. My body reacts in ways it has no business doing, knees going weak and body swaying slightly. I cringe at its utter betrayal. While I'm having an internal battle, gasps and whispers ensue all around.

Ratilda's eyes widen. "Your M-Majesty, please, come forward." She stutters on the words, clearly caught off guard by this sudden turn of events. By the formal title, I venture to guess that whoever it is rules this repulsive race of monsters and my earlier reaction to him only makes me feel worse. I can't even look out at the crowd anymore. Shame lances through me at the way a simple voice could have me acting so out of character. Boys have never been my weakness and damn sure nobody as evil, because anyone coming to this event can't be anything but.

While everyone is preoccupied, I decide to make my move. I turn toward Stacey and motion for her to follow me. Her eyes widen, but she acts, taking off her shoes just as I am. I don't want to bring any attention to us, and the clanking of those heels could do just that.

When both our feet are free, I tilt my head toward the back of the stage and we both tiptoe that way.

"Do you think this is a good idea?" Stacey whisper-hisses.

"No clue." My head snaps left to right, searching for the best way. "Follow me."

I go right, the opposite direction from which we entered the auditorium. We're sprinting down a hallway that runs behind the stage when we come to a door.

It's chained shut.

"Shit," I screech. "Shit. Shit. Shit."

"Now what do we do?" Stacey asks, eyes wide and mouth stuck in an O.

"Think you could get away that easy, did ya?"

Sarcos.

Two hulking men dressed as waiters come out of nowhere, pinning our hands behind our backs and steering us toward the stage.

I grit my teeth and attempt to jerk my arms out of the man's grip, but it doesn't work. He's too strong.

When I'm back in position, staring out into the sea of vampires, I take one last chance, and stomp my bare foot down onto the waiter's foot. I know it won't do anything, but it gives me some satisfaction when he tightens his grip on me.

Not entirely immune to pain.

Assuming this guy is yet another vamp.

"You'll pay for that," Sarcos says, hand rising in preparation to smack me, but a powerful voice booms through the auditorium.

"Don't. Touch. Her."

Shivers run down the length of my spine and heat pools low in my belly at the masculine lilt.

What the hell is wrong with me?

I lift my head slowly, watching as the crowd parts, giving way to a young man who looks to be not much older than myself. He's blond and sporting a cheery disposition. Everything about him appears normal. *Don't let his smile fool you; he's still the devil.*

He waves to me as if we're old friends, and peering at him, I wonder. My eyes narrow, searching his face, which seems so incredibly familiar. Have we met before? There is something about him—something I can't place. He grins as if he knows my thoughts. My lips slam together in a harsh line, stopping the smile that almost slipped. He's charming, that's for sure.

The devil is too.

I'm still pondering his level of evil and who he could possibly be when he steps aside, exposing his companion. Much to my horror, his face matches his suave voice. He's not repulsive. No, not in the slightest. Everything around him seems to fade a bit, as if he steals the color from every part of the room. I don't hear a sound apart from my beating heart and shallow breaths. His head lifts, and bluish-green eyes pierce through me, freezing me to my spot. My breath hitches as I take him in.

He's tall and every bit royal. The black tuxedo that is

tailored perfectly to his body looks expensive. Not that I have anything to compare it to, but it's magnificent and exquisitely pressed. His dark blond hair is swept elegantly back, allowing for no obstructions to his penetrating eyes.

My gaze pushes downward, landing on his strong jaw lined with scruff. He's sophisticated, with an edge of roughness, unlike anything I've ever seen. The most beautiful man to ever be in my presence stands before me, frightening me to my very core. He may be beautiful, but he's one of them.

His stare is fierce and unyielding, causing my legs to wobble once more. I dig in my heels and will myself to stop shaking. Standing taller, I press my anxiety down. Fear is what people like this want. It gives them power, and they already have enough of that here. The right side of his cheek lifts into a small grin, as if he knows exactly what I'm attempting to mask. I glare in return.

I won't let him think he has any control over me.

"Your Highness," Ratilda says, drawing the mysterious man's eyes away from me. "We didn't realize you'd be joining us today." Her voice shakes a little.

"I didn't realize I needed to notify anyone of my plans. I thought it was high time I participated."

"You're going to bid today, after all?" she says, eyes bulging. Based on her reaction, this is something new. Why now? What's made him come to an auction he's obviously not been to in a while?

"You never know." He grins at her and she appears to relax.

"We've had better attended auctions in the past. Surely, you'd rather come when we have more of a selection," she says, motioning at Stacey and me as though we were a disgrace to her event.

"Do you wish me to leave?" His brow rises, a deep scowl marring his handsome face.

"Of course not, Crown. I wouldn't, Crown. P-please forgive me." He waves her off.

"Please, proceed with the auction."

She begins to speak, and he lifts a hand, silencing her.

My stomach plummets. I suppose some naive part of me hoped he came to end this madness, but no. He's here to watch. Or worse, bid.

His eyes meet mine once more and I do my best to show him how much I hate him and everything he stands for. I allow all the rage I've harbored for years to come to the surface, pointing it directly at him. If my glower could kill, he'd be dead on the spot.

His eyes narrow on me, searching, but for what I'll never know. If he hopes to find forgiveness in me, he never will. I continue to level him with the most lethal glare I can muster and almost falter when he shakes his head slightly.

No, what? Don't test him? Don't fear him? What the fuck does he want from me?

That's a question I won't get an answer to as he turns his head and walks away.

CHAPTER 6

"I— Um, we'll continue in a few short minutes. Those who have already made their choices, please see Ramsey in the great room."

Ratilda runs her hands down her hips, smoothing out her skirt before walking briskly off the stage and toward the Crown. She's visibly shaken. How can he evoke such fear from a woman who runs such an abhorrent business?

He's the one actually running things.

My back aches and my muscles are tight from my botched attempt at escape. Undoubtedly, the nights spent curled up on the dank, cold, concrete floor of the cell are to blame as well. The combination has made it all the more difficult for me to stand stock-still in this getup for what must have been hours.

The charming man accompanying the Crown looks me over one last time, then turns away. My body sags. With all eyes on his friend, I finally have a moment to rub my shoulder. I groan at the exquisite pain as I work out a knot.

"Psst." I look over to the blonde standing next to me. "Are you okay? Did they hurt you?"

I shake my head. "No. Nothing that I can't handle," I say.

"What's going on?" she says. I lift my shoulders in answer. My wildest guess would probably be wrong at this point.

"Who is he?" Her voice is loud, but it goes unnoticed in the noise of the crowd. They are too consumed with the newcomers to give us a moment's thought. The men and women gather around them, vying for their attention.

Ratilda is talking animatedly to the Crown, and I can only guess at the subject. She mentioned they've had larger selections other times. Just how many girls have been taken by them? What happened to those girls?

They're long gone.

The Crown stands tall with his hands behind his back, his head tilted up so that he's looking down on Ratilda. He doesn't say a word to her before turning and leaving her standing awkwardly. She looks around as if to see who witnessed their conversation and appears to be relieved when nobody pays her any mind. Their attention is solely on the two men making their way around the room and engaging with the auction attendees.

The more serious of the two stands tall and assured, while women ogle and men cast envious glances his way. He commands the room, floating from person to person. Every woman is affected. It's evident in the way some lean into him, running painted fingernails down his suit jacket. Another woman plays with a locket that hangs precariously close to her breasts. Her fingers glide across the skin of her cleavage suggestively, while she rakes her tongue across her bottom lip. My cheeks heat at the blatant way these women are throwing themselves at these two, yet neither seem interested in any of it.

The Crown peers over his shoulder, looking directly at me. I hold his gaze, not moving a muscle. I won't show fear, and I won't allow him to think he's getting to me. My face is stone as his eyes lock onto mine. Minutes pass and I don't relent. The other man leans into him, whispering something for only him to hear. Finally, his eyes leave mine and I exhale, shoulders drooping minutely. They continue to discuss something between themselves, and the boyish one looks around the room as everyone continues to stare at them.

He leans over once more, saying something that has the Crown's mouth tilting up into a smile. *What is he up to?* They walk from person to person, grabbing each of their hands and saying something that appears to relax each of the creatures. For the first time since this pair entered the room, the bidders leave their side and take to various corners and alcoves. *Why are they suddenly uninterested in these two?*

I watch them continue to command the room, but as they do so, the guests they've already spoken to, the ones who ventured off from this twisted party, begin acting strange. Their red eyes no longer glow brightly; they're muted and almost . . . foggy. It's as if they're in a daze, movements mechanical and stiff.

What did they do?

A man runs his hand up the leg of his date, pulling the material of her skirt all the way up her hip. The fact that she isn't wearing panties is obvious as he reveals a patch of hair between the woman's legs. My eyes widen as he shoves his fingers inside of her roughly. Somehow, he manages to undo his pants and they pool at his feet. It isn't long before her hand is around his length, pumping up and down. She throws her head back as his fingers slide in and out of her. I watch as the scene unfolds, my mouth dropping to the floor in shock and disgust. They are blatantly about to have intercourse right here in front of everyone.

"What the hell is happening?" the blonde next to me asks in a high-pitched squeal.

"I have no idea," I admit, unable to look away.

I hear the other donors gasping and murmuring their revulsion as we're all forced to watch the obscene actions unfold. Nobody in the room—with the exception of us—is bothered because they are all in their own states of pleasure. They have no cares in the world as to who's watching. It's turned into a freaking orgy in a matter of minutes. As ashamed as I am to admit it, I'm transfixed. It's a menagerie of sex and I can't tear my eyes away. It can't be helped. I'm an unwilling voyeur, but as I watch, I become aware that my body demands to take part.

Heat pools in my core—foreign and intoxicating. Lust envelops me like a lover, and I am suddenly desperate for something I don't understand. Nothing good can come of this, yet I don't turn away.

An invisible magic weaves through the room, championing the desire and threatening to pull me under. The man Ratilda called Crown looks up at me, watching, knowing. He doesn't turn away as more people paw at him. Instead, his eyes remain on me, his gaze intent and fiery. I'm wet in places I should not be, and my breath is coming out in unsteady spurts.

The man's throat contracts as he gulps, seemingly affected by my current state of arousal, the simple move only making it worse. Tingles have me tightening and contracting, needing a release I've never once felt before. The tension builds low in my belly, and if I didn't know better, I'd think I was going to c—

Oh God.

My hands fly to my mouth as the horror of what's happening sets in. How? Why? As I shake off every last bit of the heady feelings, self-loathing takes hold. Why would my body react like that? More concerning, why am I attracted to the man that rules this world of darkness and death?

Jerking my eyes away from the suited royal, I suddenly feel sick at what I'm seeing.

He's caused this in some way.

From the moment he walked into the room, all sensibility was wiped away. His looks have me acting like an idiot along with everyone else. For that I hate him even more. A tear slides down my cheek and I wipe it away, angry. My chin drops to my chest, eyes closing to drown out the room.

"Close your eyes," I yell to my fellow donors. "They're doing this. Don't watch it."

My lids slam shut as I refuse to be forced into seeing this. He's to blame and I know it. I'm not sure how he's managed it, but whatever he said to these creatures, his words, it did this. I have no idea of his motives, but I won't succumb to his wicked game.

"What's your name?" That masculine voice has my head jolting up. My knees quake at the closeness of the two newcomers. Unsure of their motives, I'm desperate to run.

"What's your name?" the man Ratilda had called Lawrence repeats, a little more forcefully the second time.

"You can f—." The words don't come. I can hardly think, let alone form sentences. My finger flops down at the number affixed to the floor in front of me.

"I dare say she's ignoring us, brother."

The Crown huffs. "That has to be a first for you."

Are they seriously making jokes?

"Are you afraid?" the man asks with a frown.

I consider lying, but the way my hands shake at my sides makes the answer obvious.

"Yes," I hiss through my teeth. "But I'm *pissed* too."

I'm not sure how I was able to form the last part of that, but it's not a lie. Pissed is a gross understatement of what I am, but it's the best I could do given the circumstances.

"Pissed?" Lawrence says, scandalized. "Is that not a phrase used to describe urination?" He directs his question to the other, who chokes out a laugh.

"She's using it as slang to inform us she's angry."

Lawrence furrows his brow. "Pissed," he mutters.

He knows damn well what pissed means. He's toying with me. Trying to throw me off.

It won't work.

"How did you do this?" I ask, looking out at the sexual acts unfolding.

"Perceptive," Lawrence says as if proud. "We had to keep them busy so that we could meet the donors." I growl at the term applied to me and the others, and Lawrence has the good sense to grimace at his misstep. "My apologies. It's the term the Council has given to those of you they've brought here. I'm not sure what else to call you."

He seems contrite, which is strange and unwelcome. I don't want these men to appear good in any way. I've been naïve before and I won't again. "You can call us victims," I seethe.

The Crown's eyes narrow, "Have they hurt you?"

I blink. Is he serious? Did they hurt me? I clench my hands into fists and allow the anger to take hold.

"I was taken from my home," I grit, staring him down with all the hatred my five-foot-seven frame possesses. "Thrown into a dark cell and starved for days. I witnessed a brutal murder and now I'm being paraded around to be sold to creatures that will most definitely kill me if given the chance. What do *you* think?" I bite out the words, letting the rage fuel me.

"I'm sorry," he murmurs softly. His eyes don't leave mine. He stares back, conveying to me that he means it, but it doesn't matter. He's allowing it to continue, which makes him my enemy just as much as the others.

"Unless you plan to do something to stop it, your apology is worthless to me."

"Believe me, if I could, I would."

I cringe.

"Did she not call you the Crown? Is this not your auction?" I quiz, ensuring my revulsion comes through in my tone.

"It's more complicated than that," Lawrence chimes in.

"Just go," I say, turning my head away. All hope of help evaporated with his words. He won't help and we're as good as dead.

"Tell me your name," Lawrence commands, sounding unkind for the first time. I huff out a harsh breath. He doesn't deserve anything from me, but for some reason I give in. Maybe it's because I want to hear it. Need to hear it, just like Stacey earlier. Or maybe it's some idiotic hope that, like with all serial killers, if I make myself a real person in his eyes, it will be harder for him to allow this auction to continue. *They aren't human.*

"Marina Drake."

Lawrence inhales sharply, closing his eyes, looking like he's in pain.

The other man arches a brow at Lawrence, confused by his reaction.

"Do you know her, Lawrence?"

The man named Lawrence raises his head to the other, shaking it back and forth, but not convincingly. Could he possibly know me?

"No. It's not that. My head is pounding."

"Perhaps you're hungry. Should you eat something?"

I recoil at this suggestion, palms beginning to sweat again, and a sheen of perspiration builds at my hairline.

"Dear God, girl, he didn't mean you." He motions toward the cart of glasses. "We aren't barbarians," Lawrence says, appalled by my misunderstanding. I don't say anything.

"I won't be sampling anyone today," he says coolly. If I didn't know better, I'd say there was a hint of revulsion underlying those words. Does he not like blood? Is that even possible for a vampire?

"Surely you aren't going to pass up a glass of perfectly aged type O, brother," a male voice calls from the corner of the room. Every vampire in the auditorium stops what they're doing, and all eyes fly in his direction. A tall man with long, jet-black hair stands menacingly just inside of the door.

"Marcellus," the Crown says. "I didn't think we'd be seeing you this month."

Marcellus huffs. "I rarely miss." He picks at his fingers, seemingly uninterested in having this conversation. "It's been —what—a century since you've participated."

"I found it high time I attend. It is *my* auction, after all."

Having it confirmed that this is his auction makes me sick to my stomach. What sort of a creature would allow innocent girls to be kidnapped and sold off to sadistic blood-sucking monsters? There are blood banks for a reason. Why couldn't they do something more on the up and up? There have to be plenty of crazy people out there that would willingly give their blood in order to not be kidnapped, tortured, and killed.

Yet, there are plenty of willing women for sex, and trafficking is still a thing. Humans can be just as monstrous with their vices. Ratilda confirmed this auction was done for similar reasons as sex trafficking. For convenience and because they can.

Taking a deep breath, the Crown steps forward, grabs a

flute from the tray, and brings it to his nose. In a strange turn of events, the room goes silent. Everyone in the room watches in anticipation. He inhales deeply, sighing at the scent of my blood. A collective gasp rings across the room as every onlooker awaits his next move. Has it been a long time since he drank blood? Why is everyone so entranced by this? What am I missing?

Despite myself, I'm holding my breath, waiting to see his reaction when he drinks me in. Everyone else appears to be on the same page as they all lean in, not moving, speaking, or even breathing. Moments pass, and the suspense is killing me.

"What I find most interesting is that you actually considered sampling a donor. Isn't that against your principles, dear brother?" Marcellus's brow rises in question.

Brother?

These two couldn't be any more different where looks were concerned. Both are attractive, but one is far scarier than the other. The newcomer has my skin crawling in ways no other in this room has. Not even the wicked couple from before.

"We are vampires, Marcellus. Sampling blood is our lifeline."

"Indeed. Yet, you don't." Marcellus's lips press together in a thin line, eyes narrowing in his supposed brother's direction. "Don't let me keep you, Julian. Taste her." He grins. "She looks succulent."

Julian.

I say the name several times in my head, for no other reason but to remember who I need to take out.

Julian glowers in the man's direction.

"Fine. Fine. If you won't, then I will." Marcellus moves toward me and my back straightens. Being in a room surrounded by vampires would tend to make a human tremble, but I'm going to do my best not to show fear. It's not easy. Something about this particular vampire has me on edge. If I had to guess who's the worst of the worst, my bet is he's at the top of the evil hierarchy.

Julian's arm shoots out, stopping Marcellus in his tracks.

"Don't," Julian growls, eliciting an eye raise from the evil vamp.

Julian brings the glass up to his lips, looking pained. His eyes meet mine and I see the conflict. He doesn't want to, but he's been called out. I know this as if he himself is saying the words. How, I have no idea . . . I just know. He's waiting for my approval and I don't want to give it. I want to refuse, but if I do, will he protect me from his brother?

I nod my head, giving him permission, as though anything I say matters. I'd rather it be him than the other.

He tips his head back and the dark red liquid runs into his mouth. His eyes close and I watch as he inhales and exhales. A look of bliss transforms his beautiful face. When his eyes meet mine, they glow red, and I can't help but bare my teeth, glowering. I knew he was one of them, but the confirmation makes my insides turn.

While Julian stares at me, Marcellus grabs a glass, sloshing a bit out the side. Without fanfare he tips the glass back, downing my blood as though it were a fine wine. When he's done, he groans, licking his lips in satisfaction. Julian's drinking had done nothing to stop this monster from taking what he wanted.

"She's heavenly," he practically sings. "I do say, Julian, this one may be exactly the distraction I've been looking for."

I grimace, knowing full well I'd suffer at his hands.

"It will never happen. They are spoken for." Julian snarls.

Ratilda steps forward, like the bumbling idiot she is. "No.

No— There are two remaining, and she's one of them." I want to tear out her hair for imparting this information to wicked Marcellus.

"Wonderful. I plan to bid on her. Shall we get started?" Marcellus coos.

My body trembles at the declaration. I don't want him bidding on me. In fact, I don't want any of these vile people taking me anywhere. I'd rather die right here, right now, than go anywhere with any of these monsters.

"Tonight shall be fun. It would appear we will have a bidding war on our hands, friends." Ratilda calls out. "Give me a minute to prepare our last two donors."

They all cheer in excitement, while I internally map out plans for revenge against all of them.

"Come with me," Ratilda barks at Stacey, as she lifts her number from the floor and carries it toward me. "You need to stand next to her and hope to God you bring in as much money as she will." She blows out a breath. "The fucking Crown is here." She doesn't direct this to either one of us. She's simply talking aloud.

"Are you okay?" I ask Stacey, as she slides in next to me. Her eyes meet mine, with a *what the hell do you think* look. "We'll be fine," I say mostly to calm myself.

"What do you make of all this?" she says quietly, so that Ratilda doesn't hear us talking.

"I'm not sure, but it looks like the ring leaders of this whole circus are here and ready to bid. Just keep your head held high and try to act like this isn't affecting you."

"Un-fucking-likely," she bites out.

"Shall we get on with the main attraction?" Ratilda shouts, eliciting a round of hoots from the crowd.

Julian nods and steps aside. Lawrence bends down, whispering something into his brother's ear. Julian's eyes taper into slits as he listens.

"Which one should go first?" she coos. "Blondie or Jessica Rabbit?" The crowd snickers at her moniker for Stacey. Looking over, I see her sway, and I reach out and grab her hand, not caring what any of them think. I'll offer comfort with or without permission. We're in this nightmare together.

"I guess it'll be Goldilocks first," she laughs, looking at me with a sporting grin. "Bidding shall begin at five million dollars." She raises a brow in Julian's direction. "Would you like to claim the first bid?"

He nods, and she beams in response. My eyes widen at this turn of events. I didn't think he'd bid on me himself. *This is bad . . . very, very bad.*

"Ten million dollars." the scary couple from earlier say in unison.

The woman is now seemingly committed to taking me home. Keeping up with the Crown, so it would seem.

"Fifteen." Julian says, furthering this game and driving up the bid.

"Fifteen," the announcer repeats. "Do I hear twenty?"

Julian and the creepy couple volley back and forth in five-million-dollar increments. My heart pounds in my chest. The frightening fact that I'll be leaving with one of two evils in a matter of moments has me near hysterics. Getting away from either of these vampires won't be easy. Sweat drips down my hairline. I wipe it away, stopping my hand at my temple to rub away the impending headache.

"Fifty million dollars."

My eyes shoot to the back corner, where the dark-haired demon stands tall and assured.

The crowd gasps.

My hands fly to my mouth in shock, head shaking back and forth as the fear threatens to consume me. Fifty million dollars? He's worse than the couple. *I'm as good as dead.*

My eyes land on Julian, and our gazes hold. I don't blink. Don't move. The first to turn away is the weakest, and I won't lose this silent battle. My face is blank but my head is screaming, *I dare you,* sonofabitch.

"One hundred million." Julian's eyes remain fixed on mine, but it's not over yet.

"Prince Marcellus, would you like to trump your brother's bid?" Ratilda taunts, and I don't dare breathe.

"No." His snakelike voice slithers over my body, causing me to tremble in response. "I think I'll give him this one."

"What about you?" she says to the couple in the middle of the room.

The creepy man raises his hands in defeat and everything in me relaxes. I almost fall over in relief.

"Seven-seventy-six to the Crown, Julian Bellamy, for one hundred million dollars."

"Ratilda, I believe that concludes our evening," Marcellus intones from the corner, arms crossed and brow pinched.

Ratilda's lips pull down in a frown.

"We still have one donor remaining," she says, confused, if not a little scared.

"I'll be taking her for fifty million. I doubt anyone here wishes to bid against me." He looks around the room, challenging them to argue. They don't.

Ratilda looks to Julian, who simply nods in agreement.

"No," I yell out. "He can't have her."

Ratilda takes a threatening step toward me, hand raised as though she plans to hit me. "Shut your mouth. Do you have any idea—"

"Don't touch her." Julian's cold tone is chill-inducing, effectively silencing Ratilda and everyone else in the room.

Her eyes widen and true fear is etched on her overdone face. "A-all right. That concludes today's auction. We'll convene back here in one month for more options. Thank you," she says before walking off the stage on visibly shaky legs.

My head snaps to Stacey's. Her eyes are wide, and fear like I've never seen before shows. I turn toward her just in time to catch her as she collapses into my open arms. Her body shakes violently as I lower her and myself to the ground. I'm hoping the floor will open up and swallow us whole. Anything to keep us as far from those men as possible.

"Don't let him take me," she whimpers, and I hold on tighter.

"We'll figure out something, Stacey. We'll figure something out," I repeat, trying to convince myself as much as her.

She cries out, smashing her head into my shoulder as if trying to burrow inside me.

"I'm going to die. *We're* going to die," she shrieks.

Her fear is warranted, and I wonder why I'm not as frightened. It's not that I'm *not* scared, I'm just numb. We've been auctioned off as blood donors. *Unwilling* donors. They take what they want and come back for more.

"You have to stop talking like that," I coo into her head. "You're strong. Be that girl I met in the showers."

She looks up at me, blinking the tears away and swiping at her nose. "You're right."

I don't want to let her go. We don't know each other, but being in this situation has somehow made me desperate to stay with her. To hold on to anything and anyone who came into my life before this moment. Being victims has imprinted her on my soul. We're kindred and that's not something I want to lose, because when I do, life as I know it is over.

It was over the moment you were taken.

My wish is not fulfilled. Firm hands grab me from behind, pulling me away from a screaming Stacey. I'm pulled roughly to my feet and moved toward a step down off the platform.

"Stacey," I yell out, desperate to get back to her, but a hard smack to the face has me sobering and pulled back to my captor.

"Shut up, girl," Sarcos barks, and I growl in response.

"If I were you, I'd never touch her like that again," Julian grits through his teeth.

"Sir Crown, I'm sorry," he mutters, clearly afraid of the man in front of him. "What would you like me to do with your purchase?" Sarcos asks, head lowered.

"Prepare her for travel."

"Yes, sir," he says, bowing low.

"And Sarcos," Julian says, drawing the evil creature's gaze toward him. "You touch her or any donor like that again, I'll kill you myself," he warns.

"Y-yes, sir," he says, bowing twice more before placing his hand on my back lightly and ushering me back toward the hallway by which we'd entered the auction.

My eyes land on Julian's and his soften. I glare in response. I don't want his false sense of security. He's as bad as Sarcos and every other vampire in this place. I'll fight him to the death.

"Same with mine," Marcellus orders, drawing my attention away from Julian's.

Marcellus sneers in my direction before he pivots, stalking toward his brother.

I look to Stacey, who stares absently as she's placed next to me by Ramsey.

"Move," we are commanded.

We descend the stairs we climbed earlier for the auction.

Sarcos appears to be leading us back to the room where we were dressed. At the last minute, he steers in the opposite direction. Stopping in front of a small door, he pulls out a key and unlocks it. When the door is open, he tosses us in, slamming and locking it shut behind us. Placing my ear to the door, I listen as heavy footsteps retreat. When I can no longer hear them, I push off the door, searching the room.

"Help me look for a way out." I say to Stacey, running my hands along the wall.

"What?"

"Snap out of it, Stacey." I bark. "We have one shot to get the hell out of here. Help me."

I continue searching the room for any means of escape. There's not so much as a vent to be seen. We've been put in a room that is nothing more than a boxed-in cell.

"We're going to die," Stacey cries, losing her once-stoic persona.

Grabbing her by the shoulders, I sit her down on the nearest chair.

"Stop," I command. "Strong. Remember? Now is not the time to lose our heads. You have to pull it together."

"We're going to die," she repeats.

"No. We won't," I yell back.

"You saw *him*. I'm as good as dead," she says between sniffles. "He's dangerous."

She's right. He is. And as much as I'd love to believe that she'll make it out alive, the truth is, she probably won't.

"What's your name?" I ask, trying to get her to remember who she is. The strong girl from earlier. She eyes me wearily. "What's your name?" I repeat.

Her eyes blink several times before she finally whispers, "Stacey Ryan."

I nod, "That's right. Stacey Ryan. Say it again."

"Stacey Ryan."

"Again, with more conviction," I taunt.

"Stacey Ryan," she yells.

"Good. Now, we need to get out of here and I need your help. Can you help me?" I ask, and she takes a deep breath.

"Yes."

"Okay." I smile. "Let's find a way out of here."

I help her stand to her feet and she pulls me into a hug. "Thank you, Marina."

"For what?" I ask, confused.

"For helping me find myself again. For not allowing me to be scared."

I sigh. "There is plenty to be scared about, Stacey. I'm scared too. But right now, we need to form a plan."

"Okay." She nods her head. "What do we do?"

"We search this place."

A short time later, we've come up empty-handed. The place is no more than a fancy prison cell. We're both sitting on the ground feeling defeated when the door creeps open and two bags are thrown in. I scramble to my feet, but the door is closed quickly, locking us back in.

I pick up one of the bags and open it to find clothes. A pair of black yoga pants, a white tank top, white undies, and a sports bra a size too large are now littering the floor. Stacey dumps her contents as well, finding the same things.

"What am I supposed to do with this?" Stacey grits through her teeth. I eye the contents and can't help but smile.

"I don't know about you, but I can run much better in these," I say, grinning for the first time in days. She grins too.

Hope.

It might be a horrible tease, but it's the first sign of hope either of us have had in some time. I decide in this moment to cling to it, fiercely. We both hurriedly change into the new clothes.

The door opens once more, and Sarcos comes in with two covered dishes.

"Glad to see you chose to get dressed. I wouldn't want to have to beat you into submission," he threatens, lowering the dishes to the ground in front of us.

"I'm pretty sure you were warned not to touch me," I grit out, and he takes one menacing step toward me.

"You bitch," he seethes. "You might be safe for now, but you'll wish I'd killed you before this is all over with."

"Leave," Stacey snaps from beside me. "Just do what you came to do and leave us alone."

He peruses her body.

"Nobody ever said I couldn't touch you." He licks his lips and Stacey recoils.

"Touch her and I'll scream for Julian. You won't make it out of here alive," I promise, not knowing if my threat is even valid. He stops, face turning red. He doesn't come closer, which leads me to believe my words do in fact have merit. Without another word, he lifts the lids to the covered dishes and pulls two bottled waters from his cargo pockets.

"Eat. You leave in ten minutes."

When the door is shut behind us and I no longer fear he's near, I take a look at what sits before us and my mouth begins to water. Steak, a baked potato, and bread sit atop the silver dishes. Stacey and I don't waste time. We're starving and the food calls to us. There is no silverware, but I don't care. I shovel pieces of bread and potato into my mouth as if this is my last meal. *It won't be.*

I don't linger on that thought, instead continuing to stuff my mouth full of food. Not even five minutes later, my plate is clean. I open the water bottle and gulp greedily. That's when it all goes south. Something is off. The room is swaying and my vision is getting fuzzy. My eyelids grow heavy.

"Stacey, are you feeling strange?"

"Yes. You too?"

"I . . ." My words trail off.

The room goes in and out of focus. Before long, the fight bleeds out of me and I succumb to the dark.

CHAPTER 7
JULIAN

I pace the floor of this hellhole, wearing the treads thin. The room I'm in is a prison cell, meant to hold the innocent girls who've been stolen away from their families. From their lives. The whole fucking thing makes me sick, but what the hell can I do? I'd need an army to change things, and with half the vampire population at odds with my rule, my best chance of effecting change is to gain more alliances and earn the loyalty of more of my subjects. As it stands now, the vampire army's allegiance rests with the Council, and half the Council would do anything to see me overthrown.

It'll take time, and time is something these donors don't have. The truth is, almost every single one of them that stood on that stage today will be dead within the month. The vampires who bought them are some of the worst in our society. They're the true evil that lurks in the shadows and feeds off the fear they cause.

They don't need these girls. They own clubs and houses filled to the brim with willing donors. Yet this is their choice. They want the fight . . . the fear. They want the chase. They have the money to pay the going rate, just for the sport of it. To have slaves at their beck and call. They'll abuse these girls in horrific ways just for fun.

My stomach turns at the thought and the knowledge that all of that blood money goes to my family. It's my legacy.

A legacy I never wanted.

"What's going through that head of yours?" my brother Law asks, sounding weary.

"Don't ask," I growl, trying hard not to lose my cool on him. He doesn't like this any more than I do. But he's even more powerless than I am.

"There's nothing you can do, Jude. You've saved one. Can't that be enough?"

"It'll *never* be enough," I bark, turning on him. His hands fly up in surrender. "Why the fuck did you bring me here, Law?"

He sighs. "I didn't want to, but the Council is getting agitated. Every month that goes by and you're missing from the auction and the meetings, the whispers about overthrowing the monarchy grow."

"And you know this how?" I grit through my teeth, angry that this is the first I'm hearing of such talk.

"I have my sources, Jude. And they're not happy about the traitors." He sighs again. "But you and I both know that your absence only looks like weakness in their eyes. It won't be long before there's a full mutiny, with the Council leading the charge."

I run my hands through my hair roughly, pulling at the roots. I know what he says is true. They think I'm weak. They believe I'll be the fall of the vampire race.

They can all fuck off.

"So . . . Marina . . ."

I give my brother the side-eye, not wanting to discuss Marina Drake. That was an unexpected turn of events. I had absolutely no intention of participating in that fucking auction, but there was something about her. I couldn't—no, wouldn't—allow them to have her. Then when I drank her blood . . .

"Earth to Julian . . . what the hell, man?"

"We're not talking about this," I say, starting to pace yet again, but Law gets in my face, grabs me by my shoulders, and forces me to stop. "Don't," I warn, but he only smirks.

"Her blood was *that* good, huh?" he chuckles. "I saw the way your eyes practically rolled back into your head. There's something about her, isn't there?"

I watch my brother closely. There's something he isn't saying. There's something he's hiding. He's never tried to get me to these auctions before, and despite his words, his insistence today was completely unlike him. He's never given a shit about anything, especially when it comes to family affairs. Even if we are overthrown, money will never be an issue for us. We have compulsion. We can take what we want, even if it's not our preference. Law has made it clear that he'd prefer that to mutilating humans. We both would.

Except more humans would die.

"You knew her," I accuse, continuing to watch him for signs. His face gives nothing away.

"I thought I did. Turns out, she wasn't who I thought," he shrugs all nonchalant, but it's bullshit and I know it.

He's definitely hiding something.

A knock sounds on the door and I call out, "Come in."

"Sir, your donor is ready," Sarcos says, bowing like an idiot.

"Shall we?" Law asks, motioning toward the door and effectively ending my questioning.

Whatever he's keeping from me, I'll get to the bottom of it, but for now, I need to get Marina out of here.

I sway on my feet, feeling lightheaded. Law's hands come under my arm, helping to keep me standing.

"Whoa, brother. What's going on?" he asks with a raised brow.

I jerk out of his grasp and smooth my suit back into place. "I'm fine. I need to get out of here," I lie. Something is off. It has been since I drank *her* blood.

I wouldn't admit that to Law, and certainly not here, where the walls undoubtedly have ears. We've already said too much. Law continues to stare; what he's searching for I can only begin to imagine.

"What the fuck are you looking at?"

"You sure you're okay?" he questions, and I scowl.

"I said I'm good. Let's get out of here." He nods, never taking his eyes off of me.

Law sees too much and it's a real problem. There's something connecting me to Marina Drake. I felt it the moment my eyes landed on her. I tasted it in her blood. The question is whether this connection is a good thing or a bad thing for me. By the way my stomach is turning and sweat beads at my temple, I can only assume it's not good.

I need to figure out who this human girl is and why she has any hold over me.

CHAPTER 8

Hazel eyes bore into me. Hungrily. He reaches out, brushing my hair from my neck. Leaning in, he runs the tip of his nose delicately up the arch of my neck, nipping lightly at my ear. A shiver of ecstasy works its way through me.

"Please," I beg.

Trailing kisses down the same path, he stops at the crook of my neck and shoulder.

"You're mine, Marina," *he whispers into my skin like a prayer.*

The dream ends abruptly, and I'm left feeling cheated, in a fog of lust. I snuggle into the soft sheets that cover my body. The smell of lavender infiltrates my nostrils. I sigh in contentment, stretching my hands above my head and groaning at the exquisite stretch of my aching muscles. I run my hands down my face and my eyes flutter open.

An ornately decorated ceiling has me sitting up quickly and pulling the blankets tightly around me. My eyes dart wildly around the foreign space, searching for interlopers.

Where the hell am I?

Perspiration builds on my upper lip, and I wipe it away. The room is empty, save for the traditional bedroom furniture. Every item decorating the room is lavish and expensive-looking.

The auction.

As the initial confusion subsides, I'm able to truly appreciate the magnificence of the room. The four-poster bed I'm currently perched atop is rich mahogany that reaches almost to the top of a twelve-foot ceiling. The intricate carvings on the bed and large armoire are in the Baroque style. I know this from working in the antique store a town over from Liberty for an entire summer in junior high. It was my favorite job, and to this day I can still name certain pieces and styles because of it.

The windows are free of bars and sunlight streams in, surrounding me in warmth.

My momentary fascination with my newest prison quickly vanishes with the sight of the heavy wooden door. I rush from the bed, grabbing at the knob and twisting . . . but nothing happens. It shouldn't come as a surprise that I'm locked in. Obviously, they aren't going to make this easy on me.

I need to get out of here. To see the layout. Forge a plan.

"Open up," I yell, banging my fists on the door. "Let me out."

I'm more likely to piss someone—a vampire—off, but that's the price I'm willing to pay to get a peek outside this room.

"Julian, open this fucking door," I scream, sounding unhinged even to my own ears.

When nobody comes and not a sound is heard on the other side, I spin around, my back hitting the door, and slide to the floor with a huff. My head falls backward, colliding roughly with the strong wooden frame, and I relish the sting.

It means I'm alive.

Tears glide down my cheeks in a river of frustration. I'm trapped. And after being stuck in that dungeon for who knows how long, I'm done with confined spaces. The unknown claws away at the fortress I've built around my mind. All the awful possibilities play out in my head, worse than any horror movie I've dared to watch.

I know I'm living with the king of vampires and it's only a matter of time before he comes for me. To feed from me. *You have to be ready.*

"What do you want with me?" My vocal cords strain from the force with which the words are screamed. I know damn well what he wants, but I'd say anything to get him here.

Standing, I turn back to face the door, bringing my fist up to pound the wood over and over again. "Let me out. Let me the hell out of here," I repeat hysterically. A rustling on the other side stops me short. My body tenses. *Someone is out there.*

"Open the goddamn door, you sadist," I shriek, and then freeze when I hear a key going into the lock on the other side.

My eyes search the area around me, looking for anything to use as a weapon. I might've been asking for this, but now that someone is actually coming in, I realize my error. I'm not prepared.

I almost collapse in relief when my gaze falls upon a door on the adjacent wall. Throwing it open, I'm disappointed to find it's only an en suite bathroom. One conveniently lacking a lock. Without time to contemplate my next move, I enter the bathroom, closing the door behind me and crouching in the large stone shower. Not two seconds later, I hear footsteps on the wooden floor on the other side of the bathroom door.

He's come for me.

Several seconds go by and then the door to my room closes. I release the breath I was holding, thankful that I avoided this run-in for a little while longer. Time enough to get my act together.

"Excuse me, miss. I came to bring you breakfast."

My body jolts at the foreign voice calling through the bathroom door. It creaks open and I call out, "Go away." As if that's going to work.

"Please, miss. I won't hurt you," the deceptively nice woman promises.

Don't trust anyone here.

"Come out and eat before it turns cold."

I know better than to fall prey to the false politeness in her voice. To relax and do as I'm told would be a mistake . . . yet I can't help it. My stomach is ready to revolt from a lack of food. It's either die from being too trusting or die from starvation. I'm not sure which would be worse at this point.

Cracking the door open a little wider, I see a girl not much younger than me carrying a tray full of silver platters. She appears pale and fragile, much like the people clad in black back at the auction. *Another victim.*

She seems harmless enough, so I slowly exit the bathroom. When our eyes meet, she makes a small curtsy, which is odd, as I'm the prisoner. I search her face for signs of anything sinister, like red eyes or sharp canines.

When I don't find anything out of place, I lunge forward. "Get me out of here. *Help* me," I beg, pulling at the skirt of her dress. The silver platters clink as the tray shifts.

"Miss, please. You'll get us both in trouble."

"Help me escape," I plead once more, desperation taking over.

Her lips pull down and a crease forms between her eyes.

"There's no way out," she whispers. "You belong to the Crown now."

My hands release their hold on the girl. She won't help me.

"Stacey. Where's Stacey?"

"I don't know who you're talking about."

I see it in the way her eyes quirk. She doesn't know Stacey.

"I just bring breakfast."

"Please. Help me get out of here." I try begging once more.

She purses her lips and narrows her eyes at me.

"The Crown is a generous man if you abide by his rules. Do as you're told, and he'll bring you no harm." She smiles, but it doesn't reach her eyes.

"Is that a rehearsed statement?" I say harshly, losing all sense. If I'm going to die, better to go out fighting than lying down and taking it. At least that's my motto. There is no room for fear here. I need to channel all the rage inside of me, and God help this girl, because she's about to be on the other end of that rage. "Where is he?" I demand, grinding my teeth in anger.

"I'm only to bring you your food, miss." She places the tray on a small round table next to the bed, not even fazed by my menacing glare.

As she turns to leave, I grab her sleeve and pull her toward me, barring my teeth.

"Who is Julian Bellamy?" I grit out, desperate for answers and knowing she's my best chance at getting them. I need to keep her here for as long as possible. She has to have information on my captor.

"Who?" She quirks a brow at me, grinning as if I'm pathetic.

I remain silent, wanting—no, needing—answers. If I lose my cool, it's unlikely that this girl will help me, and I need help.

"The Crown. Who. Is. He?"

She steps out of my grip, smoothing out the sleeves of her threadbare apron. "He's our king." Her lip curls into a grin.

Our?

It was a benign world days ago, but now it's laced with so many dark possibilities.

Making a mental checklist of all the options, I almost miss the way the girl's eyes darken. My inner voice screams, but I can't get my mouth to cooperate. *She's one of them and I didn't even realize it.*

Her eyes aren't red, but she's on his side. She's no victim. This girl is here of her own free will. She reveres him, if her wide grin and sudden hostility toward me are any indication.

"You're a fool if you try to leave," she says, turning away and leaving me once more.

My body sags with regret. I did *nothing*. It was a missed opportunity to escape. The door had been wide open, and the girl was smaller than me. Maybe she's a vampire with hidden powers, but she would've been my best chance to try.

Better to go out by her then to be sucked dry by the king of them all.

My hands grip my hair by the roots and pull. A scream rips through my chest as I grab the small, round table by the bed, throwing it to the ground. The metal platters clatter against the floor, scattering food everywhere. Chest heaving and breath ragged, I stand in the middle of the room trying to pull myself together while tears stream down my face.

Hope bleeds from me with every sob. At some point, I collapse in a heap on the floor, falling fast asleep, not caring what or who comes to find me.

When I awaken, I'm lying on the bed, covered in soft linens once more. How I got up here I haven't a clue. Last I remember,

I was curled in a ball on the floor. Not that it matters. I'm thankful to at least feel rested.

The sun has set and my room is clouded in shadows. My stomach is turning from a lack of food and water. It's my fault, as I spilled the contents of the trays brought to me earlier, but in truth, I don't know if eating anything they give me is a good idea. Would they poison me? It's unlikely if I'm to be their food, but still, how am I to know? I ate what Sarcos gave me at the auction, and I don't have a clue what happened to me or for how long I was out.

If I'm to escape, I need to keep my wits about me, but I also need strength. Right now, I don't think I could fight off the small girl from earlier if I needed to. I'm weak and dehydrated. I decide to try to round up some of the spilled food from earlier, but as I stand from the bed, I see that the mess from earlier is cleaned up. The table is righted, and two silver dishes sit atop it. I don't waste time removing the covers and sighing at the replacement food waiting for me.

Someone has been in here, and as much as I want to dissect that truth more, I'm not going to waste the chance to finally eat. Poisoned or not, I'm starving. The trays are filled with chicken, pasta, bread, and a variety of fruits. I want to gorge myself, but I learned my lesson in the dank cell of the auction house. I eat only what I think my stomach can handle, but I drink every last ounce of the water in the full pitcher.

When I'm done, all I want to do is sleep, but curiosity wins out. I need to pull apart this room to see if I can find anything to help me understand my surroundings. Anything that could help me get out.

I begin by looking under the bed. *Nothing.* Then I pull out every drawer in the armoire, only to find it stocked with comfy socks and panties in every color. The last drawer is empty. As I pull out a black lacy thong, I check the tag and then I grab another, checking that size too. Every single piece is my size.

How can that be?

Why would this room be stocked full of essentials that aren't mine in my size? Did he arrange this before I got here? And if he did, how the hell did he know my size? Tingles crawl up my spine at the thought of him or any of them looking at my underwear for sizing purposes. Did they strip me down while I was out?

"Ugh," I yell out, frustrated that yet another day has gone by and the questions without answers just keep mounting. I stalk toward the one door in the room I haven't yet opened. It's a large walk-in closet and it's stocked to the brim with everything any girl could need. From beautiful blouses to sundresses, pantsuits to sweatshirts; no expense was spared based on the designer tags.

Every freaking piece sized perfectly.

"That son of a bitch," I screech, for so many reasons. All the ways he could know what size I am. The fact that I'm going nowhere—nobody would spend this type of money if they had any intention of letting me go. Not to mention the outrage of being kidnapped and the indignity of being sold like livestock.

Better here and alive than out there and dead.

Sometimes I hate my inner voice. That stupid, optimistic bitch, who loves to act like the voice of reason, when all I want to do is lash out. She isn't wrong. With a closet this full, I can only hope that Julian, the king of monsters, might not plan to drain me of my life. At least not quickly.

I've managed to find nothing to help me with my efforts to escape, and there are still no hints as to where the hell I am. I could be in Asia at this point. And where the hell is Julian? Am I to be shut in this freaking room forever? Frustration and anger collide as I begin tearing clothes off their hangers and throwing them about the closet. I grab a gray jumpsuit and pull at the seams, needing to rip it to shreds. With every stitch that comes loose, the tension in my shoulders wanes momentarily. Destruction feels good. It feels necessary to channel my fury.

"You shouldn't have done that." The alien accent winds its way up my spine, leaving chills in its wake. *Not Julian . . . a woman.* "That *was* a perfectly gorgeous, one-of-a-kind Chanel."

I spin around, glaring at the intruder. Her hands fly up daintily in surrender as she chuckles at my blatant hostility.

"Who are you?"

The woman's perfectly sculpted eyebrow rises to a point.

"Formalities aren't important right now, little girl. We need to get you cleaned up right away. You're expected in the throne room immediately." She picks at her long, blood-red nails contentedly, belying her words. "And I'll need to get someone in here to clean up this mess you've made." She tsks.

"I'm not going anywhere," I challenge, pushing back my shoulders in an effort to look menacing.

She barks a laugh, and that's when I catch sight of the pointed canines, indicating she is one of them too.

"Who are you?" I repeat, narrowing my eyes.

"I'm Ka-tee-na." The woman's head bounces in time to her name being sounded out phonetically.

My brow furrows, signaling that her name means nothing to me.

"The Crown's right-hand woman," she explains, running her hand slowly down the side of her neck, pausing at her clavicle. *Bizarre.*

In fact, everything about this woman is wacky. Channeling Cruella de Vil, she's sporting the black-and-white skunk coiffure, shaved on one side and chin length on the other. She's dressed in black from head to toe, with the distinct exception of red patent leather pumps that match her nails. The heels add to her already tall frame. Upon closer inspection, her face looks familiar.

"Have we met?"

She throws her head back, mouth open.

"You have me confused with Ratilda."

My brow rises.

"From the auction," she offers. "She's my sister. We look alike-ish." She crinkles her nose.

"Ahh . . . yep, that's it."

"We might look similar, but appearance is where it starts and ends. She's a royal bitch."

I snort. "I'm to believe you're any better?"

"Obviously," she deadpans. "I don't want anything to do with that dreadful auction."

"For real?"

I eye her skeptically, not wanting to be naïve and fall victim to some game. She's clearly a vamp, based on her elongated teeth and pale-as-death skin. *I can't trust her.*

"It's barbaric and *I* am no savage." Her hand comes to her chest.

"Noted."

I won't believe anything she says. To survive, I need to remember that nobody here is a friend. Until the day she helps me escape, she's an enemy.

"Anyway, no time to waste. You have somewhere to be."

"I'm not going anywhere." My words come out weak and pathetic, exhaustion taking over.

My mind is invaded by all the possibilities that could await me in the throne room. Torture, shackles, blood drainage—each is as terrifying as the last.

"You will if you value your life."

I roll my eyes. Call it self-preservation. Call it moronic.

Either way, I won't allow her to see me any other way but irritated by this whole situation. Everyone in this world of vampires and auctions is my enemy. I can't be seen as a weak human to any of them.

"How about we not play games, little girl. Despite your actions, I can smell your distress.

I feel all the blood leach from my face at her words. No matter what I do, these creatures will always have the upper hand.

Katina frowns, pursing her lips as she considers me.

"There, there. I didn't mean to frighten you. I only meant to warn."

She sounds sincere, and her eyes are wide and concerned, which only manages to befuddle me more. At the auction, I knew everyone was my foe. Here, I could very easily be duped into thinking that Katina could be a friend. That's dangerous and only a trick of my mind. It's typical Marina, wanting to see the best in people, even when there is none to be seen.

"Your distress is palpable; you must learn to control it. Vampires can smell your emotions. Here you might be safe, but out there"—she motions toward the windows—"that will get you killed."

Out there. Does that even mean something to me anymore? As a prisoner, how long will I be cooped up here before I'm disposed of and another unsuspecting person is stolen to replace me? *You won't allow that.*

Katina turns on her heels, going toward the walk-in closet. I hear her sifting around until she finds something that pleases her. I don't even need to look to know that her idea of what works and mine are going to be entirely different.

"You have to try to cooperate, Marina."

She knows my name. What else does she know about me? My blood type? My grades from school? Was I being followed before I was abducted? Or was it just a case of wrong place, wrong time? *Were these the monsters from my past?*

"There are always eyes, watching, waiting for a reason to swoop in and end you. The Crown will protect you if you behave. If you don't, not even he can save you."

Save me? Does he think buying me from the auction was saving me? No. Saving me would've meant stopping the auction. Or at least allowing me to go home afterward. He didn't save me. Nobody can do that but me. I'm on my own here.

"What's that?" I eye the blood-red dress she holds in her hands. It looks like something out of the eighteenth century. "I'm not wearing that," I say, crossing my arms over my chest in defiance.

She sighs animatedly. "You will, or you'll go naked. Your choice," she shrugs.

"There is an entire closet full of normal clothes," I say, pointing toward the door. "Where the hell did you find that, anyway? I looked through there and I don't remember seeing *ancient* clothes."

She rolls her eyes. "It's beautiful and you'll look . . . well . . . better." She purses her lips and I scowl. "You're having dinner with the Crown and his brother. Royalty, my dear. You need to look the part."

"Will they be dressed like this?" I say, motioning toward the offending garment.

"Doesn't matter." She waves her free hand. "I was asked to dress you, and dress you I shall. Now, take that off and let's get started."

"Absolutely not." There's no way I'm getting naked in front of this vampire. Not happening.

Now she rolls her eyes. "My dear Marina, you are not my taste. Now, move along and drop that sheet you're wearing."

Twenty minutes later, battered and bruised by the horrific corset dress Katina shoved me in, I'm already regretting that I was sold off to someone intent on torture before simply killing me. I'm a ball of fury and I'm ready to unleash it at this dinner with evil royalty.

I won't leave this world without a fight.

CHAPTER 9

"Where are you taking me?" I try desperately to sound brave, when internally I'm quaking in fear. All the bravado from earlier is gone as I inch closer to Julian and whatever nefarious plans he has for me tonight.

"I already told you—the throne room."

I know nothing about these creatures, yet they seem to know everything about humans. They have an unfair advantage. It's hard to tell if any of the fictional books and movies I've watched and read have depicted vampires at all accurately. I'm going in blind and completely helpless. I've never so much as taken a self-defense class, which means I'm thoroughly screwed and at the mercy of the monsters.

"What's going to happen to me there?"

She stops and turns toward me.

"That all depends on you. The Crown wishes to have you dine with him." Her hands fly up as if to say *duh*. "If you behave, I'm sure no harm will come to you . . . today. However, if you step a foot out of line, you'll take your last breath." Her red claws rake tenderly down my cheek, almost affectionately.

"It's a shame you're human. We could have so much fun together." She licks her lips seductively.

"You said I'm not your type," I say, eyes narrowed in on the fingernail trailing across my jaw.

"You're not." She removes her hand from my face. "But I'd give it a go. You've got great cheekbones."

My nose scrunches at her peculiarity. I can't tell if she wants to kill me or kiss me at this particular moment. Neither is favorable. We continue to march down a hallway lined with red carpeting and gold walls. The place screams wealth, in a gaudy, masculine way. The walls are filled with aged portraits of ghastly men. The sneers plastered across their faces and evil eyes that appear to follow me as I continue past make them even creepier. *Always watching.*

As we descend further down the long expansive hall, male voices fill the air, growing louder by the second.

"Shall we share, for old times' sake, brother?" a familiar jovial voice questions.

"I'm in no mood for sharing, Lawrence."

The husky voice of my captor curls around my insides, torturing me with unwanted tingles. I stand tall, pushing all the foreign feelings away. I won't let this man corrupt me. He can't own my thoughts or sensations if I don't allow him to. And I won't. He may take my blood, but he'll never take anything more from me.

"Here we are. Remember what I said. *Behave.*"

Everything about this vampire is over the top. From her style to her words, she's drama personified.

"Do I have a choice?" I snap.

She drills me with a look of admonishment.

"Make no mistake, little girl . . . you will pay with your life if you don't fall in line. I'm a peach compared to the company you're about to keep. Be quiet and keep your head down unless you're told otherwise. I'm not saying this to be mean, but like I said, to warn you. The people you'll encounter in this world won't take kindly to your lip."

I don't say another word. If there is one thing I've learned over the years, it's that silence is, in fact, golden. Besides, these creatures don't deserve my attention, so I intend to play my part, but otherwise give nothing. *Survive.*

"Here she is, Sir Crown." Katina bows low, sweeping her hands outward in a graceful maneuver I've seen plenty of times in the movies.

The Crown—Julian—quickly sits up, looking flustered at my presence. Didn't he summon me here? Why is he acting out of sorts? It's me who's internally trembling.

"Katina?" Julian says, biting his bottom lip as he looks me over. "What, pray tell, have you done to her?"

Katina blinks. "I . . . Well . . . You see . . ." She shakes her head as if clearing away the cobwebs. "What are we talking about?"

Lawrence snickers, quickly bringing his hand up to his nose to cover his laughter. My face remains stone, not giving anything away.

"It's the dress, isn't it?" I ask, pursing my lips.

Lawrence full-on laughs, head thrown back, smacking his leg. "It is. It's horrendous. Where the hell did you get that, Kat? Did you dig up an ancestor?"

Katina huffs. "I think she looks rather distinguished." She snaps her head away from Lawrence to look at Julian. "Don't you think, Sir Crown?"

She's fishing, and based on Julian's expression, he's about to let her down easy.

"Please, Katina. How many times must I remind you? Julian will suffice."

Julian. It's not news to me, but hearing it from his lips does something unwelcome to me. An unnamed emotion squeezes my heart, tightening, promising to squeeze the last beat from the steadily thumping organ. Why does he elicit such strong reactions from me? Is it that invisible magic—like at the auction—causing it? Whatever the cause, I won't let it win.

"Forgive me, Julian." She beams up at my captor, who appears to have relaxed. "If that'll be all, I have things to do." He nods, dismissing her.

Now I'm alone with them and my eyes are trained on Julian. He sits on a large throne-like chair, drinking from a golden chalice. His mannerisms here in this room are so different from the way he behaved at the auction. There, he was commanding and royal. Here today, he's aloof and laid back, almost . . . cocky.

"Well, well, brother, . . . she is just as stunning as I remember." The golden-haired man sits perched upon an identical throne next to Julian, smiling wide. I don't return his smile, continuing to fix my icy stare over their heads. "Dress aside, that is."

"You find all things woman stunning, Law," Julian says matter-of-factly.

My eyes lower, curious about my captors. In this light and away from all the scary people at the auction, I really look at Julian and Lawrence and I get a strange feeling. There *is* something eerily familiar about Lawrence. Lawrence stares back at me, and every second that ticks by, the feeling grows stronger. I've seen him before. It appears to be a reoccurring theme here, and now more than ever I wonder if perhaps I was right. *These were my monsters.*

"Marina, do you see that guy over there?" Maggie asks from behind me.

"Which one?" I lift my eyebrows twice in a suggestive manner. There is a group of good-looking guys directly in front of us.

"Not them. Him." She nods with her head. "He's following us."

I search for the perpetrator and my eyes land on a tall blond on the opposite side of the food court from us. He's watching Maggie like she's his next meal. Every step she takes, his eyes follow.

"Yeah. I'd say he's got it bad," I joke.

"No, Marina, you don't understand. He's one of them."

There's nothing unusual about the man. His eyes aren't red and his canines aren't elongated. He doesn't have overly pronounced veins, nor is he sprouting hair all over his body. We've had to deal with monsters our entire lives, but this guy doesn't appear to be one of them.

"It's okay, Maggie. He's just a normal guy with a hard on for you," I giggle.

"It's not funny, Rina. He's been following me for weeks."

I eye her suspiciously.

"You haven't said anything about anyone following you."

"Would you be surprised? I've been followed since I was three years old. And probably before then."

I frown.

"You usually tell me these things."

"This one is different."

I shake the memory from my head. There's no way. But the resemblance is uncanny.

"Do I know you?" I say, quavering.

His eyes narrow as he considers the idea. Bringing his finger to his chin, he taps twice before responding.

"Yesterday." He grins. "Although I'm sure you dreamed of my dashing good looks overnight. Don't worry; I don't blame you."

"That's not it," I say, shaking my head. "I've seen you before."

"I'm afraid you're mistaken," Law drawls, seeming almost bored.

Julian appraises his brother with narrowed eyes, but eventually his features soften, and he turns to me, but I wonder. What is Lawrence Bellamy hiding? He brushed it off easily enough, but I saw the way he shifted in his seat. Julian sensed something was off too. His reaction is filed away for me to examine while I'm locked in my room later.

"How did you sleep?"

The attempt at idle chit-chat is strange. Why on earth should I tell him anything? I should demand he return me to my room. Or get on with the blood drain. Or better yet, release me.

"About as well as anyone who's been kidnapped would," I snap, drawing a frown from him. Katina's warning flits through my mind. Everything inside of me wants to yell, fight, demand to be released, but maybe she's right. Maybe playing the game will help me out of here faster. He hasn't shown any signs of hostility, and although he deserves every ounce of mine, I truly don't have a death wish. It goes against every fiber of my being, but I decide to heed her warning.

I can do this. I've played games with Dr. Tilney my whole life. This should be a cake walk.

They can smell your emotions.

Ugh.

I lower my eyes to the ground, trying to appear apologetic for my outburst.

"You don't have to pretend with us, Marina. We know you've been through an awful ordeal, and I for one don't expect you to embrace this situation immediately."

My eyes snap up, caught off guard by his acknowledgment of my inner thoughts. He couldn't possibly know that's what I'm thinking, but I'm sure it's not too hard to guess. He's undoubtedly done this before. *How many times? How many other girls?*

"I'll never embrace it," I bite, deciding to be honest with him.

"Right now, I'll accept that, but I hope you'll give us a chance."

He's out of his mind. *Never.*

"This isn't . . . a habit of mine. I don't partake in the auction."

"Then why did you this time?" I bite.

"Politics," he offers, but doesn't elaborate.

Screw his politics. Whether this was a one-time thing or a habit, attending for any reason makes him disgusting in my book.

He frowns, biting his cheek and looking over my face as if he can read my every thought. *Well here's one for you, buddy. You're a dick.*

Julian snorts, laughing as though he did, in fact, hear my thoughts. *Oh my God. Is that possible?* I'm internally freaking out, but doing everything imaginable to remain cold and unmoved.

"Marina, I asked Katina to bring you down so that you could dine with us." He continues to chuckle, but at what I'm unsure.

"Is something funny, brother?" Law asks, with an amused smirk.

If Law isn't reading my mind, then Julian isn't. What the hell is he laughing at, then? Julian clears his throat and schools his features. *Perhaps he's losing it?* As opposed to before—when he was just abducting girls? Who am I kidding? Insanity is his middle name.

He stands, showcasing an athletic body in a pair of gray chinos and a white Henley shirt. For a moment, my breath catches. He is incredibly attractive, and I hate that I think so. There is surely nothing appealing about evil. It's only a glamour of trickery to fool unsuspecting prey. Serial killers have been known to lure their victims with their good looks, and I'd bet that's Julian Bellamy's superpower. *No. I won't be fooled.*

"Why are you dressed like that," I say, motioning to his clothes, "while I was forced into this damn torture device?" I snap, as I realize that Lawrence is also dressed normally.

"I was going to ask if we were having a ball I didn't know about." Lawrence's eyes widen, looking me over. "You outdid yourself. And just for us?" he chuckles, and I glare.

"I did *not* choose this, and you know it. Katina is a sadist," I bite through my teeth. "That . . . vampiress did this."

They both break out into laughter at my expense and I'm pissed. *To hell with playing at nice.*

"Vampiress? Katina will love that," Law barks.

"Let's not give her any more reasons to prance around here like a queen," Julian says, swiping at his eye.

"I'm glad you two find this so funny," I say, placing my hand on my hip. "Did you know she came onto me? Did you? Well, she did. She said we could have so much fun together." I crinkle my nose in distaste. "What the hell does that even mean?" I screech, losing every ounce of cool I've tried to harness. I'm losing my grip and it's all because I'm so out of my damn element with these two . . . creatures.

Jude and Law glance at each other before bursting out in hysterics.

"Ugh. You two are acting like children," I yell. "Why the hell am I even here?"

"I'm sorry," Law says, trying and failing to pull himself together. "It's been so long since we've had a moment to actually enjoy ourselves. You're funny." He waggles a finger at me and I shut my eyes and count to ten, trying to calm down. I'm equal parts annoyed and angry.

"So, I'm here for your amusement?" I say offhandedly. "I thought I was here to be your personal blood bank."

They both stop laughing immediately. Julian's eyes narrow on mine and I internally smack myself. *Why did you have to go there?*

Law clears his throat. "You're not here for that, Marina. We simply want you to dine with us."

"I'm sorry, but I'll have to pass." My tone leaves no room for argument.

Stubborn woman. Just play nice.

"You'll . . . have to pass?" Julian repeats, sounding confused.

"I'd rather eat alone or not at all."

I've gone this far, might as well thoroughly piss off the king . . . or Crown . . . whatever the hell he is. *Vampire.*

Julian sits down once more and leans back into his throne, smirking. "Then I'll have to change your mind, I suppose."

My arms cross over my chest in indignation. There is nothing he can say or do to make me change my mind. The idea of playing the game has come and gone. Now I'm back to hostile.

"Well?" he presses.

I clear my throat. "Well what?"

His eyes shine a brilliant shade of blue-green. "I asked you earlier if you like your accommodations. I put you in the best room in the house. I hoped you'd sleep like the dead."

I pale at his words.

"My preference is to stay amongst the living, if you don't mind."

My body is shaking at the mention of death. Is that his prelude to draining my blood? Is he about to kill me despite Law's insistence otherwise?

He barks a laugh.

"Will all of our conversations be like this? Will you always think I mean you harm?"

"Yes," I deadpan, feeling the need to be truthful.

"I assure you, I didn't bring you here to hurt you, Marina."

My name on his lips brings goose bumps to my arms. The way it glides off his tongue like a whispered prayer makes me shiver. For the first time ever, the word sounds beautiful, sensual even. I detest my reaction. I'm allowing his charm to get under my skin. He's my captor. He's taken me from my life. Even if it was a half-assed one to begin with. I can't allow him to warp my brain.

"Do you have magical powers?" The words sound stupid the moment they leave my lips.

Lawrence snickers. "He's full of all sorts of charms. Of that I can assure you, Marina."

"What my idiot brother means is I do possess some abilities. Mostly persuasion. I'm able to heighten emotions."

"Did you do that at the auction?"

Julian's head cocks to the side, as though he doesn't know what I'm talking about.

"When you arrived, the crowd became . . . aroused." I grimace, hating that we're somehow talking about sex in any capacity.

"I thought you noticed that. Seems I was correct," Julian's voice is thick.

I clear my throat, needing to not choke on the words.

"It was hard not to."

Julian smiles. "It was only to distract them long enough so that I could talk to you. If I hadn't kept them . . . preoccupied, I never would've had a moment alone with you."

"Why did you need time with me?" My words are whispered. Something is happening. The room is abnormally warm

—or maybe that's just me—and an electrical pull pulses between us. *That magic.*

"I don't have an answer for that, Marina. I'm still trying to figure that out myself."

"Are you doing that magic thing now?"

I pray he says yes. Every synapse in my body is firing. Tingles trail a line from my fingers to my toes. If it's not his magic, it's something else mystical. It's not normal.

"No." He says the word like a promise.

Lust. Plain and simple, it's the only explanation. It's no wonder why—he's easily the best-looking man I've ever seen. A-list actors don't hold a candle to Julian Bellamy. It's ridiculous and unfair. Why would the first man I've ever had this reaction to be the single worst person to fall for? *Karma for lying all of those years.*

I must stare for too long, because his eyes twinkle with mischief and a cocky smirk lines his face.

"You're lying. You are doing this."

He shakes his head. "Seems I don't need to persuade you to like me."

That. Ass.

Internally berating myself for being so loose with my attention, I huff out an indignant breath, determined to shield myself more effectively.

"Why did you bring me here?"

I need to know why I'm here. The suspense of what's going to happen is worse than anything. Being on unequal footing because I'm clueless as to what's going on is really getting to me. I almost feel as if it would have been better if I'd died in the cell back before the auction. At least there, I knew my life was in danger. Here, with Julian's promise not to harm me, I'm confused. I feel my defenses slipping, and that's even more hazardous.

"Yes, brother. Do tell. What are your plans for the lovely Ms. Drake?"

Julian considers me for a few moments, which doesn't help with my unease. His eyes are hard and focused.

"You were brought here for safekeeping. So, I intend to keep you safe."

Safekeeping? From what? I'm not safe with him. My shoulders slump under his intense gaze. He has no intention of allowing me to leave, which means I will fight.

Something swoops through the room, narrowly missing my head. I duck with a shriek.

"Gah," I screech.

"Aw, that's just Mosely. No need to fear a basic crow," Law says, amused.

The crow sits perched atop Julian's throne, peering down at me with such an intense gaze, I shrink back, unsettled. Slowly, memories of the night I was taken assault me. That crow . . . it was there.

I point at the crow. "That thing was there the night I was taken."

Lawrence throws his head back with a laugh.

"Mosely? Doubtful. He's a crow . . . they're a dime a dozen, and besides, ol' Mose here doesn't leave this estate."

I drill Julian with a glare. "You." My finger slides to point at him. "You did this to me. You took me from my home and made that bird follow me."

I'm not sure what gives me such gall, but my fear has evaporated, and in its wake is nothing but anger. Perhaps it's the easy demeanor these men possess today, or maybe I just don't give a crap anymore. I'm at the end of my rope with nothing to lose.

Julian sits up straight, leaning toward me as though he's going to bestow some secret on me.

"That's not my bird. I didn't have it or any other thing follow you. Be careful with your accusations, Marina. I don't take people from their homes. I simply saved you from a shortened life of being drained of blood." He sits back. "I believe a thank you is in order."

"Never." I stand tall and drill him with a glare that promises retaliation.

"You'd do best to not challenge Julian. He's a bit of a hard-ass at times." Law winks at me, trying to soften his words.

Every second of every day, I'll challenge him. My survival instinct has kicked in, blanketing me in a fog-like state. Everything is happening on autopilot, and I can't be sure what's real and what's not. It's my brain's way of protecting me. It's shutting down fear and replacing it with numbness.

He might not have sent that thing after me, but it was there. I know it. I'm learning there are very few coincidences in my life. Everything that's happening now has to be linked with all the monsters from my childhood. How could it not be?

"I'm sorry you think the worst of me already, Marina. I don't have anything to do with the . . . acquisition of the donors."

I cringe at the use of the word *donors*.

"Those girls were not donors. They didn't choose to give your kind anything. It's being taken from them by force. That makes them victims."

Julian stands from his throne, stalking toward me. Slowly. "I'm not a monster, Marina," he says, reaching out and grasping my hair in his hands. He doesn't pull, only strokes the locks between his fingers with a faraway look. Perhaps he *can* read my mind, for surely, he can see that a monster is exactly what I think he is.

Julian winces, signaling I might be on to something. The

only reason he would have to react that way would be if he heard my thoughts.

A throat clears and Julian steps away from me, dropping my hair as he goes. "Right now, I'm starving. Will you eat with us?"

The change of direction is jarring. Julian seems to enjoy keeping me off balance, and I don't like it. He still wants me to eat with him? My eyes go wide, imagining all sorts of morbid ways that these creatures eat. Law notices my expression and laughs.

"We're not beasts. We enjoy the same meals that humans do."

I make an effort to make my face blank, unwilling to allow them any more insight into what I'm feeling. I have a habit of wearing my emotions, and I can see they are good at reading me. Katina said they could smell emotions too. I'm doing everything possible to snuff all of it out. Embracing the numbness is what I need to do.

"We don't require human food, nor does it provide the nutrients that we need, but we enjoy it nonetheless," Law continues.

I'm relieved to know I won't be forced to watch them drain someone of blood or worse, become the meal myself.

CHAPTER 10

I sit ramrod straight in my chair, refusing to eat a thing placed in front of me, even when my stomach gurgles in hunger.

"Eat, Marina. You need your strength," Julian demands.

"How do I know this isn't laced with something?"

I'm starving. The truth is, I need the food. I haven't touched it because I don't trust them and I don't want to give in. *I won't show them weakness.*

"There's no weakness in taking care of yourself."

My head turns to Julian's. Eyes narrowing, I question just what other things Julian is able to do. He's read my mind too many times this evening for it to be coincidence.

"Are you reading my mind?" I say through gritted teeth.

Law's head snaps to Julian. "That's impossible, unless you are his familiar, and that's just a silly legend, right Julian?"

Julian doesn't answer him. Instead, he lowers his eyes to his bowl of lobster bisque and raises his spoon, taking a small sip, completely ignoring my question as well. Law's mention of a legend swims around in my head. What legend is he talking about?

Clanking trays have me forgetting all about legends, as servers covered in head-to-toe black place plates of steak, potatoes, and green beans in front of us. My stomach growls and I know I won't be able to resist. I can't hold out any longer. Hunger demanding, I feed myself.

Like a ravenous beast, completely lacking manners, I begin shoving pieces of potato and bread into my mouth. *Calm down. You just ate recently.*

Julian's brows raise as he watches me eat. He smothers a triumphant grin and stabs his fork into a piece of potato, bringing it to his mouth. I watch as his tongue darts out, licking his bottom lip and giving me a peek at his elongated canine. I shiver a bit at the sight of it, but that reaction is quickly replaced with something else. Something unwanted. As he opens his mouth and allows the fork to enter, his lips wrap around the morsel in the most arousing way. There is something so sensual about the way he chews, swallows . . . everything about him. He's an enigma, and I'm trying so desperately not to be fascinated.

He's shown me no signs of hostility. In fact, he's been charming all evening, and Law is, dare I say, funny. My mind is split in two. One side is screaming for me to wake up and recognize I'm amongst demons. The other is whispering to give them a chance. Charming or not, he's still a vampire. I'd best remember that.

"I'm sorry to intrude on your family dinner."

My blood runs cold at the shrill voice of Julian's other brother.

"Marcellus," Julian grates, rising to his feet.

"Please, don't stand for me. Isn't it I who should bow to you?"

A creepy-crawly feeling descends over the room at the emergence of Marcellus. He's just as handsome as his brothers, but something sinister lies just under the surface of his soulless black eyes and expertly crafted sneer. Disdain is oozing from him, and it's directed at Julian. There's a story here, but I couldn't care less what it is. I want the hell out of this house and away from the battle royale that's about to go down.

"What do you want, Marc?"

"So now the donors eat with you?" He laughs, but it's completely lacking humor. He looks disgusted by the very thought. "My, how far you've fallen, brother."

"What I do with my donors is my business," Julian says with an edge. My eyes volley back and forth, though my head is screaming at me to lower my eyes and try to disappear.

"The Council sent me to check in, and it appears they weren't wrong to worry." Marcellus grins.

"Worry about what?" Law says, sounding bored and a bit annoyed.

"It appears that not all of the elders are comfortable with your reign. They're certain you're against our ways and looking to change things. From what I see here, they might not be far off."

"Since when are you part of the Council?"

"Since I too question your loyalties. My God, Julian. You actually have that thing sitting at your table?"

My back stiffens at his obvious hatred of me. There's no doubt in my mind that he sees us as being below the vampire race. What does that mean for Stacey? Is she still alive?

"Don't make the mistake of thinking that because you're family, I won't end you, Marcellus," Julian's tone is lethal, but the raven-haired devil doesn't seem at all fazed. "Leave. You have no business here."

"This is my father's house," Marcellus hisses. "I have just as much right to be here as you."

Julian stands, stalking toward Marcellus, murder in his eyes. The rift between brothers seems to widen by the second. As they stand toe to toe, I note that Julian is an inch or two taller than Marcellus. Julian looks down at his brother, his tone deadly.

"This is my house," Julian bellows, causing the chandelier above to tremble.

"It won't be for long. I'm going to help the Council dethrone you."

"You'd turn your back on family for power?" Julian roars, causing me to slink back further into my high-backed chair. "I am your king."

"You are no king," Marcellus jeers, the words laced in venom and speared in Julian's direction.

Julian's face reddens to inhuman levels and, baring his teeth, he grabs his brother by the lapel and throws him across the room.

I gasp at the force of the throw. Marcellus is on his feet in an instant, stalking toward Julian, ready to fight.

"You really want to challenge me, Marcellus?"

Julian's voice is stone cold and his gaze cuts like knives. To be on the other side of that glare would have me peeing my pants, but Marcellus isn't deterred.

"Stop," Law yells, stopping Marcellus's advance. "Your words are treasonous, Marc. Stop."

Marcellus considers Lawrence.

"What do you care, Law? You've only ever bothered yourself with females and liquor. Am I to believe you care about the state of this kingdom?"

"Aw, come now, brother, surely I'm not without booze." Law raises his goblet in proof.

Marcellus sneers, clearly not impressed with Law.

"You're worthless."

Law laughs at his brother, not seeming to care at all how serious the situation is.

"I have a kingdom to rule, Marcellus. Show yourself out so I can get back to it." Julian says, sounding more in control than he was moments ago.

"You've never shown an interest in ruling this kingdom. That's the entire reason the Council doubts you."

"I don't have a choice," Julian's voice booms, bouncing off the walls and echoing so loudly I have to cover my ears.

Nope. He's definitely not in control.

Julian's fists are clenched at his sides. "Our father's death was no accident and I will get to the bottom of it, Marcellus. If you were involved, I promise you'll suffer greatly."

His father died. So vampires *can* die. Another piece of information for me to hold on to.

"*Now* you care about our father? Funny, you never did before," Marcellus's voice slithers like a snake in the grass, his lip quirked into an evil grin. If guilty had a name, it'd be Marcellus.

"No matter how I felt about him, I would never have conspired with the Council to kill him. If you did, you're the worst kind of traitor."

"You can't rule, Julian. You don't agree with our ways," Marcellus doesn't even bother denying the Council—with his help—killed their father. Why doesn't Julian end things now? *He is weak.*

Julian's eyes fly to mine, yet another indicator that he is, in fact, listening in to my private thoughts. Well . . . hear this, asshole. I will kill you one day.

Julian blinks and returns his gaze to his brother. "I'll decide what's best for our kind," Julian says, lacking conviction. Marcellus's cackle tells me he realized the same thing I did.

I'm on nobody's team here, but it's become obvious that one is worse than the other and the title of worst of all goes to the dark vamp. Julian needs to play this differently, because right now, he's giving this Council they speak of ammunition to overturn his rule. And that would not be in the human race's favor, if I had to guess.

"We need blood to survive and we take it. What better way is there?"

Definitely not in our favor.

Julian levels Marcellus with a glare that could burn villages. The animosity in the room is stifling and confusing all at once. Why the pissing match? Is it all about who was appointed king upon their father's death? Jealousy, greed, power, money—those things have caused more than a few family feuds throughout the years.

"There are numerous ways to get blood, Marcellus. If you think the auction is the best way, then you're a fool. All you're doing is playing into the Council's hand. They'll throw you aside as soon as you finish their dirty work." He sighs. "I'm doing my job in finding the best option for the kingdom." Julian looks tired, this physical and verbal fight catching up to him.

"You dare to undo centuries' worth of work for what? Humans?" Marcellus jabs a finger in my direction. "They're expendable. There is nothing special about them."

"There is a big difference between sustainability and greed, Marcellus." His brow pinches. "You never understood the difference."

A growl breaks through Marcellus's throat.

"You may be the oldest, Julian, and our laws might dictate you're the next to rule, but it's by a mere three minutes. That hardly makes you the best option," he spits. "You don't have it in you."

"Enough," Julian yells. "Get out or I'll throw you out."

Julian gets back into Marcellus's face. The only similarity is the matching glowers that could turn the world to ashes in seconds.

"I will rule, Marcellus, and if you keep getting in my way, I'll remove you permanently. Brother or not." Julian's tone leaves no room for argument.

"We'll see. The Council will be here soon. We'll allow them to decide what's best for the kingdom," he hisses. Turning on his heels, he stalks out of the room.

Julian's face goes ashen at the mention of the Council coming. Could they actually hold the power to dethrone Julian? Would they put Marcellus in his place? The thought makes me sick.

"Bash," Julian calls out.

A large man with a tree trunk for a neck comes walking through the same door that Marcellus just exited.

"Yes, sir."

"Please make sure my brother finds his way out."

Bash nods and exits.

"You sure know how to throw a dinner, Jude," Law snickers, but there is a hint of something else there. Law seems shaken by the whole thing, but he masks it under sarcasm and wit.

Standing, Law comes around to my side of the table. Despite the pleasant enough evening before Marcellus's arrival, I stiffen, shaken by the events that just transpired.

"No need to tense, sun—" His words trail off and he shakes his head. "I won't harm you," Law promises. "I've simply had enough fun for one night."

He grabs my hand, bringing it to his lips. I watch as he places a kiss on the top, smirking at my wide-eyed expression, no doubt.

"Until next time." He drops my hand and walks to Jude, pulling him into a brotherly shoulder bump. "I'll be in touch."

Julian nods and we both watch as Law leaves.

When it's just the two of us, the air thickens, and the silence is deafening. What's next? Is my false sense of security about to end? Will he harm me now that we're alone and he's angry? Will he drain me just to prove his awful brother wrong?

"Relax, Marina," he coos soothingly. "I can smell your fear. It's radiating off you."

"What do you expect, after that?" I motion toward the door Marcellus left through. "This whole world isn't possible."

He sighs heavily.

"I'm sorry you had to witness that. Marcellus and I have a . . . troubled past."

He doesn't seem angry anymore. If anything, he appears sad.

"I need to get you back to your room and check in with my guards to make sure the situation with Marcellus is handled."

I huff in frustration. The last thing I want is to be caged in another room.

He walks closer to me.

"Give me time, Marina. I want you to get to know me, but right now there are more pressing issues."

"I don't need to know you, Julian. I've seen enough."

He huffs, mumbling something under his breath. "We'll see."

I blow out a breath, "Answer one question for me."

He raises his brow, signaling for me to continue.

"Why did you come to the auction if you hadn't been there for years, like Marcellus said?"

"Centuries. I haven't been there for centuries," he says, running his hand through his hair. "I came because Law insisted I needed to." He sighs. "There are obligations that come with being king, and he felt that the Council would descend and appeal my rule if I didn't start acting like I planned to uphold my father's doctrines."

"Why haven't you drunk my blood?"

"That's two questions," he says wearily, but I don't crack so much as a smile. I want to know. I want to hear him say he doesn't like blood.

"Do you not like human blood?"

He shakes his head. "It's not that. Human blood is an elixir, an aphrodisiac. It warms a vampire from the inside, fuels our power, builds our vitality, and gives us our youth. Without it, we're practically corpses. We don't die, but we don't live."

"You do drink blood, then?"

"Yes, I drink blood. I was drinking it all night." I cringe at the mental picture.

Knowing he didn't drink it from a person tonight doesn't help. The thought of ingesting blood turns my stomach.

"Why then haven't you drunk mine?"

He inhales and exhales a harsh breath.

"I fear it would change everything."

I don't have a chance to ask what he means because he calls out for Katina and she enters. "Take her to her room."

With that, he turns and walks out, leaving me to ponder what he said.

Katina walks me to my room, neither of us saying a word. I quickly change into pajamas from the stocked closet and climb into bed. There is so much to process, but for the first time since my abduction, I don't want to think about any of it. He said he'd keep me safe, and for now that's the only thing I do believe. For how long, I don't know, and tonight I won't worry about things I can't change.

Tomorrow I'll start looking for a way out, but tonight, I'm going to get the rest I'll need to make it happen.

For the first time in a long time, I sleep soundly. Perhaps it's his promise of safety or the sheer exhaustion that's plaguing me, but whatever it is, I'm thankful.

CHAPTER 11
JULIAN

"Bash, I need you to keep an eye on Marcellus's estate. I want to know who comes and who goes. Take as many men as you need, but I want someone on detail at all times." I rub my temples, trying desperately to stave off the pounding. "Nobody can know," I stress, with a warning look that should say *you'll die if you're discovered*.

"On it," Bash says before leaving me alone for the first time since the auction.

I take another swig of whisky, relishing the burn as it coats my throat. I need the buzz that comes from a ten-thousand-dollar bottle of Macallan that's been aged for forty years. Like humans, vampires aren't immune to drunkenness, and tonight I'm embracing it.

Law hung around like a damn dog, all but humping my leg. He didn't leave my side once we were home from the auction. For days I've been subjected to his inquisition about Marina and what my plans were, and for days I've told him to fuck off. Law did what Law does—disregard orders. What the hell's come over him I'll have to try to figure out another day.

Tonight, my mind is solely focused on Marcellus's threats and the fact that Marina Drake is sleeping one floor above me and I don't know why I give a damn. Yes, she's beautiful and yes, her fiery attitude is intriguing, but she's a mere human. I've never been attracted to a human, and whatever this is goes well beyond attraction.

I can read her mind.

That's not a typical power vampires wield. In fact, no known living vampire has the power. It's the stuff of legends. *Familiar.*

The thought is ridiculous. It's impossible. Yet, the moment I drank from that cup, my abilities changed. They've sharpened. That knowledge would be enough for the Council to back off, but it would also start the beginning of the end for the human race. If vampires thought that familiars were more than legend, they'd scour the earth trying to find theirs. The number of innocent people who would die in the process would be catastrophic. Not only would it be the end of their race, but it would likely lead to the end of ours.

Which is the entire reason I can't give up my throne. Laws need to be upheld. Order must prevail. Otherwise, chaos would reign.

Maybe I should kill Marcellus and prove to the Council I'm not weak. Surely killing one's family would show how ruthless I'm capable of being? I sigh, knowing that no matter how easy it would be, I couldn't. Ever. That's my weakness—loyalty.

A knock sounds and I call out, "Come in."

Katina leans around the door, "Marina is sound asleep. I gave her the sleeping pills you recommended."

"Thank you, Katina," I say, growing more tired by the second. "She needs to sleep."

"She does, sir." She nods her head a little too enthusiastically, and my brow quirks.

Katina has always been strange even by vampire standards, but she's loyal and she shares my beliefs about the auction. Two traits that mean everything to me in this world where I can hardly trust anyone.

"That'll be all, Katina. Enjoy your evening."

"Thank you, Sir Crown," she says, bowing, and I can't help but roll my eyes. I've asked her repeatedly to call me Julian and to stop the damn bowing, but she can't help it. She insists on being over the top. I should be a harsher ruler, but it's not who I am. If the Council wants my father, they'll never find that in me.

I hated everything about him.

On the way to my quarters, I find myself veering down another hall and up a flight of stairs I have no business ascending. Katina told me she was asleep, and I should leave well enough alone. But I can't. I'm inexplicably drawn to her. Her blood calls to me like no other's ever has. *It's dangerous.* I'm not even sure whom it's more dangerous for at this point. Her or me.

I stagger my way down the dark hallway until I'm standing outside her door, hand pressed against the heavy wood, trying to talk myself out of crossing a line and invading her privacy. I know I shouldn't, but the need to see that she is safe and asleep after the night with Marcellus is overwhelming. I don't know how to deal with this pull. *You have to find a way.*

Cracking open the door, I'm almost disappointed to find it unlocked. Marina's smarter than that. I might not know her yet, but I can tell that much. She's strong. She's a fighter. Then I remember what Katina had said. She was given the sleeping medicine.

My hand reaches out and runs down her soft, pale cheek. The whisky's making me bold. Too bold. A strong rush of heat flows through my veins and I shiver a bit from the feeling. It's something so much greater than I understand. *Who are you, Marina?*

She moves a bit and I step back into the darkened corner of the room. I can't get caught in here. I've worked so hard to try to earn her trust and I have hardly made a dent in her armor. I know she feels something, but she's determined to think of me as nothing more than a monster. *Can you blame her?*

I crack the door open and take a step when her cold, hard voice stops me in my tracks. "What the hell are you doing in here?"

So much for progress.

CHAPTER 12

"Stay away from me," I screech, sitting up and pulling the covers up to my chin. "Stay away," I call out again, but to whom, I have no idea. I'm alone here, surrounded by vampires. My mind is hazy, my eyes aren't adapting, and everything's a blur.

"Marina, please. It's only me."

"What did you do to me?" I yell, starting to shake.

The figure in the corner moves toward me at an alarming rate and I continue to scream. Two strong hands grasp my shoulders and attempt to hold me down. I kick and thrash with all my might, trying to get out of the monster's hold. The cover that I had been using as a pathetic shield is ripped away and I slam my eyelids shut so as to not see my attacker.

Maggie always used to say that closing your eyes was a coward move. Whatever was to come was still going to hurt. You might as well look your attacker in the eyes and go out fighting. Right now, I think that's a dumb idea. Better to not see what's coming, in my opinion.

They did something to me, and I'm not thinking straight.

Fight, Marina.

All of those thoughts filter through my mind, making me thrash harder as the will to live kicks in. This isn't the end. I'm not ready. I never will be. I said I wanted to sleep, but I never said anything about sleeping forever. I want to live. There is so much I haven't done.

Whatever is above me moves off, and a second later the overhead lights flash on, blinding me in the process. I blink several times, trying to adjust to the light when I see who's in my room.

Julian.

"What the fuck are you doing?" I yell, hoisting the covers back up to my chin to hide my body.

"I . . . Katina said . . . I came to check on you," he finally manages to complete his sentence, not meeting my eyes.

"You thought it'd be a good idea to literally scare the hell out of me?"

"You were sleeping. I was only here for a moment. Calm down."

His condescending voice and invasion of my privacy has the fear melting away and the anger returning. Who the hell does he think he is? *The owner of this house and the king of vampires.*

Voice of reason, go the hell away.

He chuckles, clearly having read my mind again. Or maybe I said it out loud? Either way, there is nothing funny about this. I tear out of bed, not giving a shit that I'm hardly dressed in a short black semi-sheer nightie.

"Get out," I say, poking him in the chest with my finger. "Now."

He crosses his arms over his chest, standing tall and looking down on me. "This is my house. I don't answer to you or anyone else."

He's been cross, but never like this. I've officially pissed him off. Any other time, I'd be petrified by the look he's giving me, but right now, my brain is foggy, I'm exhausted, and he continues to piss *me* off.

"You said you'd protect me. How is this protecting me?"

He takes a menacing step toward me. "I never said I'd protect you from me, Marina. If you insist on going head to head with me, be prepared to lose the battle."

He's a mere inch from me, and I can smell alcohol on his breath. "Are you drunk?" I accuse, narrowing my eyes. I don't need him to answer. I've spent years tending to my mom and dad to know damn well when someone has had too much to drink. And when alcohol is involved, bad things happen.

The hairs on my arm rise in warning. I have to get out of here. *He's going to hurt you.* I look over his shoulder to see the door is open. If I can only distract him for a moment, maybe I can make a run for it. I step into him, turning us so that my back is to the door and his knees are at the top of my mattress.

I will myself to stop reacting to his proximity. Aside from the liquor on his breath, he smells fantastic. I find myself leaning in even more and breathing him in. His breath hitches and my eyes pop up to meet his. Distraction is one thing, but being this close to him is too much for so many reasons.

"Marina," he says my name like a prayer, eyes closing on a sigh. I know it's now or never.

I push into his chest with all my might until the back of his knees hit the mattress and he falls backward onto the bed. Any other time, I know that would never have been a possibility. He's too strong, but I caught him off guard. I don't wait around to find out how long it takes for him to realize what I've done.

I run.

The hallway is dark, and I have no idea where to go. I begin to panic at the realization, but I've already gone this far. I have to see it through, even if this is the event that leads to my end.

"Marina," his gravelly ominous voice bellows through the hall, and I look back only for a moment, startled.

I see his dark form stalking toward me, and I run faster. I make it to the grand staircase and do my best not to fall. I'm at the massive front doors when all hope is lost. A hand shoots out and grabs my arm roughly, swinging me around and into a hard-as-rock chest.

"Let me go. Let me go!" I yell, thrashing and writhing, trying to get loose.

Julian shakes my shoulders as I continue to try to get free.

"Marina..."

The next thing I know, I'm falling backward, grabbing at thin air. I twist slightly, and my temple connects with the leg of the foyer table right before another jarring smack to the side of my head has me seeing stars. My world spins and my vision blurs. I lift my hand to my aching head.

I'm bleeding.

"W...what..."

Julian staggers backward, eyes wide. "Marina, I didn't...I wouldn't."

"What the devil is going on out here?" Katina says, running out in a long crimson robe, hair askew and a look of confusion all over her naked face. When she sees me on the floor with my hand clutching my head, she gasps, running to my side and inspecting my injury.

"I-I..." Julian stutters.

"Sir, I'll take care of her," she says in a gentle voice. "Why don't you get some rest?" she suggests, grabbing me lightly by the elbow and pulling me up off the floor.

"But I—" he tries again, before Katina cuts him off.

"Please, sir. Let me handle this. You've done enough."

Julian's eyes widen before he stumbles out of the room without another word.

"Let's get you cleaned up," she coos. "You poor thing. I told you not to push him." She tsks and I don't say a word. "I'm sure this was a horrific accident. In the morning, everything will be made right."

Everything happened so fast. I'm not even sure *what* happened.

"Help me get out of here, Katina. I know he's your ruler, or whatever, but you have to know it's not safe for me here. I have to get out."

She looks down on me with a sad smile. "You know I can't, and truly, it's not what's best for you. There are things . . ." Her words trail off before her shoulders push back and she looks away. "Anyway, let's get you to bed."

Disappointment settles over me. It was a good try, but what did I expect from a vampire? Kindness? *Better.*

I allow Katina to get me back into bed. I never say a word through the whole thing. What is there to say? It's not like he pushed me, but I still blame him. I refuse to be a prisoner, which means I'm always going to try to run.

This won't be the last time.

I shake off the events of tonight, rubbing at my head. Katina turns in time to see my hand to my head and frowns.

This bothers her, and I pack that away for later. Maybe I can't convince her to help me tonight, but I'll keep working on gaining her assistance.

Despite the trauma from being stuck with a vampire, I can't help but notice how normal Katina looks without her typical over-the-top costume as she tucks me in tightly.

"Good night, Marina," she calls into my dark room.

"Katina? Could you please lock it?"

I know it's futile. If he wants to get in, he will, but I need to know I've done everything to attempt to keep him out. To keep him as far from me as possible.

I hear a click, and although I can't be sure it's anything more than the door latching shut, I close my eyes anyway. Sleep never comes.

THE SUN BEGINS TO RISE, as evidenced by the yellow and orange bursts of color shining through the windows, but I don't move. I'm too tired. Recapping the events of the last twenty-four hours has me formulating another plan. It won't be easy to escape. I learned that last night.

I've known all along not to be fooled by Julian's promise of protection, but I let my guard down. His easy smile and handsome face were enough to mask what's hidden underneath the beautiful façade. *A monster.*

I rise from the false comfort of the bed and stomp to the wardrobe. Scanning the contents, I'm disappointed to find not a single pair of pants. The romper that I destroyed had been the closest thing to it. In fact, there isn't anything left but dresses and skirts. And the longer I peruse the selection, the more I realize these are different clothes. It's as though I've stepped into some time warp and found myself transplanted to somewhere circa 1800. When did that happen? I groan in frustration.

Freaking Katina.

With no other options, I choose the lightest dress in weight I can find. I need the easiest outfit to attempt an escape in. Pulling the pale blue cotton over my head, I'm relieved to find it non-constricting. *It'll have to do.* I'm pulling my long hair into a high ponytail when Katina comes strolling through the door.

"Ah, glad to see you're up and ready."

I motion down at the dress. "What's this? Where are the other clothes?"

She shrugs. "You looked so nice last night, and the Crown gave such compliments, I thought I'd switch your wardrobe out with some of my vintage things."

"This is beyond vintage, Katina. This is antique."

She pulls a face. "The Crown would like you to join him for breakfast."

"Never," I snap, not bothering to look at her.

"Marina," she admonishes. "You're not going to ruin the day all because of last night, are you?"

My head snaps to hers, giving her my best glare. "You mean this?" I say, motioning toward the bandage on my forehead. Not only do I have a wicked cut, but a nice goose egg popped up along with it.

"Hmm." She frowns. "We'll need to get some ice on that." She busies herself arranging my sheets. "Very well. Today you can stay in."

I huff in annoyance. "I wasn't going anyway, Katina. You'd have to carry my dead body before I'd eat anything with him."

Katina stops, turning toward me. "I'm on your side on this, Marina. Last night was too much."

"You can say that again," I snap, and she purses her lips.

"You fell. He didn't push you." I don't like her tone and the fact that she's making this my fault.

I gape at her. "Are you serious? He was shaking me one minute and I was falling the next. If he didn't push me, he let me fall."

She sucks her teeth. "Didn't you strongly suggest he let you go?" She shrugs. "Last I checked you were trying to leave."

"He was drunk and rough." The words taste acrid as I recall the events that led to me being on the floor with a giant knot on my head and a cut at my temple.

"I'm not trying to make any excuses for the Crown, but he's under a lot of stress, and that whisky did not help," she says, sounding bitter. "Sounds to me like you're both at fault."

I completely ignore the part about it being a shared culpability.

"I will never allow alcohol to be an excuse for violence. I grew up in a house where both parents were addicts, and I'll never willingly live like that again. You might as well drain me now."

I wait for Katina's retort, but none comes. When my eyes lift to hers, I see pity and I hate it.

"Don't, Katina," I warn, and she balks.

"What?"

"Don't pity me. I've lived through worse than my parents," I confess.

She sits down, propping her chin on her fist. "Tell me," she begs, and I scrunch up my nose.

"You don't want to hear my sob story."

"What else do I have to do today? If you don't eat with the Crown, I'll be forced to shadow you all day."

"You really don't have to do that. I'll be perfectly—"

"Bored," she cuts me off.

"I was going to say fine. Considering where I am, bored isn't the worst I could be."

"Touché," she nods. "Well at the very least, let's have breakfast and maybe play a bit of cards? Oh, maybe I can roll in a TV and we can binge-watch something romantic."

My brow quirks at how excited Katina seems. *So strange.*

"That all sounds . . . nice," I offer, not wanting to hurt her feelings. And it actually does sound good.

Besides, it's a perfect opportunity to bond with the vampiress and make progress in gaining her help.

She rushes out of the room and is gone for several minutes before returning, sporting a grim expression.

"What is it?" I ask, already knowing I won't like the answer.

"The Crown won't accept your refusal," she says, avoiding my eyes. "He's ordered me to bring you outside."

"Outside?" I can't keep the surprise from my voice.

"Yes," Katina groans. "I'm sorry, I can't disobey his orders."

"What will happen if I refuse?"

She sighs. "Be prepared for him to storm this room and force you in ways you won't like. I'd suggest you make it easy on yourself."

"I really don't care what he wants, Katina. He can kill me if he likes."

"Wouldn't you like to go outdoors?" she presses, and I can't help but nod.

As much as I hate him, I'll never escape this place if I don't get to know my surroundings. I'll endure a morning with him in order to start my plans.

"Fine. I'll go," I bite out.

She finishes straightening my bed as I brush my teeth with the toothbrush and toothpaste she brought in earlier. Some fresh air will do me some good. If only I could enjoy it alone. Instead, I'm going to have to stomach Julian being with me. I quiver at the thought for several reasons.

"Will you come with us?"

"No. I don't like the outdoors," Katina calls from inside my room.

I deflate. Katina's a vampire, but she doesn't scare me. She hasn't so much as bared her teeth at me. She might be strange and yes, she has threatened my life, but only to keep me in line. *Don't be dumb, Marina.*

"Please," I try my hand at begging. After last night, I don't want to be alone with him. Call me crazy, but I feel less vulnerable with Katina around.

"No. The Crown wishes to speak with you alone."

My semi-good mood about getting outside evaporates. Having to deal with him tailing me is one thing, but forced conversation is entirely another.

"Do I have to?" I ask, strolling back into the room.

Katina turns toward me, rolling her eyes. "Would you really let your pride get in the way of a day in the sun?"

"It's not pride. It's survival."

"It's pride."

"Whatever." I partially roll my eyes. "As much as I need sunlight, I value my safety, and so far, this room has provided that. I'm still breathing. I'll gladly skip the sun to remain that way."

"Please," she huffs. "He doesn't wish to feast on your flesh today. He merely wants to apologize to you by allowing you some freedoms. Now hurry. I'm to have you downstairs in two minutes. Enough with the dramatics."

"Gee, you do wonders at making a girl feel better," I deadpan, but she doesn't reply. She's already on to her next task.

When we descend the stairs and round the corner, Julian is standing by the back door, looking tall and kingly.

"All set?" he asks, and I don't miss the moment he sees the consequences of last night. He grimaces, turning his gaze away quickly.

"So we're going to play it that way? Pretend like last night never happened?" I should be petrified by him, but all I feel is rising anger.

"I've told you, I won't harm you."

"Too late for that," I hiss, and he has the decency to look contrite.

"It'll never happen again, Marina. You have my word."

"Your word means shit to me," I say through gritted teeth.

He stands up taller, holding out his hand. "Give me one more chance to prove it."

I scoff at his outstretched hand. "You were rough, Julian, and I got hurt. Another chance is the last thing you deserve."

He lowers his arm to his side. "If you want to talk about last night, we will. All I ask is that you trust me enough to come outside. Having this conversation in the hallway for my staff to overhear isn't in either of our best interests."

I appraise him, looking for signs of deceit. "How do I know that I can trust you? I don't know anything about you, other than you're broody, you kidnapped me, and oh, yeah . . . I hit my head because of you."

His face hardens.

"I didn't kidnap you, Marina. The Council's men did. As for my moods, I'm under a lot of pressure these days. It's no excuse, but I am. Ruling all vampires isn't a small feat, and it just came to be my responsibility recently. It wasn't something I thought I'd have to do for a very long time." Julian looks lost in thought. *Is he thinking about his father's death? Was he close with him?* I don't ask. *You shouldn't care.*

I nod my head toward the door, signaling I'll go with him. He walks through the door and I follow him out into the warm sunlight, sighing as it envelops me. I haven't been in the sun in God knows how long. I've missed it. For a brief moment, I forget whom I have as company and just bask in the wonderful feeling a little fresh air and vitamin D can provide a person. As much as I'd love to forget about the events of last night, I won't let it go. I can't.

"The fall?"

Julian sighs. "The temper and overindulgence in whisky is not something I asked for. It's a family trait. One I'm not proud of, Marina."

"That's the worst damn excuse I've ever heard."

He stops, turning toward me. "You want the truth?"

"I deserve it," I snap back.

"I was desperate. You were hysterical and trying to leave. I didn't know what to do." He grabs my shoulders, looking into my eyes. "I never intended to hurt you. Ever. You have to believe me."

The intensity in his words has my breath catching. Not for the first time today, I try to find a hint that he's playing me. All I see is regret and self-loathing. It doesn't make sense. He doesn't know me. I'm a simple human. Why does he seem to care about how he treats me? I don't know what to do with this Julian.

I avert my eyes, refusing to succumb to whatever pull there is between us. He's still my captor. "Perhaps you should lay off the alcohol if that's how you act," I say, peering out of the corner of my eye at him.

He compresses his lips. The dimples in his cheeks explode and my knees weaken at the sight. He's so handsome, and I hate that I think so. Especially in this moment.

"You have my word, Marina. No more whisky."

He continues walking past the gardens and toward the back of the property.

"Where are we going?" I ask, not really caring, as this is giving me a tour of the property and a better sense of how to get the hell off it.

"This is my father's house," he says, motioning behind us at the palatial estate, not much smaller than a castle. "My house is just beyond that hill. I thought I'd take you there."

I want to ask him why, but the more I know the better.

It isn't long before I'm so caught up in the beauty surrounding me that I quickly forget about my mission and take it all in. The lush landscape and vibrant colors of the flowers create a visual masterpiece. Hydrangea bushes of every color line the walkway, while beautiful pink and white roses stretch out in front of me where the sidewalk splits. The limbs of a large weeping willow tree hang loosely above the garden of roses, right at the center of where the cobblestone walkway splits. The grounds are spectacular, but the manor in the distance is truly a sight to behold.

"It's beautiful," I say under my breath.

It is. It's truly magnificent. It looks like something out of an old Hollywood movie. The closer we get, the more impressive it is. No detail was spared in the design. The entire front of the stately white house consists of two wraparound porches, one on the ground level and the other on the second story. The need to sip lemonade in a rocking chair on the porch grips me. There is so much to look at. Between the sweeping magnolia trees and the line of rose bushes set in front of the porch, the scenery is something out of a fairy tale.

Nothing about this place screams evil. In fact, it's the opposite. It's bright and cheery; it looks like a home. I chance a glance in Julian's direction. He's wearing a long-sleeved white shirt and a pair of pressed black pants. Sweat drips from his brow.

"You a little warm?" I ask, gesturing to his clothes.

"Indeed. It is a bit warm today."

"Should you even be in the sun?" I can't help but put a little bite into my words.

He smirks. The bastard has the audacity to practically laugh at me.

"Not all folklore about vampires is true, Marina," he scoffs. "I can be in the indirect sun, if I take precautions."

"Sunscreen?" I ask, curious as to what he could possibly do to avoid spontaneously bursting into flames. *On second thought, fire away!*

"Something like that," he chuckles. "I'll experience a bit of displeasure later, but it's worth it."

"Good. You deserve displeasure," I say, sounding more like a spoiled brat than a victim who has every right to wish ill on her captor.

"I do," he agrees, and it only manages to piss me off. I want a fight. I don't want this easygoing Julian. It's a front and it only confuses me.

"Don't do that," I bark, turning toward him. "Don't act repentant. I'm not buying it. I might be out here with you, but it's *only* because I couldn't bear those walls for another minute."

He blows out a harsh breath. "I don't expect you to forgive me, Marina. But I thought we could try for one day to be cordial."

"Could you do it?" I ask, and his brow rises in confusion.

"Do what?"

"Play nice with the person single-handedly ruining your life?"

He flexes his fists at his side, appearing to be seconds away from losing his patience with me, but I stand tall and await his response. I won't bow down. I won't cower.

"I've allowed you to be angry."

I bark out a laugh. "Allowed?"

"Let me finish," he snaps. "I've allowed you to be angry because you have every right to be. I've taken the brunt of that anger, because I understand that you need to let it out on someone. But I'm the wrong person, Marina."

I laugh, but it's completely without humor. The actual gall of this creature is more than I can handle.

"So, who's the right person, Julian? Huh? Tell me. If not you, who?"

"My father, and he's dead. The Council, but you'd never

survive that encounter. The truth is, I am *saving* you. Half of those girls you were with are probably already dead." I inhale sharply at that, but he continues on. "I'm no damn saint, but I bid because I wanted to save you."

His words are sobering. Confusing too.

"Why?"

His eyes hold mine for several painstaking moments. I search his face for something to explain this man in front of me, but even if I had a lifetime to uncover all that is Julian Bellamy, something tells me I'd still be left with too many questions.

When he doesn't answer, I turn away, breaking the spell.

CHAPTER 13

"Let's get out of the sun for a little while," I say, gesturing toward the shaded porch. I need a minute of quiet to think and some shade to stop the perspiration running down my cheeks.

He nods his approval. "Good idea."

The rest of the way, I ponder the information I've been given so far. He said he'd just come into his rule. When did his father die? And how? I vaguely remember him accusing Marcellus of having something to do with it. Was he murdered? *So many questions.*

Lost in thought, I hardly register anything else until we approach the front stoop. I relax, seeing two giant rocking chairs sitting off to the side, just as I had envisioned it from a distance. It's unreal how normal this place feels. Surely, I couldn't have been so far off with my vision of how vampires lived. Where are the dark dungeons and coffins?

"Sit, enjoy the nice weather. I'm going to change and grab us some refreshments."

I nod my consent, not missing the fact that he's trusting me not to run. In truth, I don't know enough about where I am to even attempt it yet. There's still so much to learn and preparations that need to happen. For now, I'll bide my time and take in every bit of information I can.

He narrows his eyes, and his lips form a thin line. Sonofabitch.

He's reading my mind again.

"Just . . . please don't attempt anything, Marina. It won't end well."

I turn away, looking off into the distance until I hear his retreat. It's then that I inhale deeply, allowing nature to calm me in ways nothing else can.

Taking a seat on one of the rocking chairs, I close my eyes and enjoy the light breeze that flows through the covered porch. Sounds of birds chirping and branches rustling soothe my nerves and help me to forget for one minute all the bad in my life. It's peaceful here. It's the most normal I've felt in a very long time. If I could just keep my eyes closed, I could almost imagine I'm living a different life. One where Maggie is still alive and we're happy. *A fantasy.*

I blow out a harsh breath, opening my eyes and looking around. I continue to ruminate on how off this scene feels. If you'd told me a month ago, I would be living with a vampire, this beautiful place is not what I'd have imagined. Nobody would. It's completely opposite. It's light and beauty. It's full of life. Despite the darkness within.

This is exactly what I'd choose for myself if money were no hindrance. The very care that has to go into maintaining the flowers and shrubs must cost a fortune. The paint on this house is pristine, as if it just got a fresh coat recently. Nothing is out of place. It would take a full staff to keep this up. Does he have humans to do that? Or is his entire staff vampires?

Several minutes later, the screen door shuts and there stands Julian, wearing a pair of navy shorts with a white polo shirt. He looks young and normal. Too normal. I could easily forget the danger that is Julian Bellamy, and that's something I can't afford to do again. In his hand is a tray with two tall water goblets filled to the brim with lemonade. *Mind reader.* A tray full of fruit is situated in the center of the tray.

"You did all that in the time I was out here?"

He smirks. "Uh, no. I have a housekeeper who stocks fresh fruits and vegetables out here."

He sets the tray down and takes a seat. "Before your arrival, I only stayed in this house. I prefer it. My father's place feels like a prison."

"You don't say," sarcasm oozes from me. "Try actually being locked up."

He frowns.

"I don't want to lock you in, Marina. But I'm not sure I can trust you not to run."

"Can't you let me go? If you don't want to drain my blood, why keep me here?"

He looks out toward his father's estate.

"I can't. You've been marked," he says the words as if I know what the hell they mean.

"Marked?" I press, because it didn't seem like he planned to elaborate. Apparently, I'd be pulling information from him.

"Once you're taken by the Council, you can never go home. Think of it as tracking. You, your family and friends. If you tried to leave, they'd hunt you down and kill you and anyone you got close to. There's no leaving this world unless you're dead."

"Wouldn't you have to give them reason to track me? If you didn't tell them, how would they know I was gone?"

He huffed out a harsh breath. "It's not a risk worth taking, Marina. The spell they placed on you monitors your vitals. They'll know when you die because the spell dies when you do.

If my brother pokes around and sees you're still living, but not with me, he'll invoke the hunt."

"Spell?" I ask, grabbing my neck reflexively. "Vampires can cast spells too?"

"When you were captured, they put you out during the transport. That's when a black witch that works with the Council placed the spell on you. Like I said, it only ends when you die."

"It doesn't make sense. Why would they care if you let me go?"

He laughs, but it's not humorous.

"You have information about a race of people that are things of fable. If you were to escape and tell anybody, it could shine a light on us. They'll stop you at any cost."

It's my turn to laugh. If only he knew how long I've tried to convince humans that his kind exist.

"Your kind doesn't understand humans then. If I tried to tell people that you exist, I'd be locked up in a mental hospital," I huff. "Humans don't want to know the truth about what lives out there under their noses. They'd prefer to be in the dark."

I pull my lips to the side and bite my cheek, thinking about all the times I was almost institutionalized for talking about what I would see. All the times I would wake to glowing red eyes at the end of my bed.

"Do vampires stalk victims?"

He narrows his eyes.

"Some do, but not for long. Vampires tire of the chase very quickly."

I blow out a breath, trying to make sense of my childhood. Monsters haunted Maggie and me for years. Could it be possible that it was something else?

"Are there other things, aside from vampires?"

He nods his head, chewing on his tongue.

"Yeah, sure. There are lots of creatures. Werewolves, pixies, fairies, goblins, demons, banshees—you name something from lore, and chances are it's real."

This should frighten me, but at this point, I'd be surprised to hear differently.

"Do any of them have red eyes, besides vampires?"

He seems to contemplate this for a moment. "I believe demons have red eyes. Vampires do, but only right after they've drunk from a human. Other than that, I don't think so."

The list has been narrowed down to vampire or demon. Neither one makes me feel any less creeped out.

"Do demons tend to hunt victims for years?"

"Why are you asking this, Marina?"

I contemplate lying, not knowing what information I should impart to him. I've yet to determine whether he's going to kill me or keep his promise and protect me. At the end of the day, I have nothing to lose but a lot to gain in the information I can obtain from him.

"Growing up, my sister and I saw monsters. Creatures with elongated canines and red eyes. They were in our rooms at night and sometimes they followed us elsewhere. They never made a move to harm us; they just scared us with their presence."

He frowns.

"That doesn't sound like a demon. Their sole purpose is to possess and take. They don't play with their meals. Once you've been chosen by a demon, you don't get away."

I sigh heavily, not being any closer to the answers I seek. "Do you think it could've been a vampire?"

"It's very unlikely, given you still have a pulse, but maybe." He looks deep in thought. "If you were allowed to live without being made a blood bank, they would've had to be after something."

"What could they possibly want with a human other than blood?"

"That's the part that doesn't make sense."

We stare at each other for a few minutes, each trying to decode the mystery of my past. Eventually, we both seem to give up, lowering our gazes.

"You're the king, right? Can't you override the Council? Reverse the spell?"

"I'm barely hanging on to that title, Marina. If I were to let you go, it would be the end of my rule and the beginning of a war on humanity. The Council would do everything to overthrow me, and if that happens, no human is safe."

My body shudders at the thought of vampires running rampant. I want my freedom back, but at what cost? My life has been a series of unfortunate events. It hasn't been a great life by any stretch. Without Maggie, it's hardly a life at all.

"So unless I want my family and friends to be hunted down and killed, I'm stuck here? Is that what you're telling me?" I ask, not sure what to believe at this point.

Is he saying these things to scare me into staying? Or is there truth in it? I need to uncover the answer to that question before I leave. I won't put anyone else in danger by leaving.

"Yes, Marina." He frowns. "If, at some point, I can allow you to leave and you'll be safe, I will. I'll consult with a witch I trust and see if there is any way to reverse the spell. But I can make no promises. Black magic is hard to counteract."

My head lolls back and a sense of defeat sneaks its way in.

I've never considered myself a martyr, but it's hard to think about myself when the lives of millions could be in jeopardy if Julian's rule were overturned. Trying to escape Julian is one thing, but knowing I'd have more coming for me doesn't make my earlier plan of getting out of here sound feasible. My parents might not be the best, but I love them, and I won't bring vampires down on them because I'm selfish. They've lost so much already.

"You promise me that I have nothing to fear with you?"

His eyes bore into mine.

"You have my word."

"And you promise to consult with this witch, to see if there's a way out of this?" I continue.

"Yes. You have my word on both counts."

I nod my head, biting my tongue. "Let's negotiate a truce," I suggest, hoping to make my situation a little less horrible, while also giving me a chance to find answers.

"A truce," he says, as if testing the word out. "I thought we were already making one."

"Not exactly."

He clucks his tongue, seemingly annoyed by my antics.

"What would you suggest?" he finally asks.

My arms cross and I stand, walking in a circle, forming the words in my head before speaking. I want to be clear about my terms. Once I have it all laid out, I stop and look him in the eyes.

"I'll agree to give you the benefit of the doubt, and in return you give me more liberties."

"Such as?"

"I want to have free rein of the castle. No locked doors and no off-limits rooms."

"That's not possible. There are rooms in the house where we train new bites, and it isn't safe for you. They are guarded heavily, and you aren't at risk as long as you stay away, but I wouldn't want any accidents."

"New bites?" I could guess as to what that is, but I allow him to explain.

"Recently turned vampires. They need to be trained, so they don't go on killing sprees. However, being exposed to humans so soon is dangerous."

I shudder at the thought of coming face to face with a new vampire. I can agree that a situation like that isn't in my best interest.

"Fine. You can set limits on where I can go, but please don't lock me in my room. Allow me to come outside when I want."

He blows out a puff of air.

"Will you try to run off?" he asks, eyes narrowing.

"Not if you don't give me reason."

It's a lie. I can't truly promise that. If I ever feel like my friends and family could be safe, I'll run, but I'm desperate, so I do my best at being convincing, even if he can read me.

"All right. Deal," he says. "You can roam free, but you'll stay out of the dungeons and the east wing. The dungeon is where new bites are kept, and the east wing contains my father's chambers. His belongings are still there, and I'd like to keep the area preserved until the cause of his death is determined."

I nod in agreement.

Dark corridors and rooms tainted by death aren't on the top of my list of places to frequent. I'll mostly keep to my room, but having the ability to roam free makes it seem less like a cell.

"And one more thing . . ." Julian's eyebrow lifts, but he doesn't say anything, so I continue my request. "You stay out of my room. No more uninvited late-night visits."

"Agree."

"We've got ourselves a truce, Julian."

He stands, and I jump to my feet, eager to see more. "Let's walk."

We take two steps and my shoe gets caught in the dirt. I pitch forward, losing my balance, but Julian is there to catch me. He grabs my hand and pulls me forward, helping me to steady myself. I attempt to jerk out of his grasp, but he only holds on tighter, interlacing his fingers with mine. I should stop this. I should demand he let me go, but something otherworldly holds me in place.

The feeling of my fingers interlaced with his is not unlike that first freefall on my favorite rollercoaster. My heart races, doing a steady gallop in my chest. My face flushes and every nerve in my body feels electrified. If his hand is cold to the touch, I don't notice it. I'm warm all over. *What the hell is going on?*

I don't want to analyze my reaction too closely. I'm afraid what I might find. Then again, maybe I'm experiencing Stockholm syndrome. *It's the only thing that makes sense.* Or perhaps it *is* something supernatural. At the auction, upon his arrival, the air shifted, and the creatures were affected by it. *Yes. This is some magic he's weaving.*

I pull my hand from his grip, and his face pinches. He doesn't like my rebuff, but that's too bad. We have a truce, but that doesn't mean I'm going to walk around holding his hand. No matter what magical pull there is to him.

We stroll the grounds in silence for several minutes. It's tranquil here. I wouldn't have ever dreamed that I'd find peace in this prison, yet out here, the shackles from inside are gone and I feel a false sense of freedom.

"What state are we in?" I ask, finally breaking the silence. I'm curious how far away from home I am.

"Just west of New Orleans in Louisiana."

My stomach drops. "Far from Ohio, then." I kick at the dirt in frustration.

He stops and turns me to look at him.

"I really am sorry, Marina. If I had any choice . . ." His words trail off.

My eyes meet his. "I believe you."

I don't know why, but I do. He's shown me nothing but kindness since I arrived here. I could've had it so much worse. The couple from the auction could be torturing me as we speak. Or worse, I could already be dead, as I fear some from the auction already are.

His head lolls back and a sigh escapes his lips.

"I'm relieved. There are so many reasons why you shouldn't, but I promise you I'm not a bad guy. You're mine to care for." His voice is soft, soothing even. His eyes shine bright with the promise of protection. I know in my heart he believes what he says, and that confounds me more than anything.

I tear my gaze away from his, needing distance from his penetrating stare. I could get lost in his eyes, and it's not healthy for me. Living in denial is something I refuse to do. He might be offering protection, but no matter what, I can't start looking at him as a good guy.

My eyes are drawn to a beautiful bush full of small red buds. The color instantly reminds me of Stacey and her gorgeous hair. My stomach plummets thinking about what hell she must be in. *She's likely dead.*

"What about Stacey?"

"Stacey?" he says, sounding confused.

"The redhead that was with me at the auction. She went to your brother," I spit.

He groans.

"Unfortunately, my views on how vampires should live is in the minority. My brother doesn't share my opinion, as I'm sure you've guessed. I can only guess what's happened to her."

I turn to Julian, looking him straight in the eyes. "Please. Help her."

His shoulders rise as he inhales.

"I'll see what I can do, but I can't promise anything. My brother is not merciful, Marina. She's likely dead."

I hate that he's voiced my inner fears. A growl escapes my throat at the thought of what could be happening to Stacey right now, or worse, what has already happened. If she's still alive it will be a miracle. I've seen her captor, and Julian isn't fabricating. Marcellus is the devil.

"Just try, Julian, please. It'll mean everything to me. I don't know her well—we're practically strangers—but in that hellhole we bonded. How could we not?"

"I get that. Only someone who's endured what you have can truly understand."

"Please. Just try," I whisper.

He leans in, wiping a lone tear from my cheek.

"For you."

Our gazes lock and that same pull from the auction is there. I close my eyes to break whatever spell I'm in, and when I open them back up, I find that it's worked. He's looking off into the distance, lost in thought.

"Julian," I say, garnering his attention and taking my shot at one final request. "Can you see about reining in Katina with this?" I motion toward the getup I'm wearing. "Is it possible for me to have some clothes that aren't . . . this?"

He chuckles. "Katina is eccentric."

"She's a nut."

He smiles. "She's something."

The promise of new clothes isn't spoken, but somehow I know he'll come through on the request.

"Come on," I say, grabbing his hand without thinking. "Let's go back and sit," I motion with my free hand to the porch off in the distance.

Back on the porch, I lean over and pluck a juicy piece of

pineapple from the tray and pop it into my mouth. I can't help but moan around the sweet fruit. Julian's lip quirks.

"That good?"

"Yep," I say around a mouth full of pineapple, looking anywhere but at him.

Juice slides down my chin and as I'm grabbing a napkin to wipe it off, Julian leans forward and wipes it away. My cheeks heat.

"Thank you," I say, sounding breathy. I want to crawl under the chair at how easily this man makes me lose my senses, despite that I know what he is and what he's capable of.

We're so close, neither of us moving. I wait for him to give a sign that he's read my mind and the fact that I all but called him a monster yet again, but nothing comes. There's no sign he's reading my mind.

"Julian, can you read my mind?" I just up and ask. Why the hell not? If he's giving answers freely today, I might as well shoot for the moon.

"No," he says, but I can tell he's lying. He won't look me in the eyes, and he's suddenly shifting in his seat.

"No?" I press, hoping he'll come clean. If he can't tell the truth about something like this, how can I trust him with his promises?

"No. I can't read your mind, Marina."

I bite my lip, wanting to call him out, but sensing it wouldn't go well if I did. The day has been amicable, and I have been offered a truce for more freedoms. As much as I want to push, it's not worth it right now.

I'll be patient. As it is, I have all the time in the world.

"Tell me about your parents," he says.

I grimace. "What's to tell? They've hardly been part of my life the past few years."

He shoves his hands in his pockets, looking even more boyish when he does. He doesn't say a word, so I continue.

"Both of them have addiction issues," I say, and he winces.

"And I was drunk the other night. I'm so sorry, Marina."

I glance over at him, not sure what to say to that. He should be sorry, but I feel like I've beaten that horse enough for one day. He appears to be genuinely remorseful for his actions, and although it'll never be all right, I believe in forgiveness. I'll never forget, but I can forgive if it's earned.

"They've both had a tough life. They've lost two children, and now I'm missing."

"I can only imagine what they must be going through."

I scoff. "That's assuming they've even realized I'm gone."

"It's that bad?" he questions, as though he can't fathom it.

"It comes and goes with my dad. My mom has been numb my entire life."

"Have they tried to get help with it?"

I shake my head, even though he isn't looking at me. "I have, but the cost was too much. We couldn't afford to help them both, and my fear was if one got clean and the other didn't, it would only be a matter of time before they were both back at it." I pause for a moment, thinking through the problem as I've done thousands of times before. "It's better this way. At least they aren't worried about me."

"I don't believe that. No matter what state they're in, they care about you. I know it."

"Truly doubtful. Our life wasn't normal. Our family . . . not normal."

He stops and spins toward me. "Let me help them."

My eyes pop. "What?" I ask, baffled by his words. "Why would you help them?"

"It's the least I can do, Marina." He waves his hands

around. "And if you can't tell, money is no object for me. Let me do this."

I am speechless, confused . . . skeptical. Clearly, money grows on trees for this man, but I don't understand. Evil people don't do kind things for others. Evil creatures don't offer to pay thousands of dollars for rehab for their captives' parents. What's his angle?

"Stop, Marina."

"Stop what?"

"Overthinking this. I'm offering because I want to help, and I financially can. I'm not a bad guy. I don't expect anything in return." He chews on his bottom lip. "Well, except for one thing."

Here it comes.

"All I ask is that you give me a chance and don't try to leave. You staying here is what's safest for you, but it also buys me time to figure out how to appease the Council."

I'm completely mystified by Julian. I so badly want to believe he's evil. It would make it so much easier to hate him, yet at every turn—with the exception of last night—he makes me question everything.

Could I have it all wrong? Could he really be the exception to the rule of vampires? Judging him by the collective race of vampires is as unfair as him judging me by my parents' choices. Just because my parents are addicts doesn't mean I'm destined to become an addict. So maybe not all vampires are bad?

"If you can help them, Julian, I'd be forever grateful."

And I mean that with every fiber of my being.

CHAPTER 14
JULIAN

The place smells like death, and I'd know all about that. I step over the threshold, not having a clue what I'll find. A solid inch of dust coats every surface, and the overall state of the house is in desperate need of attention. It's falling apart. Paint is peeling off the walls and the wood underneath is rotting. Upon closer inspection, I realize it's due to an ongoing leak from somewhere upstairs.

The thought of Marina growing up here bothers me. Based on the level of decay, things have been like this for a long time. Despite the obvious neglect, she loves her parents. It was evident in the way her eyes crinkled at the corners and her lips were downturned when she spoke of their addiction. She was attempting to hold back tears and it almost broke me.

I'm not used to giving a fuck about someone else. Especially not a human. But Marina is different. Why? I have no idea, but she is. I'm still trying to figure out the connection I have to her, but for now, my focus is on this current issue.

It would be easy for me to end both of their lives for the

abandonment of Marina, but I promised her I'd get them help, and I'll keep that promise.

I continue to walk through the house, looking for any signs of life, but so far, nothing. Things are worse here than Marina let on, and no matter her feelings about being at Castle Bellus, I know now she's far better off. I'll take care of her.

There's finally a noise and I strain to hear where it's coming from. Someone moans unintelligibly. I walk toward the sound and come to a half-opened door, swinging it open, gagging at the putrid smell.

A vampire's sense of smell is more acute than a human's, and this is beyond rank. Feces and vomit coat every inch of the dark space. My hands feel along the wall until they come upon a light switch. With a flick upward, low light filters through the small space. A tiny frame covered by a thin sheet lies still.

I swipe away a strand of greasy blond hair to reveal a face unlike Marina's. The skin on this woman is weathered and gray in color. Pulling the cover back, I flinch at what remains of the woman. How long has it been since she's eaten? She's a step away from death. If I don't get her to a hospital soon, she'll die.

I take out my cell phone and call for Bash. "I need you in here."

He doesn't reply, but the line goes dead. Bash had set up a lookout for Marc. There had been nothing in days, so I brought him with me for backup, in case the Council is having me tailed.

"My God," he grates. I turn to see him covering his nose. "Is it dead?"

"Almost. I need you to get her to the hospital. I'm going to make some calls and arrange for her transportation to a rehab clinic in Arizona, assuming she survives."

"Her father?"

"I haven't found him yet," I snarl, thinking about what kind of man he must be to have allowed things to get this bad.

I stalk from the room, leaving Bash to tend to Marina's mom while I search for the bastard she calls Dad. It takes only a moment before I find him passed out on a recliner in the living room. He's in no better shape than her mother. How the fuck did they get this bad?

It's then that I sense it. *Black magic.*

It coats the air like a film. How did I miss it?

Something sinister is going on here. This isn't a simple case of addiction but something far worse. Someone has done this to them. Someone has made sure to keep them like this. The questions surrounding Marina Drake keep piling up.

With the state that her parents are in, I don't have time to waste. I'll get to the bottom of this, but right now, I have to save them. For her.

"Bash, we have another one in here," I call out before dialing the nearest hospital. I give them the heads-up that two critically ill patients are headed their way, so they can be prepared.

The magic I sense is a simple circle spell. I spent a long time working with black witches to know what they're capable of and to recognize such work. A circle spell holds its victims in a type of loop, a perpetual state of only half living. They likely wake, eat just enough to keep them alive, and abuse their drug of choice enough to keep them in a catatonic state.

The question is why. Who are these people and what have they done to catch the attention of a black witch?

CHAPTER 15

Days have passed since my walk with Julian in the gardens. I've spent my time staring out the windows at the well-groomed grounds, wishing to be anywhere but in this room. The boredom gives way to thoughts I'd best not have. *Has anyone begun looking for me? Does anyone even care?* The possibility that I've been forgotten weighs heavily on me.

Katina tells me that Julian has been away, but where he's gone, she won't say. I've wondered what he does for blood. He claims to be against the auction, but I haven't asked what method he uses. I envision something akin to the movie with the teenage vampires. Perhaps Julian is out running after deer and other wild animals. I file the thought away for another day.

"Hello hello, glorious morning," Katina singsongs as she walks through the door. "Why on earth are you still in bed?"

"For one, it's not glorious." The sun is masked by clouds for the second day in a row. "And beyond that, I'm bored."

"Tsk tsk, little human. You need to find something to do.

You can't sleep all day. You'll get bedsores." She scrunches her nose.

"Noted."

Katina has come and gone, keeping me company when she can. I've come to learn that her responsibilities in this house are extensive. She practically runs the vampire monarchy.

"What do you have to do today?"

"I'll be busy with staff training today. We've gotten a new shipment of new bites, and they always take longer."

My eyes widen, hands coming up to my neck instinctually. Julian's comment from the other day—about the basement dungeons being dangerous and off limits—rings loud and clear.

"They won't be anywhere near you, little human. Calm down." She shakes her head as though I'm ridiculous.

"What? Julian made it sound like those creatures can't control their thirst. Since I'm the only one with the blood they crave running through my veins, I'd say I have a reason to steer clear. I value my life."

"You're dramatic but not wrong. You'll be fine. They're not getting out of the dungeon."

I decide to try once more to find out where Julian is. "Is Julian back?" I ask, picking at my fingers.

"He is. He just returned early this morning."

"Are you going to tell me where he was?"

She purses her lips, which I've come to learn is a habit of hers. "Why do you care so much about someone you supposedly hate?" she asks, eyebrow rising in inquisition.

"I don't hate him, Katina. But I don't trust him." I blow out a breath. "I asked him to save a girl from the auction. I'm curious if he's even attempted."

She nods her head, not to say he has, but in acknowledgment. "He's had more pressing matters on his hands."

"The Council? Has there been another auction?" I ask, dreading her answer.

She sighs animatedly. "No and no. Things have been quiet in those respects," she stops what she's doing and comes to me, placing her hand on top of my shoulder and pushing me to sit. "Listen, it's not my place to tell you anything. His Crownness," I pull a face at her use of a nonsense word, but she continues. "would not be happy with my interference. However, I'm growing tired of your resolve to believe he's evil. He's not, Marina."

"I didn't say I think he's evil," I say, avoiding eye contact with Katina.

"Liar," she quips. "You think we're all evil."

"Are *you* reading my mind?"

She huffs a laugh. "Silly girl, that's impossible."

"Okay . . . Julian," I press, trying to get back on topic.

"If you must know, he went for your parents."

I stand up, feeling sick. "What do you mean?"

"See," she says, motioning to me. "That's exactly what I mean. You immediately jump to the wrong conclusions. I don't know why I even bother." She grabs a tray and goes to leave, but I rush to her side, needing her to finish.

"Please. Help me understand," I beg. Her hard glare softens and eventually she smiles.

"He kept his promise. They're both recovering and will soon be at the best addiction center in America."

I stagger back, shocked. He said he would, but I never really believed him. Why would he?

"Why?" I ask, and Katina rolls her eyes.

"Because, little human, he's not evil. There are many of us that aren't."

I've come to question my prior stance. Spending the time that I have lately with Katina, I've started to see her less as a vampire and more as a . . . person. A very strange and abnormal person, but likable. Kind. Funny.

I've been struggling with the warring parts of me. One side wants to keep them compartmentalized as evil, and the other is starting to see this world isn't so black and white. Just like every human I've ever met. There are good and bad sides to us all. Vampires are no different.

How can I continuously demonize an entire race due to the actions of a few?

You shouldn't.

At the end of the day, these people might be the ones to help me figure out who I am and why vampires have targeted me my entire life. It's clearly not normal, which means there's a reason, and it's imperative I figure it out. The first step is extending an olive branch to those that appear to be allies in my quest. Katina and Julian, for starters.

"How do I repay him?"

She smirks. "It's pretty simple, really. Give him a chance. Stop looking at him like he's the devil."

My lips flatten in irritation. "I don't."

"You do."

"I've had reason."

"And now you have reason to give him a chance," she says, smiling.

There's a knock at the door. "Come in," Katina calls out, and in strides Julian, stealing the air as he enters.

"Good morning, Marina."

I haven't seen him in days, and I almost forgot how breathtaking he is. Perhaps even more so, knowing what he's done for my family. Everything that Katina said runs through my head, and although it'll be a long road, I intend to try to give him the benefit of the doubt from here on out.

Julian is an enigma, a complete paradox. He's shown me a

kindness I've never experienced in all my life, yet he's part of a world that's ugly and cruel. He's ruler of an evil kingdom, but no matter how many times I remind myself of this, it doesn't seem to matter. He defies all odds and despite my resistance, I'm drawn to him.

That part, I need to get under control. It's one thing to slow down on the hostility and see how far it gets me; it's quite another to continuously turn into goo whenever he walks into a room.

"Good morning." I grant him a small smile.

"I hope you slept well."

"I did. Thank you."

He seems perplexed by my lack of attitude. I'm sure it's quite the change since the last time he saw me. We'd had a good day, but not without our fights.

"Katina," he growls, and she yelps in response.

"Have you been gossiping today?"

Her eyes flit about the room, lashes batting uncontrollably.

I smother my laugh at her reaction to being called out.

"Sir Crown. I wouldn't. I—"

He cuts her off. "You have. Leave us," he orders, and she scrambles out.

"She told you." It's not a question.

"She did," I admit. "But please go easy on her. I forced her into it."

He quirks a smile at that. "I have no doubt. Your ability of persuasion is unlike anything I've seen in all my years."

I chuckle at the playfulness in his words. Something is different. It's not just him, but with me. My walls are still surrounding me, but they're lowering inch by inch, with every second I spend here. Maybe it's foolish, but I can't help it. I'm thankful for what he's done for me. For my family. With every move he makes, it becomes harder to hold on to my grudges.

He steps toward me and I still, not knowing what to do, how to react. The closer he gets, the more it feels as though the oxygen is being sucked out of the room. My heart is thudding in my chest, and tingles cause the hairs on my arms to stand at attention.

It isn't fear, but something . . . different.

"Thank you," I whisper. I clear my throat, and internally shake off the spell he has me under.

I will give him a chance. I will play nice. I won't be a lovesick puppy all because he did something good. He's incredibly attractive, I'll give him that, but whatever this reaction to him is has to be reined in. I'm not that girl. Never have been, and I refuse to be now.

He simply nods.

"I'm sorry I've been absent. There was much to do." He bites his lower lip, and flutters begin in my belly. I'm a live wire buzzing with energy. *Good grief, this is ridiculous.*

"I— Um. It's fine."

I've been reduced to a blubbering idiot. My eyes close as I try desperately to get a grip. When I open them, Julian is staring at me, a smile lighting his face.

"I'll be around tomorrow, and I'd like for us to spend some time together." He looks expectantly at me, as though I might refuse.

I work to harden my voice, just a bit. "I'm at your whim," I say nonchalantly, but Julian cringes.

"Shall I serve her breakfast early, Sir Crown?" Katina asks, poking her head back in the room. I smother a chuckle at the exasperated look Julian throws her way.

"That would be great, Katina. Thank you."

She bows and exits the room again with a flourish only Katina can manage.

"She is always . . . interesting." His brow quirks and a small smirk graces his cheeks, showcasing his dimples.

A laugh escapes my lips.

"That she is," I agree. Our eyes meet and warmth spreads up my neck. Everything stills, and I can't pull my gaze from Julian. Breathing shallowly, I force my head to turn away from him, feeling suddenly claustrophobic.

I trust that he's not imposing his magic on me, but there's something about him that's causing this. It's not me. I'll have to do better at controlling whatever this is.

Julian clears his throat.

"I have business to attend to, but I brought you a present." His words come out sounding shy, unsure even.

"You did?" My head tilts to the side, my mouth a thin line.

He nods, offering a smile.

"I'm sorry it took me so long, but when I make you a promise, Marina, I swear I'll do my best to keep it." He turns to go. "Bash," he calls. "Bring her in."

My nose scrunches in confusion, but before I have a chance to question anything, the door opens and Stacey walks in. I gasp.

Stacey runs toward me, arms stretched wide, while Katina follows with covered trays. She places it on the table and exits the room without another word.

Stacey and I embrace for several minutes before either of us speaks.

"Are you okay?" I hold her shoulders at arm's length, so I can inspect her neck for any bites.

Her neck is bandaged, signaling she hasn't fared as well as I have.

"No." Her words are broken. "They're monsters, Marina."

I nod my head, not knowing what to say.

"He drinks from you?"

"One of them does. Every. Day."

It's then that I notice the bruising around her neck and cheeks. My hands fly to my mouth and I will myself to not break down in front of her. I've had it so easy in comparison, and the guilt hits me immediately.

"I'm so sorry, Stacey." The words come out as a cry.

Her hand comes up to halt my apologies, and she shakes her head, signaling for me to stop talking.

"I need to forget just for a few minutes."

The request is not too much to ask, but I have a hard time ignoring what's right in front of me. The truth of the matter is, only one of us is in dire danger. She's the real prisoner. I don't say anything. I'll allow her to lead this.

"This place is . . . nice." Her voice is hollow.

I purse my lips while widening my eyes. The company is great, but this place is . . . dark.

"All things considered, I'd take this place any day."

I instantly regret my complaining. She's right. This place is heaven compared to where she's come from. Julian has gone out of his way to make me comfortable; meanwhile she's being tortured.

"Can we please pretend we are two normal girls having a normal day?" I beg. "It might be denial, but I need that, and I think you do too."

She nods.

We sit and talk about our past lives as if we're still living them. The fantasy of normal life feels good, if only for a short time. It's as if I'm chatting with an old friend. I haven't been this relaxed since before Maggie died.

"So, wait, you're telling me that Andrea was the Tomato Queen? That's a thing where you're from?" Stacey asks, bemused.

"It's definitely a thing. Every township in the area has a contestant, and she won it all."

That was a great day. Shannon, Jill, Maggie, and I were so proud of our friend. She was radiant in her evening gown and smoking hot in her one-piece bathing suit. Guys never missed Andrea when she walked into a room. And I got it after that night, seeing her shine. She is beautiful.

Talking about the Tomato Pageant makes me think about the county fair, since that's where it was held. It was the one thing I looked forward to each summer. It allowed me seven whole days of avoiding my parents. From the animal barns to the dozens of vendors, I could spend all day every day with my friends, having fun and being normal.

"I was with them the night I was taken," I tell Stacey. "I left early because I felt so out of place."

"Why?" she asks.

"They've had normal childhoods. They've experienced college. I haven't. It was that night that I realized how different we were. How different I was."

She frowns, looking sad, but she doesn't say anything.

"I walked home. I tried to hide in a cornfield, but they found me."

Going down this road isn't easy for me, but at the same time, it might be therapeutic for both of us.

Stacey takes a deep breath. "I was at the mall, shopping for a gift for my mom's birthday. It was dark out by the time I left. When I got to my car, I was unlocking my door and I heard the door to the van next to me slide open, but I didn't even have time to turn around before someone pulled me into the back."

"Did you have the feeling like someone was following you? Or do you think you were just in the wrong place at the wrong time?"

I'm curious to see if she has a similar story to Maggie's and mine. We've been followed—more like stalked—our entire lives. Could she have endured what we did all these years?

"No. It was a case of parking too far out and next to the wrong psycho."

I huff. "Psycho is a good word for the beasts at the auction."

She smacks her lips together, nodding all the while.

"Julian said that it's not random. He says that we were likely watched for some time."

She chews on her cheek. "It's possible. I was so into myself I probably wouldn't have even noticed," she admits.

"How did you get here?" I ask, hoping this question will divert us onto a different path.

"Julian came for me. All I know is that he made a deal with Marcellus." Her eyes darken as she says his name. "I've been here for a few hours. I was hanging out in the throne room with a vampire named Katina." Her eyes widen, and her brow rises in an exaggerated expression that screams the eccentric, over-the-top vampiress.

"Has she put the moves on you?"

Stacey's mouth drops open slightly and the confusion on her face has me giggling.

"Why the hell would she put the moves on me?"

I shrug.

"I think she swings both ways."

"She's a vampire, Marina. I think they're all batshit crazy."

"Good point," I agree.

"Just for conversational purposes . . . how exactly did you come to this idea that she likes girls?" Her brow rises.

"It's just a feeling. I don't know. She . . . looks at me like she wants to eat me." I crinkle my nose.

Stacey snorts.

"Duh. She's a vampire. Of course she wants to eat you," she says through her laughter.

I can't help but follow suit. We're both practically rolling around on the ground laughing. Not that our conversation regarding Katina is particularly hysterical, but the ridiculousness of the entire situation has us each at our manic breaking point.

"I'm only half serious. Katina has been awesome. In truth, I've really grown to like her. She's over the top, but that's what makes her so unique."

Stacey makes a face. "Unique is an understatement."

I decide to get to the bottom of just what's going on over at Casa de la Pain.

"When do you have to go back?"

The air seems to chill by ten degrees at the thought of Stacey leaving.

"I'll die before I go back there, Marina."

I contemplate her words. I don't doubt it would be better for her, but the thought of Stacey dead sends a shock of sadness deep within my core. I might not have known Stacey long, but we're kindred spirits through this hellish ordeal, and I can't let anything happen to her.

"Do you think you could talk him into letting me stay here? I can't go back there. I'll die."

Her words have my blood running cold.

"I'll do whatever I can, Stacey."

She takes a deep breath.

We sit in silence for a few minutes before either of us breathes a word. It's me who finally caves.

"Where did you live?" I ask, out of curiosity and a need to talk about normal things one more time.

She frowns at my sudden change of subject, but answers anyway.

"Indian River, Michigan."

"I've never been," I say. "But I hear Michigan is beautiful."

She smiles warmly.

"It is. I love it."

Channeling all the Pure Michigan ads I've seen on the television over the years, I recall the beautiful lakes and sand dunes and send a silent prayer to any god listening that someday I'll be able to visit Stacey's home.

"We'll get you back there. I'll do whatever it takes."

The lie rolls off my tongue so easily I almost believe my own words. If what Julian said is true, she can never return. Not unless we find a way to break the black magic tracking us. It would put everyone that she loves in danger if she tried to return. I make a mental note to fill her in on all that before she leaves, but right now, I just want to relax and talk about normal things.

Stacey and I spend the day hanging out in my room. Katina brings us snacks while we try on every ridiculous dress in my armoire. Stacey's two inches taller than me—making all the dresses a little short for her—but it's a good distraction.

"Why the hell do they dress you in these?"

I purse my lips. "Long story. I'm hoping that's changed soon."

Around dinnertime, Katina brings us in pizza with two Cokes, at which we both squeal. Apparently, we share a love for greasy pepperoni and a cold Coke.

We end the day with a card game of War, and part only when Katina forces us to, saying we need rest. She's right. I only agree when Katina promises that Stacey will be here in the morning. Even though she's only been here a day, I can't go back to the loneliness I had before Stacey's arrival. I spent the past year—prior to my abduction—being painfully alone, and it almost broke me.

I almost beg for Stacey to sleep curled up next to me, but I don't want to sound pathetic. This will likely be the first time since she was abducted that she'll actually sleep. She deserves her own comfortable bed. She deserves what I have.

CHAPTER 16

The next morning, I rise early, eager to see Stacey again. I shriek when I find her already in my room, grinning at me from the table.

"Morning, sunshine."

"You scared the hell out of me." My hand is resting over my beating heart, trying desperately to convince it to calm down. "When did you get here?"

She checks her watchless wrist. "I've stopped caring about things like time."

I frown.

"Katina let me in about an hour ago. I ate while you slept." She plays with her fingers. "Sorry for the intrusion. I didn't want to be alone."

The happy girl from moments ago is replaced by someone who's been through more than I can imagine over the past few weeks. I've been living in luxury in comparison, and the guilt weighs heavily on me. *What did he do to her?*

"I'm glad you're here."

She smiles.

"Get dressed. We're going exploring." Her excitement is contagious.

I do as she says and dress quickly. Before long, Stacey and I are being escorted by Katina to meet Julian. We're practically skipping, we're so giddy for fresh air. The small things in life are what I miss most, like the freedom to choose where and when I come and go.

"Ladies," Julian says as we round the corner. "Thank you for joining me."

I nod, feeling tongue-tied at his presence. Just as every other time, I have to work hard not to overreact to him. Stacey nudges me in the side.

"Stop ogling and move. I want to see the sun."

My lips purse and eyes narrow at her insinuation. The fact that my emotions are so obvious is annoying. *If she can tell how affected I am, can he?*

"Where are you taking us today?" I ask Julian as we walk out the back door.

"I thought I would share something with you. Something that might help you understand my kind." His hands are in his pockets and he's rocking back and forth on his toes as if he's excited. He looks young and carefree. It's a look I love to see on Julian.

"I'm intrigued."

He looks triumphant. Turning to Stacey, he asks, "Do you mind if I borrow her for a moment?"

She looks at me, mouth pulled to one side, as if she's debating whether or not she should leave me with him.

"It's fine, Stacey. Go enjoy your sun," I laugh, hoping she'll feel all right with going off on her own.

"I'll just be over there." She points to the flower garden. "If you need me, yell."

She narrows her eyes at Julian. His hands raise in surrender.

"She's safe with me, Stacey. You both are."

Her hard eyes soften and a smile forms on her lips. She doesn't say another word as she bounces off to enjoy a moment of freedom. I can't contain my own smile at her momentary happiness. In truth, Julian made it happen and he deserves my gratitude.

"Thank you, Julian. This means . . . everything."

His head bobs, but he doesn't say anything, hands in his pockets as he walks ahead of me.

We walk for a few minutes in silence until we approach two gravestones worn with age. My head turns to Julian, the question dying on my lips.

"These are the memorial stones of my mother and sister. Their bodies aren't here, of course, but it's become a place of solace for me and my brothers."

He leans over, wiping away dust and dirt from the stones. One is engraved,

Sylvia Bellamy
beloved mother and wife
September 20, 1321 – October 4, 1346

The second reads,

Winnifred Bellamy
cherished daughter
March 14, 1341 – March 18, 1342

"What happened to them?"

"My sister died from the plague. She was one of the earliest victims," he says sadly. "She would've been the oldest of us all."

The plague. The reminder that he isn't mortal is a kick to the gut.

"My mother died during childbirth with the three of us boys, just four years later."

Triplets. Just like me and my sisters.

"I was a triplet too," I confide, feeling like I should share something, since he's showed me this.

His head pops up to mine, eyes wide.

"You . . . were a triplet?"

"Yeah, it's not that uncommon," I titter at his surprise.

"Where are your sisters?"

My face falls at the question. I wanted to share a piece of me, but this feels like too much too soon. There are some things I hold close, and the story of my past is one of them. Julian must read this on my face, because he continues on quickly to get an answer.

"Were they taken too?"

I shake my head vigorously, thankful they weren't auctioned off to a monster like Marcellus.

"Molly was stillborn, and Maggie died a few months ago." It's all I'll offer. I won't go into her death, and the fact that I'm finally admitting that she's dead isn't lost on me. It breaks me in two.

"I'm sorry, Marina."

My shoulders lift. Words escape me.

"It appears we have a lot in common." He peers at me out of the corner of his eye. Mine are lasered on the tombstones as I try to prevent myself from cracking.

We've both lost people we love, but where I'm alone, he still has Law. I'd give anything to have my sister back.

Julian turns me to him.

"You're in pain. I can feel it." My eyes squint as I try to understand how he'd know that. Is it that obvious? "What can I do to help? Name it. I'll give it to you," he promises.

I stare at him for several moments, not knowing what to say. Why is he being so kind to me? How long will it last? Then something occurs to me. *Stacey.*

"Can Stacey stay here with me?"

Julian frowns, not appearing happy with my request.

"That isn't something I can give you, Marina. If I could, I would."

"He's evil, Julian. He will kill her. She's my friend. The only one I have," I channel every ounce of sadness into my words, hoping it'll have the effect I'm gunning for.

He sighs.

"It wasn't always like that. Over the centuries, a lot has happened to him. His heart has hardened."

The shift in conversation isn't to my liking, but it has me wondering what did happen to Marcellus to make him what he is today.

"He's lost much over the years." His eyes are sad as he relays his brother's story. His hand is at his heart, as if he's trying to stave off his own pain.

"Someone he loved?" The question comes to me out of nowhere. What else could turn someone so cold?

"Yes. The one person who would've held his heart for a lifetime."

That kind of love is foreign to me. I've never felt anything stronger than lust. At twenty years old, I have less experience with the opposite sex than most. Love has always seemed unthinkable.

"I've never been in love. I wouldn't know what that's like," I admit.

"Love can be harsh. Especially for vampires."

The pain that crosses over his face forms a pit in my stomach. What has he been through over the centuries? That kind of pain can only be from personal experience. Who has he lost?

"The brother I loved is lost. This Marcellus wants to overthrow me. He's protested my standing to the Council." He brushes his hand back through his blond hair. "I'm under a microscope these days."

"Can he do that?"

"He has."

I wonder what that all means. Who does the Council consist of and what can they actually do to Julian? In the end, I don't ask. It doesn't matter in the scheme of things. My only focus for today is to secure Stacey's safety.

"Is there any way to keep Stacey here, Julian?"

He grunts.

"Outside of demanding it, no. He hardly agreed to one month."

My hands clench at my side. "Then demand it. Please."

"Is it worth a war, Marina?" he asks harshly. "Do you know her enough to potentially put millions of humans at risk?"

"You think that by demanding she stay, you'd start a war?"

"Marcellus is looking for a reason. He'd turn it around and make it appear to the Council that I'm going soft on humans. He'd convince them that I'd jeopardize our race for one girl."

A tear drips down my cheek at the realization that I can't save Stacey. No matter how much I promised, I can't deliver. I swipe it away, pissed that I can't seem to keep my emotions in check these days.

I've spent years donning a mask—one that even a professional had a hard time seeing through—but here, I'm practically naked and vulnerable. It's unnerving and a real damn issue.

"Hey." He grabs my cheek softly, turning my head toward

him. "I'm not saying I won't try, Marina. I will. I'm just asking you to know that there is a chance it won't happen. If he pushes back, I can't fight him. I can't risk everything for her, no matter how much I want to. One month. That's what was agreed."

I nod, turning my head out of his grasp. In truth, I understand his dilemma, but I hate it.

We walk along the path in silence, both lost in our own thoughts. The two-story historical dream house helps me to relax. There is something soothing about this place, but we don't stop today. We walk past, coming up to the large woods.

"What's beyond the trees?" I press my luck, digging for information on what lies on the other side.

"It separates this property from my brothers'."

The mention of his brothers makes me think of Law. He's been nothing but nice since the auction.

"What does Law think about all of this?"

"Law tends to stay out of matters dealing with Marc and the Council. He agrees with me and doesn't feel the need for an auction. He has his own line of volunteer donors." Julian's eyes roll. "Women tend to throw themselves at his feet willingly. He prefers to snack and leave them alive."

"Gross," I scrunch my nose.

"I suppose it would be to you. To us, it's merely a form of foreplay. There is pleasure in blood sharing." He looks at me sideways again.

"I doubt that." My hand comes to my neck, massaging the phantom pain.

"Truly, Marina. It's very erotic and sensual when both participants are willing."

"I'll pass."

Julian straightens, his face a mask of stone. What's going

on in his head? I've certainly offended him, judging by the way he's shut down.

"I think it's time we head back," Julian says, voice rough.

I instantly regret my reaction. Will this affect our truce? Regardless, I can't lie. To me, the thought of someone taking my blood from my body is anything but sensual. It's painful and uncivilized.

It's a reminder of the girl who lost her life in the cell next to mine.

I'd like to be friends with Julian, but at the end of the day I won't pretend to understand his culture. It's strange and disturbing to me. Especially when their kind embrace the practice of kidnapping and stealing blood. No, there is nothing sexy about that.

CHAPTER 17

The past week with Stacey has been the most fun I've had in more than a year. We've done nothing but eat and talk about our lives pre-abduction. Stacey's life was the all-American one. A beautiful, educated, loving mother. A doting, breadwinning father. One brother, a dog, and a white picket fence. I listened raptly as she told the stories of her childhood with unshed tears. She'd give anything to have that life back.

As I sat there listening to her, I realized how different we were. I might not want to be a prisoner of vampires, but I'm not begging for my old life either. It was far from perfect. In fact, at times, it was a nightmare.

Stacey's going on about high school and her friends. I laugh, because even in that aspect we're polar opposites. She had more friends than I had kids in my class. My life pales in comparison.

"So, what you're saying is you were a mean girl," I say in response to Stacey's high school antics.

"I wasn't mean, per se."

I purse my lips, tilting my head to the side.

"Okay, fine. I was mean, and karma is an epic bitch, based on our current situation." She crosses her arms over her chest, pouting at karma's revenge.

No debating that. There is nothing either one of us has done in our past to justify this. Stacey's life has literally been turned upside down. I've just traded one form of hell for another. *Your current situation is better than life before.*

"We wouldn't have been friends in life," I say, thinking about how different we were in our pasts and being thankful that we've met, even under the unfair circumstances.

"You don't know that."

I laugh. "Oh, yes I do. I was the town weirdo who saw monsters as a child. If that wasn't traumatic enough, I watched my sister commit suicide. The whole antisocial thing—I had it pegged."

"Jesus," she croaks. "We weren't cruel. The people we picked on had it coming to them."

I raise my brow.

"Seriously. You weren't a weirdo, Marina. What you saw . . . it was real," she says, motioning around. "Vampires are real. Your monsters—real," she says to emphasize her point. "It was the rest of us who were in the dark."

I nod. She's right. Everything Maggie and I saw growing up wasn't our imagination. All the medications they made us take were for nothing. We were right, but in this moment, I wish we had been wrong.

We're quiet for several moments, each lost in our own thoughts. The silence makes the air thick and awkward. Stacey, being Stacey, attempts to lighten the mood.

"Let's play a game," Stacey says excitedly.

"Um . . . okay? What do you suggest?"

She taps her finger on her chin a couple times before opening her eyes wide.

"I've got it. Let's play tag and seek."

She can't be serious.

"I'm serious," she laughs.

Okay, so she is.

"In here?" I question, not seeing the fun in that.

"No. He gave us permission to roam—let's roam."

"What the hell is tag and seek?"

"Just what it sounds like. A combo of tag and hide and seek. Come on," she says, grabbing my shoulder and turning me toward the door. "Rules of the game. We remain on this level. I hide first, but you have to give me ten minutes before you come in search. Got it?"

"Do I have a choice?"

"Nope," she singsongs, clearly excited about this child's play.

"Then you'd better get going."

I begin to count out loud and Stacey smiles widely before dashing off, giggling while she goes.

My stomach growls, alerting me to the fact I've yet to eat, but it will have to wait. Stacey was so excited, and if playing games helps her to smile, I'm going to participate. I can't pretend I get it, but I never really was one for games. Right now, though, I'm willing to try new things. It's something I should've been doing a long time ago. We need a little fun in our lives, after all we've been through.

Giving her another two minutes, I quickly shove a strawberry into my mouth. The need for more is intense, but I told her I'd play, so I repress the urge to continue to stuff my face full of food. Entering the hall, I look left and then right. I've only ever been down the right hall. It leads to the throne room and outside, the only two places I've been on the estate, outside of my room. Curiosity has me turning left.

The hall is lined with doors. I open each to find empty

rooms. I've just finished looking under the bed of the current room when a noise from behind has me spinning around. The room is dark, and with the light of the hall, I can barely make out the figure of a girl.

"Stacey?" I call out. No answer.

She turns and takes off in a sprint. Getting to my feet, I fly to the door, trying to catch her. When I reach the hall, I catch the backside of her rounding the corner. I pick up my pace, eager to catch her.

"Hey, come back," I yell down the hall. She giggles and I throw my head back, jubilant laughter escaping for the first time in years. I feel carefree. *Alive.*

A simple game of tag has transported me back to the days of my childhood that are worth remembering. Memories of Maggie and me playing the same game. I channel that and live in the moment, running around the curves of the hallway, not even bothering to check the rooms I pass.

When I come upon a large set of iron doors, I throw them open without thinking twice. Looking back over my shoulder, I check to make sure Stacey isn't creeping up on me. I lost sight of her and she could've easily ducked into any of the empty rooms. She could be in pursuit of me now. I chuckle at the thought.

Walking backwards, keeping my eye on the door in case she tries to sneak up on me, my calves hit something soft. I turn around and all the excitement I felt quickly turns to dread. A scream rips from my throat at the sight in front of me. My hands come to my mouth to smother any additional shrieks of terror.

Lying in a massive bed is a corpse, charred from the inside out. I can't tell if it's a man or woman, the body is so badly burned. Empty eye sockets and a mouth that gapes open make for a horrifying sight. I gawk at the morbid sight, trying to wrap my head around what I'm seeing. The blood's pumping in my ears so loudly, I don't hear anyone approaching. Strong hands come down on my shoulders from behind and turn me around.

I yelp and Julian pulls me into his firm chest, rubbing his hand down my back in a soothing gesture.

"Shhh. You're all right. I've got you," he whispers into my ear, likely thinking I'm about to lose it. I am shaking, but who wouldn't be, stumbling across a dead body?

I push off his chest. "I . . . I'm fine. It . . . that," I say, gesturing to the bed, "caught me off guard. That's all."

"You weren't supposed to be here, Marina. I never wanted you to see this."

With those words I know I've entered the east wing, one of the forbidden areas of the estate. He said it was his father's chambers. Realization hits, and I feel even more queasy. Why the hell would they just leave him in here like this?

"Things are different for vampires, Marina. We can't just call a crime lab and have them investigate," he says, and I ignore that he's read my mind again. "The onus lies with me to uncover what happened. I'm waiting on a friend—a witch—to come examine the body."

"What happened to him?"

I'm staring at the body of Julian's father, the former king of vampires. He's been reduced to near ashes. If I so much as touched him, what's left would undoubtedly crumble into a pile of dust, which is likely why he hasn't moved him.

"That's what I'm trying to figure out." I look up at Julian in time to see him shake his head. "We found him in here like this. It looked like he had been cooked from the inside out."

"Who would do this?"

Julian drops his hands from my shoulders, walking closer to the bed and peering at the remains of his father.

"The list is extensive. My father was not a good man."

My nose crinkles. "I mean no offense, Julian, but he's a vampire. I'm not sure, based on the few I've met, that it has anything to do with him being a good man."

"Touché," he says. "And you're right. It likely had more to do with power. Someone wanted his."

"The Council?" I offer.

"Some are at the top of my list," he admits. "He wasn't easily swayed to follow the group, which led to many disagreements. It's likely they're trying to groom Marcellus to take his place because he's the most easily influenced. They'll have their way with him running the Crown."

"Why even have a Crown in the first place?"

"Even the evilest of our kind appreciate the delicate balance of things. If we exposed ourselves, our numbers are not great enough at the moment to take on the military. We'd be wiped out if they uncovered how to end us." He sighs. "And that's not the greater threat."

"What is the greater threat?"

He looks at me, holding my stare. "Humans going extinct. The source of our power being depleted."

I gulp, thinking about the utter chaos that would reign if vampires exposed themselves.

"My father didn't want that. He felt strongly that there was another way for vampires to live without ending humanity."

"Such as?" I press.

Julian shrugs. "He harbored secrets that the elders of the other families were trying desperately to uncover. I believe my father died protecting those secrets."

My eyes narrow on Julian. "Do you know these secrets?"

"No."

The way his eyes shift tells me his father was not alone in

keeping secrets. Julian's guilt-ridden face shows the truth. He knows something.

"What are you hiding, Julian?"

He turns from me, probably trying to formulate his lie, and I'm not going to let him.

"If you want me to trust you, Julian, now would be a good time to start being truthful."

He turns around, and I see the dark circles under his pale eyes. The way his eyebrows hang low over his lids tells me that he's exhausted. Julian looks like a man with the weight of the world on his shoulders.

"There are things that aren't safe for you to know, Marina. If they assassinated my father to unearth the truth, they won't hesitate in killing you."

I huff. "They wouldn't hesitate in killing me period. I might as well be caught up on what's going on here. Maybe I can help."

He eyes me wearily. "You're very brave, Marina, but I wish you'd value your life more."

My spine straightens. *What does he know about my life?* His eyes widen at my change in demeanor.

"I didn't mean to offend you; I just don't understand. What happened in your life that makes you so quick to throw yourself into the thick of danger?"

"I haven't thrown myself into anything. Do I need to remind you that I was forced into this? That I've been stalked by creatures that were likely vampires my entire life? I'd like some answers because based on everything you've told me, that isn't normal."

His sigh is long and harsh.

"And that's exactly why you can't know my secrets."

A strange feeling washes over me, crawling up my spine and settling at the base of my neck. An inner knowing that somehow these secrets pertain to me in some way, and Julian is shutting me out. He's keeping secrets that could answer why my life's been a shit show.

"Marina," he says, voice low and cautious.

"You know what? You're right, Julian. I don't want to know. Keep me in the dark. You seem to have this all under control." I shoulder past him, pissed and ready to get far away from Julian Bellamy.

I'm halfway down the hall when Stacey comes sauntering out of a dark room.

"Whoa. What's wrong with you?"

I push past her, not wanting to stop.

"Marina," Julian calls out, but I ignore him, wanting to put as much distance between us as possible. I'm angry because I thought we'd turned a corner. He asked me to trust him, and to me, trust is earned. Trust comes from being open.

Trust comes from admitting when you know more about *me* and how I ended up thrown headfirst into this vampire world.

"Please. Stop," he commands. Coming to a halt, I whirl around and go toe to toe with the king of vampires.

"Why? You made your position clear. I'm choosing not to beat a dead horse. You won't tell me? Fine. I'll find out your secrets on my own, Julian." His eyes widen at my harsh tone and deadly glare.

"No, you won't. I'll lock you in that room before I allow you to put yourself in more danger."

I take a step toward him, teeth bared. "That's how this is going to go? Your whole promise of a small amount of freedom here is gone?"

"If it must be that way to keep you safe, yes. If you don't heed my warning to stay out of things that don't concern you."

"Don't concern me?" I laugh, but it lacks humor. "You and I

both know that I'm not here just because of bad luck and horrific timing. I've been stalked by creatures that you say don't behave that way. Creatures that would've already killed me years ago. So, tell me, do you know something about me concerning your kind or not?"

His lips part but then slam shut again. Swiping his hand back through his hair roughly, he grunts his dissatisfaction with this entire scene.

"Why must human women be so difficult?"

I blanch at his words.

"You're kidding."

"No, Marina. I'm not. I'm doing everything I can to keep you safe, yet you've been nothing but combative."

My eyes widen and my mouth drops open. "I'm being combative? I only asked for you to be honest with me." My voice rises. "I'd say, all things considered, I'm not being combative enough. I was stolen from my life. A life I'm told I can never go back to," I yell.

"I've told you a million times, *not* by me. I have nothing to do with any of that."

"Fine, then I think we can agree that this situation more than sucks for both of us. Let me in. Let me help figure all of this out."

"I told you I can't. What do you want from me, Marina?" Julian yells back.

"The truth. That's all."

My words come out defeated. I'm tired. Tired of fighting for the day, tired of lies, tired of getting the same answers. Most of all, I'm emotionally spent. Maybe I'm being unfair, expecting too much too soon, but what I saw today has me unraveling. The questions spiraling.

I'm living under a roof with the corpse of the ex-Crown. A

creature that was obviously cruel—given he started and ran the auction—and merciless.

I turn around and start heading toward my room.

"Marina," Julian barks. "Where are you going?" I stop, turning halfway around to look at him.

"I'm trying to walk away so I don't argue with you, Julian."

"What's there to argue about?" he says, arms flying into the air.

I close my eyes, inhaling deeply. I'm not going to start this conversation all over again. I'm tired. He's tired. It's time to call it a day, before something bad happens.

Julian takes a deep breath, moving toward me slowly.

"I will never harm you, Marina. Everything I've done is truly to protect you." His shoulders sag, the fight leaving him. "But if you insist on knowing things—things that will put you in further danger—I'll tell you."

I stop breathing. "Everything?"

He nods, resigned.

"Everything." He turns away. "Go clean up. We'll have dinner, and then I'll tell you whatever you want to know."

I walk to him, placing my hand on his back.

"Thank you, Julian." He looks over his shoulder, gives me a nod, and walks away.

"What was all of that about?" Stacey asks with wide eyes.

I contemplate how much to share with Stacey. The more she knows, the more danger she could possibly be in. I weigh my words and opt for the truth because at this point, I don't know any more than whoever is involved in the ex-Crown's death would, from what Julian said.

"I saw his father. He was killed, and his body remains at the scene of the crime. Julian says he thinks it's because of some secret that his father was hiding. I want him to tell me the secret."

She narrows her eyes, pursing her lips. "Why? What good can possibly come from you entangling yourself further into the vampire web, Marina?"

I consider Stacey's words. She isn't wrong—the more I know, the more entangled I am. But, If I'm to believe Julian, I've been marked. I'm stuck here and in the direct path of the vampires. If I try to leave, they'll come for me. Then again, I'm already involved in this fucked up web, and I have been since childhood. The more I know, the better armed I am. Knowledge is power, right?

"What if it's something that could help get us home? Don't you want that?"

She sucks her teeth. "Yes, but I think we should listen to Julian. He hasn't given us any reason not to trust him."

"He's keeping secrets."

"Probably for our own good." Stacey's hands shoot up, frustrated. "I for one really don't want to know what kind of monsters are out there."

"You'd rather be in the dark?" I ask, seriously curious.

"Yes. Being in the dark isn't always a bad thing, Marina. Could you seriously go home and turn your back on it all if you know everything?"

"I'm not sure I understand the question," I say, curious as to what she could be told that would have her more scared than knowing vampires exist.

"There could be worse things that vampires and their auctions," she says. "Hell, humans do that shit, and not every girl ends up in the back of a fucking van. If I knew more, I couldn't go home and live a normal life," she continues angrily. "I'd constantly be looking over my shoulder. Paranoid. You know what happens to paranoid girls? They end up killing themselves or they get institutionalized."

My face pales. She's just described Maggie. Paranoia led her to do just that. Stacey isn't wrong. In fact, she makes the most sense I've heard in some time, but it doesn't change anything for me. The fact is, I do know monsters exist. I've been living with some sense of that knowledge my whole life. I need to know everything. It's about more than just curiosity. It's about knowing that Maggie didn't die in vain. What she saw, the things she said, it was all true, and a nagging voice in my head says that this place, these people, have something to do with her death. Now it's personal.

Julian promised me answers after dinner, and I plan to hold his feet to the fire.

CHAPTER 18

"Thank you, Julian," Stacey offers for the delicious meal we were just served. "You don't know what it means to me that you saved me from your brother."

Julian's eyes lower to the table. It makes me wonder how long Stacey will be safe. Can we keep her here and away from Marcellus?

"You're welcome," he says bashfully, cheeks reddening, which is strange to see on a vampire.

"You do have blood," Stacey muses.

Julian chuckles. "What did you think, we were hollow?"

"Every movie I've ever watched, the vampires were unnaturally pale." She considers him. "You do have the pasty white skin going on, but your cheeks just turned red. So you have to have blood flowing."

"If nothing, you are observant. And yes, we do have blood flowing through our veins."

"Can I ask you a question without you killing me?"

Julian's brow lifts in amusement at Stacey's forwardness.

"Please. This I have to hear," he says jokingly, motioning for her to continue.

"Did another vampire bite you? Is that how you're . . . well . . . a vampire?" She grinds her teeth.

"Not exactly," Julian admits, which draws narrowed eyes from both Stacey and me.

"You weren't bitten?" I question, shocked to hear this. If not bitten, then how?

"Some humans are born with DNA that, when exposed to certain viruses, can result in vampirism."

"Wait. What?" Stacey says, perplexed.

"Our parents both carried the gene, but they were humans for most of their lives. My brothers and I were the first of our kind. We're called Borns."

"I don't understand. Are you saying that there is a vampire gene that lives in humans?" Stacey asks for clarification.

"Some humans. Not all. We know very little about the start of our kind, but what we do know is that select humans have a gene in their DNA that makes them susceptible to the change, given the right circumstances."

"You've had centuries to figure this out and you haven't?" Stacey says, flabbergasted. Why wouldn't efforts be made to pinpoint the origins of the species? I'm no scientist, but it seems ridiculous that they don't have this figured out. What if there is a cure?

"You'd be surprised how quickly a century goes by, Stacey. It took my father nearly a century to cope with the change. He couldn't stave off the hunger and he had three newborn vampires to care for—on his own. The origins weren't first on the list."

This is a touchy subject for Julian. I can tell in the way his eyes are narrowed and the way he grits his teeth. I imagine those days aren't ones he wishes to remember, based on the tone of his voice. There's an edge to his words. I hope Stacey won't press that subject because it doesn't matter, and I don't want to shut him down before our discussion.

"Go on," she presses.

His nose flares at her insistence that he continue. My guess is that Julian is not used to being ordered about. I'm about to jump in and change the subject, but he continues.

"My mother at the time was carrying triplets. It's believed that when she went through the change, our fetuses did as well."

"Oh my God. How in the hell did she survive that?"

"She didn't. She died during childbirth."

I bite my lower lip, remembering the memorial gravestones we visited. He told me that she died during childbirth. I want to ask how she was able to die given he said she had the gene, but I don't. It feels insensitive to pry into such a clearly painful thing, and in the end it doesn't matter. She's dead.

"I'm sorry, Julian," I say, and Stacey follows with her own condolences.

A horrible sting rips through me. I feel like shit. I've been so focused on what I've been through that I've not considered how much he's endured over several lifetimes.

"I don't expect you to feel sorry for me, girls. You've both endured a lot yourselves."

Worse. I feel worse because he continues to be so kind, when I don't deserve it. When he doesn't have to be. The bottom line is, he holds the power, yet he keeps giving it all away. Why?

"Continue, Julian," Stacey says, giving me the stink eye, and I have no doubt she'll tell me why later.

"A century later, dysentery swept through Sweden, and another family of vampires rose to power. To this day, only three families have been born, not bitten. The descendants of these three families were thought to be immortal. No blade, gun, poison, or arrow ever did the job."

"Not even a stake through the heart?" Stacey asks.

Julian rolls his eyes. "Definitely not a stake through the heart."

"Are those families the Council?" I ask, trying to piece everything together.

"Some of them. Over the years, other families have made alliances, and gained power and influence in the meantime."

"So you're a Born," I say out loud, still trying to work everything out.

He nods.

"The new vampires are called . . ." Stacey waits for an answer.

"New bites."

"Original," she says sardonically.

Julian laughs for the first time since we started this conversation.

"We were not the most innovative, I suppose."

"I'd say," Stacey laughs, and we all join her.

She sits back, clucking her tongue several times. Julian and I watch her, looking to each other in question.

"Let's play a game," she says, and I groan in response.

The last time she suggested we play a game, I came face to face with a dead body.

"I'm intrigued," Julian lies. I can tell by the way he cringed when she suggested a game.

"It's simple. Never Have I Ever."

It's my turn to cringe at the memory of the last time I witnessed this game take place. It

only further shows how different Stacey and I were before we were taken. She'd definitely fit in with my old friends, more than I did.

"No way," I say, wanting to run from the room.

"Why not?" Julian asks me. The way he says it doesn't indicate he wants to play, but more that he's trying to understand me. I don't want to answer him.

"Tell us," Stacey insists. "Why don't you want to play?"

I cluck my tongue. "For starters, it's a college game that I've never been interested in."

"You didn't even go to a traditional college," Stacey says, and I level her with a glare.

"I'm sorry. I didn't mean it to sound rude," she says, reticent.

"You're right. I didn't, and the constant reminders of all that I missed out on only hurt more," I admit. "Games make me feel isolated from others my age. I never got to be a kid, and sometimes that reality stings."

"I'm in," Julian says, and I scowl in his direction.

Traitor.

I know he's going along with it because he thinks that it'll help me feel connected. His heart is in the right place, but that doesn't stop me from grumbling.

Stacey claps her hands in excitement, while I mumble all the ways I'm going to kill her myself tonight.

"It's just a game, Marina. Maybe by playing you'll see you aren't missing out on much," Julian says with a smile.

Stacey harrumphs.

"How do you play?" Julian asks Stacey.

"One of us starts by saying something they've never done before. If you have done it, you put up a finger and take a drink of whatever your poison of the night is. If you haven't, you don't do anything. The last person to put up four fingers wins."

"Marina doesn't drink," Julian points out, and I can't help but smile at his thoughtfulness.

"She doesn't have to," Stacey says, grabbing her own glass full of red wine.

"Thank you," I mouth to Julian, and he smiles.

"What are we betting?" Julian asks with a raised brow.

"Whoever wins . . . gets to leave the estate with you on a date."

My eyes go wide in shock at her suggestion.

"What?" I screech. "A date?"

Stacey rolls her eyes. "A dinner date off the premises."

My head snaps to Julian's, eager to see his reaction. He's stone-faced.

"Is that even safe?" I question, based on all the times Julian has alluded to my not being safe outside of these walls.

"With precautions, a quick trip into New Orleans would be fine," he admits.

"Does that mean you're game?" Stacey presses.

He's silent for a moment.

"Can I trust that whichever of you wins, you won't try to run off?"

Stacey and I exchange glances.

"Promise," we say in unison.

"Then I can agree to that. But what if I win?" he says, quirking a brow.

"If you win, you have your choice of whatever it is you wish." Stacey adds. "But no biting, draining blood, or any other form of torture . . . please."

Julian grins. "Agree."

Stacey smiles wide. "Okay, let's start. Never have I ever drunk blood from a person's neck." Her cheek raises in a smirk and I return it with my own. Julian, however, groans, lifts a finger and takes a drink of his water.

"All right, ladies, my turn," Julian calls. "Never have I ever sunbathed."

Stacey and I grunt in turn, each lift a finger and take a drink from our glasses.

It's my turn and I think long and hard. There are so many things I could say, but only one that I'm more than positive would take out both of my competitors. As much as I hate to admit it in front of Julian, I know it's the right choice.

"Never have I ever had . . . sex." I practically whisper the word and regardless, my entire body heats in embarrassment.

"Ugh. You would pull out the big guns," Stacey whines. Julian averts his eyes. They both drink.

It's not like everyone doesn't know. I was called out at the auction, but it's more mortifying in this intimate situation. My cheeks are aflame, and I want to crawl under the table, but I don't. Instead, I push down the humiliation and forge onward. I'm in this to win. A night out in New Orleans isn't something I'm giving up easily.

"I believe it's your turn again, Stacey," I say without looking at either of them.

"Never have I ever kissed a vampire," she offers.

Stacey and I watch as Julian inevitably raises another finger and takes yet another swig of his drink.

"Story you want to share?" Stacey probes, smirking.

"No. Thank you."

I'm not surprised that Julian has kissed another vampire. In fact, I'd be surprised if he hadn't. I might be the only one in this entire room who has never even kissed another human. Well, outside of my parents and sister.

"Never have I ever been to an amusement park," Julian admits, and both Stacey and I fall.

It's my turn, and it occurs to me that Julian and Stacey are both on the line. Julian has admitted to kissing another vampire; surely he's kissed a human at some point. And I would be floored if Stacey hasn't kissed a bevy of boys. The realization that I probably should've started with this isn't lost on me, but what's done is done and either way, I'm winning this.

Whispering, because no matter what, it's embarrassing, I admit to them both, "I've never been French kissed by a human."

"By a human?" Julian asks, brow raised.

I roll my eyes. "By anyone."

"Are you freaking serious?" Stacey screeches. "Being a virgin is one thing, but you've seriously never even kissed a boy?"

My hand comes to my forehead. "Never had the interest," I say. "I was a little preoccupied with therapists and hospitals."

"There's nothing wrong with that, Marina," Julian offers. "You've had bigger things to worry about." I nod in silent thanks.

Then I look between the two of them, a grin spreading across my face.

"Unless one of you two is about to confess to never being kissed, I believe some fingers need to rise and some drinks need to be consumed." A smirk overtakes my face. I get to leave this place for a little while. I've never been to New Orleans, and the idea has me damn near dancing.

"When can we go?" I ask Julian, hoping it's soon.

"Next week," he laughs, catching on to my excitement. "We'll go into New Orleans for dinner. I'm sorry you won't be joining us, Stacey." She crosses her arms over her chest, sitting down in a huff of jealousy.

"I'm done with this game for good," she says. "None of those kisses or"—she clears her throat—"nights in the sack were worth it."

I chuckle, feeling sorry that Stacey has to sit home while I'm out roaming the town with one of the best-looking men

I've ever seen. She's been through so much, it hardly seems fair.

"You can go, Stacey. I'll stay back."

She scrunches her nose and shakes her head.

"Hell no, you won't. I win fair and square, and I lose the same way."

My shoulders lift in a *whatever you say* motion and I turn to catch Julian's eyes on me. He's looking at me like he's seeing me for the first time. I wriggle under his intense gaze. He's truly a work of art. His chiseled features twist my insides up in knots. The good kind. The kind that have the power to break you when they disappear.

This is clearly a side effect of winning and the euphoria that comes with it. Julian is proving to be a good guy, but he's still a vampire and I'd do well to remember that.

The tension is broken when Julian's lackey, Bash, comes flying through the door.

"Sir, we have an issue."

Julian stands, walking quickly to the door to speak with Bash in private. Stacey and I exchange glances of concern. After a minute, Julian comes back to the table.

"Ladies, Bash will escort you to your rooms. You'll lock yourselves in and not leave until either Katina or I come to get you. Do you understand?"

"What's happening?" I ask, and Julian raises a hand.

"For once, please just do as I ask, Marina."

His expression is grim, and I know better than to push at this point.

Nodding, I link arms with Stacey and we follow a quiet Bash.

"What do you think's going on?" Stacey whispers.

"No clue, but Julian looked angry. Whatever it is, it can't be good."

We reach Stacey's room first, she gives me a big hug, "Good night. Listen to Julian, Marina. Don't leave your room."

I squeeze her back. "I promise."

She enters her room and closes the door, and a deadbolt sounds from inside the room.

"What am I supposed to do?" I ask Bash. "My room only locks from the outside."

"Julian has ordered me to stand outside your room. You'll be fine."

Bash seems nonplussed despite his earlier manner, so I don't worry.

After quickly undressing, I put on my nightgown, brush my teeth, and crawl into my warm, cozy bed. I reflect on the game and realize that Julian was right. I haven't been missing anything. If that's what college life consists of, it was never meant for me.

For the first time in a long time, the pang of hurt caused from missing out and friendships changing is gone. I feel lighter, freer, and I have Julian to thank for that.

Exhaustion overwhelms me, and I swiftly fall asleep. Dreams of kissing golden-haired, brooding vampires keep me entertained all through the night.

CHAPTER 19

I'm informed bright and early by Katina that Julian will be gone for the next week. Why he didn't mention this last night is beyond me. He has a habit of disappearing. It makes me wonder what he's up to. I don't have long to think on this, because Katina's second tidbit of information grabs my attention.

"Lawrence Bellamy will be coming to stay at the estate in Julian's absence."

"Why?" I ask, not understanding the need for a babysitter. Does Julian think we're going to try to escape?

"There are valuable things on this estate and he doesn't want to take the chance of anyone trying to come and claim them. When the Crown is traveling, the estate is most vulnerable. Lawrence is well trained in military tactics. He served in the Continental Army in 1775 under George Washington."

I'll never get used to hearing that these men are hundreds of years old. Mostly, I question the need for a soldier to protect the place. What is so valuable on this estate?

His father's crisp corpse?

"Right. Well, Stacey and I will have lunch in my room."

"No, that won't do. Lawrence has decided to have a little soirée at his estate once Julian returns, and has requested your help in preparing," Katina says, sounding exasperated.

"Stacey and me?"

I know nothing about throwing a party for humans, let alone vampires, and if I'm being honest, I want nothing to do with it.

"Lawrence is a bit of a playboy in New Orleans. He's managed to compile a Rolodex full of high-rolling Louisianans who'd fall over themselves to attend one of his parties. You'll be in good company."

"Humans?" I ask incredulously.

"Stupid, arrogant, frivolous humans—but yes," she says, picking at her fingernails.

"Don't go getting any ideas, Marina. They won't help you escape."

I huff a laugh that's anything but humorous. "I gave up that idea when I heard the Council would come after me. Seems safer here for now. I'll stay."

"Good girl," she praises, patting my head. "Now, go wake your friend. She's sleeping like the dead."

I throw a reproachful glare at Katina for her terrible choice of words. In a house of vampires, jokes about death are not funny. She rolls her eyes, which seems to be her signature look as far as our interactions go.

"You have the next three hours free. You'll need to be in the dining room for lunch with Lawrence," she says, preparing to exit. "Please put on some clothes," she finishes before going out of sight.

Forty minutes later, Stacey and I are dressed and in the library, scouring shelves that line every wall, floor to ceiling, with leather-bound books.

"What exactly are we doing in here?" Stacey asks with a raised brow. "Unless they have an entire wall dedicated to romance, I'm not interested." She crosses her arms over her chest.

"We're here to talk. I'm not sure if our rooms are safe," I admit.

"Safe from?"

"From being overheard. This place might not be any better, but I'm hoping it is. We need to do some digging. Lawrence is here to protect the place and something valuable in Julian's absence. We need to figure out what it is."

"Their father's dead body?" Stacey suggests, parroting my earlier thoughts.

I purse my lips. "Maybe, but I don't think so."

"What's the plan?" she asks, sounding bored.

"Let's start by searching for house plans, something that shows us every room. That could help us navigate where to start looking."

"Is this going to get us killed?" Stacey asks with wide eyes.

"No. I won't get you killed. Anywhere that's off limits, I'll search myself."

"Great." She throws up her hands. "So, you'll just get yourself killed."

"I'm not going to set out to, but I need to know what's going on here."

"Can't you just be content, Marina? You've hit the vampire lottery here. Julian seems like a good guy, Katina is hysterical, you're fed, clothed, not hurt or bitten . . . what more could you want? All things considered, I think you have it pretty damn good here. If we can't be home, at least we have each other."

"For one month, Stacey. Julian only got Marcellus to agree to one month."

Stacey goes still, her face growing pale.

"Maybe we can find what his father was hiding. With that, we can barter with the Council for our freedom."

I have no plans to barter with the Council. They're evil and would likely end humanity, but I need to give Stacey a reason to go along with this.

She sighs. "Fine. I'll help."

We go in separate directions, Stacey searching the far-right stacks of shelves, while I go left. After an hour of finding nothing but book after book of poetry, I descend the ladder and slide down to a sitting position. My head falls back into the shelf. "Ouch," I groan.

"Find anything?" I ask Stacey.

"Nothing. They're all history books over here."

I sigh, feeling as though this entire idea was pointless. Not that we had anything better to do. I'm about to suggest we head back to my room and clean up for lunch, when the large mahogany desk that sits in the middle of the room catches my attention.

Standing, I walk toward it as though it's beckoning me. I open drawer after drawer, rifling through the papers to find nothing of significance. My gut tells me not to stop. Pulling open the bottom drawer, I find it empty save for an emerald-green decorative box embellished with ruby jewels. It sits in the palm of my hand, heavy and awkward. It's so familiar—like something I once owned—something I lost. The top pops open in my hands and I'm disappointed to find it empty.

Why would Julian or his father have something so insignificant from my home? It doesn't even make sense. There's no way it's mine. I probably had something similar to it at some point. Lowering it to its place, my hand hits the bottom of the drawer. The reverberating sound is deep, as if the drawer is hollow beneath. My hand slides across the wood, looking for a catch, but the wood slides backward, unveiling a secret compartment.

"Stacey," I hiss. "Come here."

She comes to my side, peering down at me.

"What did you find?"

I pull a worn, brown leather journal from the dark crevice.

Standing, I place the journal on top of the desk and open it to the first page.

A̲p̲r̲i̲l̲ 1994

Something has changed. Julian and Lawrence are filled with joy. Everything from their birth on has been overshadowed by the thirst. I don't know that I've ever seen them happy. At the same time, Marcellus has fallen into a deep despair. He hasn't left his chambers for weeks. The last I saw him; he was disheveled and crazed. He said it felt like his heart was being ripped out.

Could it be? Could the legends be true?

I s̲k̲i̲p̲ to the next page, eager to see if it speaks of the legend referenced on the last page.

J̲u̲n̲e̲ 2000

Lawrence came to me the other day and asked if he could be excused to take an extended trip. When I questioned where he was going, he said the Midwest. Why would he feel compelled to go to the Midwest of all places? More concerning, Julian also made an off-handed comment about wanting to visit Ohio. What could make two brothers wish to visit an area that neither have ever been before or shown an interest in? A place with very little to attract them. I wonder. Could it be happening?

October 2000

I saw them. They were asleep, curled up in their beds. The smell of their blood pumping through their veins made it almost impossible to linger for long. If they are the key, draining them of their blood would not be wise. There were only two, though. I'm undecided as to whether these children could be the answer to our family's survival, but I have hope. I found Lawrence nearby, which means one of their blood is beckoning him. I would've stayed longer, but one woke, seeing me. I fled—like the coward I am. I took a souvenir. I'm not sure why.

When I finish reading the last entry, my breathing is heavy. So many coincidences—Ohio, two girls, a vampire waking a child—I can't dismiss the possibility. Could he have been watching me?

"Does any of this mean anything?" Stacey asks.

"I don't know yet, but I think we're getting close to something."

Closing the journal, I reflect on the words. Julian's father's journal admits that he and Lawrence were in Ohio. I think it's time I get to know Lawrence Bellamy a little better.

CHAPTER 20

Stacey and I eat in silence.

I've been thinking about all the reasons why the Bellamys might have been drawn to Ohio—and I keep coming up short.

A slurping sound grates on my nerves. Out of the corner of my eye, I see Stacey with her spoon positioned in front of her lips. Lawrence and I exchange glances. His brow is tilted upward in amusement, while my eyes are narrowed in on Stacey. She's one of the most poised people I've ever met. The sucking of the soup is very unlike her.

"Everything all right, love?" Lawrence asks Stacey.

Her head lifts, and the spoon comes to rest atop the bowl.

"Fine. Why?"

"Do you have something against that soup?" Lawrence smirks.

"Oh." She tilts her head back in a laugh. "Was that awkward? No more than the silence in this room. Can somebody please start a damn conversation?"

I snort, then quickly try to smother it with my arm. I've

only known her for a short time, but one thing is for sure—she doesn't hold back, no matter the company she keeps.

"I apologize. I've been distracted."

"The party?" I offer.

"Indeed. It shall be a fantastic night." Lawrence beams. "I've invited twenty of the New Orleans elite to dine and dance with us at my home. Opulence is the theme."

Stacey and I smile because Lawrence's excitement is infectious.

"What can we do to help?" Stacey asks, eager to help party plan.

I'm also interested in what lengths a vampire goes to in order to host a dinner party with humans.

"Mostly, I'd love some suggestions on the menu. Everything else is done. I was hoping to have a few hours to get to know you better."

"Bacon-wrapped shrimp, chicken skewers, egg rolls, mini quiche, crab cakes, and a massive dessert table." Stacey rattles off, obviously having food on the brain.

"What kind of desserts?" Lawrence prods with a hint of a smile.

"All the desserts." Stacey says matter-of-factly.

I laugh. "Lawrence, you'll have to excuse us. We've been deprived of sweets of late."

"Please, call me Law. As for the deprivation of baked treats, I will fix that."

Stacey and I both smile.

The lull in the conversation gives way for my thoughts to wander to Julian and where he might be.

"Will Julian be back soon?" I ask, knowing that Katina said it would be a week, but hoping it'll lead to some information.

"I'm afraid not until the end of the week. He has quite the drive ahead of him."

"Drive?" I press.

"He's in Seattle, dealing with some pressing issues." Law provides an answer, but he doesn't elaborate. I should leave it be. A smart girl would enjoy the freedoms she's been given, the food she's allowed to eat, and the life that has yet to be snuffed, but not me, not now. I go for it.

"What is he doing in Seattle?"

Law puts his fork down, grabs his napkin from his lap, and gingerly wipes his mouth.

"There are some things I'm not at liberty to discuss."

My eyes remain on his, not backing down.

He huffs in exasperation but acquiesces.

"He's helping new bites transition. In cities, vampires are often created and left to wreak havoc on an unsuspecting urban area. Julian has made it his mission to step in when an issue arises and the death toll begins to mount. Many times, a city will think they have a serial killer on their hands. They aren't wrong—it's just not a human."

My stomach flips at the thought of Julian stepping in to essentially tame a wild vampire. He's saving lives and the thought has my heart softening where he's concerned. If he wasn't there, more innocent bystanders would die. Admiration for a vampire is not something I ever thought I'd possess—yet I do.

"There was an outbreak in Seattle?" Stacey asks. "I have an aunt who lives there."

He shakes his head. "Seattle is our home base to rehab new bites. It's something Julian set up when the first big outbreak occurred on the West Coast."

"Wow. That's . . . pretty cool of Julian," Stacey says, glancing at me for my take.

I nod. "It truly is."

"He's quite remarkable, my brother," Law remarks with a

proud smile. "I only wish I could be there to help him. Alas, I'm on guard duty."

Which brings me to my next topic of discussion.

"What exactly are you guarding, Law?"

He grins. "That, Marina, will have to remain my secret." He winks at me.

For now, I won't press. He was good enough to fill us in on Julian's whereabouts. That's a win for today.

"Let me ask you ladies, if you could do anything today, what would you do? Mind you, it has to be on this property."

Glancing out the window, I see the overcast gray sky threatens rain and eliminates all possibility of going outdoors.

"I'd love to watch TV," Stacey says hopefully.

I nod my head in agreement. Television would be amazing.

"That can be arranged. I need to finish up some last-minute details for the party, then we shall watch a show."

Stacey squeals in delight, and all the while my mind is hundreds of miles away on the West Coast with Julian.

"Let's revisit the evidence," Stacey suggests, while we wait for Law to come get us for the show.

"The journal. That's all we found, and it gives very little away."

"Recap what it said. Paraphrase, please," she insists.

My eyes lift heavenward.

"In April of 1994, something happened to the boys. Julian and Law had a rebirth of sorts, while Marcellus didn't leave his room. Six years later, Law wanted to go on an adventure and their father questioned whether it had something to do with the legend."

Her brow lifts in question.

"Legend? What legend?

"No idea. I've heard Lawrence and Julian reference a legend before, but I don't know what it is.

"Strange," she says, deep in thought. "You lived in Ohio. You saw vampires. This has to be connected to you, right?"

Inhale. Exhale.

"I don't know," I admit. At the same time, there are a lot of questions. "I awoke one night to a vampire at the end of my bed. After reading the journal and considering everything, I wonder—could it have been Julian's father? What if it was me he was talking about? Or Maggie?"

Stacey remains quiet for a couple of minutes. Whether she doesn't know what to say or is deliberating what this could mean, I can only guess.

"Why didn't he kill you?" she asks.

My mouth forms a straight line and my eyes squint. Something pokes at my psyche, just out of reach.

"I don't know, but we have to figure out what this legend is."

"Legend?" Lawrence says from the open doorway.

Stacey's eyes widen at Law's voice. He overheard us talking, so now would be the time to press for information.

"Is there some vampire legend, Law?" Stacey asks.

He walks in with his hands clasped behind his back. His blond hair is pulled back into a low ponytail, making him look like a modern-day Thor.

"You'd rather discuss things of myth than watch reruns of *Castle*?" he asks, brow raised and dimple appearing.

"Nope. I'm over it. Let's watch it," Stacey chirps, eliciting a scowl from me.

Oh, how quick she is to turn away when we are so close. Something deep within tells me that Law will tell.

"Just a few questions, Stacey. Then we'll watch."

She huffs and crosses her arms, but ultimately allows me to continue.

I understand her need to do something normal, but our lives aren't normal anymore.

We need to embrace the change and uncover everything we can. If we don't, there is no hope of her returning home someday.

"Tell us, please."

He seems to consider my request for a minute. Is he forbidden from talking about vampire legends?

"Every Born has a familiar—or so they say."

"A familiar?" My eyes squint in confusion. "What's that?"

"It's a vampire's one true blood match. If I were to find mine and drink from her, I'd come into more of my powers—what those are, I haven't a clue. It is said if my match drank from me, she'd have all of my abilities as well. That's really all I've been told." He narrows his eyes. "Why the interest in familiars?"

I can't tell him I was snooping and uncovered his father's journal, yet I don't want to get Julian in trouble either. What if he wasn't supposed to tell me about it? While I'm contemplating what to say, Stacey opens her mouth.

"We have reason to believe your father might've been stalking Marina and her sister, Maggie. The only thing that makes sense—because she's still breathing—is that she has something to do with this legend."

I shoot daggers in Stacey's direction, but I don't miss Lawrence's reaction. His eyes widen before he schools his features.

"I don't know. It seems unlikely. If, for example, Julian was your match, he would be drawn to you in ways you couldn't understand. Besides, you're not a triplet. Our perfect matches would have to be triplets."

Stacey's eyes meet mine.

The air whooshes from my body. *Triplets.* My stomach turns while my mind races with the possibilities. This whole time, were we being watched by their father because he thought we were the legendary familiars to his sons? No. It's ridiculous. *More ridiculous than seeing vampires?* Nothing about my life has ever made sense. It's not too far-fetched to believe that a vampire could've mistaken us for the key to his family's survival, but he was wrong.

I don't hold any special powers, and Maggie is dead. If the legends were true and we were the legends, another brother would be broken, just like Marcellus. Yet, here is a perfectly sane Lawrence, and Julian doesn't appear to be affected.

Law sets up the television in my room and Stacey watches with rapt attention, not saying another word. Perhaps she desperately needs to process all of this. Or maybe both of them have forgotten that I am a triplet. I can't concentrate on anything other than what Law has said. The truth is, a part of me aches to be something special—something more than a mundane human.

Stacey appears to be in her happy place, curled up in my bed, watching the television. All the while, Law's steady gaze never wavers from me. He sees too much.

"Marina . . . Marina!" Stacey yells across the room, garnering my attention. "Look." She nods her head toward the TV screen.

A news reporter with long dark hair, wearing a tight black pencil skirt and white blouse, talks animatedly into a microphone.

"Jerry, I'm here just outside of Toledo, Ohio, where a small village has banded together to look for clues in the disappearance of a third young girl this year. The town's population is only twelve hundred, so this string of bizarre events has rocked their small community. They are now in search of a serial abductor, and Mayor Callum Stahl urges residents to stay vigilant."

I listen to the reporter, but my eyes are fixed on the photo on the screen. My abduction has made the national news.

"Marina Drake went missing almost two months ago, only six months after the disappearance of her twin sister, Magdalena Drake, who was last seen jumping from Widow's Peak—a cliff overlooking the river."

My heart thumps as Maggie's picture flashes across the screen. Still, after everything I've been through, the loss of her cuts deep. The screen goes back to the reporter.

"Just last week, the town suffered yet another shocking disappearance, when twenty-four-year-old Shannon Cline went missing after visiting the home of Maggie and Marina Drake. Shannon's mother, Susan Cline, said she went to check on her friends' parents, Lena and Kolton Drake, and never returned. Shannon is the niece of Senator Thom Cline of Michigan, and he's offering a reward for any information the public might have that leads to her whereabouts. Investigators are asking for any tips in helping locate Marina and Shannon. Local law enforcement believes that the fall from Widow's Peak took Maggie's life, although a body was never recovered. This is Annabel Starr reporting live from Liberty, Ohio. Back to you, Jerry."

I'm numb. *Shannon is missing.* This can't be happening.

"Marina, do you know her?" Stacey asks in a whisper.

I nod, unable to speak the words. Why? Why would anyone take her?

My head turns to Law. "Could this be the auction? Law, you have to find out. She's my best friend. Please."

His eyes are narrowed on the screen; he's no longer looking at me.

"That made the national news," Stacey says. "Your people are getting sloppy."

"They are not my people," Law declares. "I'll get to the bottom of this, Marina. You have my word."

A sweat breaks out across my forehead, hands shaking and legs bouncing with unrestrained nerves, as I do my best to not break something. What could have happened to Shannon? Is she all right? Have vampires taken her? Could she be dead?

The last thought makes my heart thump loudly and my throat go dry.

Stacey comes to me, pulling me into her side. "Law will find her," she promises, petting my hair in a soothing motion. He has to. If they have her, this is my fault—again.

CHAPTER 21

By Sunday night, Julian has come back and Law has returned to his home. I'm pacing my room, waiting for word about Shannon, when my door creaks open and Katina pops her head around the doorframe. "May I come in?" she asks, sounding unsure.

I motion with my hand for her to enter.

"Where's Julian? Has he come to the estate yet?" I spit questions rapid fire, wanting to speak with him immediately. If Law hasn't found anything out about Shannon, Julian will.

"He's at his home," she says, tipping her head up and watching me closely.

"Go get him," I demand. "I need to speak with him now."

Her head moves back and forth. "He's asked me to come retrieve you. Stacey is dining in her room tonight. Lawrence left the television for her, so she'll be entertained all evening."

She doesn't move, but continues to stand here, staring at me.

"What are you waiting for? Let's go." I walk past her,

heading out the door, when her next question stops me in my tracks.

"Is something happening between you and the Crown?"

I turn slowly, not sure what to say to Katina. She's been good to me—a friend when I've needed one—but right now, she almost sounds angry. "Nothing is happening between us. My friend is missing, and I need his help in finding her."

Katina's eyes narrow as she bites the inside of her cheeks. "Be careful, Marina. This world is dangerous—especially for a human. You don't want to get yourself caught in the crossfire of the warring families. It won't end well."

"Why does it sound like you're threatening me, Kat?"

Her eyes widen and her mouth flops open like a fish. "H-how could you think that? I'm only looking out for you, Marina. The Crown's appeal is not lost on me—I am a woman who prefers the company of men." My eyebrow lifts at this declaration. There was a time I questioned that. She waves a hand at me. "I enjoy all company. But I do prefer a di—" My hand shoots up.

"I got it. All about men. Noted."

She sighs. "My point is that I've seen the way he looks at you, Marina. I've only seen that starry-eyed gaze once before, and it did not end well."

My stomach turns, and I feel like I could be sick.

"See . . . and then there's you," she says, pointing at me. "You look like a lovesick, emphasis on sick, puppy. I mention another woman and you get all woozy. You care for him."

I swallow, nose scrunching up at her words.

"I do not. I mean . . . I care about what happens to him, but that does not equal *care* care."

She rolls her eyes. "Lie to yourself all you want, girly, but you've got it bad and you haven't even put the pieces together yet."

Could she be right? I feel off-kilter around Julian, but that could very well be magic. I've seen him use it before on others.

You know damn well he isn't using it on you.

It's what I've feared from the beginning. I've gone and caught feelings for him.

Yes, he's otherworldly gorgeous, but it's more than that. He's kind and patient. He's gone out of his way to help me and my friend. There's a pull to him I've felt since day one, against all my better judgment. But he's proven to be different from the rest of his kind.

"Oh, Marina." Katina's voice is full of concern. She's witnessed me working out my feelings and knows where I've landed.

I look up at her. "Julian and I come from two different worlds, and I know that. I'll deal with whatever these feelings are later, but right now none of that matters. I have to try to help Shannon."

She blows out a breath. "If you say so."

I nod. "Please take me to him."

I've been over the details of the news report three times with Julian.

"Does this have something to do with me?" I question, feeling like it has to. Why would vampires continue to stalk girls from the same small town? Easy prey? Perhaps, but my gut tells me it's more.

"Maybe," he admits. "But I don't know. I haven't run the auction. That's Marcellus."

"Take me to him," I demand, ready for a showdown with the creepy brother. "I have to know if his men have her. If this has something to do with me, I need to see him. She isn't involved with this."

"We don't know if this has anything to do with you. By confronting Marcellus, we are only opening up Pandora's Box," Julian says. "This needs to be handled with care. If they have her and we go about it the wrong way, it will ensure her death."

I grab at my hair, pulling at the roots, frustrated and tired, yet ready for a fight.

"What do I do, Julian? How do I help her?"

He pulls me into his arms, blanketing me in the comfort that only he can provide.

"We wait. We strategize. And when the time is right, we act." He lifts my chin so that our eyes meet. "Can you trust me with this? Let me handle it and keep you both safe."

A tear glides down my cheek. The feeling of helplessness is so intense, it threatens to crumble me.

"I trust you," I promise. "But please act fast. Her family are good people. They don't deserve this."

He kisses the top of my head. "Very few do."

With my head plastered against his chest, I listen to the steady rhythm of his heart. For all the differences, there are some things that are the same. We both bleed. Our hearts both beat. We both have the ability to feel deeply. I'll hold on to those. His willingness to help me has my heart swelling and emotion I'm not ready to entertain taking center stage. Julian Bellamy makes it so easy to fall.

Trust your instincts, Marina.

Maggie's voice calls to me and I shiver knowing she's here even when she's not. It tears me apart, but comforts at the same time.

"Marina, I . . ." His words trail off.

"Don't say anything. I don't want to talk any more. I want to not think about any of it. Just for a while."

We sit in silence for several minutes. It feels so good in Julian's arms. *Safe.*

"Come with me."

Julian's house is magnificent. Two staircases lead up to a veranda overlooking the foyer.

A giant chandelier hangs above, reflecting light as it hits each crystal. The floors are white marble with pale gray swirls throughout. You'd think the elegance of the place would make it stuffy, but the décor throughout makes it feel like a home.

He leads me around one more corner and through a door to a game room.

"Seriously? You have a man cave?"

His brow furrows. "Man cave?"

"Julian. You may be centuries old, but you can't tell me you don't know what a man cave is."

"My time amongst humans has been very limited due to my place in the family. Unlike Law, I haven't been privy to all the luxuries that the years have brought. I've been sheltered, if you will."

How sad. It does explain why he seems so much more formal than Lawrence. To think of Julian shut off from the world makes me angry. What were they trying to do? Limit his interaction with humans so his empathy would be stifled? *Of course.*

"This is a man cave. It's a room filled with things that men enjoy."

"Man cave," he tests out the name. "I like it."

"So, what do we have in here?" I say, walking around and taking in the various games and collectibles. Air hockey, foosball, table tennis, pool, a television—you name it, it's here.

"Seriously?" I say, confounded by this room. It's completely unlike Julian. Maybe I don't know him at all.

"I guess you can say it's my way of trying to play at being human," he shrugs. "It's weird, I know. It's never been used."

"It's not," I say, understanding more than I can even explain. It's much like my attempt at drinking games. I had little interest, but for a chance to feel normal—or what's seemingly normal—I participated.

"Want to play?" Julian asks, pointing toward the table tennis setup.

I have little to no experience playing table tennis. There is a very real possibility that I can't even hit the ball. I'm about to divert his attention elsewhere when he calls me out.

"Don't be scared. I'll teach you."

I roll my eyes. "Who says I need to be taught?" I ask, feigning skill.

He smirks. "You have no idea how to play. It's written all over your face."

"Fine. Teach me," I acquiesce.

He runs through the rules a couple of times until I feel comfortable enough to start.

"It sounds to me like you've been around humans plenty, if you know all about this," I say, motioning to the table.

"I was taught by a friend ages ago. It's been a while since I've played, but we did often back then. Let's hit the ball back and forth for a few minutes until you get the hang of it," he suggests. He hits the ball onto my side and I swat it back over the net toward him. "Good job," he praises, eliciting a smile from me.

Several minutes go by as we're volleying back and forth—or so Julian calls it—before I'm finally ready to play.

"Okay, let's do this."

He serves the ball to me and I miss . . . pathetically.

"It's all right. Try again," he says, trying to encourage me.

I send the ball back so that he can serve again. He bounces it once and sends it back toward me. I swing and this time the paddle flies out of my hand and slams into a wall, making a loud clunk. My hands come to my mouth. I've managed to put a nice dent into his drywall.

"Oh my God. I'm so sorry, Julian."

A grunt breaks through his chest, followed by bubbling laughter. He finds this funny.

"Stop laughing. I nearly put a hole in your wall," I say.

His head falls back and he barks, he's laughing so hard. My arms cross over my chest and I groan in irritation. When he finally stops laughing, he wipes a stray tear away from his eye.

"I don't care about my wall, Marina. It was your face. You were so serious when you swung. I'm glad it was a ball and not my head in your path. You looked positively wicked."

No matter how hard I try to contain it, a chuckle breaks through my own lips. Julian mimicking my face is hysterical. I do have a tendency of going overboard, and I'm sure his impression isn't too far off.

"Maybe we should do something less dangerous," Julian says, pointing toward the television.

"A movie sounds good," I reply, ready to be done with table tennis. I'll leave games to people who are good at them.

We spend the rest of the evening curled up on his couch watching some black-and-white movie that I can't remember the name of. It doesn't matter. I'm content. We're not touching, but the close proximity of our bodies isn't lost on me. I can feel the heat coming off him. His deep breaths make my heart skip a beat or two. Julian and I exchange glances occasionally, but I do my best to turn away, not wanting him to see how he affects me. Feelings that don't make sense bubble inside of me, threatening to burst out. I stuff them down. Nothing good can come from loose lips.

CHAPTER 22

"You're such a witch," Stacey says, pulling a brush through my tangled hair.

I wince as the brush gets stuck on a snarl.

"I offered my spot to you and you refused. You don't get to be bitter."

Watching her in the large mirror, I see her smile. She isn't really mad, just a bit jealous. I don't blame her. I would be too. A night out on the town with Julian Bellamy sounds like heaven. The past week has crawled at a snail's pace while I waited for him to get back.

"As much as I wanted out of here, I think you and Julian need some alone time." She wiggles her eyebrows suggestively insinuating more than a platonic dinner date.

"You're insane. There's absolutely nothing going on between Julian and me." On my end, there is attraction, but that's where it starts and stops. He's simply too handsome for his own good.

Liar.

"It's ridiculous. He's a vampire," I add, to make my case. I'm not sure who I'm trying to convince at this point.

"A sexy one," Stacey says off-handedly.

"Not human."

The truth is, no matter how attracted I may be to Julian, we would never make sense. "While he never ages, I'll grow old and wrinkled."

She pouts her lips. "Who said anything about the future? I was merely suggesting you lose that V-card."

I groan at her lack of decorum in bringing up my chastity.

"I'm not interested in losing my virginity to anyone, especially not someone I have no future with."

Her lips thin into a straight line. "I hate to be the bearer of bad news, but there's a good chance you don't have a future, period. Don't miss out on your chance to experience something mind-blowing because you're stuck in ways that no longer matter."

She's right. We've been so secluded here that the auction and evil vampires seem like a nightmare from long ago. Julian has alluded to the Council trying to overthrow him. What happens if they do? *You'll die like the others.*

"You're missing something," I divulge. "Let's say I was all about your absurd suggestion, and I plan to try to seduce him. He'd have to want the same thing."

She throws her head back and laughs. I scrunch my nose, trying to piece together what's so funny.

"Oh, he wants the same thing. Trust me." She chuckles again. "There's one thing I have learned over the years, and it's how to read a man. And that man can't keep his eyes off you."

My cheeks turn warm. A swelling begins in my belly and works its way up my chest. *Could she be right?*

"Ladies, ladies. I've brought some goodies," Katina calls from the doorway, entering with a flourish and carrying a garment bag. "I brought you something more appropriate to wear. If you're going to be seen in New Orleans, you need to look like you belong."

Her eyes trail up my current dress.

"Right now, you look like you stepped out of a time machine circa 1779."

It's my turn to purse my lips.

"Thanks to you and your sense of humor," I scowl.

"Who? Me?" she asks, acting like she has no clue what I'm talking about. I let it go. I'll never win with Katina. She doesn't even realize how eccentric she is.

I'm just glad she recognizes that these clothes won't do in the outside world. Maybe this is the start of her actually coming to terms with the century outside of these walls. I'd love to see a massive clothing upgrade when I get back.

"You went shopping?" Stacey says with a hint of longing in her voice.

"I do enjoy it every now and then." Katina perks up. "Plus, I have a friend that works at a boutique in town. It's been a while since I paid her a visit. She was getting lonely." She wiggles her eyebrows.

"All done," Stacey says, patting my shoulders. "Time to get you dressed. Cinderella can't be late for the ball." I stand and walk to the bed where Katina has laid the garment bag. Unzipping it, I find a black knee-length dress with a crisscross front and pleats. I pick it up and feel the fabric beneath my fingers. It feels comfortable. Cotton or polyester, or maybe both. It's casual and cute. In the bag is a pair of knee-high brown boots and a brown bag. It's covered in Ls and Vs, which means nothing to me.

"Oh my God. Is that the Artsy?" Stacey squeals, getting a smile of appreciation from Katina.

"Obviously. Louis and I are very close."

I watch as the two go on and on about the bag as if it's the best thing they've ever seen.

I've never been one to care about fashionable things. Especially not accessories. My family was lucky to keep the roof over our head. We certainly didn't have extra to spend on insignificant things.

Continuing through the garment bag, I find another bag that looks like jewelry, dangling from the hanger. I go to pull it off and Katina slaps my hand away.

"Put on your dress first. We can worry about this later."

My eyes cross and I stick my tongue out at her.

"Ever the boss," I say teasingly.

I slip on the dress and allow my wavy locks to fall down my back. Understated and classy—I love it. I'm not overdone, like at the auction. Katina and Stacey did a great job between the clothes and the hair and makeup.

Katina checks her watch and tsks. "We're running out of time. Come here." She pulls something out of the bag that she took away from me earlier and goes to stand behind me. When her hands come around to the front of my neck, my blood runs cold. It's a collar, like the slaves at the auction wore.

"What is that?" I ask, knowing full well, but wanting her to admit what she's doing.

"It's a precaution, Marina."

I step away from her. "No. Absolutely not. That was not part of the deal."

"Marina, if you're going off of this estate, you have to wear this. There's no way around it."

"Then I'm not going," I say, growing angrier by the minute. That collar reminds me of the woman who did my hair being dragged off to likely die. It stands for everything wrong in this world.

I sit on the bed, cross my arms over my chest, and sulk. I

should've known there would be stipulations. But I never thought he would actually try to collar me.

"Are you seriously going to refuse to go out of this place just because you have to wear that?" Stacey asks, looking annoyed by my actions.

"Stacey, this is what all of those servants at the auction were wearing. It's what they use to control people. I already promised I wouldn't run. If he doesn't trust me, then maybe he shouldn't take me."

Stacey shrugs her shoulders. "Suit yourself. I'll go in your place," she says.

"You stubborn girl," Katina chastises, walking out the door and slamming it shut behind her.

"I'm sorry, Stacey, but I just can't do it. I have done my part and stayed inside these walls. I have forgiven Julian for his part in all of this, but this is asking too much. Expecting me to be okay with this is too much. It's a reminder of all the other girls who are being tortured right now or are already dead. I won't wear it."

Ten minutes later, there's a knock on the door.

"Come in," I call out.

Julian peeks his head around the corner. "May I come in?"

I motion for him to enter. He comes to my bedside, sitting next to me. He doesn't say anything for a second. "Marina, I never asked Katina to bring the collar to you. I had planned on talking to you about it myself."

"Why? You had to know I'd refuse."

He sighs.

"The chance you'd put up a fight was high, but you have to know that it's very dangerous for me to take you into New Orleans without one."

I huff.

"It has nothing to do with me trying to control you, and

everything to do with the way it looks to anyone we encounter. If the Council sees you without it, it's bad news for us both."

"They won't see me," I bite.

Julian sighs heavily. "New Orleans is riddled with vampires and people who work for the Council. Council members themselves frequent the place. They would smell your blood from a mile away, and the first question they would have is why I would walk around without having you in a collar."

I narrow my eyes at Julian. *What isn't he saying?*

As if reading my mind, he continues, "It would look as though I'm weak. That I've ignored my better judgment because of a human girl. We've been over this."

"Am I to believe that no vampire has ever enjoyed the company of a human without a collar? Couldn't I just be having dinner with you under the assumption that you are a man and not a vampire?"

"It's not that simple. As I said before, you're marked. Being marked gives you different qualities. Things you can't see, but vampires can. A vampire would know you came from the auction, and the fact that I'm allowing you to roam free wouldn't bode well for me if it got out."

"So, we're at an impasse."

"Can we compromise? Could we remove the batteries, and have you wear it? That way, from afar, it would look like I'm following policy? If someone gets close enough and notices, I'll deal with the consequences if they arise."

I don't like it. The idea doesn't seem like a compromise to me at all. He's still expecting me to wear a symbol of the very center of my abduction. However, I also can acknowledge I'm being selfish and difficult. I'm trying to give, but it's difficult. There are some things I'll never be able to agree to without a fight.

"I want you to join me, Marina. I've been looking forward to this all day."

"You have?" His words warm my insides and help to drop the wall I've erected in the past few minutes. I might not love his compromise, but at least he's trying. If he can give a little, so can I.

"I'm sorry. Old habits," I say sheepishly. "I'll wear it. With batteries. You've explained the reasons and it's unfair of me to chance any of this."

"Thank you, Marina," he says, sounding relieved. "I brought you something," he smiles. "May I?" he says, gesturing to my hand.

I nod.

From his pocket he pulls a diamond tennis bracelet.

"It's beautiful," I muse. He clasps it around my wrist and I can't help but stare. It's vintage, with diamonds all the way around. I wonder whose bracelet this was, as it is definitely old. Beautiful, timeless, but ancient. I don't ask, for fear I won't like the answer. I'm determined to turn this night around and enjoy myself. It's not every day I get to break loose.

I stand from the bed, pulling Julian with me. "Let's go on our date."

He smiles boyishly. "Date," he grins. "I like that."

CHAPTER 23
JULIAN

We're driving through the countryside and it takes everything in me to keep my eyes on the road and off her. There's something different about her. She looks younger. *Alive*.

There's been something brewing between us since the auction, but it's not simple attraction. She holds some power over me, and I've been trying to uncover its source ever since. I want to tell her all that I've learned about vampire lore and my suspicions concerning her, but I can't. Not yet.

Even I don't fully understand it.

Her head is resting back on the seat, eyes closed and carefree. I love seeing her like this. I wish I could always make her this happy. Tough times lie ahead for us. When Stacey leaves, it'll break Marina. They've formed a bond through their experience that is unlike any friendship she's ever had. If I could keep Stacey safe without bringing the Council down on us, I would.

Marc won't budge. I never thought he would. He only agreed to a month because I swore to attend two auctions next month. I only agreed because I've heard murmurings that they've abducted twice as many girls. They're sitting in cells,

God knows where. If there is a second auction, the Council will be too preoccupied with the planning to keep tabs on me. Money is more important than anything—with the exception of blood.

With them off my back, I can recruit twice as many new bites for my own army. Now that I know how to reach the small human part of them that remains, it's taking half the time to train them. The more I train and the more who swear their allegiance to me, the better. I have to act fast, because I know it's only a matter of time before Marc makes a move. He's becoming desperate.

I have to keep humans safe. *I have to keep Marina safe.*

CHAPTER 24

We're in the heart of New Orleans in a restaurant that has an old-world charm. White linen tablecloths adorn the tables. Beautiful chandeliers hang overhead in various locations. Waiters scurry about the room wearing head-to-toe black. The room is dim, lit by the glow of candles. It's romantic.

Julian has ordered a bottle of the best merlot they stock, and we're sharing a side of gnocchi, waiting for our dinner plates to be served. I look up at Julian from under my lashes, and my breath catches. Every time I see him, he's more impressive. Strong jaw, steely eyes, and that smile. God, that smile does things to my stomach. Nobody before him has ever come close to giving me butterflies, let alone whatever this is. For the first time in my life, I feel like a woman. A woman who is struggling to deny the feelings taking root for the man across from her.

It's foolish. A childish dream. We live different lives and we come from different worlds, but I can't help but yearn for a connection with him. I'm pulled from my reverie by Julian's smooth, masculine voice.

"Tell me more about your life, Marina."

And just like that, the spell is broken. Nothing is less sexy than my life pre-abduction.

"If you don't want to talk about it, you don't have to," Julian amends, sounding unsure and concerned. He's taken me into his home and kept me safe, so I feel it's only fair I share a bit more of myself with him.

"I told you about one of us triplets dying at birth." Julian nods, not saying anything, allowing me to continue. "After that, my mother became paranoid and delusional. She claimed our sister was taken from her."

"Grief is different for every person. I'm sure your sister dying was traumatic for your mother. Especially with all the hormones coursing through her at the time," Julian offers.

"It was more than that. She believed the hospital had faked Molly's death and her baby was stolen from her. My entire life, my mother wavered between helicopter parenting and months of isolation and neglect."

"Why did she think Molly was taken?" Julian's brows are furrowed.

"No clue. Nothing she ever said made sense."

"There are a lot of things in this world that do not make sense, Marina. You of all people should know that now."

The words sting, but only because I have never considered that my mother might have actually had good reasons to believe what she believed. There was a body—I know that much. My father said many times through the years that they buried Molly. He held her dead body in his hands. But what if something did happen that led my mother to think otherwise?

"The truth?" I wince, because it isn't favorable for me. "I never listened. Nor did I ask." For so many years, I tried to make people trust that I was seeing monsters. Every one of them did exactly as I did to my mother. They pushed my words off as delusions. I'm here today knowing they were wrong. Could I be wrong about my mother and Molly?

"I need to speak to her, Julian. What if I can help my mom?"

He bites on the inside of his cheek, eyes hard and mouth in a straight line.

"It's dangerous. You'd be putting her in danger too, Marina. For right now, I don't think it's a good idea. She safe and getting the help she needs in Arizona."

"She probably thinks I'm dead, Julian. After everything she's been through, I'm not sure she will survive another loss."

"What if you could call her? Tell her you're all right, but you had to get away. Then she'd know you were safe. Could that be enough... for now?"

I consider his offer. If I called her and told her I was all right, I think she'd be okay—since she's now sober. Could it be the thing that sets them back in their recovery? Could it really put them in danger? I can't do that. "I think you're right. I need to keep them out of this."

He nods.

Done talking about me, I turn the tables on Julian.

"The other night, what happened that you had to run off?"

Julian looks puzzled before recognition forms on his face.

"A new bite got loose. It was the first time that's happened."

A cool wisp of dread fills me at the thought of a bloodthirsty vampire being loose in the very place I was.

"He never made it out of the basement. Bash stopped his attempt and Charlie, another guard, held him down until I was there to sedate him."

"How did you do that?" I question, not understanding what he could've done that Bash or this Charlie guy couldn't have done themselves.

"I gave him some of my blood. It has a calming effect, almost like a sedative, for other vampires. Only Borns possess those blood properties."

"He drank from you?" I ask, trying hard to keep all signs of repulsion from my features.

"From my wrist. You can't even tell if you look today," he says, lifting the sleeve of his shirt to show a perfectly unblemished wrist. "Borns have healing properties that are superhuman."

"The other vampires don't have those things?"

He shakes his head. "Not exactly. They have swift healing, strength, and speed, but nothing compared to what I possess."

His chest is puffed out in pride, and I have to smother the smirk on my face. I don't want him to think I'm poking fun. I'm not. It's just that seeing him this youthful and carefree is liberating. I don't feel like I'm with my captor, but a guy that I like. One that I want to know more about.

Our dinner comes, and we eat while discussing mundane topics. The weather in Louisiana versus Ohio, his lack of interest in politics and religion, and more importantly, the fact that he doesn't seem to have any hobbies outside of table tennis and billiards.

"No Netflix?" I cringe, not knowing how I'll survive another few weeks, let alone months, without it. It was my source of comfort when my parents had shut me out. While they spent days locked in their own prisons, high and drunk, I binged on Netflix.

"I'm afraid not." His head pops up, as if he has a brilliant idea. "I'll purchase it tomorrow. Would you like that?"

My head bobs in excitement.

"I can go shopping tomorrow and buy a larger television. You can introduce me to your favorite shows?"

"Could Stacey and I join you?" I say, lowering my head, not

wanting to see the answer before hearing it. "I feel bad that Stacey missed out on tonight, and she loves to shop. It would really brighten her mood."

"It's done. Tomorrow we'll drive into town and buy a new television and take Stacey shopping."

I squeal, before looking around in embarrassment at the eyes watching me. "Sorry," I mouth to the nearest table occupants. I receive some raised brows and a few smiles in return.

I'm acting like a child, but I can't help it. These are luxuries I thought I'd never have again, and Julian is offering them to me left and right, when I've done nothing to deserve it.

We finish up eating, Julian pays, and we're walking out the door into the cool night air of New Orleans. Swarms of people line the streets. Laughter and raised voices bring a smile to my lips. This feels normal. Without thinking twice, I grab Julian's hand in mine. He looks to me, smiling. Giving my hand a gentle squeeze, he moves us through the crowd. We walk aimlessly, Julian pointing out famous landmarks and restaurants. We stop and grab beignets for Stacey at Café du Monde and continue around the square.

Everything about tonight is wonderful, until a voice has Julian going stiff.

"Julian, wait up," a man's voice calls from behind us.

"Remain quiet. Look forward at all times unless I speak to you," Julian commands, sounding worried about whoever is approaching.

"Vzar," Julian says coldly.

"It's been some time since we've seen you around these parts. What brings you into town?"

I do as Julian said and remain still with my eyes locked forward. I'm unable to see the man that Julian converses with, but something tells me I wouldn't want to anyway.

"Dinner," he says, nodding his head in my direction. I see

this action out of the corner of my eye and have to try very hard not to react to his suggestion.

"Good catch. It's a rare occasion when a human that delectable crosses our paths," he says covetously. "Rafael will be disappointed if you don't come by the club. He was just saying the other day how different things are, now that you're in power."

His words cut through the air like a shotgun, challenging.

"Please give Rafael my apologies for missing the club this visit. I'm sure you can imagine how eager I am to . . . snack."

My stomach drops. I know he's doing this for show, but I can't help but be disturbed by it.

"If I might say, Julian, it would be very advantageous for you to show your face at Levine, especially with this human on your arm, submissive. It would show any naysayers that Julian Bellamy is the right heir."

"You speak very loosely to your king, Vzar."

"My apologies," he says, not sounding apologetic at all. "I thought we were friends. We have been for so long. I didn't think that a throne would change that."

"If only friends shared the same values they always had." Julian's voice is harsh. His words are a riddle to me.

The man's voice drops to a whisper. "Not all of us have the luxury of disappearing for years, Julian. I had my own legacy to step into. It doesn't mean my stance on things has changed, but I can't make changes from the outside."

Julian's shoulders relax, hand shooting out toward Vzar.

The man bypasses Julian's hand, pulling him into a tight man hug. I relax, hoping this means we've run into an ally.

"What's going on here? You've started bidding and taking donors?" The man sounds slightly disgusted, which bodes even better for me.

"Vzar, this is Marina. Marina, my friend, Vzar."

I look at him out the side of my eye, silently questioning whether I can break the act.

"Marina. It's fine."

I turn my head toward the other man, realizing instantly that he too is a vampire, as I suspected. I nod my head in his direction.

"The collar?" Vzar says with a laugh.

"For safety."

The guy chuckles, "Nothing ever changes with you."

"She wanted dinner and I wanted to keep her safe."

Vzar narrows his eyes, smiling at Julian, but he doesn't say anything.

"What's the word on the streets tonight?"

"I'm serious when I say you need to make an appearance, Julian. The Council is all over you, and if word gets out that you were here and didn't make an appearance, it will be another strike on a long list of strikes. They're determined to find a reason to start the proceedings to try to extract you from the title. And it doesn't help that your brother is at the forefront."

"How do I do this and keep her safe?" Julian says, looking toward me.

"You're still king. For propriety's sake, they'll all obey. The Council isn't in town, only Rafael. Say she's off limits, and she'll be off limits. If anyone steps out of place, I'll be there to help intervene. Besides, on a Friday night, the place will be teeming with humans. Her blood won't be any more potent."

Julian nods, turning to me. "I'm sorry you're in the crossfire, Marina. I shouldn't have ever brought you here."

"What's going on?"

"We have to make a pit stop at a club. It's not your normal club, Marina. It's—"

"Crazy," Vzar cuts in. "There will be vampires everywhere drinking from humans."

My eyes go wide and my face pales. "I-I can't do it. I can't watch that."

"It's not what you think. The humans that are there want to be. New Orleans is a very different town, Marina. Will you trust me?"

I nod, because I don't want to appear weak. Being in a room surrounded by vampires sounds anything but safe, but in the end, it doesn't sound like we have a choice.

I trust Julian.

He'll keep me safe. *I hope.*

Vzar leads us down a sidewalk, the crowd on the street thinning with every step we take. Eyes dart in our direction, but Julian and Vzar remain facing forward. Neither of them speaks, which doesn't help my nerves. After a while, the streetlights begin to fade, and the night swallows us whole. In alleyways, there are people making out or doing other unsavory things, but they don't pay us any mind, and we continue on.

Eventually, a large warehouse appears to our right. Julian ushers me toward it, and a feeling of dread fills me. When we get to the massive doors, Vzar bangs his fist twice. A slot opens and a pair of eyes surveys us from behind the door.

"Magnus, you ass, let us in." The man on the other side chuckles a deep, rumbling laugh and the door bangs open. Red lights and music filter out.

"Welcome to La Luxure Levine." Vzar motions with his hands for us to go first.

The moment we're through the door and it's closed on us, my senses are on overload. The room is dark. The only light comes from a few sparse candles and the red strobe lights that work around the room. A sensual bass thrums beneath my feet, snaking its way up my body. The smell of sex is heavy in the air. When my eyes adjust, the reason is evident. Bodies are everywhere, gyrating together. *This is a sex club?*

My eyes narrow in on one couple and a gasp gets caught in my throat. The man has his head in the girl's neck, drinking from her. The most concerning part is that she appears to be enjoying it. Her head is thrown back, and she's licking her lips and moaning.

"What's going on?" I ask Julian over the noise of the music.

He eyes me warily. "This is a place vampires of New Orleans come to . . . enjoy human interaction."

"What does that even mean?"

"They come here to have sex and drink," Vzar explains, not sugarcoating it at all.

My cheeks warm at the imagery. There are no exposed body parts, but hands are in places they shouldn't be in public, tongues are down throats, and moans and grunts surround me. The lust is thick in the air and it spins around me, beckoning me to succumb.

No matter how little experience I have, my body reacts. Wetness pools between my legs and there's nothing I can do to stop it. My eyes meet Julian's and his nostrils flare. *Oh God. Does he know how I'm feeling?* My breath hitches at the heat in his gaze. It's as if endorphins and oxytocin are being pumped through the room. Julian's hand shoots out, grabbing mine and pulling me toward the back.

"Are you okay?" he asks.

"I'm fine, Julian. I'm not such a prude that this would bother me. Nobody here is being tortured," I say, lifting my brow and pursing my lips. Indeed, everyone here is enjoying themselves. Immensely.

"I'm so sorry, Ma—"

His words are cut off and his eyes widen at something behind me. I turn my head to see a beautiful, exotic woman approaching. Going straight to Julian, the woman embraces him.

"Mon amour, tu es ici."

All I could make out from that was my love. I speak very little French, but the fact she called him her love makes me queasy.

"Addy, I didn't realize you were in town," Julian says affectionately. The way he looks at her—so familiar, so intimate—makes my stomach plummet. There's history there, and I'm not sure I want to know anything about it.

"I just got into town. I'm so glad to see you, Jude."

Jude. I haven't heard anyone call him that but his brother, and the smile he wears for her guts me.

I clear my throat, trying to unclog the bile lodged there.

Julian turns, remembering I'm here for the first time since Miss Exotic showed up.

"Marina, this is Adèle Dupré, a very good friend."

"Oh, Jude, don't be so casual. I'm his very best friend." She smiles widely, showcasing a row of brilliantly white teeth. Julian grins in response.

"We should dance," Adèle suggests, already making her way toward a large room where swarms of people grind their bodies together seductively. Turning to look over her shoulder, she gives Julian bedroom eyes, running her pink tongue slowly, provocatively across her lips. Julian's back straightens, eyes coming to meet mine. My eyes are narrowed, mouth dropped open in shock at her blatant perusal of him.

There is no doubt in my mind that these two have been together. Multiple times, if I had to guess.

"Go," I motion toward her. "I'll be here, trying to stay alive." My words are dramatic; no vampire has so much as looked my way since we entered this place. All of them are currently involved in some state of sexual bliss.

"Marina, I wouldn't leave you. I want *you* to dance with me."

Butterflies tickle my stomach at his words. He wants to dance with me.

"But, your friend." I motion toward a confused Adèle.

"She'll be fine. She always manages to find someone willing to dance with her," he grins.

"As for you, there will be no other dance partners." He winks and I all but fall to the floor. "But first, a drink?"

I nod, needing something to wet my parched lips.

A waiter hands me two glasses of something that's frothing.

"What is this?" I scrunch my nose at the green foam.

"Trust me, you don't want to drink that."

"What is it?" I question.

"It's called Sacristan." He takes it out of my hand. "It's a liquor of sorts."

"Drugs?" I raise my eyebrows.

"It's not illegal, not that we abide by such standards, but it will heighten your current feelings."

"How so?"

"If you're happy, it will make you joyous. If you're sad, it will make you inconsolable. If you're angry, it will make you murderous," he smirks.

"That seems a bit dangerous to give to a room full of vampires," I raise my brow.

"Here, vampires are nothing more than gluttonous and lustful. It's only dangerous for you if you show them any interest." His cheek rises in a smirk. "Like I said, not for you."

I take a look around the room, feeling more out of place than I ever have. Not because I'm surrounded my vampires, but that I'm practically in the middle of an orgy.

Vzar comes barreling up next to us.

"Incoming. You'd better start looking like you're enjoying

the place, or shit's going to get real very fast," he says, eyes wide and pointing toward the back.

Julian's eyes are mere slits. Who could be headed this way? Whoever or whatever it is, isn't good.

Vzar grabs a glass out of Julian's hand and stuffs it into mine.

"Bottoms up, Marina," he says, lifting the cup to my lips. Without thinking, I open my mouth and ingest a bit of the liquid.

"Marina," Julian says with wide eyes. "What have you done?"

CHAPTER 25

It's too late to go back now, so I tip the glass of fizzing liquid back and shudder as the rest of it slides down my throat, cold at first but gradually warming the farther it travels. When it hits my stomach, my entire body is heated. Momentary lightheadedness overcomes me, followed by a feeling of exhilaration.

"Julian, what's happening?" As much as I should be freaking out, I'm not. I'm too free to care.

"Fuck," Julian says, running his hands back through his hair. "Do you trust me to take care of you?" he asks, looking pained.

I consider his question for a moment, but in actuality, the answer is immediate.

"Yes," I say with a lazy smile. "I trust you implicitly."

He nods, tipping his own drink back. With all the cares in the world gone, and a slight buzz blanketing me, I allow my body to sway with the music.

"Will I be hung over tomorrow?" I ask out of curiosity, because everything I know about alcohol has always included a day of headaches and blackout curtains—at least where my mother is concerned.

"No. This is not your typical alcohol, Marina. There's a witch bartending."

My gaze flies to the bar. A male that looks younger than thirty, sporting a Mohawk and a nose ring, looks up and smirks at me, as if he heard our entire conversation.

"A witch?"

"Like I said, there are many things out there that humans don't know about."

I nod my head, believing him.

"Come, let's dance," he says, grabbing my hand and dragging me out onto the crowded dance floor.

Perspiration, perfume, and some other smell linger in the air all around us. The lurid music pumps beneath my feet, making the whole room feel like it's pulsing. Julian pulls me in close and my body sinks effortlessly against his. We move in time to the music and a sheen of sweat quickly builds on my neck. My hand comes up, lifting my hair, allowing the air to cool my body. Julian's eyes heat, looking at me like he may devour me. *Please.*

Bending, he runs his nose up the curve of my neck. I shiver at his touch, wanting so much more.

"You smell amazing, Marina," he says into my ear.

I wonder if he's referring to the perfume Katina bought for me or something different. At the brush of his lips on my skin, I lean in closer, demanding more. His teeth nip at my skin and a moan escapes my mouth. I should be scared, given he's a vampire, but I'm not.

"I don't think you know how badly I want to kiss you," Julian admits, and my knees go weak. The voice in my head is screaming, *Do it.* But my mouth won't cooperate. I simply whimper in response.

He pushes me back gently. He smirks at whatever he finds. Clearly, my feelings are written plainly all over my face. Pulling me in again, he wraps his large hands around my hips, sliding them up and down over the small of my back. Looking over his shoulder, I catch a glimpse of Adèle's curious stare. She watches us very closely. It would be unnerving if my inhibitions weren't so low.

I push her out of my thoughts, no longer wishing to think about anything other than the music and the way my body flows with it. Looking at Julian, a hunger grows inside of me, threatening to burst. A throbbing thrums low in my gut, and I can hardly stand it. The need to rub against him is so strong it's maddening. I grind into him and immediately moan at the exquisite contact.

Julian groans in return, grabbing my leg and hoisting it around his waist, opening me to him. Every rock of the hips has me falling deeper and deeper into a pool of desire. My head is thrown back and Julian's mouth comes down onto the hollow between my neck and shoulders. My breath hitches, not out of fear, but out of want. Pure unadulterated want.

I *want* him to bite me. I *want* to feel the sensual pain, and more than anything, I want to know what it feels like to be consumed body and soul by Julian. There is no doubt that right now, there's nothing he could do to me that I wouldn't want, even beg for.

"Do it," I moan. "Please."

Julian's hands tighten around me. I feel his canine trailing up my carotid artery and I feel him shiver. The tension builds low in my belly, working its way downward. I'm at a fever pitch, ready to plead at any moment for him to put me out of my misery.

"I ache to give you what you want, Marina."

A whimper gets caught in my throat at his words and his

touch. It's too much. The dancing, the touching, Julian . . . it's more than I can handle.

"Please," I repeat, sounding more desperate by the minute.

Julian's eyes meet mine, dark pools promising things that my mind can't even comprehend. My tongue darts out, swiping across my bottom lip, and that's when I see Julian's patience run out. His mouth descends on mine, hard and hot. Our tongues unite in a symphony of pent-up hunger. Everything around us fades until it's just him and me. His hands tangle in my hair, tilting my head so it's at the perfect angle, allowing him to explore my mouth deeper.

I feel every kiss, every caress. Wetness pools in my panties as though he's touching me *there*. All sensibility has left me as I grab his hand, placing it between my legs. My eyes roll back into my head at his touch. I don't know if it's the drink or something supernatural, but it's unlocked something in me that's never existed there before. Something primal and predatory. Marina Drake is no more, and in her place is a girl desperate to be claimed and made a woman.

"Taste me, Julian."

He stills at my words, pulling away and leaving me feeling cold and confused.

"I'm sorry, Marina. I should have never—"

My chest heaves, embarrassment filling me.

"It's fine. Maybe we should leave?" I question, feeling out of my depth here.

"Marina, please. Don't do that," he says, grabbing my hands in his. He leans in so that his lips brush the shell of my ear. "This isn't right. You wouldn't want this if not for the Sacristan."

Embarrassment is quickly turning to resentment. Not at him, but at the alcohol.

"It's fine, but we should go. I don't want to be here."

My entire life, I've never allowed anyone in. Tonight, I was willing to open myself to Julian, but he thinks it's because of Sacristan. He's not entirely wrong; the old me would be mortified at my behavior. No, she never would've acted in such a manner to begin with. The drink lowered my defenses, but it's not why I wanted him. No matter how much I tried to stave off feelings for him, they keep barreling through, and tonight, with the help of Sacristan, I owned them.

It backfired.

I turn away, heading toward the exit. Julian catches up, grabbing my arm and spinning me around.

"Marina, stop. You don't understand."

"I said it's fine, Julian. You're right. It's the Sacristan." I pull my arm out of his grasp and continue toward the door, desperate for air.

"Please. This isn't the place. I'm begging you to listen to me." His pleading gives me pause. We are in a room full of vampires and he is under a microscope. As confused as I am in this moment, he's right—this isn't the place to go running off. My survival depends on his, and now is the time to be showing these vampires that he's in control.

I nod and walk back toward him, trying to right any damage that may have been caused by my outburst. I take a quick peek around, but it appears that nobody is attuned to our issues. They're still riding their highs.

"Come sit. We'll talk somewhere more private," Julian suggests, and I comply.

"There you are, darling," Adèle's sensual voice swoops through the air. "I've been looking for you." She takes one look at my face and frowns, peering at Julian. "Is something wrong?"

"We're fine, Adèle. Go have fun." She purses her lips in a pout.

"I thought you might dance with me. For old times' sake," she flirts, and my stomach coils in something akin to jealousy.

"Right now isn't a great time, but perhaps later."

"Fine," she sulks. "I'll come to collect in due time." Pivoting on her toe, she's off, heading toward the bar.

"How do you know Adèle?" I ask, drawing Julian's attention back to me.

He blows out a harsh breath as if he's desperate to talk about anything else. *Curious.*

"She's been a family friend for years. We were very close growing up. She's always been the one person I could confide in." His eyes avoid my gaze. "The one person I could trust."

"How nice," I say, not wanting to know any more.

"She has a fancy for the finer things in life."

"You don't say," I drag out, eyeing her red-soled shoes that I know have to cost in the thousands. "Does she have a boyfriend?" I ask, hoping she's spoken for.

"No. Her love is travel. Always has been." I detect a hint of derision.

"She pops in and out of the States a few times a year, but mostly she's in Europe. I'm waiting for the day that she decides to plant her roots there for good, much to her family's disapproval."

"Why wouldn't her family like that?"

"She's the heir to their kingdom. They're one of the royal families. Her parents were the second family in our race. Adèle is a Born."

I look at the beauty again. She's currently grinding into some tall dark-haired stranger. Her movements are fluid and graceful; she looks like a professional dancer. Her long black hair drops down her back in thick waves. A tight black mini dress hugs every inch of her body perfectly. Every man in the room has their eyes on her.

Except Julian. His are on me.

"I didn't pull away from you because I didn't want you, Marina. Quite the opposite. You have to know that." Julian says assertively but affectionately. "I'd never take advantage of you, and while you have Sacristan in your system, you aren't in full control. I never want you to regret your decisions."

My chest swells. Mortal men don't act with such chivalry. Perhaps that's why I've never been inclined to give my all to one of them. "Sacristan might have made me bold, but it wasn't directing my actions," I admit, looking into Julian's eyes.

I watch his throat bob, and when my head lifts, he blinks.

"We'll discuss this in the morning, all right?"

I nod, offering a smile.

Julian has earned my trust and admiration in such a short time. I once believed it to be Stockholm syndrome, but it's not. It never was. Something deep within me, an innate yearning, began the moment I saw him. It's as if my soul recognized its counterpart, but the call was overshadowed by the circumstances. It's been through his protection and candor that I've come to recognize my feelings for what they are. True. Deep. Everlasting.

Everlasting?

How am I to convince Julian that he belongs with a mere human?

CHAPTER 26

The sun bathes me in its warm glow as I sit atop the bottom step of Julian's porch.

"You should come under the shade," Julian suggests from a rocking chair behind me. "Your fair skin is turning pink."

I twist around to face him. "You can't tell that from clear over there."

"I can. Your cheeks are rosy."

He's not wrong. My entire face is warm, but I'm not ready to leave the sun. It's been raining for the past four days and I'm desperate for as much vitamin D as I can get.

"You couldn't see my cheeks before," I say with a grin and a quirked brow.

"Must you always challenge me?" he says with a smile that turns my insides to goo.

"It would be boring any other way."

Turning back around, I inhale deeply, basking in the fragrance of lavender that floats through the air. My eyes close and I just enjoy being still. All the worries of the world disappear for the moment. After a couple of minutes, I decide that

Julian is right, and if I don't get out of the sun, I will be dealing with a nasty sunburn.

"Ah, so now you listen," he goads.

"You look like you could use some company."

I want to spend time with Julian alone, and now is my chance. Stacey was with us all morning, but decided to head back to the estate for a nap. You know she was tired if she decided to scrap a shopping trip to take a nap.

Ours was delayed due to Julian having to rush off to meet with Law about our night in New Orleans and the run in with Vzar, followed by the visit to the club. That turned into another two days of working with the new bites on premises so that they could be moved.

I'm not upset. It gave me more time with Stacey.

With her back at the main house, I have some time alone with Julian. I have questions, which isn't anything new. Turning my chair toward him, I voice the first and most pressing one of them all.

"Have you found out anything about Shannon?" I ask, needing to know. I've wanted to ask so many times, but I didn't want to push. He said we'd have to be smart, and I'm trying to keep my promise of trusting him.

"I spoke to Marcellus. He doesn't have her, Marina. She wasn't at the auction." His voice is sad. Regret radiates off of him. My heart stops for a moment. If they don't have her, where is she?

"I'll keep looking, Marina. She's got to be out there somewhere. I'll find her," he promises. My heart breaks for my friend and what she might be going through—if she's alive. Julian says he'll continue to look for her, and that's the best I can ask for. He'd find something before the police. I have to trust that he'll uncover where she is. The need to change the subject presses on me.

"Tell me something about you," I ask with the most pleasant smile I can conjure, hoping it'll entice him to share.

"What would you like to know?" His shoulders push backward, chest puffing out.

"What was your favorite time period?"

I figure he's been through so many different eras, he has to have a favorite. Living vicariously through him seems like a fun thing to do today.

His nose scrunches. "I've had many, Marina."

"Indulge me," I beg.

He rubs his head, eyes pointed toward the sky, seemingly contemplating his favorite era, while I internally make my own guess. I can picture him in the nineteenth century, at court, dancing with all of the prettiest debutantes. A smile graces my lips at the mental picture.

"Yes, I did enjoy those days, although the dancing—" he grimaces. "Ladies in those days would have you dancing until your feet wanted to fall off," he says, causing goose bumps to rise on my arm. He's responding directly to my thoughts. And he expects me to believe he can't read my mind? Whatever it is, it's unnerving.

"It sounds wonderful," I muse. "I can picture it all. It's hardly fair you've experienced all of these years."

"They weren't all great, Marina. I've lost many friends along the way to old age and illness. It's hard to watch life move on while you're standing still."

I sigh. I don't doubt his words. It had to feel lonely at times.

"You said you didn't have time for human things the other day at your house." I recall his declaration when we were debating whether he truly knew what a man cave was.

"I didn't have many, but those I did were long ago. When my father was ruling, I had more freedom." He looks heavenward and smiles. "Addy was behind most of my friendships. She has a soft spot for humans."

I school my face, trying not to give away my unease surrounding the beautiful vampiress. He must not notice, because he forges on.

"Then there was 1903, when I bought my first car. It was incredible, but nothing like what we have today," he smirks.

I can only image what that smirk implies. I'm sure he has a garage full of cars somewhere, based on the enthusiasm he's showing now. An image pops into my mind of a carefree Julian, driving a red BMW convertible with the top down through the countryside. A smile graces my lips at the image.

"My favorite, though, was 1994."

My breath hitches. *The year I was born.* There is nothing incredibly memorable from 1994—with the exception of OJ and some pretty killer songs being released. No, 1994 is definitely not a year that most would remember as being one of the best ever. So, what could Julian Bellamy possibly have gotten up to?

"Why?" I'm holding my breath awaiting his answer. A part of me hopes that something about my birth made it his favorite year, but that would be so inconsequential for an immortal. Someone who has lived for hundreds of years would surely find more important things to remember. Besides, he didn't know me until the auction. I haven't spoken of his father's diary, because I'm not sure how he would react to my snooping and honestly, it's not worth discussing until I have solved the riddle of what it even means.

Julian continues to stare at me, not saying a word. His gaze is hard and unyielding—as though he's trying to make out the words in his head before he speaks them.

"It was just a feeling I had," he starts, running his hands down his face. "It was like waking for the first time. Colors less dull, sounds sharper, my sense of smell more acute. I don't know, it was . . . living."

"One day you just woke up and things were better?" I say doubtfully.

"Yes," he insists. "It was like being reborn. I remember the exact day."

Everything hangs in the balance as I wait for him to continue. It's as though I'm standing at the edge of an airplane door, thirteen thousand feet above land, waiting to free-fall into the air. My stomach tightens, and my breathing becomes heavy.

"You do?" I whisper, feeling light-headed.

"April 13, 1994."

I gasp, hands flying up to cover my mouth. *My birthday.* He said *my* birthday.

Tingles start in my toes and work their way up my body, warming me as they go. This has to mean something. It's too many coincidences. It's starting to make sense why his father thought it could be us. Triplets born on the day at least one of his sons changed.

At that thought, the tingles cease, the muscles in my face relax, and dread fills me. If only Mr. Bellamy were here today to see what a disappointment we turned out to be. The only thing Julian will get from me is type O. I bleed like everyone else, and it's nothing special. I push all my energy into keeping him out of my head. I'm not sure if it will work, but some part of me believes I have more power than I know.

"Marina, what's wrong?" Julian asks, coming to my side, concern lacing his voice.

It worked. Oh my god, it seems to really have worked.

I'm not ready to admit out loud that I fear his father died in vain. If the secret he was harboring involved my sisters and me, then what a massive waste of a legend we were.

"Look at me," he commands, lifting my chin so that our eyes meet. "Whatever is going on in that pretty little head of yours, stop it. I can't read your mind and it's killing me because I can tell it's eating you up inside."

I blink, slowly, frowning all the while. "April 13, 1994, is my birthday."

He smiles. "Definitely my favorite."

My ears warm at his flirtatious tone.

"You don't find any of this strange?" I ask. "You had some sort of rebirth on my birthday?"

He frowns. "Many things are strange, Marina, but I'm not sure what you're insinuating."

I want to tell him what I'm thinking, but I don't. There's still too much I need to uncover. And besides, I'm not sure I believe that he doesn't know more than he's letting on. If he's keeping secrets, I can keep mine for a bit longer.

"Come here," he says, pulling me up from my chair and into his lap.

Since the night at the club, we haven't been close enough for intimacy. If anything, I'm still licking my wounds at being rejected—even if it was for my own good. Julian stopping things from going any further the other night stung. My body was on fire for him, but he resisted so easily.

"Now you want me?" I tease, allowing all my lingering bravado from that night to rise to the surface.

He groans. "Marina, stop."

I turn in his lap so we're facing each other once again. I narrow my eyes at him, although I'm not mad.

"It wasn't easy, and I did not reject you. I simply wouldn't have continued with an inhibitor in your system. It's not right."

I smile at his words and his insistence that it was only to protect me from going further than I would've chosen without the witch potion—or whatever it was. Without a second thought, I lean in and brush my lips with his. All thoughts of mind reading vanish.

"There may have been something in my system, but it's not why I wanted you, Julian. I already told you that."

His teeth nip at my bottom lip. "Soon," he promises, smothering any protest from me by joining our mouths in a heated kiss.

As I melt into him, I forget all about witchy drinks, legends, and vampires. Right now, in this moment, we're two people who can't get enough of each other. There's no worry about the future—or lack thereof. Everything is perfect. He's perfect.

"THERE'S SOMETHING DIFFERENT ABOUT YOU," Stacey says, drawing my attention.

"What?" I ask, puzzled.

"You're strangely content."

I think about it for a minute, and realize that yes, I am content. Maybe it was my epiphany about how I feel about Julian. Or more likely, it was our afternoon, locked in each other's arms, kissing the day away. Either way, it's simple. I'm falling for Julian Bellamy.

"I care about him," I say, chewing on my lip nervously.

She tips her head back and chuckles.

"Duh. You're just now figuring this out?" she teases.

"He's a vampire who is most likely immortal. It could never work. Right?"

"That's like saying Wolverines and Buckeyes could never be married."

"What?" I ask, eyes narrowed.

"Michigan and Ohio State." I lift an eyebrow to signal I'm still lost. "Football."

I shake my head. "How is that even similar?"

"You know, good versus evil."

A corner of my lip tips up, insinuating I'm on to her. She shared with me that her family lives and breathes Michigan football. I might understand the rivalry, but she'll be seriously let down to hear I couldn't care less about either team.

I raise my brow. "Not all Ohioans care about the Buckeyes, Stac. I am one of them."

"Oh, come on, you know what I mean. You're changing the subject and trying to find reasons to push him away. Stop."

"Maybe I am." My hands fly up in the air in frustration. "Even if I tried, my concern still stands. I'll die, and he'll live forever. He has powers, I don't."

Stacey rolls her eyes, clearly annoyed at me.

"He wants you, Marina. The way he looks at you, it's . . . hot as hell."

My head falls back in defeat. Knowing how I feel and believing he might feel the same doesn't change the facts. How can we get past all our differences?

"He's the king of vampires. I'm a human being tracked by vampires. Why would we even put ourselves through that?"

"Love's worth it, Marina. No matter how much time you have—years or days—love is worth the pain."

What I wouldn't give to have all of him for any amount of time.

"Plus, he's probably a rock star in bed."

I shake my head in exasperation. That may be true, but it's so much more than physical at this point. There is an inexplicable pull—one I've felt since the first time I saw him. There is no part of me that believes in love at first sight, but with Julian, there was something there from the very beginning. Lust? Maybe. Magic? Perhaps. No matter what it was, I felt it.

"You're ridiculous," I say, smiling wide.

"I'm not, and you need to jump on that before I do."

"Oh my God. You're insane. And I might kill you if you try."

She huffs dramatically, then bursts into laughter.

"I'm dead already as long as I'm here. One of us might as well have some enjoyment."

"What do I do?" Standing, I begin pacing the room.

She bites her cheek in thought.

"For starters, you can't wear that. It screams prude."

I narrow my eyes at Stacey's appraisal.

"If you want him to make a move, you have to look the part. Think vixen, not virgin."

Grimacing, I watch as Stacey heads to the wardrobe, likely to see what she can find. She's in there for several minutes scanning through the options. I can hear the hangers scraping across the metal bar they're suspended from. I know she'll find a lack of lewd garments, which I know is what she's looking for.

She appears holding up a blood-red corset dress. Her eyebrows lift up and down. Stacey,

"Uh . . . no."

"Yes," she says ardently. "You'll kill him dead in this."

"More like make him laugh."

Julian seems to know me down to my marrow, no matter how little time we've spent together. One look at me in this and he'd know I was up to something. It would be more than obvious.

I internally cringe, not liking this one bit, but unwilling to lie to myself anymore. Julian is what I want, and if putting my assets on display will help, shouldn't I give it a shot? Even at the cost of looking foolish?

Do it.

"Help me into it," I bark.

Once it's on and she's tied up the corset bodice, I take a look in the mirror and gasp at my reflection. It hugs my middle and pushes up my already ample breasts. If hussy is what we are going for, I nailed it.

"Oh God." I bellow. "This is ridiculous. I can't—I won't."

"You'll be fine," Stacey promises. "The whole point of this was to help your chances."

"I'm serious, Stacey. I don't even know what to do. This is . . . beyond." My cheeks flush pink and my hand comes to my forehead to stave off the impending headache.

"Let's hope you rise to the occasion and don't embarrass yourself."

"That's reassuring," I deadpan.

"There's a chance that sex is just sex for him. There's a chance he might not break you in half," she snickers.

"Oh my God. I didn't even think of that. He's not a man, Stacey. He's supernatural."

"He has the right parts, he's a man."

The thought of Julian and said parts has my face heating to inferno levels.

"He seems gentle with you, Marina. You'll be fine."

She isn't wrong. Julian has been very careful with me. He's even sworn to protect me. I trust that he'd never do anything to hurt me.

"What if he bites me?"

"Then there's that. I don't know. Knee him and run like hell. Pray you can get away."

"I'm serious. I don't want to be a vampire."

Yet another reason we are doomed. She grabs my shoulders and turns me to face her square on. "Do you think he'd take that choice away from you?"

I shake my head. "No."

"Then just live in the moment and stop worrying about things you can't control."

A knock sounds at the door, followed by a boisterous voice that can be none other than Katina. "Ladies," she draws out. "I hope you've had fun, but the Crown wishes to dine with Miss—" She stops talking and narrows her eyes in my direction. "What in the hell are you wearing?"

Stacey snorts.

"A dress?"

"No, dear child, that is no dress. The appropriate amount of fabric required for a garment to be considered a dress is missing from that"—she gestures wildly to the dress—"frock."

"Is it really that bad?"

"Are you trying to seduce Satan?" Katina's lips thin into a straight line as she wobbles her head back and forth.

"You're the one who put it there," I accuse.

She pulls her lips to one side. "Yes, well . . . I forgot that was in there. I've tried for many years to block out my time in the brothel."

"What?" My voice pitches. "You can't be serious."

"And you can't seriously be trying to do what I think you're doing," she says.

"The jury's still out on that one," I admit. "Not the Satan part . . . but . . . seduction."

Stacey is practically rolling on the floor in tears. Katina looks horrified, and I suddenly feel like shit.

I straight-up lied to Katina the other day, and I just gave myself away.

What the hell was I thinking?

"My dear Marina, I mean no offense, but you're not cut out to put the moves on anyone, especially not the king of vampires. Kissing, you can probably handle. Seduction—no."

"Katina, this is a new thing. The other day when you asked, I was still trying to work out my feelings."

She purses her lips. "I know. I'm no vammy."

"Vammy?" Stacey asks.

Katina wobbles on her heels. "Vampire dummy."

I pull my bottom lip into my mouth, trying to avoid laughing at her. I can tell she's miffed at me, and I don't want to make things worse.

"Do I have time to change?" I say, trying to change the subject.

"You're not changing. You look great. Go knock his canines out," Stacey cheers, eliciting a scowl from Katina.

"I don't even want to remind you of my warnings," Katina scolds. "This certainly won't end well."

She's not saying anything I haven't thought myself, but I've gone this far. No turning back.

"Just take me to him."

I'm eager to see him after last night, and desperate to get out of this stuffy room. More importantly, I want to see Julian's reaction to this dress, because why the hell not? If it gets me a new wardrobe, it'll be more than worth it.

CHAPTER 27

When I reach the backyard, Julian's back is turned to me.

"Hello, Julian," I say, standing tall and forcing my chest forward to really sell the brothel vibe.

Julian turns, and my breath hitches as his eyes sweep over me from head to toe. The dress does not have the effect I imagined it would. His eyes darken and everything around us blurs into black and white. Once again, he steals the color from everything around him.

"Marina."

My name has never sounded so sensual. All the hairs on my arms stand at attention, electrified by the caress of his eyes.

"Wow—I don't know what to say." He steps forward until there are only inches separating us. "You're beautiful."

My cheeks warm at the compliment.

"But what are you wearing?"

And just like that, the sensual atmosphere gives way to something lighter. My shoulders shake and laughter bubbles up my chest. My hand coming up in a *I don't have a freaking clue* gesture has him snickering.

"Stacey dressed me, but I blame Katina. The whole closet needs to go."

He chuckles.

"That makes sense. It doesn't look like anything you'd choose. I'll see about getting you appropriate apparel."

"Thank you," I say, expelling a breath of air.

Julian stands in front of me and runs a finger down my cheek. "You look stunning, Marina. Dangerously stunning," he grits through his teeth, as though he's in pain.

My eyes meet his and I see the heat pooling behind his eyelids. He's affected by me as much as I am by him.

"Julian I—"

He cuts me off. "You stole my breath the moment I saw you. This dress could get you into trouble, Marina."

"How so?" I ask, taking a step closer, our chests nearly rubbing.

He groans.

"Let's just say I wouldn't want you seen in this dress in public. Men would not stay away, and I'd be forced to protect you in ways you wouldn't like."

I purse my lips, laying on the flirtation, suddenly emboldened by his words and his appreciation.

"It's just you and me, Julian." I lift my hand and run it down his chest, channeling every heroine from every movie I've ever seen. I'm slightly awkward, but he doesn't seem to notice. His eyes are wide and mouth dropped open into an O. "Should I fear you?"

His chest rises and falls in deep breaths.

"You never need to fear me, Marina."

I lean up on my toes and place a kiss on the corner of Julian's lip and cheek.

"Thank you, Julian."

"For?" His voice cracks, like that of a teenage boy. I smile, loving the effect I have on him.

"For never making me feel less than."

"Never, Marina."

I smile at him, wanting desperately to confess all the feelings bubbling inside me. Instead, I decide to steer the conversation toward additional answers. Things that might help me to understand his world a little more.

"Let's walk," I say, grabbing his hand and leading us through the garden. "What happened the other night with Vzar? Why did we have to go to Levine?"

"Every turn I make, the Council seems to know it. They have eyes everywhere, even in my own castle."

"Vzar would've told them?"

"I never know whom to trust, Marina. I believe him to be a friend, but I've been fooled before."

I wring my hands.

"What secret was your father keeping, Julian? You never told me, and I can't help but feel like this is all connected somehow—your father dying and now the Council wanting you out."

Julian sighs. "You're probably right, but knowing his secret won't keep you safe. The more you know, the more of a target on my back. If the Council finds out I told a human, they'll kill you and find a way to dethrone me."

"If they have their way, those things will happen regardless, Julian. I'd prefer to die not in the dark. Trust me. Tell *me*."

We've been through this exact conversation before. I'm growing tired of it, and he has to be as well. We're at a crossroads, and his decision will speak volumes as to where this thing between us can lead.

He bites down on his lip, looking at me intently. I hold my breath for what feels like too

long. Finally, I see a break in his resolve.

He chooses forward. He chooses you.

"For as long as I've lived, there have been legends that each vampire that is Born has a familiar."

The air rushes from me.

"If you were the first Born, how would someone know this?"

"Witches. Back in the day, my father and the other families used witches to conjure spells to enlighten them on all the powers of our kind."

I shiver at the mention of witches. If vampires rely on them for information, they have to be even more powerful and even more evil than vampires, right?

"I know what a familiar is, Julian," I admit, trying to be honest and move the conversation forward and into new territory.

"How?" He demands, not angry, but not happy either.

"I've heard you and Law mention it, and then I found a journal in the library. I think it was your father's."

"You did? That's . . ." Julian begins to pace. "Where is the journal now?"

"It's in my room, hidden."

"We need to go get it right now. If it falls into the wrong hands—"

I cut him off. "It won't, Julian. It doesn't go into the specifics of the legend. I asked Law while you were gone."

Julian swears under his breath. "He shouldn't have talked to you about this. He doesn't even know the specifics."

I put my hand up to slow him down, as he's getting worked up.

"He only gave me the highlights. I know very little about it. So, please, tell me more," I suggest, hoping he'll calm down and do what I ask.

He sighs heavily, looking weary and uncertain, but ultimately, he continues.

"According to the witches, familiars are entities that help supernatural beings come into their power. My father believed that for a vampire, it was something more. He believed we had one perfect mate, connected to our souls."

"Why was your father keeping that a secret?"

"When I came across another of his journals and confronted him with it, he said he didn't have all the answers, but I didn't believe him. He wasn't Born. If one of my brothers or I came into that kind of power—or worse, another family of Borns—his rule could've been easily overthrown."

"He really was power-hungry."

"You have no idea."

"You're nothing like him, Julian. You know that, right?"

He looks off into the distance. "You don't know that, Marina. I could end up like him one day."

The only time I've ever seen Julian even angry was with Marcellus. He's not a bad guy.

"I don't believe that. I *can't* believe that. I wouldn't feel the way I do about you if you were anything like him."

The words are out of my mouth before I even realize it. My cheeks heat with my admission. I've bared my feelings to him without any indication that he's feeling anything more than lust for me. My stomach sours at the thought that this is one-sided.

You know it's not.

Grabbing my chin in his hand, he forces me to look at him. His touch is soft, caring.

"Marina, when you are in the room, nothing else matters to me. Every sound is sharpened, every color brighter. I have never experienced anything like it in all of my centuries." He leans into me, nose in my ear, and I shudder at his nearness. "I feel the pull too."

My knees shake, and my eyes roll back into my head at his words. I feel it *all*. Everything he's described times ten. When he's near, my body comes alive. I've never felt this. I didn't know it was possible to feel like this. And he feels it too. Happiness fills me.

He pulls me into him, my entire body sighing at his touch. Our eyes are locked together, his begging permission, but he doesn't need it. He knows what I want. What I need. It's him. The missing piece of my soul has always been him.

Without another thought, his lips crush against mine, and for the first time in twenty-one years, I feel alive.

I'M SITTING in the library, leafing through an early copy of *The Secret Garden*, when I hear voices. My eyes narrow and I lean toward the door to figure out where they're coming from. I stand, walking toward the sound.

"Help me," a woman cries out, begging for someone to come to her aid, and I stand rooted in my spot. *It can't be*. He wouldn't. A barrage of thoughts run through my head, all painting a very grim picture of Julian.

Who could possibly be screaming for help on these premises without his knowledge?

Stop, I berate my traitorous mind. Julian wouldn't hold prisoners. He doesn't participate in the donor auction. I follow the sounds, twisting around corners and descending stairs, until I come to a door, clearly leading to places I've been forbidden to go.

New bites.

I should turn back. Something tells me that once I go

forward, there is no unseeing. I've come to like Julian, perhaps even love him, and he warned me to stay away from here. Voices in my head scream for me to turn around, but something compels me forward. I feel like I don't have control of my own legs.

"*Go back!*" Maggie screams, but I push her away.

Tired of the warring emotions about what hearing her voice means. I couldn't stop if I wanted to. I'm practically floating on air, driven to move forward. I put on a brave face, straighten my shoulders, and open the door. Narrow steps tilt steeply down a dark and dank passageway. I take a deep breath and descend carefully. The farther down I go, the louder the voices become.

At the bottom, there's a large metal door separating me from the people yelling for help. I'm about to go through when heavy footsteps sound behind me. *Someone's coming down the steps.* I duck into a dark corner to the right of the door, slinking as far back as I can, out of sight. Moments later, Bash is standing at the large door.

He raps three times and the heavy door creaks open.

"What took you so long?" a deep voice says, questioning Bash.

"I had work to do," he says gruffly. "With Julian in town, someone has to guard the entrance."

The unknown man scoffs. "And that's always gotta be you?" the man challenges.

"I've earned his trust," Bash replies coldly. "Why is everyone yelling down here? They've got the staff on edge."

"They're hungry. They need to eat, Bash."

"Katina is working on it. She'll be down soon."

They move farther into the room, so I come out from the dark corner and get as close to the entrance as possible, wanting to see what's going on. *Needing* to see the new bites.

I wait for a few long minutes until it appears the coast is clear and peek my head around the door.

The basement is lined with cells, much like the auction facility. The voices stopped as soon as Bash made his entrance. I can't even be sure they're still in this room.

"Psst. Come here," a honeyed voice calls from a cell midway down. I crane my neck to try to see the woman, but Bash's husky form plods my way, forcing me to hide behind the door once more.

"Whadya want?" he drawls.

"Come closer," she prods. "I want to tell you a secret."

Her lovely voice is hypnotic and calming. For someone trapped down here, she doesn't sound distressed. She couldn't have been the person screaming.

"There's nothing you could say that I want to hear," Bash replies, blowing the woman off.

A shrill scream echoes off the walls and damn near blasts my eardrums to shreds. My hands come up, covering my ears in protection from the horrible sound.

"Help," the woman screams.

I stand corrected. She's definitely the culprit from earlier. Chancing a glance, I look around the door and see her. Hands wrapped around the cell bars, she continues to screech at the top of her lungs, thrashing wildly. She looks possessed, animalistic.

"Stop that," the other man commands in a booming voice.

The woman slinks back, dirty brown hair hanging in her face.

"Are you done?" he asks in a much softer tone.

A hiss sounds from the woman's mouth and she bares a set of canines.

I'm thirsty.

The words ricochet through my mind as though she's screaming them right next to me. *What the hell.*

"I'm going to piss, and then I'm grabbing lunch. I'll be back in an hour," the other man says to Bash, who merely grunts.

I quickly hide back in my corner until he's ascended the stairs. A few minutes later I return to my post, only to hear Bash snoring loudly. Seeing my only chance to approach, I step inside.

"Come closer, girl. I can smell you," the freaky vampire woman says shrilly.

I walk closer to the cell, working hard to keep my footsteps light and soundless.

"Who are you?"

She throws her head back, cackling. Bash jerks, but remains asleep.

"Who am I?" she jeers, spearing me with her inhumanly black eyes. "Who are you, is the better question." Her nose crunches and her teeth grind together. She's frightening.

"Why are you screaming? They're trying to help you." My voice quakes, fear winding up my body, squeezing the life out of me.

"I'm trapped," she grits through her teeth. "They're keeping me here, forcing me to drink cow's blood." She hauls off and spits in Bash's direction.

My nose wrinkles in disgust at her gross behavior, but I don't question why she's mad. Being caged is horrible. At this moment, though, I'm glad for it. This vampire is nothing like Julian and Katina. No. This one would rip out my throat and drain my body of its blood.

Why would Julian try to help a creature like her?

They deserve a chance to be like him. Good.

"What are you doing down here?" Katina's taut voice from behind catches me off guard.

"Gah," I screech, whirling around in fright. "You scared the shit out of me."

"You stupid, stupid girl," she says, grabbing my arm and pulling me away from the cell and back through the door.

"Everything all right out there, K?"

"Fine," she barks. "Close the damn door, Bash."

She points a bony finger toward the stairs, directing me to move. I do as instructed, feeling thoroughly scolded. I was caught snooping around in an area I was warned never to be in. I stumbled upon a vampire prisoner. What will Julian say?

My quick steps have me well ahead of Katina, but she's gaining ground.

"Stop right there, Marina."

I pause, refusing to turn back to look at her. I'm embarrassed and a little shaky.

"What were you thinking going down there?"

I slowly turn to find Katina appearing concerned. It's better than the rage I saw moments ago.

"She was screaming. I heard it from the library and followed the sound," I say honestly.

"There are reasons you are not to go in certain areas, Marina. For your safety, you should've listened."

"Maybe if someone had told me what was down there, I wouldn't have felt inclined to snoop." I glare back at Katina.

That's not entirely true. I had been warned, but I won't tell Katina that.

She sighs heavily, not looking fond of having this talk with me.

"There are some things you are best not knowing. Being in the dark is not always a bad thing, Marina."

I've heard those words in the past, but the truth is, I don't believe them. The right to live my life in the dark was stripped from me. If I have to be aware that the things of nightmares roam the Earth, then everything else should pale in comparison.

"It couldn't be helped," I admit. "My body was slightly out of my control."

She scoffs. "That's ridiculous. What you did is stupid, Marina. What you saw is the entire reason the Council is all over his back. If they somehow got a hold of you and used persuasion to learn his secrets, they'd drag him out of here and end his rule."

"But why? Wouldn't the Council want the new vampires to be controlled?"

"No, silly girl. They're likely the ones behind the outbreaks." She rolls her eyes like I'm the biggest idiot she's ever met. "They are new bites. With the new bite comes thirst. Julian is trying to help them control it. Marcellus and a few unnamed Council members want the uncontrolled vampires."

And to kill all humans in the process.

He's trying to teach them to be like him. My heart swells at Julian's heart. He's not torturing them; he's trying to help. Some on the Council would allow their thirst to go unchecked until they set them free on innocent humans.

"Marcellus is trying to build an army of new bites. He wants to create more vampires so that they can eventually take over the world and live in the open."

"Does he not realize that if his pets kill off humans, the vampires' blood source is gone?" I ask, wondering how Marcellus and the Council could be so stupid.

"He won't listen." She shakes her head. "Creating more vampires with that newborn thirst is a recipe for disaster. We would have difficulty controlling them, and before too long vampires would begin to go rogue. It would be chaos. Julian knows this and has tried to reason with his brother. Eventually, they would deplete every source of food, just like you said."

My body shivers at the picture she's painting. Anarchy, fear, and death for the human race.

"Does everyone on the Council agree?"

"Not with his method, per se. They believe in a controlled process. Think larger scale blood banks and auctions. Humans would be made to live as blood slaves."

I shake my head.

"They can't."

"They could. We are faster and stronger. Humans would be no match. Julian spends his evenings tracking them down and bringing them here, so he can help them through the process and teach them how to survive on animal blood, but the rate at which humans are being turned is increasing to levels Julian can't keep up with."

"Why is the Council against Julian's method?"

"It goes against everything our kind has ever believed. In the Council's eyes, we are superior and we should not have to hide from anyone."

"Do you agree?" I ask, not believing she does, but needing to hear it from her.

She shakes her head. "I'm here with Julian because I believe in *him*. I think he could start a revolution for vampires. One that doesn't include hysteria, people dying, and evil ruling. Because believe me, some of the Council members are pure evil."

Her eyes darken, and something crosses over her face. Something happened to Katina. I don't know what, but it involves members of the Council. Having pushed my luck with her enough today, I let it go for now.

"How do we stop the Council?"

She laughs. "*You* don't do anything. Allow the immortals to fight this war, Marina. You'd never survive it."

I don't doubt what she's saying, but I'm dead regardless if this is allowed to happen. I'd rather do something and feel like I helped save mankind in some way.

"The fate of the world rests in Julian's hands. As long as he's the Crown, we're all safe."

"How do we keep him in power?"

She clicks her tongue and flips her eyes toward the ceiling, probably annoyed that I included myself in the equation again.

"The best way would be for him to fulfill his obligation and marry Ms. Dupré. That way, the two oldest and strongest families would be united. He'd have their allegiance and other Council members would follow."

Fulfill his obligation. Marry.

"Adèle?" My voice cracks, stomach coils, and chest feels so tight it might explode. He is engaged to her? All this time, he's been engaged, and he failed to tell me?

"Are you all right?" Katina asks, but I barely comprehend her words. My heart has been pulled out of my chest. *He's engaged.* My traitorous mind keeps replaying the words, as if the first time didn't break me enough.

"Marina, I'm—"

"Katina, we have a problem," Bash calls from somewhere, but I'm not focused on anything but my mounting grief.

"Marina." Katina grabs my shoulders, trying to snap me out of my stupor, but it won't work. Nothing will work. "You need to go to your room. Now," she barks, turning me toward the stairs.

CHAPTER 28

On autopilot, my feet carry me down the hall toward my room, but I hardly register it. Memories of the night at the club replay before my eyes. The way she looked at him; the way *he* looked at *her*. I'm sick. How did I not see it? Why has he led me to believe he cares for me?

You're a human; he's a vampire. It never would've worked.

I wish I could tell my brain to shut up and take a seat, but instead, I allow all the thoughts to consume me, until it's too much. Tears are falling down my face like water flows over a dam. Mine has broken, leaving nothing there to stop the flood. The pang in my chest is near debilitating. Crouched down, back against the wall and knees pulled up to my chest, I let it all out.

Stacey's door creaks open.

"Marina? Are you all right?" she says, voice thick.

"No."

She bends down in front of me.

"What happened?"

"He's going to have to marry someone else," I say, voice brittle.

"Who?" she asks, confused.

"Julian." I only manage his name.

"I got that part, but who is he marrying?"

My head falls back, smacking the wall behind me. I close my eyes as tears continue to stream.

"Marina. Talk to me," Stacey insists, sounding more worried by the minute.

"A vampire. Someone like him."

The one thing I've feared since the moment I admitted to myself that I cared for him was that it would never work because we come from different worlds. This just further proves there is no shot for us. It's not just a matter of caring about him, not when the entire world is at stake. He's made it clear that the Council wants him out, and if that happens, there will be chaos.

It doesn't even matter if he wants to marry Addy. He has to if it means saving the world.

Julian's reign is as important for the safety of humanity as it is for the survival of vampires. If he marries Adèle, it would solidify an alliance between the two most powerful families. With her family backing him, maybe he can stop the auction. But I can't explain all of that to Stacey. Not tonight. Not when I'm this emotional.

"Her family is the second oldest vampire family," I continue, wanting to give her something. "Their marriage was decided long ago, but they've yet to follow through with it."

"That's good news, Marina. If they haven't gotten married yet, there's got to be a reason. Maybe he doesn't love her."

I huff, knowing with certainty that's not the case. It was there in the way he smiled at her. It might not be love, but it's not nothing.

"I met her. She is exotic and cultured *and* gorgeous. She's the complete opposite of me in every way." I wipe a tear off my face. "She's also been Julian's best friend since they were young. I *cannot* compete with that."

"You're not trying to compete with that. You don't have to. I saw how he looked at *you*, Marina."

"Maybe he just wanted a plaything in the meantime. A last hurrah before he settles down."

I know that's not true. I'm being dramatic and I'm not even sure how to stop. This is new territory for me. I've never cared about anyone like this—at all. I'm out of my depth and drowning.

Stacey frowns at me. "Do you really believe that? Because I don't," she says roughly.

"The truth is, he could've had you whether you agreed to it or not. We're prisoners *and* we're human. He could've forced you into anything, but he didn't. He's been kind to you and to me."

I let out a long, deep breath. "What am I gonna do?"

"Well, I'd suggest you go get some sleep, because you look terrible."

I chuckle. "I am exhausted."

"And then tomorrow, I think you should talk to him. Be honest for once and tell him how you feel. Tell him you love him, because you might not admit it to me, but it's written all over your face. You love him and it's time you fight for him."

"I don't love him."

She cocks her head to the side, like I'm a horrible liar. And she's right, I am. I'm a horrible liar, and I am madly in love with Julian Bellamy.

"You're right," I admit, eliciting a huge smile from her. "I'm going to go sleep, and then tomorrow I'll talk to him."

"That's my girl," she says, helping me to my feet. She pulls me into a tight hug and places a kiss on my cheek. "I'm proud of you. I hope that someday I can meet someone who makes me feel like that."

"You will."

Stacey smiles. "Go get some sleep."

I move toward my room, ready to fall into my warm sheets. I'm not feeling much better, but I have a plan. I know what I need to do.

When I open my bedroom door, I take off my jewelry and place it on the nightstand. After fiddling with the lamp on the side table, I finally flip it on.

"Hello, human." A familiar voice makes my blood run cold.

Turning slowly, I come face to face with the vampire from the cell. My blood pressure drops and I feel like I could faint. *The new bite.* The one with uncontrollable thirst stands before me, canines bared, looking like she hasn't eaten in years.

"You," I say on a shaky breath. "How did you . . ."

She cuts me off, cackling. "Your friends aren't very smart. Turning a hedge witch into a vampire," she huffs. "I found that it strengthens my power."

A hedge witch? I don't even know what the hell that is. And what kind of powers does she possess?

"Powers?" I can't stop shaking. If I thought she was creepy closed off behind a cage, she's so much worse now. Her oily hair hangs down the front of her face, making her look akin to the girl in the movie *The Ring*. Her clothes are tattered and filthy. But her sneer is by far the worst. It chills my bones.

"Strength, speed," she says, walking toward me, calculated and unhurried. "You know, the typical vampire traits." Her hands come up as if she's weighing two items in the palms of her hands, shifting them up and down, all while her narrowed eyes are fixed on me. "Mix it in with a little witch's blood, a few incantations, and poof, the lock popped."

My chest tightens, feeling as though someone is sitting on top of my diaphragm and pushing hard.

"Why are you here?" I don't even know why I asked the question; it's pretty obvious she intends to kill me.

"I followed your scent. It's nothing personal, just hunger. Cows' blood doesn't cut it," she snarls.

"He's trying to help you."

"I don't want his help," she roars, and I jolt back, caught off guard by the shift in tone. "You're not very smart, are you, human? Angering me won't bode well for your survival."

"I've very rarely been in situations where my life is on the line, so please forgive me if I'm freaking the hell out right now." I'm not sure how I was able to form the words in my head, let alone speak them, but the witch actually chuckles.

"I think I might've liked you in my former life. You have spirit." Her smile transforms into a hideous grin. "Your blood will taste delicious running down my throat. I will savor it all."

I turn to run out the door, but with a flick of her wrist, it slams shut. Everything in me goes cold, and the shudders begin again. I've never seen Julian do such a thing. What in the hell is she?

If all the tales of witches are true, she may possess some sort of magic. There is no way I could escape a normal vampire, but one with magical abilities? *Fight, Marina.* I stand tall, refusing to cower any more. She glares. Her hands come up, and with them so does my body. With a power I can't see, but can feel all the same, she lifts me off the ground and hurls me toward my bed.

My body smashes into the bedframe with a harsh thump. I wince at the pain shooting down my back from the impact.

"Surely, you'll put up a little more fight? This is rather boring," she says, picking at her gray teeth. A long finger runs down an elongated canine and I know she's set out to frighten me.

"I'll drain you of your blood and then feast on your flesh," she says, licking her chapped lips. "Julian will regret the day he came for me."

At the mention of Julian's name, I get an idea. Keep her talking. "He didn't turn you. Your hatred is misplaced."

"Stupid girl. I asked to be turned. I wanted to join the army Marcellus is putting together. If you can't beat them, join them." The words slither from her lips like a snake. "Julian is only getting in the way."

"Why would you want this?" I ask, not understanding.

"Julian will be overthrown. It's only a matter of time. When that happens, vampires will roam the earth out in the open. The first thing they'll do is come for us witches. It's either be a vampire or be a slave to their will. I'm nobody's slave," she hisses.

"Julian will win the war." My voice shows no signs of concern, even though I'm quaking inside.

Her head falls back and she cackles, loud and rough. "He has no chance. He's living under the same roof with the key to his survival, yet he's too daft to know."

"Key?"

"Hush now, human," she says, flicking her wrist once more. This time I fall forward, clutching my stomach. It feels as though I've been kicked. She strides in my direction, slowly, like a cat playing with a mouse. "This will all be over soon," she says, smiling wide in victory.

I don't dare blink for fear she'll gain more of an edge. My brain funnels through ideas of how to fight this creature as the seconds tick by painfully slowly. Her hands grab the collar of my dress and pull me up so that my feet dangle off the floor.

She leans in, inhaling with her face pressed into the curve of my neck.

The smell of rotting flesh coming off her breath roils my stomach. Bile rises to the top of my throat. It's now or never as she leans in, running her canine down my carotid artery. She's toying with me, making the entire experience more agonizing than it needs to be.

"I won't go down without a fight," I growl, throwing my head back and slamming it into her crooked nose.

The witch howls and my head spins. I'm seeing stars and my legs wobble underneath me. I need to pull myself together long enough to run from the room and yell for help.

"Your death won't be short," she bites through her sharpened teeth.

The sound of a loud crash ricochets off the walls, and my head swirls toward the door. *Julian.*

In her surprise, the hedge witch drops to her knees, crouching in preparation to attack. The breath I was holding comes out in a harsh whoosh, and oxygen begins to flow again. I shake off the fog in time to see Julian has the hedge witch by the throat, but she doesn't appear frightened. Her head is thrown back, maniacal laughter bubbling from her lips.

"You're not as strong as me," she singsongs, to which Julian huffs his own laugh.

"Witch, you're talking to your king. The first Born."

"You're nobody's king," she says stridently. "They're coming for you."

My heart beats fast at her declaration. Is she talking about the Council?

I don't have a chance to ask. Julian's arm twists, separating her head from her shoulders. It drops with a noisy thud to the floor.

"Is-is she dead?" My voice quakes from adrenaline and emotion.

He doesn't speak, motioning for me to come to him.

I do. I run into his arms and shake in his embrace, the adrenaline taking its toll. Fear, relief, and love vie to be the central concern. Tremors rack my body as Julian runs his hands soothingly down my back.

She can't be dead. It can't be that easy, considering his father had to be charred to die.

I vaguely notice Bash and another man come in to drag the hag away. I wonder what they'll do to her. *Hopefully take her far from here.*

"I've got you," he whispers into my hair. "I won't let anyone hurt you. I will *never* let anyone hurt you."

I look up, his eyes meeting mine. Love wins out over everything else. All the pent-up feelings for him, all the things I want to say, threaten to explode from my chest. But none of them come out, because Julian's lips are on mine before I can say a word. His kiss says everything. He feels the same. He's my oxygen and I'm his in this moment. Our tongues tangle around each other, neither one of us coming up for air. We don't need it. We don't need anything but each other right now.

Eventually, he pulls away, breath heaving. His hands come to my face, cupping my cheeks in his palms.

"I was so scared, Marina. I've never been more scared in all my years. When I think about what could've happened..." His words catch in his throat. "Immortality wouldn't have stopped my heart from breaking in half, had she hurt you. My heart, my soul. It's yours."

He crushes his lips to mine once more. I don't want to stop, but the events of tonight are catching up with me quickly, and my knees buckle. I'm lifted off my feet by Julian's strong arms. I don't look up, keeping myself buried in the safety of his warm chest. He carries me for several minutes. *He's taking me to his home.*

My back is placed gently onto his soft mattress, and a warm blanket laid across my body. Not long after, Julian lays next to me, continuing to whisper soothing words into my ear. At some point, I doze off and dream of horrible monsters. And worse, my death.

I awake sometime in the night, after what feels like hours' worth of sleep. My body is achy and my stomach grumbles from hunger. I stretch and my hand hits something next to me. Popping an eye open, I remember that I'm not in my room at the main house. Julian brought me to his.

The reminder of how gentle he was, how affectionate, warms my heart. I turn to find Julian assessing me with concern.

"Did you sleep well?" His face says he knows I didn't. "You did a lot of tossing and turning. You cried out a couple of times for Maggie."

My eyes close at the mention of her name. I came so close to being reunited with her tonight. But if I'm being honest, I'm not ready for that.

"I'm so sorry that happened, Marina. It should've never happened," he says, clearly upset.

"It's not your fault, Julian. You were just trying to help her."

He falls back roughly to his bed, staring at the ceiling, putting his hand over his eyes in frustration.

"I knew what she was. I should've taken proper precautions to make sure she was unable to get out. I put you and everyone else in danger."

"You ended it."

He scoffs bitterly. "It's far from over. She'll be dealt with, but not here." He shakes his head. "To think what could've happened if I hadn't heard your scream. She could've killed you."

"But she didn't, and I have you to thank for that," I say, truly meaning it. I don't have the energy to question the what-ifs at this point. So much bad has happened over the past few weeks that I just want to hold on to the wins. I'm breathing, and I have him to thank. He is my most unlikely savior, yet a savior is what he is.

"I want to talk to you about something else," I say, needing to get this all out before I change my mind.

"Shh," he says, quieting me. "We have all the time the world, but you need rest right now."

I shake my head.

"No, Julian. This needs to be said." My voice leaves little room for argument. "When were you going to tell me that you're engaged?"

He sits up quickly, eyes wide.

"How? Who?"

"Katina," I offer, to prevent the guessing game. "I hate to throw her under the bus, but I'm not going to lie to you. Just... don't blame her. I would've found out somehow." I lick my bottom lip, trying to formulate my words. My thoughts are so jumbled, I'm having a hard time deciding where to begin. "I know we're temporary. It wouldn't work out long-term for us. But I wish you had told me."

I pray that he says it's not true. If he admits it, I might die right here of a broken heart.

"You're more than that to me and you know it. Don't belittle what you mean to me, Marina. Nothing about this is temporary." His eyes soften. "Please don't ever question that you are *everything* to me."

I take a deep cleansing breath, relieved at hearing exactly what I needed to hear from him. Right now, I don't want to hear about Addy or an engagement. I want to lean into what I feel is real between us.

Sitting up, I bring my lips to his without warning. The need inside me grows faster by the second. My lips move urgently with his, hands working quickly to undo his pants. I'm in uncharted territory here, acting on autopilot, but I know what I want, and it's him. Now. Always. Until my last breath.

We're in sync, both lost in each other, until Julian pulls away, leaving me confused and gasping for air.

"Whoa," he says, putting up his hands. "We . . . can't do this."

I frown, heart stopping momentarily. Is he refusing me?

"But I feel the same way. You just said—" My words come out jumbled and rushed.

"God, Marina. It's not that I don't want this. You've been through so much, and I don't want our first time to be when you're under duress. I want you to be of sound mind. You deserve my patience."

"My mind couldn't be any clearer, Julian. I don't know when it happened, but at some point, I fell in love."

He takes my cheeks in his hands, leaning his forehead against mine. "It's you. Only you, Marina.

"Adèle?" I ask, needing to put my fears where she's concerned to rest. She's the only thing standing in our way.

"That's been something that our families have pressed since her birth. Neither one of us wants it."

"But she makes sense. You two make sense."

He pulls back, frowning down at me. "Can't you see, Marina? She's not you. She'll never be you."

"Then please don't push me away. I need you."

I watch the war in his eyes. The need to care for me and not push versus the need he has for me too.

"Are you sure?" His penetrating eyes beg me to be certain.

I bob my head. "I've never been more sure."

Slowly, he lowers me to the bed, bringing his head down to plant soft kisses on my cheek. His canine trails a line down my neck, stopping right at the curve. He inhales deeply.

"Julian." My words come out breathy. "If you bite me, will I turn?"

"No," he whispers into my neck. "But there will be no biting tonight."

I'm suddenly nervous. Not because this isn't exactly what I want, but because I'm afraid he'll be disappointed in my lack of experience. He knows I'm a virgin, but still.

"Stop," he breathes, knowing I'm worrying.

"I don't want to let you down."

"You couldn't, Marina. I'll take care of you."

His promise calms me. With all my heart I know he speaks the truth, and right now I just want him.

He lowers his lips to mine and our tongues join in a dance that I will not soon forget. His teeth nip and suck at my lower lip, drawing a moan from me. This seems to excite him more until eventually, he lifts off me and lowers himself to my calves. Grabbing the hem of my dress, he pulls it upward. His knuckles trail a line up my thighs, over my hips, and up my ribs, leaving goosebumps in their wake.

I lift my hands in the air and allow him to pull the dress up over my head. I lie before him in simple white undergarments. His breath hitches, but he doesn't say anything. I see the desire in his eyes—the reverence—and I know he's affected. He wants me just as much as I want him.

He continues to worship my body, placing kisses anywhere and everywhere, lighting my skin on fire and making me buck beneath him. He pulls off the last scraps of my clothing and wriggles out of his own. I moan as he finds purchase on my most sensitive areas. My hands run through his hair, gripping the strands as his tongue does things to me that have never been done before.

"You're beautiful, Marina," he says reverently.

I close my eyes and bask in the feel of his mouth on me. I will never be the same. With every nip, every lick, every kiss, I've become Julian's. He positions himself at my entrance and everything in me tightens in anticipation.

"Open your eyes, Marina."

I do. He's looking at me intently. "Are you sure this is what you want? Because once this happens, you can never go back home. Not even if I find a way for it to be possible. I won't allow it. You can't leave me, Marina."

The vulnerability in his voice stuns me. I take a deep breath, letting his words sink in. I allow my thoughts the opportunity to battle, but it's not even a question. I've nothing to go back to. My life was over a long time ago. My parents deserted me, and my relationship with my friends is no longer the same. He's what I want. He's my new life, and there's no question . . . I need him.

"Yes, Julian. I'm sure."

With a single thrust of his hips, I am forever changed. Marina Drake is no more.

CHAPTER 29

I lay in his arms all night, deliciously sore and eager for more of everything he offers. Sleep would be impossible. He has awoken in me a savageness. A need beyond anything I've ever experienced in my life. But it doesn't stop at the physical contact we've already shared. I want something darker—more intimate—something only he can give me. I want to feel his bite.

"What are you thinking over there?" he asks from beside me.

I want to tell him, but I know now is not the time. Julian is so concerned about me, there's no way he'll agree to that right now. Soon.

"Everything," I say, and he pulls me in close, placing a kiss on my forehead.

"Julian, how is this ever going to work?"

I despise the words as soon as they leave my mouth. Why would I feel the need to ruin what just happened between us with talk of our future? I should've just lived in this moment with him.

He lets out a deep breath. "There's plenty of time to talk about that, Marina. Tonight, I just want to hold you."

He's right and I know it. That's a conversation that's going to be very difficult, because there are only so many options. We stay together until it doesn't make sense anymore and then I leave, or I turn. Neither sounds like a viable option at this moment.

"My brother is having a dinner party tomorrow night, and we've been invited."

Julian does his best to change the subject away to better things, and I silently thank him for it. After what we just shared, I don't want the night to be ruined by what-ifs and hows.

"I'm invited too," I say, remembering the conversation about said party with Law. "We sort of helped him plan the menu."

"So I've been told." He grins. "It will be enjoyable, I suppose. Law loves to entertain, and he's been asking since your arrival to throw a party. I figure it's high time I give in. He's been very insistent, and he's a pain in the ass when he doesn't get his way."

I smile. "A dinner party with Law would be great."

"Then it's done. I'll inform him to expect us tomorrow evening. But I want to do something for you today." He smiles. "If you could do anything, what would it be?"

I think of all the possibilities. Without a doubt, it would be getting off this estate just for a little while. I would love to do something for Stacey too.

"Stacey was really a great sport about our dinner in New Orleans, but I felt horrible leaving her behind. She's had it far worse than I have, Julian. I'd love to do something and include her, if that's all right with you?"

"Anything you want. It's yours."

"If we have a dinner party tomorrow night, could we go into New Orleans and shop?" I scrunch my nose, not knowing what the answer will be. The last time we went into town, we were accosted by vampires.

"I don't think New Orleans is safe right now, but I do know another place that we could go. Maybe have lunch at a small café and do a little bit of shopping."

My mood brightens immediately. "Yes," I say, popping up on my knees and throwing my arms around him. "Can we tell Stacey now?"

He chuckles. "It's three o'clock in the morning. I think we should probably let her sleep." I roll my eyes. "I'll sleep when I'm dead."

"Once you're changed, you won't be dying, so let's enjoy sleep now."

It looks like we'll be having *that* conversation sooner than I planned.

"Okay, why are you flushed and glowing?" Stacey narrows her eyes at me, trying to work out the puzzle.

"No reason," I lie.

"Oh my God!" she exclaims, bringing her hands up to her mouth. "You slept with him." She points her finger at me, squealing. "Dish, girl, dish."

Part of me is thrilled at having someone to spill all the details to, while another part of me has this strange need to keep Julian all to myself, almost smothering. Watching her eagerness, I decide to cave.

"While you were curled up in your bed, I was almost killed by a new bite."

She gasps. "Oh shit." Her eyes are wide, and her skin has turned a sallow shade.

"Yep. She got loose from the basement, which by the way—don't ever go down there."

Stacey raises her hands up. "No worries. I'm staying far from the basement. Keep going," she urges, eating up every word.

"She was in my room and she was going to kill me. Julian came to my rescue."

I continue telling her the events of the night as she sits with her hands on both sides of her cheeks, thoroughly engrossed in every word I say.

"Wow, some people have all the fun," she muses.

I frown. Nothing about almost dying at the hands of a new bite hedge witch is any fun.

The parts that came after? That's a different story.

"Did he tell you he loved you?"

I have to think back. He said a lot of things that alluded to it, but the actual words, no. Is that something a vampire that's lived for centuries would even say to a human? The truth of the matter is, I still know very little about his way of life.

"No, but it doesn't matter. I know how I feel about him, and that's all I need to know." She smiles, looking gleeful at my declaration. "I'm glad that you fessed up, and I'm glad that the V-card is no longer." She laughs. "If what the witch said was true and war is going to come down on the vampires, then by all means, I am glad to know that we're going out with a bang. Well…at least you are."

I smack her shoulder.

"Stop. It was more than that. It doesn't feel like meaningless sex with Julian. It's special."

I think back to our night together and heat floods my cheeks. The way his muscles rippled under my touch. The solid

V that bled into his boxers. His impressive length—though I have nothing to compare it to. The whole thing was . . . magical, and I want so much more.

"I want him to bite me, Stacey."

Her face is very serious. "You want to turn?"

I shake my head. "No. I don't want to turn. It's a conversation we haven't had, but I never want to turn."

"How is that going to work? I mean, at some point, you'll die."

I sigh, not wanting to have this conversation, but knowing it's something I can't avoid forever, and it was me who brought it up.

"I'm content being by his side until it doesn't make sense anymore. I know that I'm going to age and at some point, he's probably not going to be attracted to me."

"Doubtful. That man has googly eyes for you."

"Doesn't change the fact that things will change as I age and he doesn't. At that time, hopefully, he'll have figured out a way to remove the mark that the Council has on me, and I can leave."

"You could do that? You'd be willing to spend your whole life with him and walk away because you have wrinkles and gray hair?"

"I'll leave before that. The thought makes me terribly sad, but it's inevitable. Until then, I'm going to enjoy my time with him."

"I think you're crazy. That will never work. He won't allow you to leave."

She isn't wrong.

"We'll cross that bridge when we get there, I guess."

She's frowning, clearly not agreeing with my plan. It's not what I want, but it's the obvious solution. I won't turn, and he can't age with me. What else is there to do?

"So, you want him to bite you?" she says, changing the subject. "That sounds . . . painful." She scrunches her nose.

"He mentioned one time that a bite is sensual for both vampire and human. He made it sound like a very personal and sexual experience." My cheeks heat, telling Stacey something so personal. Other than Maggie, I never shared such intimate information with anyone. Not even Shannon. "I also witnessed it at a club in New Orleans. There were humans lined up to experience it."

"That's kinky shit," she says, waggling her eyebrows. "Go on. Tell me all about this sex club."

I roll my eyes, switching the subject. "I want that with him. Is that strange?"

She lifts her shoulders. "I don't know. People are into all sorts of kinks. I guess even humans enjoy biting at times. Guess you're just one hell of a freak," she snickers. "He's unleashed something in you."

"Dear God," I cry, shielding my face in embarrassment.

"Oh, come on. There's nothing wrong with that. It's normal. Go for it."

Lowering my hands, I consider what Stacey is saying. She's right; I've heard of couples doing all sorts of things during sex. How is this any different? I'm consenting to trying something my partner enjoys. What could be wrong with that? *Something could go wrong, and you could die.*

I push that thought out of my mind. Julian would never hurt me. I trust him. Tonight, I'm going for it.

Looking at the clock, I see we're running out of time. I came here to tell Stacey about my surprise, and somehow, we squirreled away from that subject and landed on sex and kinks.

"You need to get ready. We're going to Law's party tomorrow night, and Julian is taking us to lunch and shopping today."

"Are you serious?" Stacey yells in excitement. "I mean, you're for real?"

I laugh. "Yes. It's already in motion. He's going to pick us up in thirty minutes, so you need to get ready."

"I'll be to your room in fifteen," she screeches, running toward her bathroom.

We're driving with the top down, wind blowing through my hair. My head is thrown back in laughter as Stacey mimics the scene from *Titanic* at the front of the boat. We're carefree and enjoying life. A couple of months ago, this wouldn't have been in the realm of possibility. Yet here we are, sitting in the backseat of a red BMW convertible—just like I imagined—with a vampire in the driver seat.

It's eighty degrees, perfect weather. The sun is shining down on us, and we are basking in it. Julian has a baseball cap pulled low over his forehead, shielding him from the sun, along with a gray long-sleeved Henley shirt.

The fact that he can't just enjoy this beautiful day is horrible. Yet another reason why I'm not inclined to turn. What's the point in living if you can't enjoy a beautiful sunny day? There is none, in my opinion.

"Julian, do you want to put the top up? If the sun is bothering you, I don't want it down."

"No, I'm fine. Enjoy yourself."

I sit back, crossing my arms over my chest at his insistence to burn himself for our pleasure. Peering at him through the rearview mirror, I get chills. There's something crazy sexy about Julian in a hat with a pair of Ray-Bans. He looks so normal—though warm. Thankfully, there's a good enough breeze with the top down, it's probably not that bad for him.

We're driving down country roads when houses start to appear more frequently, and before too long we're approaching a sign for Albita Springs. We pass through the small town lined with cafés and trinket shops until we're on the outskirts, pulling up to a large white home with black shutters, surrounded by a white picket fence. Stacey and I exchange looks.

"All right ladies, let's go." Julian says, getting out of the car and extending an outstretched hand to offer help. I take his hand and he squeezes affectionately. My cheek warms as heat flirts up my neck and onto my face.

We follow him as he walks to the door, but before he can even knock, it swings open. A dark-skinned woman dressed in loud colors greets us.

"Julian," she says with a raspy voice, sounding like she has been smoking since she was ten. "I didn't think I would see you in these parts anytime soon. Come in," she says, standing aside and allowing us to pass.

When we enter, it looks like your standard home—sitting room off to the right, formal dining room to the left—but we bypass all of that and go straight to the back of the house. She pulls a curtain aside and steps through. Stacey and I look to Julian, who nods for us to follow her. On the other side, my breath hitches. A huge room with cathedral ceilings is lined wall to wall with all sorts of treasures. Gowns and clothing of all kinds are along one wall, while on the other end, glass cases full of what look like crystals have Stacey and I quirking our brows.

"Ladies, this is Madame Shante. We've known each other for over one hundred years." My head jerks back at the information, questioning whether she's a vampire herself.

"I'm no vampire, child. Just an old woman."

Does she read minds too? Are any of my thoughts my own around here?

Julian chuckles at her self-description and most likely my inner struggle about the lack of privacy.

"Not that your magic would have anything to do with that," he smirks at Madame Shante, still not acknowledging whether he can read my thoughts.

She smiles. "All right. So, I may weave a bit of magic every now and then that helps me stay young and alive, but let's keep that our secret." She winks. "Julian tells me you need something for one of Lawrence's soirées. Seeing as how this will be your first, I must warn you, Lawrence loves the pageantry of a dinner party. He forgets it is the twenty-first century and insists that your dress is that of a debutante going to her first summer season." She rolls her eyes. "You are going to be stepping back in time for this event."

"That sounds . . . fun." Stacey says, surprisingly chipper to hear that we have to wear corsets and multiple layers. It's essentially a costume party, which is just ridiculous. And completely tracks for a Law event.

"You'll find what you're looking for. Go ahead and poke around. Try anything on that you'd like. I have some business with Julian," she says, grabbing him by the elbow and walking out of the room.

He offers us a smile as he goes.

"That was strange," Stacey admits. "What kind of business do you think she has with your vampire?"

My vampire. I suppose that is exactly what he is. Mine. I'm okay with that. God only knows what a witch and a vampire would have to talk about. There's still so much I don't know about this whole world. I shrug, not having the slightest idea.

"While they're gone, we might as well find our dresses."

We go about sorting through racks of clothes. Stacey

chooses an emerald-green dress with a corset back, trimmed in white lace, much like what she wore at the auction. With her red hair, she looks stunning. There's no question that emerald is her color. I continue to search, pulling off a yellow dress, which Stacey scrunches her nose at. I keep looking, and finally I see it.

Tulle in navy blue with a strapless sweetheart neckline, beaded bodice, basque waist, lace-up back, and matching bolero has me stopping in my tracks. It's beautiful. I step into the small room, calling out for Stacey. She helps me step into it, making sure it's laced up so that I know it fits properly. And it does. It fits perfectly.

"Yes. You're breathtaking," Stacey praises, sidling up next to me. "Julian won't know what to do with you." I smile widely, hoping she's right.

I take off the dress and hide it, not wanting Julian to get a peek of it before tomorrow night. It's not like it's a wedding dress, but I want to surprise him. With the help of Stacey and Katina, I'll be transformed into a vixen that any vampire would have trouble resisting. At least, I hope.

Twenty-five minutes later, a stone-faced Julian comes walking in with an equally melancholy Madame Shante.

"Are you ready?" Julian asks, without looking at me.

I frown, not liking this sudden change in demeanor. *What was their talk about?*

"I'll wrap up your purchases. Have a seat in the parlor," she says, ushering us back through the curtain.

We sit in silence for several minutes, Julian avoiding my gaze. Stacey twiddles her fingers, looking anywhere but at the two of us. The awkwardness of this moment is thick and smothering.

"Here you are," Madame Shante says, walking out with two large garment bags. Julian takes them in his hand, leans over, and places a small kiss on her cheek. She waves him off, directing her stare at me.

"Marina. Take care and heed Julian's requests. They will be vital for your survival."

With that she turns, walking out of the room and dismissing us.

Her words fall around me, chilling my bones and confusing the hell out of me. What can that mean? I look to Julian, who's appraising me warily.

"What was that about?"

"Not now, Marina. Later," he says, making me even more nervous. I don't want to spend the rest of what should be a fun day worrying about what some hundred-year-old cuckoo's words of warning could mean.

"She's a seer and she's given me some valuable information that I will share with you later. For the rest of today, don't focus on that. Live in the moment."

The words help. If he can read minds, this is the one time I'll forgive it.

CHAPTER 30
JULIAN

I can hardly look at Marina. She reads me too well, and this is one time that I won't be convinced to share what I know. It's too dangerous. Knowing her, she'd try to intervene. Change something. She can't. *I can't.*

Shante's visions can't be messed with. They always come to pass. There's no dodging fate, no matter how much I want to. Shante and her family have been trusted advisors of my father and now me. She came to him years before his death, warning that there was danger. Every vision she's ever imparted has proven true, making her incredibly reliable.

I never should've brought them here. The plans had already been made for me to see Shante, and I should've left them behind. I'd scheduled this particular meeting to speak with her about the black magic residue I found in Marina's parents' house. I know it's connected to their addiction, but I want to know who spelled them.

I could've rescheduled, but given everything that's happening, it didn't seem wise. But I wanted to make Marina happy. After everything she's been through, she deserves some happiness. Now she knows something's up, and I only hope she heeds my warning and doesn't press for answers.

"I'm starving," Stacey whines from the back seat.

"We'll stop soon. I know a place nearby you'll both like."

Stacey pats my shoulder. "Good man."

I look over at Marina, who's smiling serenely at me.

"Yes. He is," she agrees, and I relax, hoping this means she's not angry.

I smile back and she blows me a kiss. My God, if my chest doesn't swell and ache for things I don't deserve.

I've fallen for her and it's more than some infatuation. What I feel is innate. It runs through my veins. It's taken me lifetimes to find her, and I won't let her go. No matter how I've felt for anyone, there was always something that held me back. Something wrong about the relationship. Outside of Addy, nobody has ever gotten close.

If Shante's prediction is right, I'll die to protect her.

CHAPTER 31

Sitting at a small café, Stacey and I are on one side of the table, and Julian sits directly across from me. We've all ordered—I opted for a lemonade and a small chef salad. We sit silently, waiting for our food, everyone enjoying the peaceful day. My foot taps lightly at Julian's foot. He grins, brushing my shoe with his. I run the toe of my shoe up his leg to his knee. He jerks under my touch, a little ticklish.

Stacey looks back and forth between us. "What's going on, guys?" There's a teasing lilt to her voice. "Do you think you two could keep it together while I'm in your company? You're kind of making me nauseous." She scrunches her nose in mock illness. "I'm kind of hungry and I don't wanna lose my appetite."

Julian chuckles. "You need to speak to your friend. She's the one playing games."

Stacey laughs. "Doesn't surprise me. The girl's been glowing ever since yesterday."

My cheeks heat to inferno levels. Stacey's allusion to the things I told her from the night before makes me want to crawl under the table and hide. Julian doesn't seem to be fazed. In fact, he seems to be thrilled I told Stacey.

"So, she told you about that, did she?"

"Are we seriously talking about this at a table, in a café?" My voice pitches.

"Not at first. It was written all over her face, so I called her out," Stacey says, ignoring my distress at the topic of conversation. "Whatever you did changed her. Got any friends?"

"Oh my god. Please," I murmur, placing my head in my hands.

Julian splutters, clearly not having the same conversation she was. "I'm sorry, what were we talking about?"

Stacey tilts her head. "Se—"

"Okay, Stac," I say, cutting her off. "Could we possibly talk about something else? *Anything* else?"

I'm shifting in my seat, becoming antsy very quickly.

"Don't be embarrassed, Marina," Julian says, offering a small smile. "There's nothing to be ashamed of. We care deeply for each other," he says reassuringly, clearly having caught up.

Stacey snickers. "This is new for her, though. It can be embarrassing."

My mind runs away with itself. *Just how many people over the past few centuries has Julian been with? Has he been in love before? Does he love me?* All of these thoughts compound until my chest feels heavy. So many mounting questions.

Not noticing the sudden awkwardness, Stacey stands, informing us she needs to use the ladies' room. When she's out of earshot, Julian leans across the table, grabbing my hand in his.

"Marina, breathe," he suggests. "I'm sorry we talked about those things. It was inappropriate. You have my word it will never happen again."

Pulling my hand out of his grasp, I sit back, taking a good

hard look at Julian. "It wasn't your fault, Julian. I'm not angry, it's just . . . not a subject I'm entirely comfortable with yet."

He chews on his bottom lip, nodding in response. "To answer your question, there haven't been many."

I scrunch my eyebrows together, trying to figure out what he's going on about.

"You shouldn't worry about those things. My feelings for you run deep. That's all that should matter," he says.

He's given himself away. There's no possibility that he can know that's what I was thinking. Unless he's reading my mind. I glare.

"How? I know you've been able to read my mind this whole time."

Julian's eyes bug out, realizing what he's done. "I should've told you. It was wrong of me not to. It happened when I drank your blood at the auction."

My eyes widen. "Is that normal?"

He shakes his head. "No. It's not normal. I can only guess that it's your blood that binds us. Since I consumed it at the auction, I've had additional abilities present themselves, and I'm trying to get to the bottom of it."

"If that's the case, why can't I read your thoughts?"

"The only person who can read my thoughts is my familiar. She'd have to ingest my blood to have that capability. Or so the legends say."

"What happens if you find this mythical familiar? Is that the end of us?"

I'm only half kidding.

He sighs. "Marina. I've lived hundreds of years and I've never experienced what the legend says. Neither have my brothers, and neither have any of the Borns from the other families. It's a myth. One that's been passed down by people who are jealous of our powers. They hope it'll drive us insane. They want us to go chasing a unicorn."

He sounds angry. Almost like he's done just that, went on a wild goose chase, only to end up empty-handed.

"It doesn't change the fact that you've been reading my mind."

I realize that I always suspected, but the part that has me irritated is that it took me calling him out to get the truth from him. How are we supposed to have any kind of a relationship when we're constantly keeping things from each other?

"I didn't mean to be intrusive—I don't purposely try to listen in on your thoughts. I only ever hear them when they're screaming at me. Like when you're extremely upset or frightened—it's hard to ignore."

At that moment Stacey sits back down, looking between us. "Do you need me to leave again?"

"No," I say, and at the same time the server arrives with our food. We continue to eat in silence, all while I try my hardest to shut down all thoughts. If Julian can read my mind, I don't want to give him any more of an upper hand.

I stew the whole way home. No matter how much I try not to think about anything, I think about *everything*. The half-truths. The secrets. The closer we get to home, the angrier I am. Julian drops Stacey off at the estate entrance, Katina meeting him at the door.

"Katina, please take Stacey to her room for the evening. Marina will be staying with me."

Katina's eyebrow lifts, but she doesn't say a word as she ushers Stacey away. Stacey waves her goodbye, knowing I'm in no mood to talk. She didn't do anything wrong. I'm not angry with her. No. This is between Julian and me. There are some boundaries not to be crossed and lying is one of them.

If he can't help hearing my thoughts, fine. I don't like it, but it can't be helped. It's keeping it a secret and taking advantage that I'm not all right with. If he's holding things back from me now, how are we supposed to move forward? There are so many obstacles in our way already that withholding information makes it impossible to have a relationship.

We can't exactly have the talk that needs to happen in the main house. He's said many times—as has Katina—that there are eyes and ears everywhere in that place, and I plan on being loud with my frustration.

Julian parks the car and starts up the Gator—a motorized vehicle much like a golf cart, only bigger—which is what he uses to get back to his home. We drive in silence until we are parked and I'm jumping off.

"Marina, please," Julian says to my back, but I march into the house, slamming the door open. His strong hand reaches out, grabbing my elbow and twisting me around, my chest hitting his.

"Stop. Listen to me."

I yank his hands off me and push him away. "No. You listen to me," I command. "I am sick and tired of being kept in the dark. I'm always five steps behind you, and that makes this relationship uneven. I'm not going to do it anymore, Julian. You're either going to tell me everything I need to know, or this ends here, and I don't care if the Council has marked me. I'll leave."

He barks out a humorless laugh. "Good luck trying, Marina."

That manages to piss me off more. The reminder that he has the upper hand in all ways isn't what I need right now. What I need is truth.

Looking dejected, Julian asks, "What do you want to know? I told you everything at the diner."

"How many people have you slept with?"

He throws his head back. "That's such a human thing to ask, Marina. There's no way you're going to like the answer. I can't win here. I have been around for centuries and there have been years in that time when all I could do was drown in someone else. It wasn't love. I can't be held accountable for that."

It's an unfair question, one I didn't think through. But one thing I've come to learn about Julian is that he's a shit liar. At least when it comes to my questioning. I can see through him, and I'd rather start with something insignificant. If he lies about this, he'll certainly lie about anything else. "Just answer the question, Julian."

"I know what you're doing, Marina."

"Well, then you know the stakes if you can't be honest."

"I don't know," he says, throwing his hands up. "I have not even the slightest idea."

Truth.

"Have you ever been in love?"

"Once. I've been in love once," he admits, and my stomach nosedives, vomit creeping up my throat.

Another truth.

"Who is she?" I whisper, unsure that this is a great idea. It won't change anything, and most likely, it will only hurt my ego more.

He closes his eyes. "You really don't want to know the answer to that question."

I know without a shadow of a doubt it was Adèle. He nods his head, clearly reading it in my mind. It was obvious in the way he looked at her.

"I love Adèle, but not in that way, Marina. I love her like family."

If I could see my face, I imagine it would be green. The fact that he loves her in any way is more than I can bear.

"We attempted to have a relationship more than a hundred years ago, and it didn't work. She needs her freedom, and honestly, I was all right with that."

"You're engaged to her. Am I to believe that your devotion to your family won't end in a broken heart for me?"

"A month ago, I might've tried to convince her to settle down, but then you walked into my life, and everything changed. I don't know why, and I don't know how, but you changed everything."

More truth.

"I love you, Marina. Only you. Always."

Tingles. They start at my fingertips, then work their way up my arms, over my shoulders, and down my back. *He loves me. He said it.*

He pulls me into him again. "I will say it to you a thousand times if that's what you need, because I love you." He places a small kiss on my cheek. "I love your smart mouth, and the way you try so hard to be brave when you are scared to death. I love the way you stood tall even when your knees were shaking at the auction. I love the way you care about a girl that you've only just met. The way you would go toe to toe with a vampire to keep her safe. It's the stuff of vampire legends. I would do anything to keep you safe. I would lay down my crown. I swear it to you."

The stuff of vampire legends.

"You want to know my secrets, Marina? You want to know everything my father died to protect?"

I don't say a word, allowing him the chance to tell me every detail. To fill in the missing pieces. He knows that's all I want; there is no point in saying it.

"My father knew of the familiar legend of Borns. He hunted down hedge witches for information, foretelling, but he always came up short. Until Madame Shante. She told him three sisters would be born in the twentieth century. These three sisters would harness the power his sons needed to rule all vampires. Their blood alone would be the cure."

"The cure for what?" I question, not following Madame Shante's cryptic message.

"That is what my father was trying to uncover. He was searching for the three sisters, but he never found them."

"What does this have to do with me, Julian?"

"In this century, something happened to my brothers and me. We all had a strong pull to travel. It led us to small towns all over the Midwest. We were on a wild goose chase that we couldn't explain. It started on April 13, 1994."

The room stills. My heart picks up speed.

"My birthday," I whisper.

"Something was different for Marcellus. He experienced the need, but within minutes, bone-crushing sadness took over, and he's never recovered."

I ruminate on his words, digesting everything he's said and all that he hasn't. Three brothers and three . . . sisters. Three sisters all born on April 13, 1994.

"You think it's us," I say, having already come to that conclusion, but hearing him voice the belief is confirmation. "You think we are your familiars."

"You, Marina. *You* are *my* familiar."

He leaves no room for argument, but that's all I want to do. There is no way I'm his familiar. I'm a regular girl, and he's drunk my blood, and nothing spectacular outside of reading my thoughts has happened.

"Marina. Say something," he demands.

My back straightens, and I wipe away stray tears. Anger is the prominent emotion coursing through me. I hold on to it.

"You're trying to tell me that I possess blood that can make you one of the most powerful beings on earth? That I alone can enable you to harness that capability." I throw my hands in the air. "It's bullshit, Julian. I'm just a human and you're sadly mistaken. Your father was sadly mistaken. You said earlier it was a myth. So now you're saying I'm it? I'm the legend?"

"I didn't know until recently. I started to suspect after New Orleans, but it was Shante who confirmed it. I couldn't admit it to you. It puts you in grave danger, Marina."

Shante confirmed it.

"Bullshit. I'm in danger no matter where I am. You're confusing me and for what? I can't be your familiar. I'm human. Nothing more."

"You're more special than you could ever know. My father looked for you because he knew it too. If he had found you, he would've told you all of this."

He's wrong about one thing—his father or the Council did find us. Everything from my childhood suddenly makes sense. The monsters that stalked me and Maggie, the ones who caused her death, came because they thought we were something that we're not. It was all for nothing.

"I've been uprooted from my life and for what? My sister died because vampires wouldn't stop coming. She was trying to protect *me*." I jab my finger into my chest, needing to feel pain. Anything other than the crushing sadness.

"It wasn't for nothing. You *are* my familiar. Maggie was Law's and Molly was Marcellus's. He is the way he is because he can't get over the grief of losing her."

"No," I say, shaking my head. "It can't be true. Maggie is dead. If she was Law's familiar, he'd be broken like Marcellus. Yet he seems fine."

"Law is stronger than Marcellus. He's learned to deal with his grief in other ways—alcohol, women."

I grimace, realizing how similar Law is to my parents, hiding from their sadness with some of the same things.

"I knew something was different the moment I drank from you at the auction. It was the way my body hummed from your blood. The need to protect you became so acute it was almost debilitating. But even before that, when I walked into the room, you called to me. It's what brought me to the stage. I can't explain it—it was as if I could hear your soul calling to mine. I just didn't realize it at that time."

My knees shake and my eyes roll back into my head at his words. I feel it all. Everything he's described times ten. When he's near, my body comes alive. I've never felt this way, and I knew it was something more from the beginning. It was my lack of experience with love that had me second-guessing myself, but I knew. It was different.

"Marina, I brought you here to keep you safe, but I'm keeping you here out of necessity. The Council is not merciful. If they came into the knowledge that you existed, and our bond was true, you'd endure terrible things. They'd never allow you to live." He takes a deep breath. "No matter where we could go, they'd hunt us until the end."

"If the legends are true, I can make you stronger than any of them. You've drunk my blood; why hasn't anything happened?"

"I have to drink directly from you. You're not ready for that."

He's wrong. I am. I've been ready.

All of my insecurities and fear for our future dissipate, making me feel stronger.

Somehow in my bones, I know we'll find a way. Julian's eyes darken. He walks around me, stalking, drinking me in with his eyes, and I feel bared to him in this moment. Where I would've felt insecure moments ago under his gaze, I feel emboldened, beautiful, wanted.

My need for Julian has reached a climax, and there's

nothing that I can do to stop it. I want him to mark me. To claim me. To make me his. It doesn't change that I'll never be a vampire, but I will be his human until the day I die.

"Show me what my blood can do. Make me believe."

He growls, pulling me in and bringing his lips to my neck. He breathes in deeply and exhales in a groan. Everything in me tightens and wetness pools.

"Please," I beg.

He runs his lips up the curve of my neck, torturing me in the most exquisite way.

"This will only hurt for a moment. Do you trust me?"

"I trust you," I whisper, eager for what's to come.

A tight pinch draws a swift intake of air. Heat floods my body, running through my veins.

Electrical pulses stimulate every nerve ending. Euphoria temporarily blinds me. I call out to him, needing more. He answers my cry by tilting my head, opening my neck up to him, drinking me in as if I'm the fluid he needs to survive.

There is no pain, only intense pleasure. I'm basking in it, until his voice rings loud and clear in my head.

I won't let anything happen to her. I'm hers, forever. She is the one.

His words flow like a waterfall. *I can hear him.*

He jerks back. "You heard my thoughts?"

I smile mischievously. "I did."

"Incredible. That's never happened, Marina. Even with the Familiar connection, you're supposed to drink my blood in order to share my gifts."

I don't mention how I was able to block him from my subconscious. Some things are best left unsaid. Right now, I don't want to ruin the moment.

"The legends could be a bit off then?"

He kisses me deeply, pouring every emotion into this, not

needing to say anything. Regardless of whether I am his familiar or not, we share a bond that can't be broken. I'm his and he's mine. We spend the rest of the night wrapped up in each other, cementing our love in every kiss, every caress.

Let the Council try to separate us. I'll die fighting.

CHAPTER 32

The next day, Stacey and I spend all day preparing for Law's party, both of us so excited, we can hardly contain ourselves. The revelation that I am vital to Julian fills me with a pride I've never known. After my blowup with him, followed by the bite and a night full of lovemaking, I'm on cloud nine. Elation flows through me, enough to make my chest burst.

I've never been this happy in all my life. I found my home in Julian. My smile hasn't left my face. Stacey appraises me with a grin.

"You're doing that whole glowing thing again. I'm taking it last night turned around?"

I turn to her. "Yes. It's all good. It's so much better, even."

She beams. "Honestly, you have no idea how happy I am to hear that. The two of you give me hope for a future. I know he loves you, which means he'd do anything for you." She grabs my hands in hers. "Use that to help the humans who continue to be stolen every day, Marina. You have the power to change things."

It's a lot of pressure, but she's right. Maybe Julian and I together can find a way to stop the auction.

"I don't know how much I can do, but I'll try."

Are there other vampires besides Katina who agree with him about the auction? Or would it only be leading him into a war that would end humanity? It's too much to think about, and there's no getting out of this party.

There's something about what Stacey just said that doesn't sit well with me. It's not the words, but how they were said. As if it didn't include her.

"I'm so glad I've found your friendship through all of this, Stacey. I don't know what I would do without you. You know I'll fight for you too, right? Hell, you'll fight right alongside me."

She hugs me tightly. "Same. You're like a sister to me, Marina."

I squeeze her back. In a short amount of time, she has come to feel like family.

Throwing on the finishing touches, we are both ready to dance the night away.

"Ready?" I say, taking a look at how beautiful Stacey is tonight.

She nods her head. "Never been more ready."

SHANTE WASN'T LYING. Law has transformed his castle—and no, I'm not exaggerating, it quite possibly is larger than the main estate—into something out of a fairy tale. A large ballroom lined with windows spans the entire backside, overlooking a beautiful wooded lot, adorned with rich, heavy tapestries and set up with tables lining one wall full of every type of appetizer you could think of. Another wall has tables lined with every kind of dessert, from pies to cakes to cookies.

Servers dressed in head-to-toe black walk around with silver trays full of shrimp cocktail and chicken Cordon Bleu. It's lavish and ostentatious, everything Law promised.

"Brother. I'm so glad you could join us," Lawrence greets. "I've been trying to get him to bring you here since the auction," he remarks. "He's intent on keeping you holed up in that gaudy house. I can only imagine the things he's done with you," he says with a grin.

Julian smacks him in the stomach, eliciting a grunt.

Stacey chuckles.

"Where exactly did you round up all these humans?" Julian asks.

Looking around, I notice that everyone is in fact human. The only vampires in the room, from what I can tell, are Julian and Law.

"Surely you remember how popular I am amongst the people of New Orleans. All I needed to do was send out invitations, and every human with class within a hundred-mile radius was chomping at the bit to show up."

Julian rolls his eyes. "Yes, of course. Lawrence Bellamy and his aptitude for throwing lavish affairs." His sarcasm has me smothering a laugh, not wanting to insult our host.

"Ladies, go eat. Enjoy yourselves. No need to stand around Julian for tonight. You're my guests of honor." He waves us off.

Stacey grabs my hand, running toward the sweets table. "This is incredible," she says excitedly. "I've never seen so many desserts in one place."

She begins piling a plate high with every sugary confection available. I can't help but laugh.

We eat, we dance, and we people-watch.

"I need to use the restroom," I tell Stacey, hoping she'll

come with me. Instead she simply nods her head, continuing to watch those dancing. I stand and walk toward the hallway, not exactly sure where I'm going.

Bash is standing right outside the ballroom. "Where ya headed?" he asks.

"Restroom?"

He points to the left. "Thank you," I say, taking off toward where he pointed. I walk under an arch, moving down a wide hallway. At the very end, there's a girl standing still, looking in my direction. The farther I travel, the closer I get, but she's still some distance away. The hairs on my neck rise and I almost turn back.

She's wearing a yellow dress that matches her golden blond hair, and there's something haunting about her. *Maggie?*

My eyes squint, trying to see her more clearly. She turns and walks out of sight. I go to follow her when I hear Julian call out to me.

"Marina. I was looking for you. What are you doing?"

I look back to find the hallway empty. The girl is long gone.

If there was a girl there at all.

"I was heading toward the restroom."

"Ah, well, I'll escort you." He places my arm through his and we walk another few feet before finding a door labeled *Washroom*.

"I'll be just a moment," I say, smiling up at Julian.

I lean over the sink, knees still a bit wobbly from seeing that girl, or whatever it was.

Nothing. It was nothing.

I close my eyes, taking in a cleansing breath. When I've pulled myself together, I join Julian out in the hall, completely forgoing my entire reason for being in this hallway in the first place. The truth is, I had just wanted an excuse to be alone for a moment and check my makeup and hair in the mirror. Two things I wouldn't have cared about not long ago.

When we reach the ballroom, Julian turns to me. "Will you dance with me?" He bows low, quite the gentleman. I smile, forgetting my strange encounter, and take my love's hand.

A waltz of sorts comes on, and I feel embarrassed to admit that I have no idea how to dance properly. Julian laughs. "Very few people today would, Marina. It's not exactly common anymore. I'll show you." He takes my hand, positioning me where I need to be. Leading me gracefully around the dance floor, he spins me about and makes it look easy. With him, I feel like I can do anything.

He brings me closer to him, kissing me on the side of my neck. "I can't wait to get you out of here," he groans.

I agree. There's nothing I want more than to be alone with him. We twirl and spin, having a great time and allowing our cares to evaporate. It seems as though nothing can spoil the moment..

A commotion toward the front of the room has the music screeching to a halt and Julian and I turning to see what's going on. All the joy of moments ago rushes out of me in an instant. *Shannon.*

I gasp. Marcellus has her beside him, collared and . . . leashed.

"Shannon," I yell, but Julian holds me back.

Her head doesn't even turn in my direction. Her eyes remain fixated on something in the corner, dazed and docile.

"Marina, calm down. Let me handle this."

"Julian. Help her," I beg.

That fucking liar. He had her all this time.

"Stay here," Julian says, holding me in place and then stalking toward the scene playing out in front of me.

At that moment, Stacey comes walking through the door.

When she sees Marcellus, she pales. Even from this distance I can see her body convulse in fear.

He grabs Stacey by the arm, dragging her toward the door, with Shannon in tow.

"Take your hands off of her." Julian's voice bellows through the room.

My feet move in their direction until a hand grabs my arm from behind.

"Marina, you have to leave." Law is by my side, trying to direct me to a side door. "It's not safe for you."

"No. Stop," I say, trying desperately to get out of his clutches. "I have to help them."

"You can't. Let Julian handle him. You have to go. Now."

Law tries and fails to remove me, as I fight to stay put. I won't leave Shannon and Stacey.

"I've come to retrieve my property. Surely, you'll allow me my rights, Julian," Marcellus sneers. "Perhaps we can barter. One for the other?"

He wouldn't. There is no way he'd allow that monster to take Stacey. Not after everything we've shared. Everything I mean to him. He'll protect her.

"You can't have either of them," Julian says in a murderous tone, motioning between my friends.

"Oh no, you misunderstand, brother. I want her," he says pointing to me.

I jerk back, not understanding what he could possibly want with me and not giving a shit. He won't touch me. I'll die first.

Julian grabs Marcellus by the collar and throws him against the wall. He hits it with a smack, plaster crashing. Nobody moves. All the partygoers still, watching the fight in front of them play out.

Julian stalks toward Marcellus's body, heaped on the floor, when Marcellus springs to his feet, teeth bared. Julian steps backward, acting as a barrier between me and Marcellus. Seeing that he won't get to me, Marcellus moves toward Stacey.

In slow motion I watch as he grabs Stacey, dragging her body across the room while she fights, screaming and clawing, trying to escape his grasp. *Help her*, I command myself, but my limbs don't react. My body is motionless.

"Please. Please," Stacey screams at the top of her lungs, desperate, savage. "Kill me," she begs in Julian's direction.

Julian moves swiftly to intersect them, but Marcellus sees him coming. Taking her head in his hands, Marcellus breaks her neck. Stacey's body goes limp, falling to the floor.

"No!" I scream, shaking with the vibration from the sheer force of my words.

I clutch my stomach, bile threatening to spill over. Falling to my knees with a guttural cry, I know that there is nothing I can do for my friend. Broken sobs rack my body. I'm so wrapped up in my grief that I don't see the throngs of vampires piling into the room until Law grabs my arm.

"Get up, Marina," Law screams. "You've got to get up."

My eyes rise to find Julian, and that's when I see them. Julian's being held by two beefy men with glowing red eyes. The party guests are being brutally drained of blood. Cries and screams of terror echo off the walls in a cacophony of horror.

Julian's mouth is moving as he yells in my direction. Two strong arms pull me to my feet. *Bash*.

"Get her out of here, Bash," Law commands.

Bash yanks me off my feet, carrying me toward the hall. I thrash, trying to get loose. My eyes meet Julian's. **Go.** He wants me out of here.

"He'll be safe, Marina. But you won't. We've got to move."

"I can't leave Shannon," I scream.

"He'll save her, but he can't if you're still here. We have to go, now."

I don't fight. I've lost the will, not trusting that Julian will be safe. Who are the vampires that have him? Are they the Council? Are they just Marcellus's lackeys?

We get to the hallway and Bash sets me on my feet, moving me quickly down a hallway. A raucous noise behind us has Bash spinning on his feet. Another vampire with glowing red eyes lurches forward toward us. Bash pushes me behind him.

"Run, Marina. I'll hold him off."

I stand frozen in place until he screams, "Go."

That does the trick, pulling me out of my daze.

Without a second thought, I'm running blindly down a hall I'm not familiar with, in a house I know nothing about. I can try to hide, but I'm human. They'll smell me, no matter where I am. My arms pump riotously, pushing me forward as fast as I can go. I come to a break in the hall. *Left or right?*

I'm just about to take my chances on left when someone calls my name from the right hallway. I spin on my heels and catch a glimpse of someone turning a corner. I hesitate for a moment wondering if it's a good idea for me to follow some unknown person, but they knew my name.

I take off running after the being, coming around the corner just in time to see yellow fabric from a dress swish around yet another corner. The place is a labyrinth, and the further I go, the more unease I feel. I need to get out of here. I need to find the nearest exit and take my chances getting back to Julian's land.

Instead of continuing to follow this unknown person, I turn the opposite way and head toward what I think is the back of the place. At this point, anywhere other than back where I started is the best choice.

I come to a set of massive double doors and swing them

open to find they lead outside. I sigh in relief, finally outside of those walls where death and chaos reign behind me. I take off running toward the woods, but someone grabs me from behind, smothering my cries with a hand over my mouth. Two things happen at once. One, I realize the delicate hand clasping my mouth belongs to a woman, and two, I recognize the scent. It's one I'd never forget. Not in a million years.

Spinning around, I gasp. "You."

"Hello, Marina."

Maggie.

Marina and Julian's story continues in Blood That Reigns. Grab it now!

Also by Melissa Winters

Blood Legends Duet

Click to purchase

Blood That Binds

Blood That Reigns

Blood That Burns

Blood that Serves

Fallen Hunters

Fear the Fall

Trust the Fall

The Pandora Chronicles

Secrets Legends Keep

Lies Legends Tell

Meet Melissa

Melissa Winters' debut novel, Blood That Binds, has been in the making for over a decade. She finally mustered up the courage to push publish, and now she's sitting back and biting her nails—which is one of her many bad habits. Writing and coffee keep her sane, but have also contributed to her being nocturnal! All things paranormal and witchy excite her. She hates to cook and work out, but will suck it up if it means one more hour to listen to whatever audiobook is currently on queue.

Melissa lives in the suburbs of Cincinnati with her husband, three kids and dog.

Keep up to date with my new releases and sales ➜ https://melissaholtz.com/newsletter/

Printed in Great Britain
by Amazon